D0027238

COVERT AFFAIRS

LICENSE TO THRILL • LIVE AND LET SPY • NOBODY DOES IT BETTER

ELIZABETH CAGE

SIMON PULSE

NEW YORK   LONDON   TORONTO   SYDNEY   NEW DELHI

This book is a work of fiction. Any references to historical events, real people, or real places are used fictitiously. Other names, characters, places, and events are products of the author's imagination, and any resemblance to actual events or places or persons, living or dead, is entirely coincidental.

alloy**entertainment**

Produced by Alloy Entertainment

151 West 26th Street, New York, NY 10001

SIMON PULSE

An imprint of Simon & Schuster Children's Publishing Division

1230 Avenue of the Americas, New York, NY 10020

This Simon Pulse paperback edition May 2014

License to Thrill copyright © 1998 by Daniel Weiss Associates, Inc., and Julie Taylor

Live and Let Spy copyright © 1998 by Daniel Weiss Associates, Inc.

Nobody Does It Better copyright © 1999 by 17th Street Productions, a division of Daniel Weiss Associates, Inc.

Cover photograph copyright © 2014 by Jill Wachter

Cover design by Karina Granda

Interior design by Lissi Erwin and Karina Granda

Spy Girls™ is a trademark of Daniel Weiss Associates, Inc.

All rights reserved, including the right of reproduction in whole or in part in any form.

SIMON PULSE and colophon are registered trademarks of Simon & Schuster, Inc.

For information about special discounts for bulk purchases, please contact Simon & Schuster Special Sales at 1-866-506-1949 or business@simonandschuster.com.

The Simon & Schuster Speakers Bureau can bring authors to your live event. For more information or to book an event contact the Simon & Schuster Speakers Bureau at 1-866-248-3049 or visit our website at www.simonspeakers.com.

The text of this book was set in ITC Garamond Std.

Manufactured in the United States of America

2 4 6 8 10 9 7 5 3 1

Library of Congress Control Number 2012953513

ISBN 978-1-4424-8227-2

ISBN 978-1-4424-8228-9 (*License to Thrill* eBook)

ISBN 978-1-4424-9961-4 (*Live and Let Spy* eBook)

ISBN 978-1-4424-9962-1 (*Nobody Does It Better* eBook)

These books were originally published individually with the series title Spy Girls.

CONTENTS

LICENSE TO THRILL

To Jay Brown, my superfly Spy Guy

"This is the *life*," Caylin Pike sighed as she leaned her blond head back against the plush Royal Airways seat. "There's nothing like sitting in first class to make a trip to England extra comfy."

"You're telling me," Jo Carreras exclaimed. "I mean, the service is out of control. I think I've already drunk my weight in Diet Coke, and we've only been in the air for an hour." Her ebony eyes gleamed mischievously as she hit the reading light button. Its golden glow shone down on her face, highlighting her cheekbones and rich, flawless complexion.

"I never knew how lame flying coach was until now," Theresa Hearth added with a luxurious yawn as she extended her long, tan legs in front of her. "What's the ETA?"

"Um, *I believe* we have about five hours to go," Caylin replied with a roll of her baby blues. She'd made who-knew-how-many cross-Atlantic journeys in her seventeen years on the planet, and the reminder that she'd be rooted in her seat for that long made first class suddenly feel far from comfy. She squirmed restlessly, wondering how to inject some excitement into the long ride ahead. Other than jumping out the emergency door and surfing 747 style to the land of fish-and-chips, she couldn't imagine how.

Jo let out a long sigh from the center seat. "If only there were some U.K.-variety hotties on this plane—then we could *really* make time fly. Where's Harry Styles when you need him?"

Caylin laughed. "Jo, don't your babe-dar batteries ever wear out?"

"Nope!" Theresa broke in. "They keep going . . . and going . . . and going . . ." She craned her makeup-free face up over the seat back in front of her and scanned the first-class compartment. "Whoa, Jo, check out that cutie in two-B. I bet he's Harry's long-lost twin."

Caylin chuckled as she eyed the object of Theresa's joking affections—a gray-haired guy a couple of rows ahead.

"Cut it out," Jo complained. "You shouldn't get my hopes up like that. I *don't* go for the geriatric set, thankyouverymuch."

"Oh, so you *are* selective," Caylin drawled. "I was beginning to wonder. . . ." She trailed off as she realized that the gentleman in question had turned to stare at her, causing her face to make like a fire engine. "Okay, you guys, change of subject," she whispered hastily.

"Got one," Jo began. "What do you think our first mission is going to be?"

I wish I knew, Caylin thought, her heart pounding in anticipation of the adventure that lay ahead for her and her two new gal pals. Just four months ago Caylin, fresh out of high school in Maine, had been recruited by The Tower, a super-secret organization that was rumored to be a joint venture between the CIA and the FBI.

Hardly what I expected, Caylin noted silently as she recalled arriving in Washington, D.C., for what she had been led to believe was a post-high-school, see-the-world-while-you-help-it program like the Peace Corps. She had been all set to use her extensive mountaineering skills to teach underprivileged Tibetans how to become more self-sufficient or maybe employ her clout as a champion snowboarder to bring excitement to the sunlight-deprived lives of teenagers in Iceland.

Instead she was hit by an unexpected bombshell. Top secret government operatives had been watching Caylin since the seventh grade with the idea that she would someday make a perfect international spy for the U.S. government—and right there by her side in D.C. had been Jo and Theresa, two complete strangers who had undergone the same scrutiny.

Once they had set foot through The Tower's doors, she, Jo, and Theresa had to put their "normal" teenage lives behind them forever. Now, with sixteen weeks of Bondstyle training under their collective belts, the trio were on their first real mission. In the short time they'd known one another the newly christened Spy Girls had become best buds—and, Caylin hoped, an awesome team.

We definitely work well together, Caylin thought. Her

ability to put on a good act for authority figures—honed over years spent sneaking out past curfew for late night street skating—blended perfectly with Theresa's high-tech problem-solving prowess and Jo's expert knowledge of foreign languages. But Caylin couldn't help wondering if friendship and teamwork would be enough to sustain them through a mission they hadn't been told one iota about.

Let the fish-and-chips fall where they may, baby, she resolved, a smile of barely suppressed excitement playing on her lips. I'm ready to go wherever the wind carries me—and I can't wait to get there!

"I bet it's some sort of unsolved murder," Theresa guessed. "Maybe in a school. That way we can pretend to be students and go undercover. Get the inside scoop."

"Mmmm, that would work for me," Jo breathed, her tone growing dreamy. "I can see it now—London prep schools, yummy boys in uniforms, those awesome accents. . . ."

"But why would the U.S. government get involved in something like that?" Caylin asked. "Think about it—we're going to the U.K. I heard the British government is cracking down on their out-of-control tabloids, so perhaps the U.S. is trying to help out. Maybe we're going to pose as paparazzi to find out what kind of practices go on behind closed doors."

"That would be cool," Theresa said. "Plus it doesn't sound *too* dangerous."

"Hey, I'm looking for danger," Caylin exclaimed. "Those paparazzi can get kinda nasty."

"*Completely* nasty," Jo agreed. "They can put on a pretty good chase—and I'm all into that."

Theresa shook her head. "Not me. You guys may be thrill seekers, but I'm a thrill *freaker*." Her stomach lurched as she imagined how she would function in a truly tense situation—one where she wouldn't have time to analyze, only act. Sure, she'd had plenty of experience during her Tower training, but now for the first time she'd be expected to perform in a totally uncontrolled environment.

Trial by fire, she thought, glowering. Not my style at all. There was no question in Theresa's mind that her partners would be able to get the job—*any* job—done and have a fantabulous time along the way. But Theresa, a computer fiend her entire life back in Arizona, was more used to working on the sidelines than being in the eye of the storm. She dealt far better with inanimate objects than with real people—not to mention people who could put her head on a silver platter.

"Well, we'll just have to loosen you up, girl," Jo enthused.

"Yeah," Caylin agreed. "A few days in London with us and you'll be looking at danger in a *totally* new light."

"Hey, speaking of looking," Jo began, "that guy is still staring at us."

"What guy?" Theresa and Caylin asked in stereo.

"My new *boyfriend*, remember?"

Theresa inched up slightly in her window seat. Sure enough, the gray-haired guy she'd joked about earlier had his eyes on her like white on rice. She shivered, her mind racing with possible theories as to why this total stranger would find three teenage chicks so fascinating.

Sinking down slowly, Theresa whispered, "Do you think he's . . . onto us? Like, he knows who we are or something?"

"Let's not freak quite yet," Caylin replied, her tone

suddenly all business. "We'll just monitor his movements and figure out what to do from there."

"Sounds like a plan, Stan." Jo ran a manicured hand through her glossy black locks and exhaled deeply. "Look—he's reaching for the Airfone."

"Maybe we should listen in on his phone call," Caylin suggested.

"Can you rig up our Airfone to tap into his?" Jo asked Theresa.

She shook her head sadly. "No. My gear's stashed down below."

Caylin leaned into the aisle, her eyebrows furrowing in concentration. "Shhh—he's muttering something," she whispered. "And it ain't English."

Jo leaned an ear between the seats. "It's French," she diagnosed. "I'll translate. No prob."

As the swoosh of the man's credit card through the Airfone's pay slot echoed ominously in Theresa's ears, Jo casually set her drink on Theresa's tray, motioned for Caylin to get up, and scooted past her into the aisle. Theresa's heart thump thump thumped out of control as Jo snuck up the red-carpeted aisle, slid into the seat behind Mr. Suspicious, and pretended to search for a magazine in its deep velvet pocket.

Caylin glanced at Theresa and shrugged. "That guy's speaking way too fast," she whispered. "I can't make out a word. Then again, I was never at the top of my class *français*-wise."

Theresa nodded. "The only French I've ever mastered involves fries, so I'm totally lost." She watched nervously as Jo glued her twice-pierced ear to the back of the guy's seat. Suddenly Jo's sparkling eyes lit up, and a smile played on her pouty lips.

"What could she possibly be smiling at?" Caylin murmured. "This isn't a game, for Pete's sake!"

Theresa shook her head, dumbfounded. "Beats me."

The man quickly hung up the phone, and Theresa's blood ran cold with worry. But Jo simply sauntered back to her seat. Forced casualness, Theresa noted unhappily. We're sunk!

"So what'd he say?" Caylin demanded, her blue eyes glittering with impatience.

Theresa gnawed on her thumbnail. "He's onto us, right?"

"Well, he *did* mention us several times," Jo began as she reclaimed her drink from Theresa's tray and took a sip.

"Oh no," Theresa lamented, her mind ticking off countless scenarios, none of them good.

"I *knew* it!" Caylin whispered, her fists clenched tightly. "Who does he work for?"

"Weeellllll," Jo drawled, "he said he couldn't help looking at us because . . ."

"What is it already, Jo?" Caylin snarled. "Spit it out!"

"I don't think you can handle it," Jo said gravely.

"Please, just get it over with," Theresa begged.

Jo took a deep breath. "Okay. I don't know how you're going to take this, but . . . apparently we remind that guy of his daughters, and we've made him feel horribly homesick."

"What?" Caylin cried, sending Jo into a fit of self-satisfied giggles.

Theresa leaned back in her seat and exhaled slowly.

"Please, don't *ever* do that again, Jo. You almost gave me a heart attack."

Caylin punched Jo on the arm. "*Not* cool, Jo," she complained. "I was about ready to go over and take care of the guy myself."

"Okay, I'm sorry for bugging you guys out," Jo apologized. "Maybe it wasn't cool, but it was a much needed reality check. We can't let paranoia get the best of us, and we shouldn't freak out without good reason."

"A little paranoia can be helpful sometimes," Theresa murmured as she gazed out the window. There wasn't much to look at—they had flown into the middle of the night, and she couldn't see anything but lacy gray clouds against the black sky. How many more bizarro situations am I going to end up in? she wondered, biting her lip. And how many of them *aren't* going to be false alarms?

"Here you go," the flight attendant said as she woke Jo from a long nap and handed her a disc. "Special delivery."

"What is it?" Jo asked with a yawn. She couldn't recall

ordering a video—not even in her sleep. But the woman had already disappeared down the aisle.

As Jo began examining the DVD Caylin stirred awake and squinted into the bright sunlight streaming through the window. Meanwhile Theresa napped on, lightly snoring.

Jo nudged Theresa with her elbow. "Wakey wake," she sang. "Looks like we have some viewing material here."

Caylin grabbed the disc out of Jo's hands and studied the label. *"Three American Werewolves in London,"* she read with a laugh. "Obviously from The Tower."

Theresa snorted. "I'm offended!"

"Well, we *can* transform ourselves in the blink of an eye," Caylin offered. "You know, with disguises."

"And I love wearing fur as long as it's fake," Jo added. She took the disc back from Caylin and popped it into the DVD player embedded in the seat back before her.

"Hopefully we'll finally find out what we're supposed to be *doing*," Caylin said as she rushed to hit the play button. "Earphones, everyone."

A shot of a black limousine filled the screen and the rich voice of Uncle Sam, their boss, filled the silence. "Good morning, Spy Girls," he intoned. "You're almost there."

Jo impulsively hit pause. "Doesn't he sound too gorgeous?" she swooned. Ever since Jo had first heard Uncle Sam's voice, she'd been dying to meet him. But neither she nor her two partners had ever been allowed to see Uncle Sam's face—it seemed to be the most heavily guarded secret The Tower held. Naturally the suspense made Jo's imagination run wickedly wild. "If he's even half as foxy as his voice is—"

"Stop drooling, Jo," Theresa admonished. "You're going to get saliva all over the seats, and they'll boot us back to coach."

Without a word Caylin reached over and unpaused the disc.

Killjoys, Jo thought, rolling her eyes. They're always obliterating my buzz!

"Once you go through baggage claim and customs at Heathrow," Uncle Sam continued, "you'll be met by a chauffeur holding this sign." The limo image was replaced with a shot of a cheesy-looking driver holding a handwritten sign reading Stevens. "That's it for now, ladies. Welcome to

London . . . and good luck on your maiden mission."

As the screen faded to black, Jo removed her earphones and frowned in confusion. "Stevens?" she wondered aloud. "Who in the world is Stevens?"

Caylin pressed the fast-forward button, but there was nothing else on the disc. "That doesn't tell us anything!" she complained.

"I can't take this suspense much longer," Theresa moaned. "Those folks at The Tower *really* know how to lead a girl on, don't they?"

"Seriously," Jo murmured, her mind returning to the day she'd discovered that The Tower was not what she thought. She had been totally psyched about having an opportunity to see the world and do good things for the underprivileged—the kinds of things her father would have been proud to see her achieve. But that dream, like her father, had been killed in an instant.

Jo winced at the memory. She'd only been a high school freshman, sweet little Josefina Mercedes Carreras, the pride and joy of her father, who had defected from Cuba as a teenager and risen to prominence as one of Florida's most powerful judges. But then came that horrible day—the day Jo knew would haunt her for the rest of her life. Judge Victor Carreras had driven her to school and was just about to kiss her good-bye when shots rang out. He was gunned down by a vicious emissary from the drug cartel he had tried so hard to bring to justice.

An orphan at fourteen, Jo remembered, holding back tears. Her Brazilian-born mother had died during childbirth, so her father was the only family she had. Or so she'd thought until her aunt Thalia—her mother's sister—stepped into her life and brought Josefina to live in Miami with her and her husband, Enrique. Her newfound aunt and uncle took her on frequent trips to Brazil and introduced her to an extended family she never knew she had.

Still, the pain of losing her father was too great to bear. After she transferred to a new high school, she rejected good-little-girl Josefina and became fun-loving, boy-crazy Jo, connoisseur of fast food, faster fashion, and the fastest cars on earth. As hard as she tried to let go of her tragic past, it jumped up and bit her at the most inappropriate times—such as when The Tower informed her she was about to become a top secret international spy. She definitely wanted to fight for truth, justice, and the American way—her father had taught her well about that. Still, she couldn't help but fear that someday she would end up meeting the same senseless fate he had.

Suddenly the speaker above Jo's head crackled, breaking through her morose thoughts and shaking her back to reality. "We are beginning our final descent into London Heathrow," the captain announced. "Please fasten your seat belts. . . ."

Caylin immediately began following his orders. "Whoo-hoo!" she cheered. "It's about time!"

"I wonder what's in store for us when we touch down," Theresa mumbled, her gray eyes lost in thought.

"My feelings exactly," Jo said quietly as she gazed out the window at the clear blue sky. "One thing's for sure— our lives will never be the same again."

TWO

"I *hate* baggage claim," Caylin groaned as she lugged her oversized bags toward customs. "My stuff is always the last to go by."

"They save the best for last," Theresa quipped.

"And now another line," Caylin moaned. "Waiting is the worst. *Especially* waiting for customs. I gotta be on the move."

"But look around! There's so much to see while we wait!" Jo said in excitement. "Everything here is so different—from the people to the clothes to the pay phones. This is just too incredible."

"As incredible as those customs boys, Jo?" Theresa asked, motioning to the two guys checking passports straight ahead.

Jo grinned. "Talk about hotties."

Caylin looked the guys up and down. "Yep, you could definitely fry an egg on them," she admitted. They looked maybe eighteen or nineteen and wore red button-down jackets with black slacks. Their short, neat dos were extra shiny, as if they had been heavily gelled recently. Basically the guys looked as if they belonged in a Brit-pop band—a band Caylin would have gladly put aside her surfboard to see, no matter how tasty the waves were.

"Well, those guys are *way* too pale for my taste," Theresa said. "Haven't they ever heard of that blazing ball of fire in the sky—the *sun*?"

"We're in England, not the islands," Jo pointed out. "Pale boys with dark hair are always the flavor of the month here."

Theresa leaned her head on Caylin's shoulder and made puppy eyes at the fellas. "Okay, second opinion. They *are* pretty cute."

Caylin shrugged Theresa off her shoulder playfully. "Take a chill pill," she murmured. "We're almost there."

"Passport?" Customs Boy No. 1 asked, his chestnut eyes boring into Caylin's own set of peepers.

"Sure," Caylin replied. As she handed over the navy blue booklet her fingers touched his for a millisecond, sending a shiver down her spine. She focused in on his shiny gold name tag: Ian. How beautifully British.

Ian opened the passport to the page with her vitals and squinted at the pic. "Length of stay?" he asked, stone-faced.

"Um, indefinite," she answered with a thousand-watt grin.

The corners of Ian's lips turned up slightly.

"Purpose of your visit?" he asked, meeting her gaze once again.

"To preserve world peace," she replied, deadpan. The second the words were out of her mouth, she heard Jo and Theresa stifling giggles behind her.

Ian chuckled. "No, seriously—what is the purpose of your visit?"

Caylin flipped her blond hair behind her shoulder flirtatiously. "Visiting my aunt . . . Stevens."

"Address while you're here?"

I have no idea, she realized. As she rolled her eyes up in cluelessness she decided to play off the move as if she had an airhead merit badge. "Um, me and my friends here, we're, like, staying in this hotel?" she replied in that statement-as-question tone she always found so grating.

"Which hotel is that, luv?" Ian asked, clearly amused.

"Oh, I can't *rememberrr*," she trilled. "My aunt, she's, like, out there somewhere?" She pointed past checkpoint security. "She's taking us there herself. I can get her if you—"

"No, that won't be necessary, miss," Ian replied. "Why aren't you staying with your aunt?"

"Well, she's kinda old. You know." Caylin rolled her eyes and feigned a yawn.

Ian winked and stamped her passport forcefully. "Very well, Miss Pike," he said. "Enjoy London."

Theresa handed over her passport with a coy smile. "If you're a good representation of the male population, she'll have no prob enjoying your fair city."

As Ian gave Theresa the same drill, Caylin sighed with relief. The getting-the-aunt thing had been a gamble, but it had worked, just as Caylin knew it would. Guys never argue with an airhead, she thought. They crumble every time.

Caylin smiled as Theresa, through with her own private inquisition, did a quick brow sweep and came over to join her. She mouthed the words, That was close.

I know, Caylin mouthed back as she watched Jo begin to flirt wildly with Ian. But just when she thought they would all be home free, the words she'd been dreading to hear boomed throughout the checkpoint.

"Would you please open this case for me, Miss Carreras?"

"Why should I have to open a suitcase when no one else had to?" Jo complained, deeply horrified. The case Ian had singled out just happened to be the one holding a few key pieces of supersecret spy equipment supplied by The Tower. If Ian uncovers any of it, she realized, good old Scotland Yard will be called in to haul all three of us off to the hoosegow!

"Because this one is by far the bulkiest," Ian explained as he put the dreaded case on the metal table with a smile. "And if you have nothing to hide, you won't mind opening it. Right, luv?"

Your cuteness rating just dropped a million points,

buddy, Jo thought angrily. She glanced over at Caylin and Theresa, who were both obviously doing their best not to freak.

"Listen," Jo seethed. "I put my blood, sweat, and *tears* into this packing job, okay? I stuffed so many clothes in this suitcase, it took, like, half an hour to zip the stupid thing up. So I'm warning you, if you open it . . . there's no guaranteeing you'll *ever* get it shut again."

Theresa gave a shaky laugh. "Yeah, she's right. I mean, the thing is so stuffed, I was afraid it would explode and blow up the whole plane!"

Jo felt as if her heart had just stopped dead. The rest of her body stock-still, she turned her head slowly in Theresa's direction. She felt as if she had turned into Robocop or something. In fact, she was almost certain that her head swivel and subsequent jaw drop were accompanied by a high-pitched robotic whine. Furious, she gave Theresa the end-all glare to end all end-all glares.

"Beg your pardon? Is—is that a joke?" Ian asked, the flat, lifeless note in his voice indicating just how hysterically unfunny he found it.

Theresa noshed on her nails as if they were covered in chocolate. "Heh . . . sorry. Not funny."

"Indeed." Ian shook his head. "Well, I'll just have to have a look, then." He motioned for Jo to undo the locks.

Thanks a bunch, T., Jo thought with a gulp. She mentally crossed her fingers, praying Ian wouldn't find the shoe cam or the pressed powder compact phone too fishy.

As Ian shuffled through the bag someone behind Jo cleared his throat angrily. She snapped her head around in alarm but only saw a line of impatient, innocent-looking travelers, all checking their watches and shooting Jo dirty looks.

"Seems like the natives are getting restless," Caylin remarked as Ian picked up the shoe cam.

Ian didn't seem to notice Caylin *or* the beads of sweat forming at Jo's temples. He ran his fingers slowly over the shoe, turning every second into an hour. Jo's palms became swimming pools. Ian looked at the heel a beat longer—too long, Jo thought—before he quickly set it back atop the mound of mussed clothes. "Thanks, luv," he said, stamping her passport and motioning her past.

"That's *it*?" Jo cried.

Ian's perfect brow wrinkled. "How do you mean?" he asked suspiciously.

Whoops! "I mean . . . aren't you going to help me shut this thing?" Jo amended hastily as she mentally kicked herself in her Prada-clad behind.

"I can't be of assistance, I'm afraid, what with the queues and all," he apologized, managing to zip it up halfway. "But enjoy your stay."

"You can take *that* to the bank and cash it," Caylin quipped as she grabbed Jo with one hand and the half-closed bag with her other. "*Ta*, luv."

"I *cannot* believe we pulled that scam," Theresa exclaimed once she and her compatriots had sprinted far past the security checkpoint. "You two were awesome! I don't know what I would have done if any of that stuff happened to me."

"Well, it probably would have gone easier if you hadn't

opened your big ol' mouth, Theresa," Jo said, glowering.

Theresa pouted. "Yeah, sorry . . . I was just trying to help, and—"

Jo shut her up with a little hug. "Hey, these things happen. I'm sorry I snapped at you like that. We made it and that's what counts."

"Yeah—sometimes you just have to go with the flow," Caylin said as she completed the zip-up job on Jo's bag with a fierce final tug. "When you get in a tense situation, your body *and* your mind work in mysterious ways. It's just that *yours* were acting a little *extra* mysteriously."

"It'll never happen again, I swear!" Theresa crossed her heart and laughed. "Wow, you were so great, Jo. Your composure was so totally . . . composed."

Grinning, Jo blew on her fingernails and buffed them on her shoulder with a flourish. "I don't know what came over me, but whatever it was, it worked."

"You just used your womanly wiles on Ian," Theresa joked. "Admit it."

"Oh, I am *so* over him. 'Miss Carreras.' 'Thanks, luv.'" Jo gagged. "He practically treated me like a *criminal*!

The only guy I'm concerned with at the moment is our limo driver."

Theresa opened her bag and took out her DSLR camera; she often used the powerful telephoto lens as an impromptu, incognito telescope. She put the camera to her eye and scanned the crowd anxiously, her heart pounding when her lens lit on a sign reading Stevens. "I found him!" she exclaimed, pointing to a tiny, shadowy figure in the distance.

"Let's hear it for the girl with the bionic eyes," Caylin cheered. "Come on!"

Her spirits back up and soaring, Theresa grabbed her bags and sprinted toward the limo driver. But an annoying voice in the back of her head kept reminding her of her little screwup in customs. When it comes time for us to really shine, she thought, am I going to be the one who spills the darn polish?

The second Jo sank down into the soft leather seat in the back of the limousine, the door shut, the engine roared to life, and the black privacy screen went up. "Privacy, anyone?" she quipped.

At the sound of Jo's voice the TV in the back of the limo flickered on.

"Whoa!" Theresa enthused, jumping to check out the setup. She pointed to a tiny patch on the speaker. "Voice recognition mike," she explained. "Turns the whole she-bang on."

Uncle Sam's voice filled the back of the limo.

"You've made it past customs," he intoned, as a surveillance tape of Caylin putting on her airhead act for Ian came on-screen. "Just barely, I might add."

"How in the world did Uncle Sam manage that?" Caylin shrieked, her face flaming.

"No idea," Theresa squeaked, clearly flabbergasted.

Jo's jaw dropped in disbelief. This spy stuff gets freakier every day, she realized. In fact, it's kinda creepy!

Caylin's image was replaced with a still of Buckingham Palace. "Welcome to London. Where you can shop till you drop at Harrods and Piccadilly Circus."

Jo's eyes lit up with excitement as different shops were shown, rapid-fire, on-screen. "Oooh," she breathed. "Maybe our mission is to masquerade as incurable shopaholics!"

That idea flew out the window as footage of a tall, ugly building began to roll. "This is the U.S. Embassy," Uncle Sam went on. "You'll be infiltrating the embassy, ladies. The mission ahead is deadly serious. The fate of the world depends on you."

Jo gulped. This was *not* quite what she had in mind for a maiden mission. She shot a glance at her partners, whose gazes were glued firmly to the thick limo carpet. We're all in this together, Jo thought, grabbing their hands in hers for strength. Theresa squeezed Jo's hand in response. Caylin met her gaze and nodded in agreement, as if she had read Jo's mind.

"Watch carefully," Uncle Sam continued. "The next face you will see belongs to William Nicholson, the American ambassador to the U.K."

The image of a ruggedly handsome man in his late fifties filled the screen. Caylin scooted up in her seat and narrowed her eyes as if she were drinking in every line on Nicholson's time-worn face.

"Nicholson is a former media mogul," Uncle Sam told them. "Born in America, he graduated from Oxford and soon gained ownership of several newspapers in the U.S. and U.K., as well as a British radio franchise and an American television network. He gave it all up for a life of politics—his countless media outlets and British education helped him earn an ambassadorship to the U.K. The next face you see belongs to his son, Jonathon."

Theresa gulped.

Caylin gasped.

Jo grinned. The tall, dark, and handsome image that was now gracing the screen had cheekbones for years, shoulders for miles, and thick, dark eyelashes for days. Jonathon Nicholson's brown eyes seemed to gaze lovingly into Jo's right through the TV, and the glow coming off his Colgate smile was most certainly *not* provided by electricity. Jo rubbed her hands together in anticipation of having a superfox like Jonathon working on the Spy Girls' side—or better yet, right by her-and-*only*-her side.

"Jonathon Nicholson is nineteen years old," Uncle Sam began, his tone ominous. "Born and raised in America, he, like his father, is being schooled at Oxford. However, last week Jonathon took leave from his studies with no explanation, winding up in the service of his father at the embassy. The Tower has reason to believe this event is linked to the murder of Special Agent Frank Devaroux, who was found dead on the embassy grounds almost simultaneously."

Jo's giddy excitement whooshed out of her like air out of a balloon. Her blood chilled instantly.

"Dead?" Theresa squealed.

"Jonathon is our primary suspect," Uncle Sam announced.

"But look at that gorgeous face," Caylin lamented. "How could Jonathon possibly be involved with icing an agent?"

"Looks can be deceiving," Jo said flatly. The man who had killed her father might have looked like James Dean, but he had the heart of Charles Manson. Correction, Jo thought. He had no heart at all.

As Jonathon's picture was replaced by a hazy one of a smiling Special Agent Devaroux, Jo instantly wished she could take back all the hormonally hysterical thoughts she'd had about the creep who had more than likely killed him. I bet Agent Devaroux never knew what hit him, Jo thought, an image of her father's face flashing in her mind. Well, once I set my sights on Jonathon Nicholson, he'll never know, either!

Caylin studied the face of Special Agent Devaroux, her heart pumping—with excitement or dread, she couldn't tell. But she ignored her heartbeat and perked up her ears when Uncle Sam continued his narration.

"After the Soviet Union broke up, a great number of nuclear warheads went unaccounted for," he began. "A rumor has been floating around that a complete list of these purloined nuclear weapons—along with their exact locations—exists and has been hidden away somewhere in Europe. Special Agent Devaroux had narrowed the location down to the U.S. Embassy in London, but as far as we know, he got no further."

"I'll say," Theresa whispered.

"The Tower has reason to believe that Jonathon Nicholson is working with terrorist forces to acquire this list," Uncle Sam went on. "The timing of Devaroux's death, so close to Jonathon's sudden arrival at the embassy, only serves to bolster this belief. If Jonathon and his terrorist allies are successful, the list could be used to jeopardize world safety. That is why the three of you are assigned to gather information about Jonathon's daily activities, his partners in crime, and what you believe to be his motivations and report back with them on a daily basis."

As Jonathon's picture reappeared on-screen, Caylin whistled. "For a bad guy he sure is looking *gooooood*!"

"He's hotter than Arizona in July," Theresa agreed, fanning herself. "You should have no problem tailing *him*, Jo," she joked. To Caylin's utter surprise, Jo remained silent and tight-lipped. She was about to check Jo for a pulse when Uncle Sam's voice-over started again.

"From this moment forward," he said gravely, "you will learn things on a need-to-know basis. You'll soon arrive at the Ritz hotel on Piccadilly. Once there, check in under the name Camilla Stevens. The desk staff has been prepped to receive you and take you immediately to your suite, which will serve as your base of operations for the duration of your mission. You'll find further information in the suite's safe, combination thirty-six, twenty-four, thirty-six."

"Barbie's measurements!" Theresa joked as Jo scribbled the info on her hand.

The screen went black, sending Caylin into a total adrenaline rush. Now that she knew the scoop, she felt light-headed enough to float straight through the limo's sunroof. "This is it," she whispered, her eyes shining with joy as she gazed at her two partners—and friends—for life. "It's finally happening. We're real Spy Girls now!"

THREE

"Whoa, this is heaven!" Jo exclaimed as she entered the busy lobby of the Ritz. Her jaw dropped as she took in the thick Turkish carpets, the ornate chandeliers, the bouquets of flowers that seemed to be everywhere.

Caylin twirled around gleefully. "I'll say."

"It sure beats Motel Six," joked Theresa, smirking. "Okay, so what's the name we're supposed to check in under?"

"I wrote it on my hand—hold on," Jo said, dropping her luggage and bringing her palm to her face. "It's—oh no! My suitcase handle must have rubbed it off. I can't read *what* it says."

Caylin moaned. "I remember the Stevens part, but that's it. Now what are we supposed to do?"

"Don't panic," Theresa said calmly. "Let's just think for a second. Was it Clarissa?"

"The name definitely started with a *C*. And I think it had something to do with Prince Charles." Caylin squinted. "What's his wife's name? Carlotta?"

"Camilla!" Jo said triumphantly.

"You rock," Theresa cheered as she followed Jo to the front desk. "Let's hope our room does as well."

While Jo told the front desk clerk their alias, Theresa held her breath and crossed her fingers behind her back for good luck.

It must have worked because they were all given card keys with no hassles despite the fact that they had no IDs whatsoever bearing the name of Camilla Stevens. Uncle Sam obviously has our back, Theresa thought thankfully, her heart rate slowing down to normal.

As the porter was called to fetch their bags Theresa gazed around the opulent lobby. She felt as if she were in one bigger-than-life dream. Here she was in London at the swankiest hotel in town, representing the U.S. government! It seemed too good to be true. So good that she floated all the way to the elevator, nearly ramming into a woman who was entering at the same time.

"Oops, sorry," she said, giving the lady an apologetic grin.

The woman gave her a cold smile and a brisk nod. Something in her eyes sent shivers up Theresa's spine. The whole way up to the fourteenth floor the woman seemed to be watching her every move. Theresa didn't like that one bit. She took note of the woman's features just in case. Early thirties. Tall and thin. Short, dark hair. Porcelain skin. Full lips—probably collagen enhanced. Looked like she could have played the vixen on *Pretty Little Liars* or something.

The woman's cold, dead stare was giving Theresa the definite creeps. How can I wipe that look off her face? she wondered, suddenly getting an idea. Still holding her gaze, Theresa casually dropped her not-so-light backpack right on the woman's foot. Theresa's blood chilled instantly—the woman's gaze was unwavering and unchanged. She didn't blink; she didn't move. After a few unbearable seconds Theresa shamefacedly picked up her backpack and stared straight ahead. This woman was *definitely* bad news.

As they reached the fourteenth floor the woman gave them one last searching gaze as they exited the elevator. After the doors closed, Theresa waved Jo and Caylin back for a miniconference while the porter continued on toward 1423. "Did you guys notice that short-haired chick?" she whispered. "She was totally evil."

"Well, I *did* like her hair," Jo said lightly. "I wish I could pull off the short-hair look. It's so glam."

"Hardly!" Theresa wrinkled her nose in disgust. "Anyway, her do is the least of my concerns. My gut tells me she's up to no good."

Caylin's heart raced as she set foot in 1423, the *sweetest* suite she had ever seen. "Not too shabby," she murmured with a satisfied nod. Growing up the child of wealthy, globe-trotting parents, Caylin was used to staying at five-star hotels. But staying in one without parental supervision felt way beyond supercool.

Jo shrieked with delight "Whoa, can we say *super-glam*?" She ran over to the baby grand in the middle of the room and began bashing out "Chopsticks."

"Check out the sound system!" Theresa cried, eyeing the speakers mounted discreetly in the ceiling.

"Glad it meets your approval," the porter said as he began leading Caylin on a tour of the three-bedroom suite. He started with the three bedrooms, each door adorned with a sign displaying each of their names. The bedrooms were amazing—with huge, pillow-covered four-poster beds, beautiful oak dressers, candles everywhere, TVs, and antique desks complete with personal phones and laptop computers.

Theresa skipped merrily into her bedroom. "I could *definitely* call this place home," she breathed.

"I'll say," Caylin agreed. She'd secretly had nightmares of staying in some roach-infested dump of a hostel during their mission, so these surroundings were all the more welcome. Although Caylin was all for roughing it if necessary, part of her still loved the plush life.

As the porter continued the tour through the two huge bathrooms, dominated by pink marble fixtures and huge, Jacuzzi-style bathtubs, Jo exclaimed, "Dibs!"

"Can I just live here forever?" Theresa asked as the

porter led them all toward the minibar, which was specially stocked with nothing but diet Coke, cranberry juice, and Evian.

"Our faves!" Caylin said, reaching for a bottled water. "I feel like Taylor Swift or something. You know how rock stars always request weird stuff to eat backstage, like M&M's with no brown ones? We have our demands too."

"Just don't ask me to sing—that could be brutal," Theresa said with a chuckle.

"For real," Jo said. "I've heard her sing along to her iPod, and Adele she's not."

Jo and Theresa's ribbing was cut short when the porter showed them the safe, where they knew Uncle Sam's top secret info was awaiting them. Caylin could barely contain her anticipation as he explained the importance of placing valuables in there.

We've already *got* something valuable in there, she thought impatiently as she silently willed the guy to speed up his spiel. As soon as he paused to take a breath Caylin immediately tipped him five pounds—"the amount I'd like to lose before Christmas," Theresa quipped—before she shooed him out the door. She could hardly wait to see what juicy details were hidden behind that silver, combination-locked door.

"'You are to report to the American Embassy at nine a.m. sharp tomorrow morning, Wednesday, separately,'" Theresa, parked on the velvet couch in front of the baby grand, read aloud from the confidential Tower memo Caylin had rescued from the safe. Her hands trembled slightly over the importance of what she was reading. This was going to change their lives forever!

"'Jo will be a personal translator known as *Natascia Sanchez*,'" Theresa continued. "'Brazil born, America raised, currently on a work visa for six months. This position will allow her to be privy to sensitive information.'"

"Natascia Sanchez?" Jo said, laughing. "What am I, a salsa singer or something? That name is so cheesy, I could make nachos with it."

Theresa cracked up. "Okay, what's next. . . . 'Caylin will be'—*no way!*—'a housekeeper from Camden Town, London, since most of the housekeepers are locals,'"

Theresa recited, noticing Caylin's falling features. "'Her alias is *Louise Browning*. In this capacity she can snoop through the trash and bug offices without suspicion.' And use that fabulous accent, too, I might add."

Caylin's jaw dropped. "That *must* be a misprint!" she cried, snatching the memo out of Theresa's hands. "I've had a few housekeepers, but that doesn't qualify me to *be* one. Hello, where's the action? Where's the adventure?"

"It won't be *that* horrible," Theresa lied, reclaiming the memo. "And you might not even have to do windows—who knows."

"And maybe you'll get to wear one of those cute black-and-white outfits!" Jo exclaimed.

"Oh, puh-*leeze*," Caylin complained.

Theresa cleared her throat impatiently, dying to find out her own assignment. "'Theresa,'" she continued, "'will be an American call-forwarding technician known as *Emma Webster*. This will allow her to track who's getting calls from whom.' All right!"

"Wanna trade?" Caylin asked hopefully.

"No way, José," Theresa replied as she silently thanked

her lucky stars. "I'm not trading a phone for a feather duster. Sorry."

"What else does the letter say?" Jo asked. "Anything about a set of wheels in there?"

"Unfortunately for you, no," Theresa said. "But there is stuff about where we need to go, who we need to report to." Theresa skimmed the page with her index finger. "Hey, get this: 'Appropriate wardrobe is already in your closets. Good luck!'"

The moment Theresa uttered the word *wardrobe*, Jo yelped and jumped to her feet. "Let's go!"

Jo and Caylin hightailed it to their respective closets while Theresa lagged behind.

"We are so stylin'!" Jo yelled. She ran out of her room, her arms laden with ultrahip office wear.

"Stylin' *and* profilin'," Caylin exclaimed. She stood at her closet, pushing aside her drab gray housekeeper's dresses to reveal totally awesome Jean Paul Gaultier club-bing clothes. "Wow, I guess British housekeepers lead pretty wild nightlives."

Theresa walked into her room, opened her closet, and

picked over her new duds with disdain. "I could pretty much take or leave this stuff."

Caylin wandered into Theresa's room, followed by Jo, who was showing off an ultraglam lime green suit. "Check out the new me!" she cheered, spinning around with the suit held tightly to her bod.

"I don't see how you get so worked up over what's essentially just a piece of material and some thread," Theresa said, rolling her eyes.

Caylin laughed. "For the daughter of a fashion designer, you sure don't like clothes very much."

"That's precisely why she *doesn't* like fashion," Jo declared. "Can we say, *rebellion* against the 'rents?"

Theresa shook her head even though Jo's statement was pretty much on the money. "At least I'm not a fashion junkie like some people I know," she said with a smile.

"Guilty as charged," Jo announced, whirling around once more.

"This is all so hard to believe," Caylin said as she shrugged off a funky fake fur pea coat. "Here we are, real international spies about to embark on our first mission.

And only four months ago we arrived at The Tower, totally clueless."

"I thought it was a scam when I found out the truth about The Tower," Jo recalled.

"Remember how they told us there would be seventeen people on our 'outreach mission'?" Theresa asked, laughing.

"Not told," Jo replied. *"Lied."*

When Theresa realized that only she, Caylin, and Jo had shown up for "active duty," she had begun to wonder if she had made a massive mistake. After all, she'd put off her early enrollment bid at the University of Chicago for what she thought would be an opportunity to put her technological prowess to good use, perhaps to help the Russian population learn job-worthy computer skills.

But that night all her questions had been answered during a top secret meeting about her true calling: to protect and serve the world on missions where a seventeen- or eighteen-year-old girl would be appropriate and/or the least likely to be suspected. The whole seventeen-member-outreach-mission thing had been a ruse concocted to keep her and her two new partners from walking out of The Tower *tout de suite.*

"It took some convincing for me to believe The Tower was legit," Theresa recalled. "But once convinced, I realized I was up to the challenge."

Are you really? a little voice in her head asked. She pushed it aside quickly. She'd made it this far, after all. It was too late to talk herself out of her decision now.

After a long, refreshing shower Caylin wrapped herself in the lush terry bathrobe provided by the Ritz, towel-dried her shoulder-length blond hair, and padded out into the living room of the suite. Theresa was hooking up her laptop and Jo was gabbing on the phone in Portuguese—probably to her aunt. Quietly Caylin picked up the memo from The Tower and looked it over one last time to be absolutely sure she had the specifics of her mission straight before she went to bed.

She couldn't wait for the morning to come. Patience, to Caylin, was hardly a virtue—and the same went for sitting still. The first week of security training at

The Tower had been held in a classroom, and Caylin had wanted to pull her hair out. If she had wanted to be trapped in a classroom all day, she would have gone to UC Berkeley, where she could have surfed and swam and actually had a life. She started to think The Tower was total Snoozeville—until the real fun began. In addition to the training in concocting disguises and learning accents there had been kickboxing, skydiving, motorcycle racing—you name it. She'd even learned yoga, which had helped her to channel her impatient energies toward a more productive goal.

Her nerves jangling and her muscles aching to move, Caylin put the memo aside and sat on the floor in the lotus position. She closed her eyes, stretched her arms above her head, and arched her back, willing the tension in her body to work its way up and out of her. When she opened her eyes, she saw that Theresa had planted herself on the floor next to her and was doing the same thing.

"Helps, doesn't it?" Caylin asked.

Theresa exhaled and smiled. "Totally. The whole physical part of our training was so brutal for me," she confessed. "I felt like I was in sixth-grade gym class again. You know, always last to be picked for the team. Stick me in a tae kwon do class and I feel worthless."

Caylin widened her eyes, genuinely shocked. "I always thought you really rocked as an athlete."

"Really?"

"Me too," Jo added, coming over to join them after her phone session.

"Me?" Theresa laughed. "It's so funny when you find out what people think of you—it's usually so *not* what you think of yourself!"

"Totally. I mean, what'd you guys think of *me* at first?" Caylin asked excitedly.

"I have to admit, my first impression was that you were a prima donna," Theresa confessed. "But I think that's because of your Barbie-perfect looks. Once I got to know you, I realized you were down-to-earth and totally not like that."

"Same here," Jo admitted. "I thought you'd be way stuck-up, but you ended up being a total doll. No offense."

"None taken—I'm used to it," Caylin said. "Everyone

always leans on the whole princess thing. I guess it's the hair."

Theresa laughed. "So . . . what was your first impression of me?"

Caylin scratched her forehead thoughtfully. "A very smart and together girl who needs to cut loose every once in a while."

"I totally thought you were some elitist girl genius," Jo admitted. "But that was probably because you had your nose buried in a book the first few hours after I met you."

Theresa shrugged. "I was bored. With all that waiting around for those fourteen invisible others, I had to entertain myself *somehow*."

"Well, what about me?" Jo asked mischievously. "Come on, hit me with your best shot!"

"I thought you were totally worldly," Caylin recalled. "Been everywhere, seen everything—that type of girl."

"Me too," Theresa chimed in. "I immediately picked up on how confident, dynamic, and pretty much unshakable you are."

"Thanks—but I'm not always unshakable," Jo confessed. "Especially around gorgeous guys. Hotties are my weakness."

"Speaking of hot, what about Jonathon Nicholson?" Theresa asked. "I know he's the main focus of our investigation, but can we say *cute*?"

"Aw yeah!" Caylin exclaimed.

"Murderers are *not* hot in my book," Jo stated angrily. And to Caylin's shock, she stood up, walked to her bedroom, and slammed the door.

"Jo? Are you okay?"

"If you don't let us in, Jo, I'm going to break this door down! I mean it!"

"I'm sure you do, Cay," Jo mumbled to herself as she lifted her tear-streaked face from the pillow. Theresa and Caylin had been pounding on the door for five minutes straight now, and the noise was hardly doing anything to make her feel better. She wiped her eyes on the corner of a pillowcase, leaving two dark mascara smears, but she didn't care. She just wanted to put the traumas of her past behind her. Why did that seem so impossible?

The moment she unlocked the door, she was wrapped in a massive group bear hug.

"Oh, Jo, we're so sorry," Theresa cried. "That was really insensitive of us—we didn't mean to hurt your feelings, honest."

"It totally slipped my mind about your father," Caylin added, squeezing Jo tighter. "I should have realized when you got so quiet in the limo today that was what you were thinking about. It was so stupid of me."

"Me too," Theresa agreed.

Sniffing, Jo stepped out of the hug and smiled weakly. "It's okay," she said quietly. "It's just that all this talk about starting at The Tower and knowing that our first big mission is about to begin—it's bringing up a lot of bad memories. I shouldn't let myself get so upset about this kind of stuff . . . because I'm going to have to deal with it all the time from now on."

"I can't imagine what you're going through," Caylin said, shaking her head sadly. "Do you want to talk about it?"

"Thanks . . . no," Jo replied. "I should just go to bed. I'm pretty worn out, I guess."

Theresa looked at her watch. "You're right—it's seven o'clock here, so it's one in the afternoon back in D.C. And we sure didn't get much sleep on the red-eye over."

"Yeah, I guess we're all a little jet-lagged," Caylin observed. "We'd better turn in so we can be fresh as daisies for our first big day."

After they'd all said their good nights, Jo smiled, thankful that her friends hadn't pressed her to discuss her father. Some people thought Jo should talk about him, as if she could get rid of the pain by hashing out the ugly details for the umpteenth time. But Caylin and Theresa seemed to understand that sometimes Jo didn't want group therapy.

She'd convinced herself that becoming a spy would be the best way for her to get over the death of her father once and for all. But she couldn't help wondering if spending the rest of her life investigating and, hopefully, *preventing* nothing *but* death—of people, of truth, of justice—was just going to make it all the more difficult.

She changed into her boxers and her old Luis Miguel T-shirt—a souvenir from the first concert her father had ever taken her to—and sat down on her bed. I'm not doing this to forget my father, she reminded herself. I'm doing this to keep his memory alive. There. With a smile on her face and an image of Victor Carreras in her mind, Jo knew she was ready.

FOUR

"It's a jolly good morning, I say," Caylin remarked on the three-block walk to the embassy on a bright and sunny Wednesday morning.

"With an accent like that, even I'm starting to buy that you're a Brit," Jo remarked as they walked past row house upon row house—council flats, as they were known in Brit parlance—along the narrow, winding road. Even though she spoke four languages fluently, Jo had experienced a few difficulties trying to perfect the accent herself; hence her *Americanista* status on the mission. Obviously Caylin didn't have the same problem.

"Before you know it, Cay, you'll be drinking tea with clotted cream and eating scones at every meal," Theresa joked. "And then all the color will magically drain out of your skin."

"Yeah, that sun-kissed look doesn't quite match your accent," Jo said, catching their reflection in a store window. What she saw staring back at her in the streaked glass was Caylin, a striking blond in an *un*striking gray housecoat; Theresa, a brunette beauty in a simple cotton sundress; and herself, an exotic, out-of-place-looking chick dressed to the nines in a black business suit. They all looked pretty darn good in Jo's eyes.

"Hey, we'd better split up," Theresa suggested. "The embassy's only a block away."

"Consider it done," Caylin said, initiating a good-luck high five. As their hands slapped together Jo, Caylin, and Theresa disappeared, leaving Natascia, Louise, and Emma to take their places.

"Emma Webster to see Ms. Dalton, the voice mail manager," Theresa told the receptionist nervously. She repeated her pseudonym over and over in her mind like a mantra—Emma Webster, Emma Webster, Emma Webster—and prayed she wouldn't blow her cover in front of her new boss.

"Let me check," said the polished redhead, motioning for Theresa to have a seat on the nearest couch. As Theresa parked it she studied her new surroundings. The large, airy lobby had the feel of a government agency but with more class and cash than those she'd had to deal with back home as a Tower trainee. The couches were leather rather than vinyl, and the art on the walls was actually quite attractive. She was so absorbed, she nearly jumped out of her skin when the receptionist called her new name loudly.

"Yes?" Theresa asked, startled.

"Ms. Dalton can see you now, Ms. Webster," the receptionist announced. "Down that hall, third door on the left."

"Thank you." Theresa stood up and smoothed her sundress. Walking down the narrow hall, she held on to her composure. She had trained four long months for this moment. She was ready. Or better yet, Emma Webster was ready.

As she walked in the office marked Nora Dalton, Theresa's heart sank. Behind the immaculate desk sat a woman with a severe silver bun and a gray suit to match. Not exactly the kind of boss who'd let the good times roll, she thought, plastering a smile on her face to mask her disappointment.

"Hello, Ms. Dalton? I'm Emma. Emma Webster," she said in a rock solid voice, sticking her hand out for the obligatory nice-to-meet-you handshake.

"Hello, Ms. Webster," Ms. Dalton said, looking her up and down with seeming disdain. "Have a seat."

As Theresa sank into the brown leather chair her spirits sank with her. By the sour expression on Ms. Dalton's face, it didn't look as if she was too keen on her *or* her casual attire.

"You've come highly recommended for the job of voice mail technician," Ms. Dalton began, "but I'd like to discuss your credentials. Could you explain to me why you feel you're qualified for the position?"

Theresa was totally confused. Didn't she already *have* the position? "Um, well . . . I just *love* telephones, and my grandmother was a switchboard operator way back when, so I guess the passion runs in the family."

Ms. Dalton looked at her suspiciously. Was the grandmother bit too much? Theresa wondered. "And, uh," she continued nervously, "at my last job there were fifty lines that were lit up all the time."

"Your last job?" Ms. Dalton asked, looking down at a piece of paper in front of her. "Which job was that?"

Theresa took a deep breath. "Well, I was the voice mail technician for Bill Gates—you know, the chairman of Microsoft? And since he's one of the richest men in America, the phone was always ringing off the hook. I was forwarding calls, screening calls, placing calls, patching people through to his cell . . . the whole nine yards."

Ms. Dalton's eyes lit up. "Well, that's most impressive. To have gone from working for Sam Walton to Bill Gates!"

"Um, Sam Walton?" Theresa asked, trying to disguise her confusion.

"Yes, how delightful to have had the founder of Wal-Mart as an uncle," she said, clasping her hands. "Your reference mentions you and your uncle Sam were quite close."

A lightbulb clicked on inside Theresa's head. Uncle Sam! It would have been nice of him to let her know the details of her resume. "Well, yes, we were," Theresa said solemnly. "May he rest in peace."

Ms. Dalton's features softened. "His memory will live on with every call you answer here at the embassy, I assure you." She rose from her chair. "Follow me, Ms. Webster. I'll teach you all you need to know."

As she trailed Ms. Dalton out the door Theresa breathed a deep sigh of relief and gave herself a mental pat on the back. Snow job one—successful!

"Mr. Nicholson, I'd like to introduce you to our newest translator," Sandra Frankel, Jo's *very* blond and British boss, announced as she led Jo into a posh office where none other than William Nicholson stood up from behind his desk and smiled welcomingly.

Jo gave Mr. Nicholson her best I-know-you-but-I-*don't*-know-you look, certain that her face showed no signs of recognition. "Nice to meet you," she said confidently, extending her arm to offer a handshake. "I'm Jo—uh, *jovial* to be here. Natascia. Natascia Sanchez."

Jo panicked momentarily, hoping Mr. Nicholson didn't notice her slipup. But to her relief, he shook her hand without missing a beat. "Nice to meet you, Natascia," he said, flashing a pearly white grin. "William Nicholson."

Sandra, also seemingly oblivious to Jo's flub, quickly reeled off Jo's extensive credentials: fluent in Spanish, French, and Portuguese; lived in Cuba, Mexico, and Brazil; degree in international relations. Everything but the language and Brazil parts were fabricated, but Jo smiled proudly as if every word were the honest truth.

"Well, I'm impressed," Mr. Nicholson said, nodding enthusiastically. "So accomplished for such a young girl. How old are you?"

"Twenty-one," Jo lied.

"I have a son about your age," Mr. Nicholson said. "He's interning here for the summer, so I'm sure you'll meet him one of these days. At any rate, Ms. Sanchez, we're pleased to have you on board."

"She'll be on call for you whenever you need her, sir," Sandra said. "When she's not working for you, she'll be translating the documents for the conference."

Mr. Nicholson nodded thoughtfully. "Good, good. That conference is creeping up on us, isn't it? Just a few weeks away."

"Yes, sir," Sandra chirped.

What conference? Jo wondered. She vowed to get the dirt as soon as possible.

"Well, I'm sure I'll see you soon, Ms. Sanchez," Mr. Nicholson said hastily. "Thanks for bringing her by, Ms. Frankel."

Sandra shook his hand forcefully. "Very good, sir."

"See you soon," Jo called, wiggling her fingers good-bye.

As she followed Sandra out Jo breathed a sigh of relief. Other than almost completely blowing her cover, things didn't go too badly at all.

"That went well," Sandra whispered, leading Jo down the fluorescent-lit hall. "Mr. Nicholson is really nice to work with. Very polite."

Jo nodded. "He seemed really sweet. What's the conference you two were talking about?"

"Oh, the World Peace Conference," Sandra said. "It's this really grand affair we're hosting two weeks from next Monday, and anyone who's anyone in politics will be there. Following the conference will be a formal ball. As a translator, you'll be invited."

"Great!" Jo exclaimed. "It sounds totally glamorous. But I'm sure there's a lot to be done before then."

"You don't know the half of it," Sandra said. "I'm running around like a chicken with my head cut off trying to get all the documents translated. But I'm sure it will all work out."

"Absolutely," Jo assured her. "I'll do everything I can to help."

"Well, I appreciate that," Sandra replied. "Actually, it'd be brilliant if you could help pick out some of the music to be played at the ball after the conference. We need some . . . you know . . . *up-tempo* numbers, and I'm hardly one to judge."

"I'd love to! Just say the word."

"Well, we've got a while to go yet, but I'll let you know." Sandra cleared her throat. "And now it's time to meet the rest of the translators." She led Jo into the large translation department. It consisted of several cubicles—one for each of the translators—and private offices for Sandra and her second in command. Enormous file cabinets lined the walls.

"This is Natascia Sanchez, our newest translator," Sandra announced. "Natascia, meet Flora, Nakita, Franz, Julius, Nana, and Antonio."

While Sandra rattled on about her "credentials," Jo made an effort to remember her new coworkers: Flora, a serious-looking woman with dark hair and glasses; Nakita, a Nordic blond girl around Jo's age; Franz, a pale brunette hipster boy; Julius, a distinguished man with salt-and-pepper hair and beard; Nana, an older woman with short red hair tucked under a black beret; Antonio—*whoa!* Jo almost seriously lost it when she laid eyes on him. Early twenties, dark hair, olive skin . . . *ouch!*

"It's great to meet you all," Jo said, directing this comment to Antonio in particular. You are utterly amazing, she told him silently, hoping her open admiration was beaming out through her ebony eyes. When Antonio held her gaze a beat too long, her heart sped up to about a million miles an hour. Was she having the same effect on him?

After everyone waved and welcomed her to the group, Sandra whisked her away for a tour of the embassy. First stop: the ballroom where the World Peace Conference was to be held. It was a massive, opulent room, with shining wood floors and luxurious patterned carpets. A huge chandelier dominated the space, creating an atmosphere of Old World elegance.

"This is incredible," Jo cooed.

"It *is* smashing," Sandra agreed. "And will be even more so when it's filled with the most important people in the world. Let me show you back to the office, where some of the old files are archived."

As Jo followed Sandra back to the far corner of the room she noticed a door marked Private next to the ladies' room.

"Uh, Sandra," she asked, curiosity piqued, "would you excuse me while I go to the little girls' room?"

Sandra grinned. "Oh, sure, the loo's right there. I'll be in that office straight ahead."

"Okay," Jo said, ducking into the bathroom. After a few moments she poked her head out to make sure the coast was clear, then slid over to the mystery door. As Jo twisted the knob to the right her pulse raced. But her heart soon

sank like the *Titanic* as she realized the knob wasn't budg-
ing. *Locked!*

"Not that door, Natascia."

Jo jumped and whirled around to see Sandra peeking
around the office door. She gulped, her heart pounding
madly. Caught red-handed!

"Here." Sandra met her out in the hall and directed Jo
toward the ladies' room door. "This one."

Jo hit her forehead with her hand, relieved that Sandra
hadn't busted her. "Duh!" she exclaimed. "Sometimes I am
such an airhead."

She walked back into the bathroom to check her lipstick, but all the while her mind was spinning. Just what
was behind that locked door that was so private? If Sandra's
cool response is any indication, she decided, maybe it's
nothing at all.

Caylin ran her feather duster along a smooth oak desk,
her mind wandering in a thousand directions. Why did
she have to be the one assigned to be the maid? The only
perk of the job thus far was that she got to use an accent.

Too bad she didn't have anyone to use it on. Her boss had talked to her for thirty seconds, tops—long enough to hand her a bucket of cleaning supplies and a garbage can and to tell her which offices she was in charge of cleaning.

Twenty offices, six conference rooms, and two suites would be spic-and-span thanks to Caylin's services by day's end, according to Fiona, a frizzy-haired, twentysomething woman who also happened to be Caylin's boss. Fiona had quickly bailed, leaving Caylin alone with her thoughts. And those thoughts were none too sweet at the moment, considering most offices were empty—their inhabitants in meetings—and the few people she had encountered had avoided her gaze, not even saying so much as hello. Caylin was used to being a center-of-attention fly girl, not an ignored fly on the wall. And now, with each office she cleaned, her mood grew more and more sour.

"Cor blimey!" Caylin shrieked as something seeped down her dress during a routine garbage removal. After some close inspection she discovered that an open soda can at the top of the overflowing trash bag was obviously the culprit.

"What a blazing idiot," she cursed the absent office inhabitant while staring at a smiling family portrait on his desk. People who leave open Coke cans in trash cans don't deserve to smile, she thought, barely resisting the urge to smash its frame to bits. During training at The Tower she had been taught that a lot could be learned about a person by going through his or her trash. It sure sounded good in theory, but actually *doing* it was another matter entirely. Basically all she'd learned so far was that the bigwigs at the U.S. Embassy had a taste for junk food and a distaste for junk mail.

As she stormed out of the office and started down the hall Caylin took a deep breath. "Keep your eyes on the prize, *Louise*," she told her alter ego. The suites, where Jonathon Nicholson hopefully lived, were her next stop.

Snooping through Jonathon's garbage will make up for all this other . . . uh, garbage, she assured herself. Her pulse raced as she got closer and closer to the door. Will he be behind it? she wondered. The possibility gave her a thrilling rush.

She reached the door of the mystery suite, opened the

lock easily with her all-access service key, and placed a trembling hand on the knob. Breath held in anticipation, she hastily pushed open the door, unable to stand the suspense a moment longer. She was dying to know what—or who—lay in wait on the other side.

"So Jonathon wasn't even *there*," Caylin complained to Uncle Sam's silhouette via videophone that evening. "After my bore of a day I thought his suite would be pay dirt. But it was practically empty—just a few shirts, a pair of pants, and that's it. Anticlimactic, to say the least."

"Well, I've got some scoop," Jo piped up. "I met William Nicholson through Sandra, the translator coordinator. It was your typical meet-and-greet, no biggie. But he did mention that I'd be meeting Jonathon 'one of these days.'"

"If Jonathon's father said that and Jonathon's suite is practically empty, then he must be out of town," Theresa deduced. "His name came up a lot in the call-forwarding area at the embassy today. Everyone in the department was told to take messages for him—and he gets a *lot* of calls. I asked around about where he could be, but no one in the department had a clue."

"Keep your eyes and ears open," Uncle Sam instructed. "Anything else to report?"

"There's this World Peace Conference coming up, and it sounds like it's going to be major," Jo said.

"It's about time you mentioned that," Uncle Sam remarked.

"What do you mean?" Theresa wrinkled her brow in thought. "Oh, I get it. You didn't tell us about the conference because you wanted us to find out about it ourselves. Just like you didn't tell me about my faked credential working for my 'uncle' Sam Walton!"

Uncle Sam chuckled. "That was quite clever, I thought."

"Oh, please!" Theresa cried. "That joke was so lame."

"All right, all right, let's deep-six this discussion," Caylin demanded with a wave of her hand. "We've got more important things to think about—like how this race for the list of nuclear warheads is timed to coincide with the conference."

"Exactly," Uncle Sam replied. "Now grab a pen, Caylin. I've got an assignment for you."

Caylin jumped up and retrieved a pen from the antique desk in the corner of the room. "Okay, Uncle Sam, shoot."

"You will go to the first-floor bathroom in the embassy," he commanded. "There will be eight bugs in the sanitary napkin machine, hidden in a tampon."

A tampon? Caylin thought, looking at Jo and Theresa in horror.

"Then you are to take those and place four in Jonathon's suite and four in William's suite," he continued. "The offices we'll do later since that will be a bit riskier and take some more planning. Any questions?"

Caylin looked up from the notes she'd been scrawling furiously and grinned, her grossed-out look replaced with one of delicious anticipation. "Nope, I got it," she said. "Four bugs each, and we're not talking about the ones you could kill with Raid."

Uncle Sam's silhouette nodded. "Okay, Theresa, you're next."

"Pass that pen over, Cay," Theresa requested gleefully. She caught it in midair and looked directly into the video cam. "Okay, Uncle Sam, give me the news."

"Will do, Theresa," Uncle Sam said. "You're to record all calls William and Jonathon receive—time, date, from whom—into your tape recorder–watch."

Her face fell. "That's it?" she asked.

"That's it for now," he said sweetly. "Even though it may not sound very exciting, it's *very* important that we have a record of who calls. It could lead us to the warheads."

"Okay," Theresa said, perking up a bit. "I won't let you down."

Uncle Sam cleared his throat. "Good. Jo, you're up."

Jo bounced up and down with excitement. "I thought you'd forgotten about me! Hang on a sec."

Uncle Sam laughed. "You're certainly in rare form tonight. Jo, you need to pay special attention to anyone the Nicholsons speak with from any foreign country since we suspect the group Jonathon is in cahoots with is definitely not a domestic one. Set up a file of people they talk to, countries they're from, matters discussed, that sort of thing."

"Gotcha," Jo said, smiling.

"That's it for now, ladies, unless you have anything else," Uncle Sam said.

"I have a mission for *you*," Jo replied mock huskily. "You have to let me know what you look like. It's a health precaution because I'm *dying* to know."

"Worry about the list, not my looks," he said, "and you'll be just fine."

FIVE

"Great, a *downpour*," Jo moaned as she walked out of the Ritz bright and early Thursday morning. "That's going to do wonders for my hair."

"Umbrellas up," Caylin said, clicking hers open.

As Theresa followed suit she spied a woman without an umbrella standing at the café across the street. "Check out that chick getting drenched over there!" she observed. "Wait—is that—?"

The short brown hair, the lean frame—where did Theresa know her from? Staring at her a moment longer, Theresa gasped as it clicked. It was *her*—the woman from the elevator. The shiny cap of hair was a dead giveaway. Without a word Theresa fished her lipstick camera out of her purse. She removed the cap, twisted up the red lipstick "lens," and hit the button on the bottom of the tube, which activated the shutter.

"Check it—it's her," Theresa whispered, clicking the lipstick cam as quickly as she could. "That creepy woman—over there." But by the time Jo and Caylin looked up, the mystery woman was nowhere in sight.

"You're probably imagining things, T.," Jo said.

"No!" Theresa looked at the empty space where Short Hair had been, her nerves frayed with frustration. "She was right there—the woman from the elevator, remember?"

"Oh yeah," Jo murmured. "I liked her hair."

"Well, now it's immortalized on film," Theresa said, holding up her lipstick cam. "I got some really great shots."

Caylin snatched the camera out of her hands. "Oh, I was so green when you got this! This is the glammest gadget going."

Jo stole it from Caylin. "How does it work?"

"Just point, click, and shoot," Theresa explained, saying cheese as Jo aimed it her way. "But, seriously, this woman is following us."

"But, seriously, you're being paranoid," Jo replied.

"I hope so," Theresa murmured. "For our safety's sake, I really do."

"I'm getting cramps already!" Caylin snickered as she crept toward the embassy bathroom. She scoped out the hall, shifty eyed; to make sure no one was around to blow her cover. But just as she was about to make a quick entrance a young executive type barreled out, high heels clickety-clacking on the tile floors.

"Good morning," Caylin said with a nod as she continued rolling her trash can down the hall, pail of cleaning supplies in hand. When the coast was clear, Caylin backtracked and ditched her supplies near the door so she could execute her operation unencumbered. Taking a deep breath, she ducked into the empty bathroom.

Operation On The Rag is now in full effect, Caylin thought as she placed five shillings into the machine and retrieved one tampon. It didn't feel all that special to her, so she dug out more shillings and cranked out more tampons to be safe.

What if someone walked off with my magic tampon?

Caylin lamented, her stomach lurching with worry. Just then her five shillings were eaten up with a sickening clank—she'd bought every last tampon in the machine.

Suddenly the door swung open and an efficient-looking woman entered the bathroom. Caylin stifled a gasp, stuffed the tampons in her housedress pockets, and pretended to clean the machine with the sleeve of her dress.

"Good morning," the woman said. She eyed Caylin's pockets curiously.

"Can't hurt to be prepared, cannit?" Caylin replied, accent pitch perfect. Once the woman ducked in a stall, Caylin slipped into a stall of her own and began ripping open tampon after tampon. The fifth one revealed gold—eight bugs, just as Uncle Sam promised. She dumped the loot into the breast pocket of her housedress. Talk about my time of the month! she thought, chuckling softly.

No one answered when Caylin rapped on Jonathon's door—a very good sign.

"Housekeeping," she hollered, letting herself in. Her pulse quickened as she noticed a brown suitcase in front of the door. Jonathon was back in town! As excited as Caylin was to finally have the chance to see him in the flesh, right now she had other priorities.

"Mr. Nicholson?" she called, just in case he was asleep. No answer, no sign, no problem. But I've gotta move fast, she thought.

Surveillance search—check, Caylin noted as she scoped around for hidden cameras or any tape recorders. When her search came up empty, Caylin breathed a sigh of relief. At least no one had beaten her to the punch.

The first bug went under Jonathon's oak desk. The second, on the bedroom nightstand. The third, in the bathroom. Caylin installed them quickly and methodically, all that security training paying off in spades.

The last bug, destined for the phone, was a tad trickier. Caylin grabbed the receiver clumsily, twisting the top off the earpiece to place the bug inside. She replaced the earpiece, already cheering her success. But with a few turns of the earpiece left to go, it stuck. Just then the doorknob rattled.

Looks like I've got company, Caylin thought. She wrenched the earpiece on tightly, the intensity of the moment giving her extra speed. Without a second's panic she replaced the assembled phone on its cradle, grabbed her orange feather duster, and started dusting up a storm as the door opened with a bang.

"Just who are you, and *what* are you doing in my room?" Jonathon Nicholson demanded angrily.

Caylin jumped, totally taken aback by both Jonathon's tone and how hot his white-T-and-khakis-clad self was in person. The tousled brown hair! The sparkling dark eyes! The way his eyebrows scrunched up when he was mad! All the excuses she had planned to make went out of her head and up in smoke at the mere sight of him. But in order to save face, she made a split-second decision to play off her moshing hormones as jitters.

"Cripes, settle down!" she shrieked. "I'm only the bloody housekeeper. Thanks a lot for scaring the living daylights out of me."

"Oh, uh, I'm sorry," Jonathon said, shutting the door with a guilty look on his face.

"You bloody well should be, giving an innocent girl the collywobbles like that."

Jonathon shrugged and approached the desk she was "dusting." "I'm really sorry. Honestly." He extended a Rolex-flanked hand. "Jonathon Nicholson."

"Louise Browning," she said, nearly falling over from the electric charge she felt as he grasped her hand in his.

"I'm William Nicholson's son," he explained, releasing his grip. "Interning for the summer."

"And scaring housekeepers to death while you're at it," Caylin joked flirtatiously.

He chuckled, meeting her starry-eyed gaze. "Yes, I guess I *am* doing that as well, Louise Browning."

She joined in the laughter. "Well, just don't let it happen again, Jonathon Nicholson."

He scratched his chin. "I just didn't expect anybody in here. The old housekeeper used to come at two o'clock every day. You could set your clock by her. Are you new?"

She nodded. "Yes, started yesterday and still trying to figure out this blasted cleaning schedule, I'm afraid. You weren't in yesterday, were you?"

"I was at a funeral in Washington, D.C.," Jonathon said, his features clouding slightly.

"I'm sorry to hear that. Family?"

"No. A friend."

Frank Devaroux, Caylin deduced. "I'll be out of your hair, then, so you can settle in."

He smiled again, his eyes crinkling at the corners. "Okay. Thanks."

For someone possibly involved in a murder, Caylin thought, he sure has looks that kill. As she gathered her things and bid adieu, however, Caylin reminded herself that she had to keep her mind off Jonathon's looks and on the mission at hand. But as she stole one last glance at him before walking out the door, she got the feeling that wasn't going to be easy at *all*.

Jo chowed down on a grilled cheese sandwich in the embassy commissary, lost in thought. Her morning had been utterly uneventful. The files Sandra wanted her to translate were endless, barely leaving her time to breathe, much less talk to any of the other translators. Plus Sandra kept bugging her about doing the music-for-the-ball thing, making Jo sincerely regret she'd ever offered to help in the first place. She desperately wanted to get the dirt on the Nicholsons. There'd been no chance thus far.

"Excuse me—is this seat taken?"

Jo jumped, startled, at the sound of the deep, sexy, Italian-inflected voice. Her heart raced and her breath grew shallow as she looked up from her sandwich into the black, black eyes of her fellow translator Antonio. While he smiled down at her over his lunch tray, she soaked in his olive skin and glossy, curly hair.

"Uh, um, yeah—I mean, no, it's not taken," she blurted, blushing slightly. Antonio wanted to sit with her! This was *definitely* enough to jump-start her afternoon.

"Thanks, Natascia," he said, sliding into the adjacent folding chair and tossing his silk paisley tie over his shoulder. "I couldn't ask for a prettier lunch partner."

Jo smiled. "Why, thanks. I bet you say that to all the girls."

"Only to translators with supermodel looks," he said, fixing her with an intense gaze before biting into his sandwich. Roast beef, double stuffed.

"Speaking of supermodels," Jo began, "what are you

doing translating? With that face you could be on magazine covers from here to Timbuktu."

He smiled, mesmerizing her with his dimples. "Flattery will get you everywhere. But all that's holding me back from a glamorous life as a supermodel are my studies at Cambridge. International business."

All those looks—and brains, too! Jo marveled with a silent sigh. "Wow, a Cambridge man—I'm impressed. Do you like translating?"

"Pays the bills."

"Do you do a lot of translating for the Nicholsons?" she asked nonchalantly.

"Yes, some," he replied, taking a bite of his salad.

"Which languages?"

"Italian, Spanish, some Portuguese," he replied, an eyebrow raised. "Why do you ask?"

"Just curious. You know, I'm new to the job, so I'm interested in what goes on."

He looked deeply into her eyes. "Well, business is not my favorite subject, especially when I'm in the company of someone as beautiful as you."

Jo's face made like a candied apple. When she flirted with a scrumptious hottie, it usually didn't affect her like this—not at all. She'd heard lines like Antonio's before, millions of times. But the depth of his gaze gave her a completely unfamiliar sensation. He wasn't playing around, even though his words were. His eyes were compellingly serious.

"Well," she said, "hate to dine and dash, but I have an important errand, so if you'll excuse me . . ."

She grabbed her tray and bailed before she could fall even deeper under his spell.

Caylin dragged her gear back to the storage closet, groaning all the way. Even though she thrived on all-out physical exertion, exerting herself while *cleaning* was a million times more backbreaking. She'd never felt so sore in her life. Not even the memory of bugging William Nicholson's suite without a hitch could raise her enthusiasm.

"This job really sucks," she muttered, throwing her bucket in the corner angrily. It knocked over a bunch of mops that had been leaning precariously against the fuse box.

"Blast it!" Caylin wanted desperately to turn around and leave the mess behind. Of course, if she ended up getting fired, Uncle Sam would be none too pleased. Her next undercover assignment would be mowing the embassy lawn or something.

She picked up the mops and leaned them back up against the fuse box. The door of it was hanging slightly ajar, so she pushed it shut. The problem was, it wouldn't *stay* shut.

Impulsively Caylin opened the fuse box to find out what the problem was. She found a leather-bound date book nestled inside.

"What the . . . ?" She grabbed the date book and began leafing through it quickly. No distinguishing names, places, or phone numbers could be found—not immediately, anyway. She closed it and noticed that the smooth finish of the cover was marred by some sort of indented scribble. Like someone had used it as a table to support a piece of paper as they wrote.

Her curiosity in overdrive, Caylin held up the cover to the light and tried to make out what the scribble read. It was a series of numbers: 2025550162.

"Oh . . . my . . . gosh," she breathed. She recognized that number. Area code 202, 555-0162. The red line. Tower speak for the number to Uncle Sam's emergency phone.

"You're so lucky, Jo," Theresa griped in the middle of a crowded pub down the block from the Ritz. "*You* get to work with a cute guy. The closest I got today was taking a call from some weird guy named Albert or Alex or something. He kept calling me Gwenna instead of Emma."

"Maybe he got you confused with Gwyneth Paltrow, who *played* Emma," Jo suggested.

"I wish—at least then I'd have kissed Brad Pitt in my lifetime." Theresa sighed.

"Oh, come on, you get to talk to guys all day long," Jo teased. "You probably take a hundred calls a day from beautiful people of the male persuasion."

"Saying, 'Hello, U.S. Embassy,' isn't exactly what I'd call 'talking to guys,'" Theresa said with a laugh. "What kind of impact am I making on this investigation, anyway?"

"Logging all the calls that come in could be totally crucial to finding the list," Jo reasoned. "And if Caylin was able to bug the Nicholsons' suites, your log will help us figure out who the calls are from and when they came in."

"And if Caylin's phone bugs fail, I'll have backup," Theresa realized. "Hey, speaking of Caylin, where is she? She should have been here fifteen minutes ago."

"Not in trouble, I hope," Jo said, biting her lip. "Do you think—"

"There she is!" Theresa waved toward the door, where Caylin had just burst in, her hair mussed and her face flushed.

"Are you all right?" Jo asked, worried.

"I'm great," Caylin insisted as she took her seat. "You won't *believe* the day I had." She leaned her head confidentially toward the others. "Not only did I bug the suites," she whispered, "but . . . I think I found Frank Devaroux's date book."

"Oh, score!" Jo cheered softly.

Theresa clapped her hand to her mouth. "Where? How?"

Before Caylin could respond, a waitress appeared with a full tray of fish-and-chips. *"Bon appétit,"* she said, setting the mighty meal on the table.

Caylin leaned back over the plate. "Listen, I'll give you the specs later," she murmured. "I had to run back to the hotel and stash that baby in the safe ASAP—that's why I'm late."

"Well, we've got the guy's handwriting samples in the safe, too, so I can run a check on that after dinner," Theresa suggested.

"Cool. I can't wait," Caylin said. "I'm so excited, I can hardly eat." She piled two pieces of fish and a handful of chips on her plate. "But I will, anyway," she added quickly.

"Okay, the conference is taking place two weeks from next Monday," Theresa began between bites. "It's the perfect place and time for Jonathon and his flunkies to announce they've got the lethal list—if they find it before we do, that is."

"Well, now that we've got a real lead, we could have this mission wrapped up by tomorrow," Jo pointed out.

"That'd be awesome," Caylin chimed in.

"Not exactly," Theresa said. "We shouldn't put all our hopes on this. We only have seventeen days until the conference, and we can't waste our time on false leads." She twirled a strand of hair around her index finger thoughtfully. "Seventeen days. It's not much time when you think about it."

Caylin gestured with a chip in her hand. "But if the world was made in seven days, we sure can solve this case in seventeen . . . can't we?"

"So Theresa compared the handwriting in the date book to the samples here in the safe, and it checks out," Caylin relayed to Uncle Sam via videophone. "It's Frank Devaroux's book, definitely."

"And get this," Theresa burst in. "At the top of last week's page he scrawled 'green disc' in big letters. So that probably means the list is stored on a disc somewhere. Was anything found on Devaroux when he was killed?"

"No," Uncle Sam replied. "If he had been carrying a disc, his killer or killers would have taken it. Obviously they don't have it and are still looking for it."

"How do you know?" Jo asked, arching an eyebrow.

"Well, I have big news for you, too, ladies. We picked up a phone conversation this afternoon between Jonathon Nicholson and someone known only as Alfred."

Theresa's eyes lit up. "Alfred! That's the guy I was talking about earlier—the one who sounded like a weirdo."

"Your instincts were definitely right," Uncle Sam said. "Take a listen."

There was a click, then some static. Then:

"Do you have the disc yet?"

"That's Alfred's voice," Theresa confirmed. "Totally."

"Negative."

"Jonathon Nicholson," Caylin identified. "No doubt."

"Any progress?" Alfred's recorded voice continued.

"I'm trying, but it's hard with everyone around."

"Well, time is ticking here."

"I know, I know," Jonathon replied, his recorded voice urgent. *"You'll get your disc, I assure you."*

"If I don't, you don't get the two million dollars wired into your account. You have until the conference."

There was a click, then silence.

After a few seconds Caylin exhaled shakily. "Man, that was—*whoa*."

"What a slimeball to put the world's safety in jeopardy for a few lousy Benjamins," Jo spat out in disgust.

"Yeah, and for way less than Jim Carrey gets for one measly movie," Theresa joked halfheartedly.

Uncle Sam cleared his throat. "Well, Jim Carrey aside, that's all we've got so far."

"Between this call and the date book, we know that the list is on a disc—and that's major," Theresa offered.

"And Devaroux probably stashed it somewhere in the embassy, just like he did with the date book," Caylin suggested.

"Speaking of which," Uncle Sam began, "you should courier that date book to me immediately."

"But what if there's more information in it?" Caylin complained.

"If you didn't find more tonight, there probably isn't any more. But I'll have my staff go over it with a fine-tooth comb and report back to you if they find anything. You don't have time to be analyzing that book. Anything else?"

"Tell you what," Theresa said. "If Alfred calls again, I won't put him through. That way maybe we can stall their operation."

"Good idea. Anything else?" Uncle Sam asked.

"Tell Uncle Sam about those pics you shot," Caylin urged Theresa.

"Oh yeah!" Theresa said, hitting her forehead with the palm of her hand. "I totally forgot—I took some pictures with my lipstick cam this morning. They're of this woman who appears to be trailing us. We've seen her two times now, and I have a bad feeling about her."

"Brown short hair?" he asked.

"Yes—how'd you know?" Theresa asked urgently.

"No reason," Uncle Sam said, voice smooth as silk. "Send the film along with the date book, and we'll investigate. But in the meantime concentrate first and foremost on finding that disc."

"But this woman could be the key to finding it," Theresa persisted.

"As I said, we'll investigate."

Theresa's brows knitted in confusion. Something very

fishy was going on. Was Uncle Sam aware of Short Hair's identity and withholding information to protect them? Who cares, Theresa thought. All that matters are my instincts. And my instincts tell me this woman is really, really bad news.

SIX

"Hey, I heard you were a wild one," Caylin sang off-key as she made her way to Jonathon's suite Friday morning. She'd been singing all morning, possibly because her whole outlook on cleaning had been changed after her discovery of Devaroux's date book. Today she found herself experiencing a sort of inner peace, as if she'd just had a good aromatherapy massage. But her chakras were quickly unaligned when she was practically knocked over by someone barreling out of the suite.

"Cor blimey!" she exclaimed as she looked up into the nearly unrecognizable face of Jonathon Nicholson. His once friendly smile had been replaced with a nasty scowl. "You almost knocked me over, there," she finished weakly.

"Well, you should watch where you're going," Jonathon growled, shooting her an icy glare.

"Looks like some bloke got up on the wrong side of the bed," Caylin said, her heart pounding anxiously. Deep inside, she was certain his mood had nothing to do with a bad night's sleep. The veins bulging at his temples and the white in the knuckles of his close-fisted hands told her only one thing: that he had found the bugs. Operation On The Rag was a bust, pure and simple.

"I don't have time to talk to the hired help," he said, his eyes slits.

"What's your bloody problem?" she asked, drop jawed.

"I don't have a problem. Just stay out of my way!" he warned, stomping down the hall.

"Don't worry—I wouldn't want to be within a hundred feet of your rude self," she muttered. But he was already gone.

She opened the door slowly, holding her ragged breath. With tightly crossed fingers she tiptoed into the bathroom. When she spotted the tiny black bug, she breathed a sigh of relief. She checked for the bugs one by one, only to find each firmly in place.

"What's Jonathon's deal?" she muttered. If he hadn't

found out about the bugs, he must have found out *something*. But what?

I really need a mental health break, Jo thought. She leaned back from the desk and closed her eyes, ignoring the boring Portuguese document in front of her. She felt a light tap on her arm and jumped. She glanced up, ready to apologize to Sandra for loafing. Instead she stifled a gasp. The eyes she was looking into belonged to none other than Jonathon Nicholson!

"Yes?" she asked, trying to act clueless over his identity.

"I don't believe we've met." He extended a hand and flashed her a smile. "Jonathon Nicholson."

Jo struggled to keep the displeasure off her face. Slimeballs like Jonathon made her want to blow chunks. "Um, Natascia Sanchez," she said, shaking his hand and noticing its silky smoothness, the firm grip. Boy, do I have mixed feelings about this guy, she thought. Like someone took my emotions and tossed them in a Cuisinart or something.

"It's a pleasure," he replied, then looked around at the

other translators. "Excuse me, everyone. I need to know if anyone here speaks Arabic."

"Um, a little," Jo lied, tentatively lifting her hand skyward. If Jonathon bought her baloney, she figured that could get her into a face-to-face meeting with the ringleader of this whole shebang. She could always get The Tower to wire her to a real Arabic translator or something so no one would ever be the wiser. She certainly couldn't do that this very second, however. "I'm . . . I'm pretty rusty, though, and I'm also *totally* busy with this document—"

"Yes, I can see that," Jonathon said, a look of genuine relief flooding his handsome features. "Well, I don't need your services just yet, but I'll definitely be in touch."

As he departed, Jo bit her lip. She was happy her boss wasn't in to witness her white lie, but she *really* hoped she wasn't in over her head.

"TGIF," Caylin said, kicking off her shoes the moment she entered the hotel suite. "Ugh! Thank goodness I've got Monday off. I don't think I can take much more of this."

"Yeah, we've got Monday off too," Theresa said with

a wave, her eyes glued to the TV set. "What's this bank holiday thing all about, anyway?"

"It's kinda like Presidents' Day, but it happens three times a year," Jo explained. "Sandra told us non-Brit translators all about it." She sighed. "Listen, change of subject. I told a huge lie today, and I'm really worried I messed up."

"What about?" Caylin asked, pausing in the doorway.

"She told Jonathon she spoke Arabic," Theresa said. "I told her it was no biggie."

"Well, he *asked*, and I said I did just in case it had something to do with the disc," Jo admitted, stomach clenching.

"You were *improvising*, not screwing up," Caylin told her. "Give me a break. You had the chance of a lifetime and you took it. I'd have done the same thing."

"Yeah, I guess it's not so bad," Jo lied. She smiled confidently, but inside she was all butterflies. "But now I hope I *don't* get to make good on it. If I have to get wired to a translator, I'll scream. Those stupid things are so itchy, and I'd have to wear a baggy blazer to hide it." She shivered. "If it ain't tight, it ain't right—that's my motto."

Theresa laughed. "Hey, hurry up and get changed, Cay. I got an e-mail from Uncle Sam, and we're supposed to check in tonight. Something about a new assignment."

"Well, do *I* have a story for him," Caylin called, voice slightly muffled. "And maybe he has a story or two for us about Devaroux's date book. I'll be out in two shakes."

As soon as she returned to the living room in a sweat-shirt and jeans Caylin dialed Uncle Sam. Jo's anxiety mounted with each digit she punched.

"Hello, ladies," Uncle Sam said, a Will Smith poster hanging in place of his silhouette.

Jo laughed in spite of herself. "Whoa, Sam, cuttin' loose!"

"I always suspected you were a Man in Black," Theresa joked.

"Okay, okay—so he's gettin' jiggy wit' it," Caylin said impatiently. "Listen, something weird happened today."

"What is it?" Uncle Sam asked.

"Jonathon was completely rude to me," she said. "This, after he was so sweet to me yesterday. The bugs are all copacetic, but still, I think he may be onto me or something."

"Don't jump to conclusions," Uncle Sam suggested. "Anyone else have any contact with him today?"

Jo nodded, taking a deep breath. "Well, he came in and introduced himself, then asked us—the translators—if we spoke Arabic. Then I, uh, told him I did, even though I don't. I just didn't know what else to do." She paused, feeling sick to her stomach. "I mean—I don't speak Arabic, obviously, but what if this is the key that we need?"

"Don't worry," he said after a beat, instantly alleviating Jo's tension. "You did the right thing. We could easily cover you when the time comes. But he wasn't rude or upset when he came into the translation office?"

"Quite the contrary, really," Jo said in relief. "All smiles."

"Well, how about you, Theresa?" Uncle Sam asked. "Anything?"

She shook her head. "Not a thing. I guess Friday is a slow day on the phones. I have absolutely nothing to report. Not even a call from Alfred."

"That's okay," Uncle Sam said. "You'll have lots to do next week after the holiday. Caylin, I'd like you to plant some bugs in the Nicholsons' offices on Tuesday—those will be ready at the hotel desk Monday afternoon in a faux tube of toothpaste."

"Check," Caylin croaked out. She sounded almost bored by the idea. "Hey, was there any word on Devaroux's date book?"

"Clean as a whistle," Uncle Sam replied. "Nothing that appears to be of any importance."

Caylin swore under her breath. From the looks of her, it was hard to tell if she was inspecting her split ends or about to tear her hair out. Theresa slumped back against the couch, deflated. She picked up a Ritz notepad and began scribbling on it aimlessly. The sight of them made Jo's heart sink along with her spirits. Getting nowhere was getting the best of them all.

"May I make a suggestion?" Jo asked, breaking the silence. "Considering Caylin's run-in with Jonathon and my little stress attack, maybe we should take it easy this weekend. See the sights, have some fun. We've been kind of missing out in those departments lately, and I think we could use a break."

"There's not much we can do in the embassy on a weekend, anyway," Theresa added.

"I have to agree," Caylin chimed in. "I'm feeling a little frustrated, to be honest. It's really ticking me off."

"Well, unless an emergency development arises, consider yourselves on vacation till Tuesday," Uncle Sam announced.

Jo cheered. The news was music to her ears. She *needed* a break, that was for sure. She looked at the others in glee. Caylin had perked up instantly, and Theresa was drawing a big smiley face on the memo pad. They were ready for London, all righty. She just hoped London was ready for them.

After a full Saturday of shopping till they dropped, Jo, Caylin, and Theresa rode the elevator up to the fourteenth floor of the Ritz, arms overloaded with packages and their weekly Tower stipends almost exhausted.

"I can't believe you bought three stuffed animals and no clothes, T.," Jo said in confusion.

"I love animals way more than I love outfits," Theresa

said, not one bit embarrassed. "These were too cute to resist."

"To each his own." Caylin laughed. "I'm just happy I got all this yummy bath stuff. This is really going to relax me."

As they entered the suite Jo said, "Right now we need to do the *opposite* of relaxing. What do you say to a night on the town? We can get dolled up and head out to the nearest club. I hear they get pretty crazy here—all ages, techno music, nonalcoholic smart drinks, dancing till dawn. How 'bout it?"

Caylin jumped up and down with excitement. "Sounds awesome, possum!"

"I don't know . . . ," Theresa said nervously. "We don't really know our way around yet."

"So we'll take a cab," Jo said, running to her closet. "It's time to let loose, Theresa."

Without a word Theresa went into the nearest bathroom and stared into the mirror. Looking back was a cute girl in the prime of her life who was too scared to live it. Well, she wasn't holding herself back anymore.

"Does anybody have a bright red lipstick I could

borrow?" Theresa called, running a finger over her naked lips. "My lipstick cam isn't going to cut it tonight!"

Meltdown, "the hottest club in the galaxy," according to the cabdriver, was crammed to the gills.

Caylin immediately dashed onto the dance floor and began tearing it up in her little red dress and stiletto heels. She didn't care that she didn't have a partner—she was sure there wasn't a guy in town who could keep up with her, anyway. For Caylin, dancing was a totally personal issue, one that didn't need to be shared. She closed her eyes, letting the ambient beats carry her far away from her stress and into the zone where nothing mattered but music and movement.

She immersed herself in full bliss, but a light body slam jarred her out of it abruptly. She whirled around and saw Theresa giggling madly in her black jeans and baby T.

"You go, girl!" Theresa hollered over the music. "How can you dance to this stuff? It's so . . . bland."

"Techno rules!" Caylin shimmied to the quickening beat. "Come on, you try it."

"No way," Theresa demurred. "I can't dance when the music's got no soul."

"I can't believe you're not into this stuff, *techie*."

"Hey, computers are good for a lot of things, but making music is *not* one of them." Theresa bounced up and down to the beat. "I feel so stupid!"

"Who cares? Have some fun for once." Caylin spun around and spotted Jo at the edge of the dance floor, looking beyond stunning in her white Armani halter dress. She was flirting madly with two guys at the same time. When another guy rushed over to give her a drink, Caylin burst out laughing.

She glanced away toward the bar, where someone appeared to be giving her the eye. A woman, she realized. She froze instantly. The brunette sat alone, sipping a glass of something orange. She looked familiar—a little *too* familiar.

The realization hit Caylin like a bolt of lightning: Short Hair! Her pulse raced out of control as she watched the woman take a dainty sip of her drink, suddenly oblivious to Caylin's stare down.

"What's wrong?" Theresa asked over the music. "Is this a bad song? I can't tell the diff—"

"Short Hair! At the bar!"

Alarm clouded Theresa's features. "What? Where?"

Caylin pointed back over her shoulder. She scanned the crowd for Jo but couldn't find her anywhere. A tap on her shoulder sent her reeling around, ready to drop-kick Short Hair in a millisecond.

"Hey! Hey!" Jo yelled, holding her hands up defensively. "Some freaky moves you've got there, *Jackie Chan*!"

"Okay, here comes the strategy," Caylin announced in the middle of the dance floor. "We chase Short Hair down and demand to know why she's following us. Tell her we have photographic evidence. Theresa's been right all along— this woman's obviously working for the enemy. Let's rock!"

Caylin darted off instantly before Jo could even begin to process the information. Shrugging, Jo followed, weaving and pushing her way through the thick crowd, making about an inch per hour. Her left ankle buckled as her platform sandal skidded on the drink-slick floor. With a sigh of lament she kicked off her sandals completely. She'd be better off with grungy feet than a sprain, after all. Barefoot, Jo struggled to catch up, grimacing as she ran over pools of sticky spilt drinks and gross cigarette butts. Suddenly the music cut off and the club went totally dark. Jo stopped in place, blinded.

"Uh, we're the Scorching Radiators," a guy announced over the PA.

Jo turned around and saw a spotlit Pete Wentz look-alike front and center on the stage. He made chopping motions at a silver guitar. "Check—one, two. *Onetwothreefour!*"

Painfully loud industrial noise filled the club as the lights went back up. A mosh pit quickly formed, clogging Jo's path to the bar. She ground her teeth in frustration as she was battered back and forth. Her bare feet were definitely in danger, but it hardly mattered. She had to find Caylin and grab Short Hair before she got away.

With a shock Jo looked up to see someone being passed over her head—someone in a tiny red dress who was kicking angrily at the moshers with stiletto heels. Caylin! In a second she was whisked away, out of Jo's reach. Undaunted, Jo pushed ahead, desperate to make it to the bar. But when she was about midway through the pit, Short Hair's gaze met hers and she instantly ducked into the thickening wave of people. Cursing, Jo turned sharply left and bulleted forward. She immediately ricocheted off a burly guy in a satin rugby shirt.

"Watch it!" he bellowed. His drink toppled and spilled all over her white dress. Probably on purpose. She hardly noticed as she squeezed past him and searched frantically for the black leather outfit, the tall frame, the pouty lips. But all of the above were MIA at the moment.

"Wait—there she is—over there!" Theresa screamed over the noise. She ran like mad after the glossy cap of brown hair and spotted a barefoot drink-stained apparition on her right. "Don't just stand there!" she hollered, grabbing Jo by the arm and yanking her in the right direction.

"Excuse me! Excuse me!" Theresa barreled into people left and right. Thank goodness I put aside my computer long enough to go to all those rock shows, she thought proudly as she slammed her way through the crowd like a pro linebacker. A supermodel-looking girlie practically bounced off her shoulder.

"What in blazes are you doing?" she screeched.

"Emergency situation," Theresa yelled, pointing back to Jo. "This girl needs medical attention!"

Jo nodded. "Appendicitis. Don't drink the cranberry juice."

"Uh, okay," the girl said, stepping aside. Others around her followed suit, clearing a path for them.

"I see her—that way!" Theresa called, pointing to the front door. She hauled tail with all her might. Short Hair was barely two yards away. Suddenly an immense shadow grew along the floor, followed by an enormous wave of excited chatter. Before Theresa could stop and change direction, a huge group of under-eighteens rushed in past the bouncer.

"Stop!" Theresa screamed. She knew the momentum she had built up was about to work against her in a danger-ous way, but she was powerless to prevent it. She careened headfirst into the crowd and was bounced clear off her feet and onto the floor. A very sturdy Dr. Martens boot kicked her to add insult to injury. By the time she clambered to her feet, Short Hair was gone.

Infuriated, Theresa threw herself back down on the floor. "I think I'll just stay down here awhile, if you don't mind," she told Jo's sorry-looking feet.

A hand dangled in front of her face. Theresa looked up to see Caylin, scowling. Her blond hair was in an insane tangle, and her right stiletto heel was missing and presumed dead somewhere in the pit. She pulled Theresa to her feet with a slight stumble. Cursing, she lifted up her left foot and snapped off the heel of her shoe as if it were a twig. "This is pointless!" she hollered, throwing the heel to the ground.

"Well . . . at least we know she's onto us," Jo said optimistically.

"A whole lot of good that does us now," Theresa muttered. If they couldn't beat the mosh pit at Meltdown, how were they supposed to stop a gang of ruthless terrorists from destroying the world?

SEVEN

"Hello?" Caylin said briskly into the phone Monday afternoon, feeling refreshed and revived after a Sunday of doing nothing but sleeping and recharging. But since Jo and Theresa had called dibs on a holiday stroll, Caylin was forced to stay in and play secretary in case Uncle Sam called in with an emergency.

"Yes, Louise Browning, please," said a woman who sounded an awful lot like her boss, Fiona.

Caylin gulped, wondering what her next move should be. She had answered the phone in her normal voice, so she couldn't just say, "Speaking."

"One moment, please," she said, adding a little bit of country twang to her own Maine accent. She rustled the phone a bit and waited about fifteen seconds for authenticity's sake.

"'Allo," she greeted Fiona in her Louise voice, adding a breathless element as if she had just rushed to the phone.

"Fiona here," she chirped. "Hate to ring you on holiday, but the weekend girl's come down with a bug. Could you possibly cover for her tonight? You'll get overtime pay."

"Why, sure," Caylin replied, trying to disguise her excitement. What better time to plant the bugs and search for the disc than when the offices were empty? "I could be there as soon as you need me, actually."

"Brilliant," Fiona said, very pleased. "Just be there around seven. I won't be there, but a schedule of offices you'll need to clean will be with the security copper. Simply ask for it when you sign in."

"Splendid," Caylin said, not quite believing her good fortune.

At twenty to seven Caylin swung by the front desk, her backpack stuffed to bursting, to pick up her "toothpaste." After she'd secured it, she ducked into the Ritz's ladies' lounge and cut the tube open with her Swiss army knife. There they were, eight more bugs. She hid them in her hair with bobby pins. This way, in the event that the security guard decided to frisk her or put her bags through the X ray, her bugs would pass for funky barrettes rather than ultrasophisticated surveillance equipment.

Caylin practically skipped all the way to the embassy. Not only was she psyched to come in on a holiday, but she'd be solo all evening, too. No Jonathon Nicholson to gripe her out, no Fiona inspecting her every move, no annoying crowds clogging the narrow halls. Bugging the Nicholsons' offices would be a megacinch!

"Nice barrettes," the security guard commented as she buzzed Caylin in.

"Thanks," Caylin replied. "I made them myself."

Without passing go or collecting two hundred dollars, Caylin headed straight to Jonathon's office. But just as she was about to bug the telephone, she heard approaching footsteps. Her heartbeat racing, she ducked under the desk and tried not to breathe too loudly.

"Hello, Louise?" a female voice—Fiona's!—screeched loudly. "Louise?"

What is Fiona doing here? Caylin wondered. She said she wasn't going to be in! Caylin bit her lip and scowled.

This certainly would throw a wrench into the works.

When Fiona's footsteps finally faded into the distance, Caylin hopped up and finished the phone job hurriedly, totally on edge. She wasn't sure if Fiona would be back or what, but she wasn't taking any chances.

After she placed a bug in Jonathon's desk drawer, Caylin tackled the huge sliding glass door that led out to the balcony. But just as she was about to apply a bug in the lower corner, she heard footsteps approaching once more. Darn, she thought, Fiona again! The desk was on the other side of the office—her only way out was right in front of her. She was balcony bound.

Caylin gathered up her backpack, nipped up the security lock on the door, and slid it open quickly; thank goodness it was whisper quiet. In a flash she stepped out onto the narrow balcony and whisked the door shut.

What a horrid view! she thought, looking down the six floors onto an empty warehouse and an alley. She listened for some kind of sound on the other side of the glass door, but she heard nothing. She didn't see any shadows on the wall, either. The longer she waited, the more impatient she became. Surely Fiona would have come and gone by now.

She peeked through the door and gasped. There, in front of the desk, stood someone who was decidedly taller, more solidly built, and far more masculine than Fiona. It's Jonathon! Caylin realized, her spine tingling. And—oh no!—he was coming her way!

Caylin pulled her head back from the door and froze for a moment. She had absolutely nowhere to hide. Her heart beat a mile a minute. Terrified, she scooted as far away from the window as she could and plastered herself up against the embassy wall. Still no sign of Jonathon at the glass door. She was safe.

Suddenly a face pressed up against the door. Jonathon! Caylin bit her tongue to keep from screaming. Her heart beat so loudly, she was sure it would give her away. She tried not to move an inch, to breathe—she even tried to use her meditation techniques to become one with the wall. But her mind kept telling her she was dead meat. She shut her eyes and waited for the inevitable—for him to come out and throw her off the balcony.

She waited for what seemed like hours. Summoning

all her courage, she opened her eyes. Jonathon's face was gone. And finally, after what seemed like an eternity, she heard the door inside open, close, and lock.

"I made it," Caylin murmured under her breath. "I'm alive. I made it." She peeked through the glass door—the office truly was empty. But when Caylin tried to open the door, it wouldn't budge. Jonathon had locked it.

"Just my luck," she muttered. What on earth was Jonathon doing in his office on a holiday, anyway? Didn't he have a *life*?

"Stay calm," Caylin told herself, taking a long, deep breath. She exhaled and began methodically removing her rappelling gear from her backpack. Thankfully she was only six floors up. Scaling down the embassy would be a walk in Hyde Park compared to the death-defying descents she'd made with her dad on some of their father-daughter mountaineering journeys. That didn't mean it was going to be easy, however.

After slipping off her gray housecoat to reveal a black bodysuit and tights, she quickly changed into her light-weight footwear and tied the housecoat around her waist.

The service key! she remembered with a start. It was useless on the glass door, but she sure needed it to get back into Jonathon's office. She detached it from the key chain and hooked it onto her hoop earring for safekeeping.

Caylin strapped on her harness, hooked it up to the line, and secured the other end of the line to the balcony rail. She tugged on it to make sure the connection was solid. After she wiped the sweat from her palms, she grabbed on to the end of the line nearest the balcony. On a wing and a prayer she boosted herself up onto the rail, swung her legs over, and dropped down over the side.

Her heart pounded fiercely—half from excitement, half from fear—as she swung freely under the balcony. The rush was intense. Her nerve endings were practically singing. With a grunt she swung her legs up so her feet met the wall. Pulling the line taut, she began walking down the side of the embassy, letting out a little line with each step.

Fifth floor . . . fourth floor . . .

As she descended she felt eerily calm—the way she always felt while doing something intensely physical. But this time the stakes were different. Her backpack was splayed out where her "boss" could find it, totally blow her cover, and bring her career as a spy to a screaming halt. Her line was hooked to the balcony of a terrorist who could rush out and send her plummeting to her death without a second thought.

Caylin's palms immediately went into a sweat. She lost her grip momentarily and slipped down the rope. In her free fall the air whooshed out of her lungs. She couldn't breathe. She couldn't scream.

With a thud she landed on the third-floor balcony.

"Third floor," she murmured. "Housewares, lingerie, and *time to get a grip, Caylin*." Thankfully the room on the other side of the glass door was abandoned. She'd hate to have all that awful explaining to do while her butt was aching.

Glowering, she wiped her palms on the housecoat and pitched herself over the balcony for the last half of the ride. She rushed herself—not a smart move where safety was concerned, but she had no time to waste. Her nerves were jangling anxiously, and she lost her foothold a couple of times. But she wanted to get her toes on solid ground and her tail back up to Jonathon's office before Jonathon—or Fiona, even—could catch a drift of her little ruse.

She slid all the way down the line from the second-floor balcony, silently cheering as she touched down. With lightning speed she disconnected herself from the rope, brushed off, and slipped into her uniform. She left her harness connected to the rope—she'd pull it up once she made it back to Jonathon's office.

If I get there in time, that is, she thought with a wince. Sheer panic flooded her body. Mortified, she unsuccessfully smoothed out the wrinkles in her housecoat and prayed no one would ask her where she got such weird-looking shoes.

Caylin knew her confidence wasn't about to return anytime soon, but she didn't have time to wait for it. She rushed toward the rear security entrance. She didn't want the woman up front wondering where she'd lost her fabulous barrettes.

"I can't bloody believe this, but I was taking out the trash and got locked out," Caylin ranted before the rear security guard could open his mouth. "Cripes, I'm not even supposed to work today and I get stuck out in the wind! Can't believe my luck. I really bloody can't."

The overweight security guard, engrossed in his *Sun* tabloid, barely even looked up during her entire monologue. Finally his gaze met hers. "No bother," he muttered, buzzing her in.

Once in, Caylin raced to the elevator and back up to Jonathon's office without encountering another soul. She removed the key from her earring and opened the door. The office looked exactly how she'd left it. And the balcony—*yes!* Her hook glimmered through the glass door. She put on her rubber cleaning gloves, undid the lock, and stepped out onto the balcony, wanting to drop to her knees and kiss her untouched backpack and even her ugly embassy-issue housekeeping shoes.

"What in the world are you doing out there?"

"F-Fiona!" Caylin whirled around and gave her boss what she hoped was a confident smile. "Well, Jonathon asked me to dust off the balcony of his suite the other day," she lied, heart pounding like crazy as she positioned her body in front of the hook. "I figured I'd do it for his office as well."

Fiona eyed her suspiciously, but Caylin's innocent gaze didn't waver one bit. "Oh, well, all right, then," Fiona said. "I was just wondering where you'd run off to. Security called me down to confirm you were the right girl and all. Everyone's high-strung round here with the conference just two weeks away, and I just wanted to suss everything out."

Caylin exhaled in relief. "Everything's right as rain, Fiona. I'm working like a busy bee. In fact, I'd climb the walls if you gave the word."

EIGHT

"I've got the munchies in a *big* way," Theresa declared. Even though she'd only made it a couple of hours past lunch—shepherd's pie, the Tuesday special at the embassy commissary—she was feeling the need for something cocoa derived to combat the starch in her stomach. Desperate, she turned to the young woman at the voice mail station to her right for advice. "Siobhan, do you know if there are any vending machines in this place?" she asked breathlessly.

Siobhan looked at her questioningly. "You mean, candy machines and the like?"

"Yes!"

"Sorry, no," Siobhan replied. "But you might try the kitchen. I've snuck in there a few times m'self when I'm feeling peckish."

"Great. Do you want anything?"

"Ta, but no. Go on—I'll cover for you."

"Thanks, Siobhan." In a flash Theresa was out of her seat and motoring down the hall, visions of chocolate cake, chocolate pudding, and chocolate chocolate dancing before her eyes. As she made her way down the hall she kept extra vigilant. She hoped no one would see her sneak in and get suspicious. As a guy passed her in the otherwise empty hallway she nodded uncomfortably. Her palms were sweaty, trembling. She needed a chocolate fix *bad*.

She burst through the kitchen doors and made a bee-line for the fridge. But as she sifted through it her spirits sank. There was nothing rich and sinfully delicious in sight. There wasn't even anything brown. She *did* find, to her amazement, some bottles of nail polish, a few prescription drug vials, and even a crystal vase. *Not* the kinds of things regularly served at the commissary. She felt as if she'd stumbled on someone's stash of goodies.

Ding! went the brilliance bell in Theresa's head. A kitchen is an awfully good place to hide something that isn't food related, she realized. Maybe I should have a look around while I have the place to myself. If Caylin found a date book in a fuse box, why couldn't she find a top secret disc in the kitchen?

She started with the cabinets, pulling everything out and feeling along the bottom of large cans and bowls for anything suspicious. She even felt along the shelf paper but to no avail. Next came the drawers. Still no luck.

Once she had removed nearly all the refrigerator's contents onto the kitchen floor for inspection, she panicked. She *definitely* heard the commissary door open. Oh no, she thought, terrified. Who could it be—and how exactly was she supposed to explain away the mess? She hoped it was just someone cleaning the commissary tables, but she couldn't rely on hope anymore. In a total frenzy she scrambled to cram everything back into the fridge. A carton of eggs opened in the mayhem, and one crashed to the floor.

"Oh, *pretzels*," she mumbled. As she searched for a paper towel she heard someone clear his throat loudly. She held her breath and looked to her left. Immaculate brown hair, a tall, toned frame, golden skin—Jonathon Nicholson!

"Who the heck are you?" Jonathon demanded, his tone nasty.

She lowered her gaze, feeling like a reprimanded schoolgirl. "Emma Webster," she answered. "Voice mail technician."

"What are you looking for?" he asked suspiciously.

"My, uh—" she stammered.

"Yes?" he demanded.

Her heart hammered, and her eyes began to water. "My, uh, asthma medication," she muttered, remembering the asthma inhaler cam in her purse. "I brought it to work, and Ms. Dalton said she'd stick it in the kitchen for me, but now I can't find it anywhere." She weakly picked up the prescription vials she'd found to support her fib. "And I—am—having—a—hard—time—breathing."

Theresa began to fake an asthma attack, gasping for breath as hard and convincingly as she could. Her best friend back home had asthma, so she had witnessed a few attacks.

Jonathon's eyes grew wide. "Oh, my gosh, sit down. Do

you need a paper bag to breathe into or something?"

She motioned to her purse, which he brought over to her double quick. She quickly retrieved her inhaler cam from the bottom of it, put it in her mouth, and pushed down. Instead of releasing medicine like a real inhaler, it snapped a pic of Jonathon. Up dose, his eyes looked puffy—so much so, she was tempted to ask him about it.

Once she got the snaps she needed, her "asthma attack" miraculously ended. "Whoa, looks like I'm getting my air back," Theresa said, breathing an exaggerated sigh of relief. "Thank you so much for your help."

"No problem."

Theresa waved, deciding to leave the refrigerator items on the floor, egg and all, for extra effect. "Well, bye."

"Bye," Jonathon said, giving her a questioning look as she departed.

Did I make him suspicious? she wondered anxiously as she tried to mentally process his look. No, maybe . . . maybe he's just worried about me! The idea made her swoon—half in enchantment, half in amusement. Imagine a coldblooded killer getting all weakhearted over a girl with asthma!

• • •

"So he looked all upset, and his eyes were red," Theresa relayed that night in 1423.

"I might know why," Caylin said, waving a printout. "This just came in from The Tower. Alfred called again at fifteen hundred hours and told Jonathon if he didn't get his disc by the conference, his father was going to be killed. Transcript right here."

"Oh, my gosh, no wonder!" Theresa exclaimed. "I'm such a jerk. That's when I was in the kitchen. Siobhan was covering for me, and she must have patched his call through!"

"Don't worry about it," Jo said. "It's a good thing you did—otherwise we wouldn't have found out this info."

"You know, you kind of have to feel sorry for the guy," Caylin commented. "He's totally in over his head."

Jo snorted. "He's a total scumbag. He puts his own father's life on the line for a pile of dough."

Theresa shrugged, not sure what to think. His swollen eyes had definitely looked as if they'd shed some major tears, so maybe he was genuinely upset. But if he was so upset about it, why was he going through with it?

"Well, no matter what we do or don't think about Jonathon," Caylin began, "the pressure's on to find this disc. At least Theresa was making an effort to find it today, unlike the rest of us. We've gotta move, and we've gotta move now."

"The key word is *green*," Theresa reminded them. "Is there anyplace in the embassy related to the color green? The kitchen's out, but maybe some of the rooms have green walls."

"Maybe it's hidden in a green book in the library," Jo said.

"Or a greenhouse, if there is one," Caylin suggested.

Theresa chewed her nails. "Too many possibilities. My brain's going to crash just thinking about them."

"Well, we've got to get on this double quick," Caylin said. "We lost our steam after that night at Meltdown, but we need to get it back. I, for one, have a surprise in my backpack—Jonathon's trash. I snagged it today when I was cleaning."

"Oh, joy," Jo muttered. All this talk about William Nicholson's possible fate gave her an ugly feeling of déjà vu, and the thought of digging through his loser son's trash did nothing to improve her mood.

"Hopefully there's nothing too gross in here," Caylin said, crossing her fingers as she laid out some newspaper on the coffee table and placed the bag on top. "Jo, would you do the honors since you have the longest nails?"

"Whatever," Jo griped, slicing the bag with a long red nail.

Caylin dumped out the contents. A receipt from a corner deli, a half-empty bag of salt-and-vinegar potato chips, a banana peel, a coffee cup, some crumbled-up junk mail, and some miscellaneous scraps of paper. Nothing terribly exciting.

"Any of this look useful to you guys?" Theresa asked.

Jo sifted through the lot with disdain. "Hardly."

"Hey—look at this business card," Caylin said, snatching it up. "It's a nearby hotel. Maybe he stayed there so he could have some privacy."

"So he could make private phone calls, perhaps," Theresa suggested. "You know, so his father wouldn't overhear him?"

"There's only one way to find out," Caylin announced. "Pass me the phone, *por favor*."

"Five Sumner Place—may I help you?"

"Yes, you may," Caylin began, putting a stuffy spin on her working-class Louise accent. "This is Veronica Carey, Jonathon Nicholson's secretary, and I believe he recently stayed there. If it's not too much trouble, I just need to confirm the day and time he checked out for his expense report."

"Very well, Ms.—Carey, was it?" the clerk said.

Caylin smiled confidently. "Yes. C-a-r-e-y. And while you've got the file handy, could you check and see if he made any calls? He never writes any of this stuff in, it's a bloody mess, and I'm left to sort through the fallout."

The clerk laughed. "My boss is like that, too."

Caylin heard the sound of computer keys clicking and crossed her fingers.

"Let's see," the clerk said, "he checked in yesterday at nine p.m. and out this morning at seven forty-five a.m. And there were four calls, all to the same international number."

"What country?" Caylin asked, hoping she wasn't pushing her luck. "I have to file them under different codes, you know."

"Hold on just a moment, please," the clerk said. "I'm looking that up for you."

Caylin held her breath.

"Ms. Carey?" the clerk asked. "That international country code indicates the call was placed to Laqui Bay."

Caylin stifled a gasp. "Ta," she said in shock before she hung up the phone.

"Any luck?" Jo asked halfheartedly.

"You're not going to like this one bit," Caylin began, her heart pounding. "But the call was made to Laqui Bay."

"*What?*" Jo shrieked, her eyes wide with disbelief.

"No way." Theresa shook her head. "This is incredible! You mean *the* Laqui Bay?"

"Like there's another one?" Caylin quipped with a snort. "Listen, if there was a different island called Laqui Bay, they should be searching for a new name double quick."

"Seriously," Theresa breathed. "I mean, it'd reek to

be mistaken for the place responsible for bombing that jet last year—"

"Or for taking all those hostages in that awful subway incident—remember?" Jo added.

"Or for threatening world security by claiming possession of nuclear missiles," Caylin suggested with a serious nod.

"That's right!" Theresa snapped her fingers. "Hey, maybe that threat was just wishful thinking. Maybe it was jumping the gun—"

"Until they got their hands on the warheads list," Caylin finished. "Well, if they think it's that easy, they've got another thing coming."

"I don't know," Theresa said, glowering. "If we think we can take on Laqui Bay, I'd say *we've* got another thing coming."

NINE

"Get out of my office and *never* come back!"

"What?" Caylin screeched, terror coursing through her veins as the brick solid figure of Jonathon Nicholson confronted her after one single baby step into his office.

"You heard me—out. From now on I'm doing my own cleaning." He stormed over to the door and held it open. His dark eyes shot sparks at her, virtually daring her to protest.

"What's your bloody problem?" she asked, hoping to get at least one tiny morsel of information out of him. If he was busting her, anyway, what would it hurt to push?

"It's none of your *bloody* business," he hollered with a sarcastic, mimicking tone. "Now get out and stay out."

As Caylin followed his orders her head spun with worry. If he had finally realized she was the babe with the bugs, he could blow the mission—and possibly the entire world—sky-high. Either that or he'd just knock her off himself. Either way she was one dead dame.

At lunch Caylin ran to the Ritz to see if Uncle Sam had been in contact. The following message was in the laptop's incoming mailbox:

> J.N. office transmitters discovered this morning 8 a.m.
> followed by suite 8:15. Static received on all stations.
> Lay low until video conference tonight.
> —Uncle S.

So Jonathon *was* buggin' over the bugs, Caylin thought with a sinking heart as she headed back to the embassy. She skulked into the utility room and jumped about a mile in shock. Fiona sat in wait for her, an evil look on her face. "Do you know anything about these silly devices found in the Nicholsons' offices and suites?" she demanded.

"What . . . devices?" Caylin asked innocently.

"The ones found in the Nicholsons' offices and suites,"

Fiona repeated slowly, as if she were speaking to a kinder-gartner. "Surveillance stuff. Spy gear. *Bugs*, I think they're called?"

"I have no clue what you're talking about," Caylin said with an edge of offense. "You know, Jonathon went off on me this morning, and I was wondering what his blimey problem was."

"That's it," Fiona said, cracking a smile. "I got the riot act myself, so don't feel bad. The suites are now off-limits to the cleaning staff, as are the Nicholsons' offices. Less bally work for us, right? And I hear they think some trans-lator did it, anyway, so there's really no need to worry. But I had to ask."

Caylin nodded understandingly, trying her hardest not to look upset. A translator? she asked herself. That could only be one person . . . Jo!

Jo sipped her carrot juice and drank in the afternoon sun-shine, a precious rarity. Pentland's, an outdoor café near the hotel, was the perfect place for a lunchtime getaway. The commissary's Wednesday meal du jour, bangers and mash, was hardly anything to write home about, and she really needed the private time. She wasn't used to being around people 24/7, being an only child and all. When her aunt and uncle had adopted her, they had given her the space and solitude she had grown accustomed to. Two things she hadn't had much of since coming to London, that was for sure.

"May I join you?" a familiar voice asked, breaking into her thoughts. Her skin tingled as she looked up from her journal to see Antonio, a charming smile playing on his lips.

"Okay," she said, figuring she could easily sacrifice her private moment for a flirt sesh. As long as she didn't let it get *too* intense. "How's it going?"

"Pretty good," he replied, taking a sip from his steaming cappuccino. "Work's been a killer, right?"

"That's for sure," she agreed, though work was the least of her problems.

"I'd give anything to jump in my Porsche right now and take a few spins around a racetrack," he said with a sigh.

"You race?" she asked in amazement.

"Oh yeah, I love it," he said. "You too?"

"That's an understatement. I *live* for it!" She leaned back in her chair and twirled the straw in her drink. "But how did a working man like you score a Porsche? I'm *dying* to know."

"My uncle left it to me in his will. He died last year."

"Oh, I'm sorry. Were you close?"

"Yes—he taught me everything I know about racing." His face pinched up for a moment. "I could sell it—I sure need the money. But driving in it reminds me of him. I wouldn't sell that for the world."

I know what you mean, Jo thought, her heart going out to him.

"Enough about me," Antonio began, understandably anxious to change the subject. "I've been meaning to ask you—how'd you learn to speak Arabic?"

"Huh?" she asked, taken aback. "Wh-why do you want to know *that*?"

"I overheard you telling Jonathon you spoke Arabic, and I don't remember Sandra saying you did. So I was just wondering how you picked it up."

She crossed her fingers under the table and took a deep breath. "Well, um, my father had this oil baron friend from Saudi Arabia who stayed with us for a while when I was little," she fibbed. "So I guess that's where it started. And I studied it a bit in college. I'm not exactly fluent, though."

He raised his eyebrows. "Whoa, I'm impressed. Your dad must have friends in high places."

"My dad is dead," she said automatically, looking down. She hoped this true confession wouldn't blow her cover.

He touched her elbow. "I'm really sorry."

"It's okay."

"Well, I'm still sorry," he said quietly. "Listen, could we meet for coffee some weekend?"

"What?" she asked, heart racing. "I mean, um, sure."

"So how can I get in touch with you?" he asked.

"The Ritz," she said. "Uh, with my aunt—Camilla Stevens." Inside she kicked herself for giving up her home base so easily. But what could she do? Antonio had a way of getting her guard down. Besides, one coffee date wasn't going to hurt anything.

"Stevens?" he asked. "I thought your last name was Sanchez."

"It is," she stammered, "but it's my aunt from my mom's side."

He nodded and looked at his watch. "Oh no—I was supposed to meet my friend Graham at the gym ten minutes ago. I totally forgot today's our gym day."

She smiled. "That's okay—go."

"I hate to, believe me, but he'll kill me if I bail on him," he said apologetically. "I'll give you a call, okay?"

As he looked into her eyes she wondered if the strange feeling in her stomach was a product of excitement over this encounter or fear she was getting in too deep. Suddenly she couldn't tell the difference anymore.

That night at the suite Theresa paused for a moment over her French onion soup. "Was that a knock?" she asked.

Antonio! Jo thought, jumping to her feet and almost upending her salad. She floated to the door, her heart sinking a bit when she found only a bellman behind it. But her spirits lifted instantly when she saw he was holding a gigantic gold Godiva box.

"Package for a Ms. Natascia Sanchez," the man said.

"For me?" Jo cheered, grabbing the megabox out of his hands. She fished a few pound notes out of her pocket and blindly tossed them to the bellman.

"Very good, m'lady," he said, tipping his hat. "Have a pleasant evening."

Jo ripped open the card with glee. "Oh, my gosh, check this out," she demanded, heart rate accelerating faster than a zillion-horsepower engine. "'Natascia, here's to fast cars and faster friendships. Antonio.' Ohhh, couldn't you just *die*?"

"Pretty profound," Theresa said, focusing her gaze on the Godiva chocolates. "Pass 'em over."

"So how well do you know this guy?" Caylin asked. "Don't forget, Jonathon thinks a *translator* planted the bugs. And that more than likely means you, Jo. Maybe Antonio is one of Jonathon's cronies."

"Antonio has nothing to do with Jonathon," Jo said, rolling her eyes. Honestly, her roomie could be such a stick-in-the-mud. "I know him well enough, I assure you. Now which one should I have first? The pink one or the heart-shaped chocolate one?"

"Come on, you guys!" Caylin cried. "Jo's life could be in danger here. *All* our lives could be in danger now that this Antonio guy knows where we *are*! Doesn't that matter to you?"

"Not where chocolate's concerned," Theresa said as she studied the chocolate map. "Okay, Jo, you've got strawberry creme and macadamia nut. But—wait a second—the strawberry creme is supposed to be in the corner, not the middle."

"Same difference," Jo said, the pink confection just millimeters away from her mouth.

"Don't bite into it!" Theresa cried, batting the strawberry creme out of her hand.

"What are you doing?" Jo demanded. "Have you gone psycho or something?"

"No," Theresa said, pointing down to the map urgently. "See, these are all out of order. Which means they might have been *tampered* with."

"Hmmm. Can we say *par-a-noid*?" Jo quipped.

"You see? You see?" Caylin said, moving in for a closer look. "I bet Antonio *is* working with Jonathon. How can we be so sure he's not a bad guy?"

"Caylin's right. Look." Theresa held a piece of candy before Jo's eyes. "There's a little pinprick in the side here. And it looks like that's not the only one."

Jo inspected the candy herself, feeling a bit skeptical. But the more pinpricks she saw, the more convinced she became. "I guess we're better safe than sorry," she admitted.

"You'd better believe it!" Caylin ran her hand through her hair anxiously. "We should send these out to the lab immediately. Find out just what kind of guy we're dealing with here."

"I'll handle it," Theresa offered.

"And if there's *any* way you can convince them to *not* breathe a word of this to Uncle Sam, please do it," Caylin begged. "Because if he *ever* finds out that *someone* gave out our home base to a terrorist, that *someone's* going to get us all declassified!"

Jo shook her head in disbelief and flinched as Caylin's

tirade sank in. Jo had let her friends down—and she'd let *herself* down, too. Clearly Antonio was bad news from the beginning. Jo had known there was something different about him, something unnerving. Still, she couldn't believe that Antonio would actually want her dead. No way. Why would the guy who made her heart do back flips want to stop it from beating altogether?

TEN

"Hey, Antonio," Jo called when she walked into the translation office on Thursday morning in her usual flirtatious fashion. "Thanks *so* much for the chocolates," she cooed. "I was just *super* tired last night, and I couldn't take a bite. But it was so sweet of you."

"Not at all," he said with a wink. "The pleasure is all mine, Natascia."

She shivered, wondering if she was only imagining the predatory flash in his eyes.

"Jo, William Nicholson needs your translating services ASAP," Sandra announced from her office. "It's urgent. He has someone in his office right now."

Oh no, she thought in a panic. Does he need my *Arabic* translating services?

The color drained from her face as she headed to his

office, feeling as if she was on her way to the electric chair.

When she entered the office, she found a well-dressed man sitting in front of Nicholson's desk. Please don't be Arabic, she chanted silently. Please don't be Arabic.

"Hello, Ms. Sanchez. This is Mr. Sandro from Portugal," Mr. Nicholson said. "If you could kindly translate our conversation, it would be much appreciated."

"Certainly, sir," she said, breathing a big sigh of relief.

As the men began to talk she mindlessly translated the rather boring conversation between them. As far as she could tell, nothing of interest was being discussed—just a lot of political mumbo jumbo.

"Could we have a tour of the green room in the basement?" Mr. Sandro asked in Portuguese, putting Jo on red alert.

Green room? she thought. Like, a perfect place for a *green* disc?

Nicholson cleared his throat after Jo translated the question. "Well, I can't discuss that with a translator present," he said, looking uncomfortable. "It's highly sensitive information."

The cat's got Nicholson's tongue, Jo realized, her heart soaring. This is the big break we've been waiting for!

"I have an amazing announcement," Jo told Caylin and Theresa the second she came through the door that evening.

"You've got a date with Harry Styles?" Theresa joked.

"No—how about you've found a good-tasting fat-free potato chip?" Caylin said, making a face as she bit into one from the open bag on her lap.

"Wrong and very wrong," Jo said, plopping down on the couch next to the girls. "I found out there's a green room in the embassy."

"A *what*?" Caylin and Theresa asked in stereo.

"A *green* room," she repeated. "I was clued in today while translating for Nicholson. Anyone else thinking what I'm thinking?"

"Green room, green disc?" Theresa said, eyebrows raised.

"Right on," Jo screeched, barely able to contain her excitement. "I mean, what are the odds? It's fate!"

• • •

"Hey, have you ever heard of the green room?" Caylin asked Fiona nonchalantly on Friday morning. Her pulse was racing in anticipation of getting the goods.

Fiona cocked her head thoughtfully. "I have heard of it but never actually seen it. And as far as I know, no one except for Mr. Nicholson himself is allowed down there."

"But do you know what's in there?" Caylin asked.

"No clue," Fiona said. "Confidential stuff—papers, documents, stuff like that. As far as I'm concerned, I'm glad it's off-limits. Just one more blasted room to clean."

Later that morning Caylin went back to the same storage closet where she'd found the date book. Even though she'd already turned it upside down, she figured it was worth another shot, like maybe Devaroux wrote out its location on a bottle of oil soap or something. She took all the bottles down from the shelves and inspected their labels closely but found nothing. Disheartened, she checked out the linen closet next.

"Uh, can I help you?"

She jumped and smiled cluelessly at the janitor hovering in the doorway. "Just looking for some bleedin' ammonia—you got any?" she asked, scratching her head.

"Try storage down the hall," he said, looking at her as if she were two sandwiches short of a picnic. "This closet's just for linens, hence the name."

"Sorry, fella," she said apologetically. "I'm new and all."

"Don't worry yourself, luv."

"Say—you know where the green room is?" she asked, deciding to take a chance. "That's something else I'm having trouble finding."

"Worked here three years, and I never heard of it," he said. "The green room, is it?"

"Yeah . . . well, maybe I sussed it wrong," she lied, her spirits plummeting. "Ta."

"Dinner reservations, eight o'clock sharp," Theresa announced the second she walked into suite 1423.

"Dinner reservations?" Jo asked. "Is that a good idea with this chocolate scare and all?"

"I took a call this afternoon confirming Jonathon Nicholson's reservation for two at eight o'clock at Simpsons-in-the-Strand restaurant," Theresa said, chest swelling with pride over her coup. "Which means we now have instant dinner plans."

"Could be a good lead," Caylin said optimistically. "But sadly, I have nothing to wear." She put the back of her hand to her forehead and swooned dramatically.

"Cay's right, you know," Jo replied. "Jonathon knows what we look like. We have to go totally incognito. Does London have any after-hours wig shops?"

"Already taken care of," Theresa said. "If you'll head into my room, ladies, I believe you'll find a shipment of goodies from a designer I just *happen* to know personally. To my room, pronto!"

Jo and Caylin ran into Theresa's room lickety-split. Theresa followed behind, chuckling.

"All right, Mom clothes!" Jo cheered as she ripped open the box. After the chocolate scare, Jacqueline Hearth's wacky fashions were just what the doctor ordered.

Caylin rubbed her hands together anxiously, looking like a kid on Christmas morning. "Bring 'em on!"

"This is too cool!" Jo cried, checking out the rainbow of vinyl clothes, fluorescent wigs, and feather boas.

"I can't believe your mom actually made these," Caylin said in awe.

"I have to admit, she *is* a splendiferous designer, even if her funky clothes don't exactly float my boat," Theresa admitted. "And Mom was hoping we'd road test these before she debuts them on the runway."

"Wow—what an honor!" Jo said, pink wig covering her black locks. She felt curiously carefree as she admired the colors, textures, and fabrics. "How did you get 'em here so quickly?"

"Mom's got a boutique here in London, so she arranged to have her samples messengered over today," Theresa explained.

"What do you think of these?" Caylin asked, pointing to the large cat eye glasses perched on her nose. "Nonprescription."

Theresa laughed. "*Très* chic." She leaned over and grabbed a chartreuse boa from the stack. "How about this?" she asked, rolling her eyes as she wrapped it around her neck. "Is it me?"

"Oh, definitely," Jo gushed, chuckling. "Watch out,

world—because the Spy Girls are glamming up tonight!"

"No way will Jonathon Nicholson recognize us under all this glitz and glimmer," Caylin chirped as she balanced a vinyl poor boy cap on top of a towering bouffant wig.

Well, one thing's for sure—we'll get noticed, Theresa mused as she checked out her too flashy reflection in the mirror. *And if* Jonathon *notices us, will he end up* recognizing *us too?*

As Caylin entered Simpsons-in-the-Strand she almost burst out laughing. The restaurant was totally pretentious—huge abstract mural on the wall, well-coiffed diners in black clothes, tiny entrees on big plates with bigger price tags. It could have just as easily been in L.A. or New York—places like this were all the same.

"May I help you?" the snooty hostess inquired, looking them up and down sourly.

"Reservation for three. Stevens," Jo replied, her tone just as stuffy as the hostess's expression.

"Yes," she said, giving them one more sweeping glance. "Right this way."

As they followed the hostess across the restaurant Caylin felt as though every person in the room had turned to watch them being seated. "Maybe we overdid it," she whispered, feeling a bit exposed in her pink wig, white vinyl dress, and pink platform boots.

"I don't think so," Jo said, shaking her cherry red wig and smoothing out her matching red vinyl jumper.

"Well, I for one feel like a Slip 'N Slide from third grade," Theresa joked, obviously referring to her bright yellow vinyl pants, matching baby T, and white Marilyn Monroe wig.

"Hey—there he is. Three o'clock." Caylin motioned slightly to a table for two in the corner where Jonathon was getting cozy with a striking redhead.

Theresa immediately started snapping pictures with the special salt-and-pepper-shaker cameras she had whipped out of her bag and placed on the table. "What's our next move?" she asked. "Maybe we should send two drinks to Jonathon's table anonymously, only we bug the glasses first."

"I don't know," Caylin began, her heart pounding.

"After what happened the other day, I think Jonathon's got his back up about this bugging thing."

"Not to worry—I've got the power accessory of the day, ladies." Jo waved a large, garish-looking costume ring under Caylin's nose. "It's really a long-range audio surveillance device. All I have to do is aim it in their direction and voilà."

"But how are we supposed to hear anything?" Caylin asked.

"The audio feeds straight into this." She pulled back a few wisps of cherry red "hair" to reveal an elaborate jeweled earpiece. "It's hideous, I know. Thank goodness it's hidden by the wig."

"Yeah, The Tower *is* kind of behind in the style department," Caylin said with a laugh.

"May I take your order?" a tall, waifish waitress inquired.

"We need a few minutes," Theresa requested.

The waitress departed, and Jo's brow wrinkled in concentration. "I'm starting to get a feed," she whispered. "Okay. It's working."

Caylin leaned over excitedly. "Are they talking about the disc?"

"Has he noticed us?" Theresa whispered, feeling like a sitting duck in her bright yellow ensemble.

"Give me a second," Jo admonished, putting her finger to her lips. She smiled. "Well, she *is* someone special."

"A coconspirator?" Caylin guessed. "A secret love?"

"Alfred's wife?" Theresa blabbed, shrugging as everyone turned to give her blank stares. "Well, he could have a wife, you know."

"Wrong on all counts. She's an old friend from high school who just arrived in London for a fellowship."

"Think it's a cover-up?" Caylin asked, eyeing the woman suspiciously.

"Highly unlikely," Jo said. "They're talking about old times—the prom, homeroom teachers, stuff like that. I think she's legit."

Theresa ran her hands through her wig frantically, sending it slightly off-kilter. "You mean I got dressed in this getup for nothing?"

Caylin smiled. "I happen to like this look and the fact that we're out together. So we went on a hunch and were wrong— big deal! At least we'll get some good eats out of the bargain."

"True and true again," Theresa agreed. "Now get that waitress over here. I'm a starvin' Marvin, and the chocolate mousse on that dessert tray has been taunting me."

Caylin's eyes wandered around the restaurant. Suddenly she spotted a familiar brunette parked at the far end of the bar. Short Hair! Their disguises weren't fooling anyone after all.

"Jo and T., there—at the bar—Short Hair!" Caylin whispered, pointing to the far end, where only a half-full glass and an empty bar stool sat. "Darn!"

"Where?" Theresa said. "*The* Short Hair? I don't see her."

"She was right there," Caylin insisted, her nerves jangling. "Let me go look around."

Caylin did a tour of duty around the restaurant but returned a few minutes later, defeated. "She's nowhere to be found. Maybe she's the one who sent Jo the chocolates. Like, she's working with Antonio or something."

Jo's face fell. "No, I'm pretty much convinced that this woman is involved with Jonathon. And if she knows we're here, then *he* might know we're here."

"At this point I think it's safe to assume everyone's

involved with everyone," Theresa suggested. "Let's blow this joint. I'll choose personal safety over chocolate mousse, no matter how painful the decision."

When they arrived back at the hotel after grabbing fish-and-chips at the neighborhood pub, the labs were awaiting them.

"Well, it was lucky you didn't eat those chocolates, Jo," Theresa said as she inspected the pages from The Tower's lab.

"What is it?" Jo asked. "Not a love potion, I'm guessing."

"It turns out the chocolate was full of an elaborate chemical concoction dominated mainly by benazathol, kyryzalophin, and phyloranine. A signature cocktail—the kind of thing only used by spies and terrorists. Your average joe couldn't get this kind of thing on the street . . . or even on this side of the world."

"What would it have done to me?" Jo whispered, trembling.

"It would have paralyzed you at first, then worked almost like a truth serum. But three hours after you ingested it, you would have been dead."

"Oh, my gosh." Jo's blood chilled to below freezing. "Death by chocolate. For real." Tears welled up in her eyes. She'd come so close. . . .

Theresa wrapped her in a hug. "Hey, I was going to eat them, too, remember?"

"But you didn't, and that's what counts," Caylin said. "Listen, these people are playing for keeps. They don't care who they hurt to come out on top. And if we let them walk all over us, we should just hang this gig up right now. I, for one, am *not* going to allow that to happen. Are you with me?"

"I am," Theresa vowed.

Jo gulped as an image of her father flashed before her eyes. "Count me in," she said, her resolve strengthening. She wasn't going to let anyone walk on her again—especially not Antonio. And on Monday she was prepared to hit him with the crudest joke she could play on him—surviving.

ELEVEN

"Antonio, you devil, you," Jo cooed as she leaned against his desk first thing on Monday morning. He looked up at her and half gasped. She could practically feel the shock radiating off him.

"N-Natascia, hi," he stammered. "What's up?"

"Oh . . . not much," she insisted. "I just have some great news for you."

"And what is that, exactly?" he asked, his expression darkening.

"I finally tried those chocolates you gave me," she said, running a finger up his arm. "I wolfed down *every single last one* of them. All by my lonesome. Mmmm . . . they really were yummy to my tummy."

"Uh, that's . . . great," he muttered. His jaw sagged a little bit to the left.

"Thanks again, sweetie." She winked at him and sauntered over to her cubicle. There. Things were out in the open now. Seeing the look on his face made her brush with death almost totally worth it. She wished she knew what he was thinking now. He was probably going nuts trying to figure out who she was, what she knew, and why she hadn't perished from his spiked sweets. Probably questioning his masculinity or something, too.

Feeling empowered, Jo began sifting through the file cabinets in the office for info about the green room. She'd avoided the files thus far for fear of being caught. But today was the day to live on the edge. Finally, after searching through three full filing cabinets, she discovered a Spanish file marked *verde*. As she opened it slowly her heart nearly jumped in her throat. There, *en español*, were all the vital green room stats.

Jo, looking around the room to make sure she wasn't being watched, smiled triumphantly and slipped the document in her purse. She was going to find that disc before Antonio did, even if she had to die trying. She'd come close enough already.

• • •

As soon as Caylin and Theresa arrived at the Ritz on Monday evening Jo immediately sat them down on the living room floor. "Brace yourselves," she said. "I hit pay dirt."

Caylin held her breath. "What'd you find?"

"This," Jo said, extracting a piece of paper from her pocket. "*En español.* Green room vitals. How many entrances the floor has, its exact location, and—presto!— the company who installed the security system."

Theresa's mouth dropped open in disbelief. "Ohmigosh, it's too good to be true!"

"Rock on!" Caylin cheered. "This could be the key to finding our disc!"

"So what do we do next?" Jo asked, rubbing her hands together.

Theresa drifted away in thought for a moment. "I know. One of us should call to confirm the green room's security system ASAP. Once we've gotten that info, we move from there."

• • •

"Hello, this is Verna Frazier," Theresa announced in a nasal voice on Tuesday morning. "I'm an insurance clerk for the U.S. Embassy, and I need to confirm some security information."

"Okay, let me connect you with someone who can help you," said the Securitech receptionist.

Theresa's heart was practically pounding out of her chest, and she hoped her nervousness wasn't detectable over the phone lines.

From the red phone booth in which she was huddled, she had a perfect view of the embassy across the street. The disc is somewhere in there, she thought, exhaling deeply. She didn't take her eyes off the building until someone picked up the line.

"This is Naomi Thompson. How may I assist?"

"Yes—this is Verna Frazier," Theresa said, making sure her voice sounded as nasally as it had before. "I'm an insurance clerk for the U.S. Embassy. I'm updating my files and need to confirm some security information."

"What sort of information?" the woman asked, sounding suspicious.

Theresa bit her lip and looked down at the handwritten piece of paper Jo had given her. "Let's see," she said, scanning the page. "It looks like I just need to confirm that the system in the green room is still the AC-Twenty, that there's a uniformed security guard employed twenty-four hours a day, and that the only person with authorized security clearance is William Nicholson, U.S. Ambassador."

"And *who* are you again?" the woman asked.

Theresa clutched the receiver a little tighter, knuckles whitening. "Verna Frazier," she repeated quickly, panic rising in her throat. "I'm an insurance clerk at the U.S. Embassy. I actually just started last week. The woman who had the job before me left the files in a wreck, and I have to turn in these reports this afternoon. So if you could help me, I'd really appreciate it."

"Certainly, ma'am," the woman said after a slight pause. "I can check that for you. Hold, please."

As Muzak filled her ears Theresa took a deep breath. Please don't let her come back and bust me, she thought, crossing her fingers.

"Okay," the woman said, returning. "The AC-Twenty

and the security guard parts are correct, but the clearance is not. Mr. William Nicholson has full clearance, and it says here the cleaning crew has limited access Thursday nights from eight to ten in the evening."

Cleaning crew! Theresa thought, her spine tingling. Looks like they're going to have some replacements this week!

"You wouldn't happen to have the name of that cleaning crew listed there, would you?" Theresa asked, attempting to sound as off-the-cuff as she possibly could. "I should probably call to confirm a few things with them—how many are in the crew, how it's invoiced, et cetera."

"Oh, sure," the woman said, totally buying Theresa's whole clueless-new-clerk act. "It's Sunbeam Cleaning Company down Hollyview Road. They're top-notch. They pretty much handle all the high-security jobs in town."

Theresa quickly scrawled the magic words on her piece of paper, then thanked the woman profusely. "You've really saved my day," she said with a laugh, "and maybe even my *life*."

"No problem at all," the woman said, chuckling modestly. "Have a smashing day."

Once I figure out how we can pass for the cleaning crew, Theresa thought, my day won't just be smashing—it'll be superfly.

"Yes, I'd love to work for Sunbeam," Caylin told the director of personnel at Sunbeam in her *Louise* voice before she left for the embassy. It wasn't the first call she'd made that Wednesday morning; she'd already called to cancel Sunbeam's Thursday night green room appointment in her *real* voice. "I hear you have a really nice outfit there, and I'm a real cleaning pro with oodles and oodles of references."

"Well, you're certainly an enthusiastic one now, aren't you?" he asked wryly. "How is one o'clock today?"

"That's brilliant," Caylin said, using the word that Brits seemed to use for everything and anything. "See you then."

The second she hung up the phone, Caylin was hit by the fact that she was supposed to be cleaning offices for Fiona at the same time she was going to interview for the

Sunbeam cleaning job. And taking a late lunch wouldn't work since that wouldn't give her enough time to get everything to the seamstress and counterfeiter Uncle Sam had hooked them up with the night before. She scratched her head and racked her brain. How in the heck was she supposed to be in two places at the same time?

"Fiona, I'm really sick as a dog," Caylin said, doubling over her cleaning bucket from imaginary cramps at 12:38 p.m. "It's that time of the month, you know."

Fiona fixed her with a glare. "I've worked here five years, and I've only called in sick once. Once! And that's when I had gallstones."

"Well, unless you want this bucket filled with puke, I'm going to have to go," Caylin said, making her voice weak and feeble. "And I filled in for that girl who called in sick on bank holiday, remember? So give me a break."

Fiona's features softened a tiny bit. "Righty now, I remember. Well, if you're sick, you're sick. Just leave me the list of which offices you haven't gotten to, and I'll see you tomorrow."

• • •

"So your references are clearly excellent, and we'd love to have you on board," Joseph Winslow, director of personnel at Sunbeam Cleaning Company, announced an hour later.

Caylin smiled brightly, thrilled he had bought her "hardworking Brit looking for extra dough" tale of woe. She was getting good at this acting stuff, if she did say so herself. If she kept this up, there could even be an Oscar somewhere in her future.

"You must be smiling in anticipation of seeing the lovely uniforms," Joseph joked. "Follow me and we'll get you set up."

"Do you chaps have photo ID cards as well?" Caylin asked.

He nodded. "Yes, but you won't need that until your first day on the job."

Caylin bit her lip. She really needed that ID card *today*. She walked along in silence for a moment, collecting her thoughts. After a few paces she said, "I know this sounds silly, but is there any way I could get my ID card today? I'm getting braces on Monday and would hate to have to look at a tin grin on my ID day in, day out. And I plan to be here for a long while, so it'd boost my morale to be able to have a picture I could be proud of." Even Caylin had a hard time keeping a straight face for that explanation.

Joseph looked at her as if she were a few cards short of a deck. "Braces?" he asked. "But your teeth are perfect."

Since she'd already endured two years of braces, he was right—they *were* perfect. She stuck her top teeth out a bit and tried not to smile. "Well, they look okay now, but my dentist says they're shifting. Happens to a lot of people, more than you'd think."

Joseph nodded as they entered the uniform closet "Hmmm—well, I *guess* it's okay. As long as you don't say anything to anyone."

"My lips are sealed," she promised, locking her lips with her fingers and throwing away the imaginary key. "So these are the uniforms?"

"Straight off the runway," he joked. They were even drabber than the one she had to wear at the embassy. The ensemble consisted of navy blue polyester pants, a navy cotton smock that had a Sunbeam Cleaning patch above the left breast, and a matching Sunbeam Cleaning ball cap. *Gag.*

"I need a size . . ." She trailed off, trying to remember what a size eight was in Britspeak. "Thirty. Yes, a thirty." She sighed and thanked her lucky stars she wouldn't have to wear this outfit for more than one evening. Life's too short to wear polyester pants—that had always been her motto.

After he issued her uniform, Joseph snapped her photo and laminated it to a blue-and-white ID card. "Okay," he said, "you're all set until Monday. See you at nine a.m. sharp."

In your dreams, she thought, but instead said with a tin-free smile, "See you then. Ta-ta!"

Once she left the building, Caylin immediately fished her pressed powder compact cell phone out of her purse to call Uncle Sam, as he'd instructed.

"Go to room thirteen eleven in the Sullivan Suites at fourteen twenty-five Plumbtree Road in half an hour," he told her. "There a seamstress and counterfeit ID maker will be waiting. Good luck."

As she snapped the compact shut Caylin hoped—in light of their upcoming green room invasion—that they wouldn't be needing any *more* luck from here on out.

"Theresa, would you be a dear and run by the stationery shop after work to pick up my order?" Ms. Dalton asked her near the end of the day. "Then you could just bring it to work with you tomorrow morning."

"No problem," Theresa said with a smile. After all, it was the first time Dalton had ever asked her to do anything outside of the office and the woman was *way* too old to be trekking around town fetching supplies.

However, once she started making her way to the store, a huge knot formed in the pit of Theresa's stomach. She was certain she was being followed. She kept looking over her shoulder warily, scared to death of what she might find behind her. Each time she saw nothing suspicious. But she still couldn't shake the eerie sensation.

She walked into the stationery shop and picked up Ms. Dalton's order without once experiencing that I'm-being-watched feeling. Her spirits lifted until she exited the store. Rain tore down in sheets all around her. Great, she thought. She was only about ten blocks from the Ritz and was wearing a raincoat, but she had no umbrella. So she stuck the sack in her raincoat pocket and made a mad dash for the tube, where at least she'd keep dry the two stops to the hotel.

A train pulled up immediately, and Theresa sank down into a seat. But as soon as the doors closed, that knot formed in her stomach again. This time, tighter.

She looked around at all the other passengers, checking to see if anyone's eyes were on her. One man met her gaze full on and held it a beat too long, totally giving Theresa the willies. How come only the wackos give me the eye? she wondered. Disgusted, she stood up to change cars.

She checked the reflections in the windows as she walked. Sure enough, Mr. Shifty had gotten up as well. He shuffled along behind her. Theresa's heart raced with fear. She sped up and bolted into the next car. When she glanced over her shoulder for a split second, she saw that he had sped up, too.

She dashed through the car, bumping into people along

the way. When she looked back again, she noticed a bulge at the man's waistline that could only be a gun.

"That man pinched me!" she screamed. "He pinched me!" She pointed at the guy in anger, still keeping up her pace. She heard a few people call him a pervert, but that was it. She decided to go for the sympathy vote and employ an English accent in the next car. Even if that blew her cover with Mr. Shifty, she didn't care. She was running for her life now.

"That bloke pinched me on the bum!" she hollered the moment she opened the door to the next car. "Somebody help me! Please!"

As she ran down the aisle she glanced back and saw a group of rugby players stand in his path. But straight ahead she saw that the next car was the last. A dead end—in more ways than one. What was she supposed to do now?

She stepped out and stood between the two cars, the wet underground air tossing her hair about her face. Theresa shot a glance back at Mr. Shifty. He had made it halfway through the crowded car—only a few scant yards, one train door, and one very chivalrous rugby player separated them. Biting her lip, Theresa studied her surroundings. She had two options: get trapped in the next car or surf the top of the train. Either way you slice it, I could definitely croak, she thought. Her heart was racing so fast, she feared it was going to burst out of her chest. But she couldn't just stand by and make herself an easy target.

As she stole one last glance at her assailant she sighed deeply. "Here goes nothing," she muttered. She boosted herself up on the safety chain connecting the two cars and placed her hands on the top of the last car, her adrenaline pumping. Gathering all her strength, she pushed off the chain with her legs and hoisted her body on top of the car in one swift motion. She was almost immediately blown away—literally—by the whooshing wind in the tunnel.

I'm gonna die, she thought. Her sweaty palms, coupled with the condensation on the outside of the train, were making it almost impossible to keep her grip. Her fingers slowly slipped from their hold. Just when she thought she couldn't hold on even one second longer, Theresa glanced up—and spotted a dim light up ahead in the tunnel. A stop! she realized. If I can only hold on until then, I can make it!

The few seconds felt like an eternity. Please let me live, she prayed desperately, and I'll never pull anything this stupid again.

Suddenly the brakes engaged. Theresa flew forward, and her grip strained under the pressure. She held on for dear life as the train ground to a halt in the station. Her body began sliding to the left.

"You're almost there," she whispered, even though she knew her hardest move was yet to come. If she got off the train too soon, there was a chance Mr. Shifty would see her and snatch her. But if she tried to get off too late, she could get killed trying to jump off a moving train.

Once the doors slid open and she heard, "Please mind the gap," she held her breath and went for it. She scooted over to the side of the car, made her body go limp, closed her eyes, and rolled onto the concrete just as the doors whooshed shut.

As she hit the ground relief flooded her body. Taking a

deep breath, she opened her eyes—and stared straight into the eyes of Mr. Shifty, now trapped behind closed doors.

She gasped. A look of disbelief overtook his sinister features, and he began to claw at the window desperately. As the train pulled away from the platform Theresa dragged herself up and gave her predator a "So there!" wave until he was no longer in sight.

"So then I jumped off the train and escaped," Theresa relayed to Uncle Sam via videophone just moments after returning to suite 1423. Although she was bursting with pride, the train adventure had definitely left her shaky.

Neither Jo nor Caylin looked as if they could believe what Theresa had just been through. But while Caylin's face beamed with pride, Jo looked upset and concerned.

"First, I want to commend you on how you handled yourself, Theresa," Uncle Sam said. "You weighed your options, relied on your instincts, and did what you had to do. Good job."

Theresa smiled. "All in a day's work."

Uncle Sam chuckled. "Second, you need to be on high

alert with the conference coming up in just four days," he continued, his voice suddenly grave. "You've given me a good description of your would-be attacker and I'll get an artist on the composite. In the meantime don't open your hotel doors to anyone. Look around when you're walking outside. Be aware of your surroundings. The stakes are getting higher, and these people don't care who they have to crush to get what they're after. So beware."

"We'll be extra careful, Uncle S.," Caylin promised. "We're crossing our fingers that the disc is in the green room and that it will be in our hot little hands mañana."

Uncle Sam cleared his throat. "I hope so too. But in the event that it's not there, I'm confident you'll recover it somehow."

Theresa wished she could say the same. She wasn't so sure she could anymore.

TWELVE

"This polyester is going to give me hives!" Caylin whispered as the trio made their way to the green room at 8 p.m. sharp Thursday evening in their custom-made Sunbeam uniforms.

As they approached the tall, wiry guard he eyed them curiously. "You aren't the ones who usually come," he said in a suspicious tone, looking them up and down.

"We're the fill-in crew," Caylin said, as they'd rehearsed. According to Theresa's plan, Caylin was to do all the talking. "Thomas, Martha, and Hugh were on a long-distance assignment and got held up, so we've been sent in their place."

She presented her ID card, and Jo and Caylin followed suit. "Well, I didn't hear anything about this, and there are strict policies," the security guard said. "Perhaps I'll just call your HQ."

"Go right ahead," Theresa said, keeping her cool only because she'd had the foresight to have Sunbeam's calls forwarded to The Tower just fifteen minutes earlier.

As he dialed the digits Theresa's hands began to shake slightly. The operator had said the phone calls would be transferred within ten minutes—but what if there was a delay?

"Yes," the security guard said into the phone, "this is James at the U.S. Embassy. I'm just calling to verify that in lieu of our regular crew being held up, you've sent over a Ms. Frazier, Ms. Hanover, and Ms. Fineberg."

He paused and looked them over closely. Theresa took another deep breath. "Okay, I see." He nodded. "Oh, they did?" When he scratched his eyebrow and smiled over at them, Theresa figured they must be home free. "Very well, then. Have a good evening."

He hung up and smiled at them apologetically. "Sorry about that," James said, his tone a million times nicer. "Policy, you know."

Caylin shrugged. "We understand."

"Just let me buzz you in here," he said, punching some

numbers into a keypad. The steel door raised up, allowing them entry. "This door will automatically close behind you. It will open again at ten o'clock sharp. If you need anything, press the red button and I'll buzz myself back in. Otherwise I'll see you at ten."

Caylin's heart sped up as she followed the guard into the green-walled room, equipped with four desks, four computers, six ten-line phones, four paper shredders, and six huge filing cabinets.

As soon as the steel door closed behind them they sprang into action. "Okay, you know what to do. And remember: Leave no surface unturned," Caylin whispered, dashing to a desk and exploring every crack and crevice.

Jo and Theresa followed Caylin's lead, beelining to the two desks on the opposite end of the room. "So should we only get the green discs?" Jo asked in confusion.

"Grab every disc you can, no matter what color," Theresa said. "The 'green' was probably just a reference to this room."

Caylin dug through a drawer like a puppy digging for

a bone. As she found disc after unmarked disc her spirits lifted considerably. She knew that going through them later would be time-consuming and that maybe Devaroux had even planted a file in a file, but it felt good holding them in her hands.

"We have too much ground to cover," Jo complained. "I don't think we'll have enough time!"

"No whining—we'll find it," Caylin said, not looking up. She had tunnel vision at the moment and was focused on nothing more than recovering the disc. This was how she felt when she hang-glided or snowboarded—totally centered and determined to be all she could be. And that's what she was trying to do in the green room, for the sake of the mission and the fate of the world.

"We'd better start cleaning up," Caylin announced suddenly. "It's nine-forty. We've only got twenty minutes."

"Ohmigosh!" Theresa cried in disbelief. She went into a tailspin of activity, putting the room back together as frantically as she had torn it apart. By 9:58 the room looked immaculate and the duffel bag Caylin had smuggled in was full to bursting.

"Anyone need to wipe her brow?" Theresa asked as Jo and Caylin struggled to replace a computer monitor they had searched under. Theresa reached into a box of Kleenex, her fingers brushing something hard, flat, and very familiar feeling. She yanked the object out of the box and screamed with excitement. "Check this out! A green disc! A *green disc*!"

Jo and Caylin froze in place and gaped, open-mouthed, the monitor still in their hands.

"This was hidden in the Kleenex box!" Theresa exclaimed. "This is it!"

Jo and Caylin jumped up and down as Theresa kissed the disc in sheer glee.

The door whooshed open and James stepped inside. "Okay, it's ten o'clo—oy, what in blazes is going on in here?"

Jo shrieked. Caylin gasped. Theresa looked on in horror as they flung the monitor away from them. It hit James squarely in the gut. His eyes went wide with shock and he fell backward.

"Look out!" Theresa screamed, but it was too late.

James hit his head on the edge of a desk with a sickening *thunk* and sank to the floor.

"Wha-what?" he muttered, giving the girls a last, dazed once-over before passing out cold.

"Is he still breathing?" Theresa squeaked. She clutched the duffel bag, terrified.

Caylin bent down over him. "Yep." She shrugged. "Well, this is our out. Let's book!" She led the mad dash down the hall and began frantically pushing the elevator button.

"What's wrong?" Jo cried desperately. "Open, stupid doors, open!"

"It's after ten," Caylin said. "The doors probably won't work."

"There's a secret door here somewhere," Jo recalled. She strained her brain but couldn't remember the floor plan. "Let's just push all the tiles. Maybe something will give."

Caylin pushed as hard as she could against the tiles on the opposite side of the hall, frustrated. "This isn't getting us anywhere. Maybe they tiled over the secret door or something."

"Oh n-no," Theresa stammered. "I think James is

coming to." Her eyes were glued down the hall at the guard's twitching foot. She looked as if she might puke. "H-Hurry up, guys."

Jo pushed tile after tile after tile until finally she felt one give. A satisfying whoosh at her feet heralded the opening of a two-foot-high hatch. "I've got it!" she called proudly. Without even thinking, she jumped in. She immediately regretted it as she slid toward oblivion in a coffin-wide metal chute.

Chilled to her core, Jo screamed in the hopes of saving her friends from suffering the same. But her cry was quickly joined by Caylin's wail and Theresa's squeal. They plunged toward certain death, their voices raised in a chorus—metallic, echoing, and terrifying. The sound plucked Jo's spine with cold fingers. Desperate, she reached out and tried to grab onto the sides of the chute, but the metal was more slippery than an oil slick.

Jo closed her eyes and prayed the chute had an end . . . *somewhere*. Visions of the center of the earth and a bed of foot-high spikes danced in her mind. She screamed even louder, her heart nearly stopping from fear. She kept screaming and screaming until her echoing wail turned into no more than a flat screech. Suddenly she realized she wasn't moving anymore.

Jo opened her eyes and squinted into the darkness. She was lying on an old mattress. The room around her was totally bare—dirt floor, dirt walls. Jo stood up tentatively. She realized with a start that the screams behind her were growing louder. She stepped off the mattress and down came Theresa with a thump, followed by Caylin right on top of her.

"That rocked—in a really weird way," Caylin said.

"Oh, stop!" Theresa cried. "Don't even joke about that, Cay. For about three full minutes I swear I was watching my own funeral on the backs of my eyelids."

"Well, you can rest easy," Caylin remarked. "Now we just have to figure out where we are."

"I don't know—there's nothing here but dirt," Jo said. "Maybe it's just your basic, average secret room. Do you think this is still embassy property?"

Theresa cocked her head. "I don't know. I think we were moving more to the side than down, to be honest.

Instead of taking us below the building, the chute shot us away from it."

Jo shrugged. "The architect must have had a wiggy sense of humor," she offered.

"No—this is probably a full-on escape hatch," Caylin pointed out. "Like in case of a terrorist attack."

"Well, I sure hope Jonathon Nicholson knows about it," Theresa said. "He's going to need it if we didn't get that disc."

"The disc!" Caylin gasped. "Theresa, do you—"

"I've got all of 'em right here," Theresa assured her, holding up the duffel bag.

Caylin sighed with relief. "Thank goodness. Now let's head down this passageway and find a way out of here." She dusted the soot off her polyester duds and grinned wryly. "At least we don't have to worry about getting our clothes dirty, right?"

"Caylin, I'm getting a bad feeling," Theresa complained. "Maybe we should sit down and rest. Or . . . maybe . . . fall . . . asleep. . . ."

"Oh, you've always got a 'bad feeling,'" Caylin griped. "Where's your sense of adventure?"

"I left it in the dryer too long," Theresa quipped. "It shrank."

Caylin chuckled, but inside she was torn. She had absolutely no idea where she was or where they all were headed. Every time she turned a corner, she expected to see Dracula or Freddy Krueger or even that weird teddy bear from those fabric softener commercials. That thing always gave her the creeps. But she put her irrational fears aside and kept walking, kept leading, kept hoping with quickened pulse that she wasn't about to set foot in a trap.

"Jeez, this is making me tired," Theresa complained. "Have you noticed how exhausting this walk is? We've only been going about twenty minutes, and I'm pooped."

"Yeah," Jo agreed. "It's an uphill battle."

"It is!" Theresa snapped her fingers. "Guys, we're heading up. Slowly but surely. This tunnel will take us to ground level!"

Or maybe ground *zero*, Caylin thought with a wince.

She hoped not. She hoped that wherever the tunnel took them, it had nothing to do with Jonathon, or Laqui Bay, or Godiva chocolates. She just wanted to get back to the Ritz, shimmy out of that itchy polyester, and sort through those discs, pronto.

Theresa sprinted past Caylin, supercharged by the fresh air blowing on her face. "We've made it!" she cried. "The end! We're safe!"

"Shhh! Don't push your luck," Caylin warned. "Just because the end of the line is outdoors doesn't mean it's not dangerous."

"I don't care," Theresa sassed, her lungs practically singing. "Oh, to be out of that musty tunnel . . . 'tis heaven." She reached the end of the line and stopped cold in her tracks, amazed by what she saw.

"What is it?" Jo cried.

"Are we safe?" Caylin hollered, hurrying to catch up. "Yell if you're in trouble!"

"I'm fine," Theresa said, dumbfounded. "It's just . . . that . . ."

"What?" Caylin reached Theresa's side and looked around. She gasped, her blue eyes widening. "I don't believe it."

"I don't get it," Theresa added.

"I don't even want to know," Jo chimed in as she reached the end of the line.

Theresa shook her head. She couldn't piece it all together. She and her partners, after a death-defying plummet down a chute and a never-ending walk through underground catacombs, were standing not on the threshold of an amazing discovery or a deadly trap. No, they were standing in the mouth of a large, defunct drainage pipe near the banks of the Thames. Totally alone. Totally confused. Totally ticked off.

"This has got to be the lamest payoff *ever*," Caylin groaned.

"I still don't get it," Theresa murmured, slinging the duffel of discs over her shoulder. "Why even bother, you know?"

"Like I said before," Jo quipped, "that architect must have had one *wiggy* sense of humor."

• • •

After two hours of watching Theresa sit at her laptop and open every single file on every single disc, Caylin's anticipation had vanished into thin air.

The first defeat had come when their trump card, the green disc, turned out to be completely empty. Now, with every disc Theresa tested and eliminated, Caylin's frustration mounted to dangerous levels. Maybe the heat coming off my head is screwing up the laptop, she thought halfheartedly.

"This is the last one," Theresa said. She stuck the disc into the drive and waited.

The ceaseless whirring of the disc drive made Caylin want to trash the suite rock-star style. Toss a few TVs out the windows, set stuff on fire, the usual. She'd never do it, of course. But it was fun to think about. More fun than listening to that darned whirring.

The whirring stopped. Caylin held her breath in anticipation until the dreaded prompt—*This disc is not initialized. Do you wish to initialize it now?*—appeared on-screen.

"Darn it," Theresa muttered.

Jo sighed. "I guess we wore polyester for nothing."

Caylin got up without a word and walked into her bedroom, slamming the door in defeat.

Friday night Jo sulked back to the Ritz after an uneventful day at work. Antonio was a no-show at the office, and Sandra had said he was sick. Sick in the *head*, Jo thought with a shudder. To make matters worse, Sandra had finally pigeonholed Jo into putting together the "up-tempo numbers" for the after-conference ball—on a *Sunday. Ugh!* What a way to spend the end of a weekend. *Especially* if it turned out to be the last weekend of her life.

A red Porsche approached the crosswalk, distracting Jo from her thoughts. What I wouldn't give to be in the front seat of that baby, Jo mused, hair flying everywhere, pedal to the metal, radio cranked to ten-point-five, no worries. To her surprise, the dream machine first slowed down and then completely stopped right in the middle of the road next to where she was standing.

As the tinted window came down she looked in, curious. One glance made her blood run cold: Antonio sat in the driver's seat. Jo took off running as fast as she could. She spotted an alleyway and ducked into it. But as she exited the alley and rounded the corner near the post office, she could see his car clearing a hill in the distance and coming her way. How were her size-seven feet supposed to compete with a Porsche? Her eyes landed on a VW double-parked in front of the post office, motor running. Without a moment's thought Jo jumped in the VW and slammed her foot on the gas.

"It's not like I'm *stealing* it or anything," she told her reflection in the rearview mirror. She was simply *borrowing* it to escape Antonio, who was now hot on her trail. She made a sharp turn onto a busy side street and erratically swerved in and out of traffic, trying desperately to lose the chocolate poisoner. This wasn't just *any* chase. She was driving for her life. And on the wrong side of the street, too.

As she wove between vehicles Jo saw red lights flashing on and off in the distance. Jo squinted to make out the sign below them: Train Crossing.

"Oh no," she muttered, stepping on the gas even harder.

That was all she needed—to be trapped behind a who-knows-how-long train with nowhere to run or hide. If that happened, she'd be dead in no time.

She looked back at Antonio and swore she saw him smiling. "You jerk!" she muttered. "I might be in a VW, but I can outdrive you any day of the week!"

She heard the engine chug slightly and looked down at the dash in alarm. "Engine—fine," she read aloud. "Pressure—fine. Gasoline—*empty*?" Goose bumps covered her arms as she realized she might not even have enough gas to make it across the tracks.

The black-and-white barriers were descending, and the flash of silver on the track was coming closer and closer. She looked down again at the gas gauge—below *E*. A glance in the rearview confirmed her worst fears—Antonio's Porsche was just inches behind. It was now or never time: Should she gun it and risk getting killed or brake and risk getting killed?

Jo held her breath, closed her eyes, and floored it. She felt the tracks bump under the wheels just seconds before she heard the train whoosh by, the brute force of its speed rocking the little VW. The engine coughed and sputtered, but she'd made it.

She opened her eyes and checked the rearview. Only a blur of silver could be seen—no Antonio. He was behind the train, eating her dust.

Trembling, she breathed a deep sigh of relief and turned down the nearest side street. Sputtering along, she was shocked to feel tears run down her cheeks. Tears of rage over Antonio's relentless pursuit. Tears for her father, who had been taken away before his time. And tears for the mission, which she feared might not be solved despite all the efforts of her and her friends. She wiped the tears away with the back of her hand, forcing herself to get it together. After all, she had gas to get, a car to ditch, a hotel to return to, and a major score to settle. There was no time to waste.

"So then I made sure I left no prints on the car and left it a few blocks away from the post office," Jo told Uncle Sam a few minutes after she'd arrived back at the Ritz, safe and sound.

"I can't believe you survived that," Theresa said, completely blown away.

"I can," Uncle Sam said. "The conference is only three days away, and things are coming to a head. With that in mind, Theresa—go to the laptop right now. I'm sending a photo of someone I'd like you to identify."

Theresa ran to the desk, where a blurry black-and-white photograph was coming up on the laptop screen.

"Does this man look familiar to you?" Uncle Sam asked.

Theresa studied the image on the screen. Her blood ran cold. "Ohmigosh—that's him! The guy who chased me on the train! But what—I mean, how—"

"Thanks to the description you gave me, this man was detained yesterday when he entered Heathrow under an alias. However, he somehow managed to escape custody when customs detained him for a passport check." He paused, and Theresa shook slightly. "We believe he's the infamous Alfred."

"Alfred?" Theresa repeated in disbelief. Not only had she escaped a madman on the train that day. The madman was also an international terrorist in cahoots with

Jonathon! "We believe he is Alfred, yes," Uncle Sam replied. "His passport was falsified, but when they searched the airport for him, he was nowhere to be found." Uncle Sam paused. "This means he could very well be in your neck of the woods, and judging by Antonio's actions, they might very well think you have the disc. You all could be in grave danger."

"I think I'm gonna be sick," Theresa said, hauling full speed to the bathroom. Before anyone could react, she was puking her guts out into the marble toilet. This is where our mission seems to be right now, she thought between hurls. Right down the toilet.

THIRTEEN

"Come out, come out, wherever you are, discie," Caylin muttered as she combed through a filing cabinet Saturday afternoon.

She'd had to scheme and scam to be able to fill in for the weekend cleaning woman, and at the very least she hoped her efforts would pay off.

But wherever she looked—under phones, through trash cans, in drawers—no disc. She even pulled out seat cushions in her mad search, but found only nada.

As Caylin glanced at her reflection in a nearby window she took a deep breath. She looked totally tired. And she *was* tired—tired of not finding the disc, of feeling inadequate, of doubting her abilities. She was used to savoring the thrill of victory, not choking down the agony of defeat.

• • •

Disheartened by Caylin's unsuccessful search, Jo dragged her feet back to the embassy on Sunday to finally perform her special music assignment. When Jo arrived, Sandra led her straight to the door marked Private—the one she had unsuccessfully tried to open her first day on the job. Jo was amazed that almost three weeks had passed since that day; she wasn't any closer to recovering the list of nuclear warheads than she had been then. The realization was beyond discouraging.

"Here's where all the CDs are kept," Sandra said as she unlocked the room. "You'll need to pull enough music for four hours—an hour and a half of dinner music, and two and a half of dancing music."

The room—maybe fifteen feet by fifteen feet—was wall-to-wall CDs. "Where did all these come from?" Jo asked. "Why not go digital?"

"You'll notice all the CDs are marked with stickers saying Property of BLC, British Radio," Sandra said. "That used to be Mr. Nicholson's radio station. He sold it to a chap a few years back, turned it into chat radio—you know, no music. So Mr. Nicholson donated the CDs to the embassy. Digital is great, but we wouldn't turn down all of this free music."

Jo nodded, still thinking that digital would be a smarter choice. But on the bright side, at least this would be a distraction from the mission. Seeing the room made her realize the dozens, possibly hundreds, of nooks and crannies the girls hadn't even checked yet, and would maybe *never* get the chance to check. They were running out of time, and she was all out of ideas.

Later that evening the girls sat on the floor of their suite, surrounded by every note and scrap of paper they'd accumulated over the past three weeks, totally at wit's end.

"What could we be missing?" Caylin asked as she picked up the green room stat sheet and stared at it in vain.

"It has to be right under our noses," Theresa said, raking her fingers furiously through her brown hair.

"But the question is—where?" Jo inquired. "There are probably a million places we haven't even looked at—"

The video chat beeped, cutting Jo off. "Hold that

thought," Caylin said, grabbing the TV remote and pushing talk. "Hello?"

"Uncle Sam here, ladies," he said, his voice accompanied by a black screen. "How are you holding up?"

"Not so good," Jo replied in a decidedly glum tone.

"Well, you've still got tomorrow," he reminded them. "You've been e-mailed the address of the FBI safe house, which is two blocks from the embassy. Go by there as soon as possible just so you know where it is. You're to report there at six p.m. sharp whether you've recovered the disc or not."

"But we don't want to go without the disc!" Jo cried.

"If you don't have it by six, you'll have to accept that sometimes a mission is successful simply because you survived it," he said. "But you can all rest easy knowing you've given it your best shot, no matter what happens."

Caylin sighed deeply. The sigh echoed hollowly in her throat. She felt powerless, as if she'd just lost a kickboxing title. When she looked over at Theresa, she noticed tears were glistening in her eyes. Uncle Sam wished them the best of luck and signed off quickly.

"What are we going to do if we don't find it?" Caylin wondered aloud. "I can't handle failing at our first mission."

"Me neither," Theresa said. "We've passed so many tests along the way. It's hard to believe we might flunk the final."

"Especially when there's who knows how many places we haven't even had access to in that embassy," Jo said. "That's what I was going to tell you before Uncle Sam called. Today I had to go through the music in a little closet off the ballroom. That room, which is pretty much locked twenty-four-seven, was a total reality check of how much of that embassy we probably haven't even explored."

Caylin took a deep breath. "Pretty discouraging, isn't it?"

"You can say that again," Theresa said. "But we're all worn-out. Maybe we'll feel fresher in the morning after a good night's sleep."

"You're right," Jo said, pulling herself up off the paper-covered floor. "I can't think about this another second."

"It's probably a good idea to get some rest," Caylin agreed. "It's going to be a big day tomorrow, no matter what."

. . .

A few minutes later Theresa shrieked loudly.

"What's wrong?" Caylin said, dashing into Theresa's room.

"Ohmigosh, what is it?" Jo screeched, hot on Caylin's heels.

"Jo! The room you were in earlier, with the music. Was it digital?"

Jo shook her head, looking perplexed. "No, they were CDs."

"CDs!" Theresa said excitedly. "Compact discs."

Caylin's eyes suddenly lit up. "Ohmigosh, could that be it?"

Jo's mouth dropped. "I didn't even make that connection. I was so focused on our possible failure, and how weird it was that the music wasn't saved digitally, that I forgot I was in a room full of discs!"

"The only thing is," Theresa said, "how many CDs were there?"

"Like a thousand," Jo replied in a dejected tone. "How would we know which one to look in?"

The girls fell silent for a moment.

"How about ones with *green* in the title?" Theresa asked, head spinning. "Like *Green*, by R.E.M., or the Jam's 'Pretty Green'?"

"Or the *Green Acres* theme!" Jo suggested with a laugh. "Or how about that wiggy old psychedelic song—you know, 'Green Tambourine'?"

"Green Day!" Caylin exclaimed, smiling hugely. "Or *Green Mind*, by Dinosaur Jr."

"Yeah!" Theresa clapped. "Or maybe that Kinks album—*The Village Green Preservation Society*!"

Jo and Caylin stared at her questioningly.

"Hey, my mom played that all the time when I was a kid." Theresa rolled her eyes. "Look, whatever, there are tons of possibilities." She smiled, her heart swelling with pride.

"Wait, how about CD covers that are green, too?" Jo asked. "That could be what he meant."

"Oh, that's good!" Caylin exclaimed. "I can hardly wait to get in there! What time could you get into the closet, Jo?"

"Sandra has to pick up some dignitaries, so she won't

be in until around three," Jo said. "But we could meet there then. I'll just tell her I need to grab more music for the ball."

"Sounds like a plan!" Theresa sang, eyes shining with hope. This was the first time in a while she'd actually felt as if they could solve this sucker. And maybe her lead was going to be the one they'd been waiting for!

"Man, if this theory is right," Caylin said, "we're going to love you forever, Theresa."

"Well, I would have never come up with it if it hadn't been for Jo going there today," Theresa replied modestly.

"Wow—mutual admiration society!" Caylin laughed. "I guess that means we're a good team."

"You guys know that and I know that," Theresa said. "But I hope we get the chance to prove it to the world tomorrow."

FOURTEEN

"Okay, so, Caylin, you go through the green CDs on the south wall, I'll take the north wall, and Theresa take the west wall," Jo instructed as she unlocked the door to the CD closet on Monday afternoon.

"Then we'll all go through the ones on the east wall, right?" Caylin asked.

"Yep," Jo replied, oozing with confidence. "And after that, if we still haven't found it, we'll go through the green names."

"But that could take a little longer since it's more abstract," Theresa noted. "And if all else fails, we'll just go through every single one until we find it."

When Jo opened the door, Caylin and Theresa gasped.

"Whoa," Caylin said, sounding overwhelmed.

"Whoa is right," Theresa said. "There's way more than

a thousand CDs in here. More like *ten* thousand!"

"Really?" Jo asked, heart sinking. "I'm just horrible with numbers."

Caylin sighed. "It's okay, it's okay," she murmured reassuringly. "We've just got to take it disc by disc and not look at the big picture. So let's do it!"

"This is a lost cause," Theresa muttered two and a half hours later, her hair sticking up every which way and little cuts from the sharp CD cover corners covering her fingers.

They'd already gone through all the discs with green covers and with *green* in a song or band title with no success and were now going through what was left in this, their final hour. CDs were flying everywhere, the room was a wreck, and claustrophobia was kicking in. Caylin and Jo looked discouraged, and Theresa was pretty much resigned to the fact that her hunch had been wrong after all.

A sudden pounding on the door made everyone jump. "Don't answer it—it could be Antonio," Jo whispered.

"Or Jonathon," Caylin added.

"Or Alfred," Theresa realized out loud, her blood

running cold. She pushed the possibility aside and got back to brass tacks. "Are you totally sure we checked that R.E.M. CD, Jo? I can't believe it wasn't in there."

"Yeah, I'm sure," Jo said as the knocking grew more insistent.

"How about Green Day?" Theresa inquired. We must have overlooked *something*, she told herself. That disc has to be in here!

"Checked. I've got their CD right here," Caylin said, grabbing it off the filing cabinet. "Jeez, that knocking is *really* giving me a headache."

"Maybe that's not their only CD," Theresa said, motioning to the disc in Caylin's hand. "Do they have others?"

"Ohmigosh," Jo breathed, gasping and looking up at the other girls in horror. "I pulled one yesterday! Sandra has them. I totally forgot—she must have at least thirty CDs. We've got to find her!"

This news flash filled Theresa with pure adrenaline. "Okay, okay," she told the knocker in annoyance, swinging the door open swiftly. But she gasped in horror when she saw not one knocker but two—Antonio and Jonathon!

"Whoa!" Jo gasped, jumping back in shock. Before the fiends could react, she barreled past them, knocking them over, and ran top speed over to the other side of the ballroom. She began grabbing the CDs off the corner shelf.

"Natascia," Sandra demanded, "just *what* do you think you're doing?"

Jo threw some CDs Caylin and Theresa's way and led them out of the ballroom without a glance in Sandra's direction. Caylin and Theresa were hot on her heels—Jonathon and Antonio were hot on theirs.

"Who's got it?" Caylin yelled, running at light speed toward the exit up ahead. "The Green Day?"

Her pace never faltering, Jo shuffled through the CDs and smiled as if she'd found Willy Wonka's golden ticket. "I got it!" she cheered. She separated it from the rest of the pile without slowing her pace or dropping CDs under her feet. Glancing back, she saw Antonio and Jonathon still in hot pursuit, their arms outstretched and ready to grab.

As she neared the exit doors Jo firmly grasped the Green Day CD in one hand, never slowing her pace for a second. "Okay, here goes," she said, voice trembling.

"Please be in there, please be in there," Theresa chanted, while Caylin went white as a sheet.

Jo held her breath as she opened the cover gingerly. And there, nestled inside, was a shiny CD-ROM reading *Classified*.

The most beautiful sight I've ever seen, Jo thought.

Theresa pushed open the exit doors—and gasped as she ran smack-dab into a man's broad chest. And when she looked up, she discovered she'd bumped into not just any man but *Alfred*.

"Dirty rotten girl chaser!" she yelled, kicking him hard in the shins. "It's payback time!" As Alfred doubled over she took off running. Antonio and Jonathon were gaining in a major way.

Theresa ran into the street. A fast-approaching Fiat screeched to a halt and swerved, just barely missing her.

"Bloody idiots!" the driver screamed out the window, but Theresa didn't even stop to react. Not with Jonathon and Antonio so close behind.

"Have some CDs, guys!" Jo hollered, her right hand grasping the Green Day CD case tightly. She dropped the extras behind her. Theresa followed suit, as did Caylin, and discs flew everywhere. The clatter of plastic on concrete mocked Jo's frazzled nerves. The guys faltered, but they instantly regained their footing. Jo ran on without looking back, desperate not to lose hold of her precious cargo.

Caylin felt fingers brushing her back. She shot a look over her shoulder—Jonathon! He was trying to grab her!

Frantic, Caylin led him toward a phone booth. Her heart pounding with fear, she stopped suddenly, sending Jonathon rushing past her and into the booth. She kicked a trash can in front of the door. "Call nine-one-one," she taunted, her adrenaline overtaking her terror. "You need some major help!"

Caylin left him pounding on the door and ran toward the FBI safe house. She spotted Jo dashing up the side-walk, the CD case held firmly in her right hand. Caylin poured on the heat to catch up, but she was knocked to the ground by a man in a dark coat who kept on running. Antonio!

"Jo! Look out!" Caylin yelled from the ground.

Jo looked over her shoulder, the action slowing her down a bit. Without a word Antonio pulled even and grabbed the priceless case out of her hand.

"I don't *think* so!" she screamed, tackling him to the ground. Her pulse pounding—from excitement or terror, she couldn't tell—she grabbed for the case in Antonio's hand.

"Hey! Over here!"

Jo looked up to see Caylin up and running and heading right toward her. Antonio did the same and relaxed his grip on the case. Propelled by sheer willpower, Jo yanked the case from his slimy hand. "I believe that belongs to *us*," she said, tossing the case to Caylin as hard as she could.

Caylin stretched out her fingers and reached for the flying case. Alfred lunged for it, too. Not fast enough. Caylin tripped him and made a successful snag. She exhaled in relief and pounded the pavement with all her might. The FBI safe house was only one block away. She was going to deliver the disc. She *had* to.

Jonathon, free from the phone booth, caught up to her. "Give—me—that," he demanded, sideswiping Caylin and hitting her hand. The case flew from her grasp.

The feeling of the case slipping through her fingers was the sickest she'd ever had. The sight of Jonathon grabbing it out of midair made her want to throw up. But she wasn't going to let that case get away. Her muscles vibrating with nervous energy, she chased Jonathon for a few feet, then—fueled by the sight of the safe house just two doors up—knocked him over with all her weight, sending the CD case flying and sending Jonathon into a cursing frenzy.

Caylin recovered the case from the gritty cement and ran like lightning to the safe house. She was halfway up the safe house stairs when Jonathon caught up to her and knocked the case out of her hands again, sending it flying onto the porch.

"Nowhere to hide, *Louise*?" he crowed as he dashed past her.

Caylin heard tons of footsteps scrambling all around her, but her eyes never left the CD prize. Just as Jonathon dove for the disc an FBI agent swung open the screen door of the house, whacking him hard on the head.

With a roar of victory Caylin kicked the case out of Jonathon's grasp and into the house, where it skidded across the floor to safety.

"Put your hands up!" the agent commanded, leveling a gun in Jonathon's direction.

"Yeah, freeze, sucker!" Caylin cheered.

A look of confusion flashed on Jonathon's face. What's he so confused about? she wondered as he was cuffed and taken into the safe house. Surely he realized he ran the risk of being arrested before undertaking such an evil endeavor. Either that or he was a first-class idiot.

Theresa, struggling for breath, made it into the safe house and ran to Caylin's side. Her heart was nearly pounding out of her chest as Jo burst in seconds later, Alfred and Antonio hot on her heels.

Theresa sighed with relief when Alfred and Antonio were cuffed and taken into custody. She checked out the black-clad, totally professional agents who were running the show. When she took a good look at *one* of the agents, she gasped. She'd know that tall frame, bee-stung lips, and *short brown hair* anywhere. Ugh! What was she doing there?

We've been double-crossed! Theresa thought, her stomach lurching and her lungs ready to burst. She looked over at Caylin and Jo defeatedly, raw terror in her eyes.

"Could it be—" Caylin muttered.

"Surely not," Jo muttered.

"Short Hair!" Theresa screeched, pointing to the woman in horror.

Short Hair glanced over and winked before returning her attention to Jonathon.

"What?" Theresa spat out.

"I don't get it," Caylin muttered. "I just don't—"

Suddenly two uniformed men busted in and trained their guns on Short Hair. "Drop your gun or I'll shoot, ma'am," one of them demanded. "Scotland Yard. The jig's up."

Theresa held her breath, terrified of what would happen next.

"Drop the gun, ma'am," Scotland Yard No. 1 repeated, his voice rising with impatience.

"Danielle Hall, Tower," Short Hair said calmly in response.

"Tower?" Jo repeated, shell-shocked.

"Release Mr. Nicholson from your custody, Ms. Hall," Scotland Yard No. 1 demanded.

"But he's guilty!" Jo screeched. "He's a huge part of this whole sick scheme."

"Do what you're told, Ms. Hall," Scotland Yard No. 2 bellowed. "He works for *us*."

"Works for *you*?" Caylin echoed. "But he tried to—"

Scotland Yard No. 1 sighed and showed his identification. "Come on, we're all on the same side here."

Danielle Hall replaced her gun in her holster. To Jo's relief, there were no further surprises.

Scotland Yard No. 1 nodded. "Good work, ladies. You too, son."

Jonathon nodded back, pride shining in his eyes, as two FBI agents set about uncuffing him.

"Wait a minute now, let me get something straight here," Jo began, waving her arms in confusion. "Jonathon Nicholson—the guy who totally tried to grind us into the pavement out there—he's in cahoots with *Scotland Yard*?"

"Scotland Yard," Antonio repeated, sounding just as stunned as Jo felt.

Jonathon walked up to the handcuffed duo and leaned into their faces. "Yes, I work for Scotland Yard," he said smugly, "and I hope you rot in prison for what you did to my friend Frank Devaroux."

"Well, I'll be darned," Caylin muttered.

"I can't believe it," Theresa whispered.

"Neither can I." Jo shook her head. "Neither can I."

Without a word Caylin embraced Jo and Theresa in a group hug. "We did it," she said, feeling exhausted and exhilarated all at once.

"I never doubted us for a second," Theresa said shakily, then paused. "Well, maybe for a *second*."

Jo laughed. "Me too," she admitted. "But we made it. For The Tower. For my dad. For *us*."

Caylin's heart filled with pride. This was better than winning a tournament, a trophy, or even a gold medal. Because tonight they really were world champions.

FIFTEEN

"We want all the details, Jonathon," Jo demanded as she cozied up to him at the World Peace Conference dinner party. If she didn't get the skinny soon, she was liable to die of suspense. "How'd you get yourself in this situation?"

"It's kind of long," he said, giving her a shy grin.

"We want every bit of the dirt," Caylin said, her voice rich with delicious anticipation.

Theresa grinned. "Spare nothing."

"Okay," he said, taking a deep breath. "Frank Devaroux was this guy I interned with last summer. He was a real genius computer hacker, totally cool, and we kept in touch when I headed back to school. So a few months ago Dad sent me some old discs they were about to toss from here and said I could just erase and use them for school. But one of the discs had a file on it that couldn't be erased and actually corrupted my whole hard drive. I sent everything back here to Frank, told him what the deal was, and asked him if he knew what I should do to fix the stuff it had damaged."

"Was it a virus?" Theresa asked, absolutely fascinated.

Jonathon nodded. "I thought so, but I wasn't sure. So when he got the disc, Frank developed a decoding program to dig into the file. He discovered it was this really elaborate code that took about four or five days to crack, then he finally found that the file contained a list of locations of nuclear warheads in Russia. He knew this list was major."

"I'll say," Theresa agreed as she noticed the gold flecks in Jonathon's eyes. "It's really hard to believe they just had it floating around on an unprotected disc."

"So he destroyed the original, burned the info onto another CD for the feds, and called a meeting with the heads of the FBI for the next day," he explained. "He hid the disc—I guess in the Green Day case you found—for safety reasons. But later that evening he was killed, anyway. By Alfred and Antonio."

Caylin gasped. "What slimebuckets."

"That'd be a compliment for those guys," Jonathon said solemnly. "We're talking the lowest of the low. So the day Frank died—totally by coincidence—I was here at the embassy to get my computer back from him. That's when Scotland Yard approached me and told me that I, like Frank, was on a list of possible Laqui Bay targets. It wasn't a hit list—just people SY thought they might contact to try to find the disc for them."

"Why you?" Theresa asked.

"Because of my age and my access to the embassy, I guess they figured I'd be an easy target. I wanted time to think about it, but when Frank was murdered that night, I agreed to help. I had no idea that Frank was a special agent for The Tower until after he was killed. Still, I was forbidden to breathe a word of my involvement to any-one—not my father, the CIA, the FBI, *or* The Tower since it was top secret and happening on London soil."

"So why did you do it?" Caylin asked. "I mean, you had to work with the guys who killed your friend."

"It was horrible." Jonathon turned his gaze downward.

"I hated pretending I was in league with Laqui Bay. But I wanted to nab those jerks—and I had to get to the list before they did. I did it for Frank . . . and for world peace."

"We were in the same boat," Jo chimed in. "I still can't believe you were on our side all along."

"I know, right?" Jonathon exclaimed, shaking his head in disbelief. "Antonio had me ask the translators if anyone spoke Arabic, thinking that would be bait for anyone who was working for another terrorist group. His theory was that whoever lied about speaking it must have a reason to lie—like wanting to get inside information. So when you bit, Jo, that's when we figured you were a bad guy."

Jo laughed. "I was afraid to lie about that, but I couldn't resist."

"Then right after, I discovered the bugs in my suite and office and in Dad's as well," he said. "So we figured you had to have been the one to plant them."

"When it was actually me," Caylin admitted.

"See, I had my suspicions about you but no proof," Jonathon said. "But about Jo we *had* proof—or so we thought. We sent someone to follow Jo, and they saw her with

Theresa. So we figured she was working against us, too."

"So then you knew Antonio and Alfred tried to kill us?" Jo asked, finding it hard to believe now that he had anything to do with that. He was so sweet—and *so* cute.

"I didn't know until later," Jonathon said. "I told them up front I'd have no part of anything like that. But when I couldn't find the disc, they threatened to kill my dad. That's when I really started to lose it."

Jo put her hand over his. "I lost my dad. I can understand the pressure."

He smiled gently. "I'm sorry, Jo. No one should have to go through that. And I didn't even lose mine, but I was biting everyone's head off. In fact, I think I yelled at Caylin at least a couple of times. And I didn't even know for sure you were an impostor."

Caylin giggled. "You were *so* mean."

"I know—I'll admit it," he said. "But I was a basket case. That was a stroke of genius, whoever discovered the Green Day CD location. I was going to give a quick look in there with Antonio because I was desperate, but I'm sure I'd never have found it."

"It was a group brainstorm," Theresa insisted.

"And what a brainstorm it was," Danielle Hall said, breaking away from her conversation with William Nicholson to take a seat with the group.

"And you!" Theresa said with a grin. "I was certain you were trailing us since day one."

"Then you had good instincts," Danielle said, "because I *was* trailing you. Uncle Sam assigned me to be your mentor, so I was never far behind."

Theresa shook her head. "It's such a trip!" she exclaimed. "I just can't believe it."

Danielle smiled. "Well, believe it. I'm your real-life guardian angel—there if you need me or are in a bind. Otherwise laying low and watching from the sidelines."

A waitress approached and delivered a round of virgin strawberry daiquiris, courtesy of William Nicholson.

"I propose a toast," Jonathon said, raising his glass. "To world peace and mistaken identities."

"I'll drink to that!" Jo cheered, clinking glasses with the rest of the gang.

Before Jonathon had a chance to take his first sip, his

cell phone rang and he snapped it up. "Hello? Yes, this is he." He nodded, then grabbed a napkin and furiously scribbled something on it. "Okay, sure, no prob." After he hit the off button, a totally perplexed expression overtook his gorgeous face.

"What's up?" Theresa asked.

"It was a message from someone's uncle Sam," Jonathon announced. "Um, he said you need to turn on channel ninety-six at midnight. And that there's some documentary about Prague he wants you guys to see?"

Jo grinned and grasped her friends' hands in hers. She could feel raw energy, pure excitement, and total empowerment pulsing from one hand to the next. At that moment she would have guessed their hearts were beating in time.

"Are you thinking what I'm thinking?" Theresa asked, a mischievous gleam in her gray eyes.

"Totally," Caylin agreed.

Jo threw her head back and laughed. "Time for another international mission!"

LIVE AND LET SPY

To Laura Burns and Michael Zimmerman,

les cool cats *extraordinaires*

Special thanks to Michael Zimmerman for his assistance

in the preparation of *Live and Let Spy*.

ONE

"Holy cow!" Theresa Hearth said as she checked out the spread of Godiva and strawberries on the huge conference table before her. "This is a diabetic's worst nightmare."

Caylin Pike grinned. "That which does not kill you will only make you fatter." She popped a plump strawberry into her mouth for emphasis.

"Like *you* have to worry about getting fat," Theresa muttered. "Run any marathons this morning?"

Caylin flipped her blond ponytail behind her and fired a roundhouse kick into the air. "Just a ten-K. But I *did* foil a few muggings on the way home."

"The world should know better than to mess with you, right?" Jo Carreras added, her dark eyes sparkling.

"Right." Caylin straightened her sweatshirt and gracefully slid into one of the massive conference room chairs.

Her every move was lithe and athletic. "So what's the deal with this room? It's big enough for a game of racquetball. And it looks so . . . *sterile*."

"No kidding," Theresa replied, scanning the high white walls and hidden fluorescent lights. The chamber had to be at least a hundred feet long and thirty feet wide. The only furnishings were the gigantic white conference table and three expensive-looking white leather chairs.

One chair for each of the Spy Girls.

"Sometimes The Tower really creeps me out," Theresa remarked. She ran a hand nervously through her tousled brown hair. "It's like they plan everything with only us in mind."

"Like they know what we're thinking at all times," Jo agreed. She approached one of the empty chairs tentatively, then tippy-tapped away in her Manolo Blahnik mules.

"Sit down, you guys," Caylin said impatiently. "I bet the show's not going to start until we're all in our seats."

Theresa snagged a piece of chocolate and slowly sat down. The chair was surprisingly soft and comfortable.

"This is the kind of room where presidents decide which countries to bomb. We trained in this building for four months and we didn't even know this room *existed*. Doesn't that weird you out in the slightest?"

"Nope," Caylin replied, popping another juicy berry.

"Whoa! Careful with that juice, Cay," Jo warned as she sat down in the last remaining empty chair. "Would you like the honor of paying my next dry-cleaning bill?"

Caylin pretended to lob a chocolate in Jo's direction. "What do you care when The Tower's picking up the tab?"

"Oh yeah . . . you're right." Jo smoothed her pristine Prada pencil skirt over her knees. "So why did we get summoned here, anyway?"

Caylin sipped from a bottle of water. "I guess we've got another secret mission ahead of us."

"But we only got back from England forty-eight hours ago," Theresa moaned.

"Yeah," Jo chimed in. "That's not even enough time to go *shopping*, let alone celebrate our first victorious mission."

Caylin grinned. "We *did* kick butt."

"You expected anything less?" Jo declared, reaching across the table and high-fiving her comrades. "The Spy Girls rule!"

"Well, we've only had one mission," Theresa said cautiously. "We're no Jane Bonds yet."

"I sure think we are," Caylin insisted. "Boy, T., you need to get your nose out of your laptop and take a good look around you. We totally saved the world last week. Didn't you notice?"

"Yeah." Theresa chuckled. "But didn't *you* notice how we almost got completely killed in the process? Hmmm . . . maybe all that bungee jumping has rattled your brain."

"And all that hacking has fried yours," Caylin said, giggling.

Theresa stuck out her tongue. "You couldn't hack your way out of a dressing room."

"Look, all joking aside," Jo interrupted with a smile, "don't forget that that's the whole point."

Theresa lifted an eyebrow. "What do you mean?"

"I mean, Caylin doesn't have to hack her way out of a

232 ELIZABETH CAGE

dressing room because *you* can. Just like you don't have to bungee jump off Hoover Dam because Caylin can. We're all here because our skills complement each other, you know?"

Theresa gave Caylin a knowing look. "Hmmm . . . Jo must have been taking notes during our orientation speech."

"Naw, Jo was just paying extra-special attention to that speechifying hottie," Caylin quipped.

"So," Theresa mused, "if I'm Henrietta Hacker and Caylin is Action Jackson, then what does that make *you*, Jo?"

Jo half closed her eyelids. "I'm the seductress."

Theresa and Caylin groaned and pelted Jo with strawberries.

"My *skirt*!" Jo yelped. "Hey, watch the couture, okay?"

Their giggling stopped when the lights suddenly went dim. That could mean only one thing.

"Uncle Sam, is that you?" Theresa asked.

A low, powerful hum grew all around them. The Spy Girls glanced nervously at one another. The sound was everywhere, as if it came from deep within The Tower itself.

Slowly, on the far wall, a panel slid open and a giant screen appeared.

It glowed eerily. Blank.

Theresa's heart pounded. She watched, hypnotized with curiosity, as The Tower's fearless leader, Uncle Sam, appeared on-screen. Fearless—and *faceless*. His image was digitally altered, pixilated like a surprise witness's on *truTV*. These tiny electronic dots mixed with black, murky shadows to create an image that was more Grim Reaper than Guy Smiley.

"Welcome home, ladies," Uncle Sam said, his honey-rich voice full of pride. "And how are my favorite international spies doing today?"

"Ab fab," Jo said with a purr in her voice. "But we had *no* idea how terribly boring London could be this time of year, *dahling*. Was it the off-season for intrigue?"

"Hmmm, I believe it was," Caylin chimed in, employing her impeccable British accent. "Do send us somewhere a trifle more challenging this time, Samuel. I'm *dying* to know what's next."

"Don't die just yet, Caylin," Uncle Sam said ominously. "There'll be plenty of time for that later."

The girls glanced nervously at one another. Theresa gulped. Was good old Uncle Sammy *serious*?

The big screen was filled with the image of a sprawling, high-tech building. "This is the U.S. headquarters of InterCorp," Uncle Sam stated. "A multinational corporation that has reportedly been behind some of the more unsavory ventures in recent history. Toxic waste dumping, chemical weapons manufacturing, industrial espionage, you name it. Although we've kept the company under surveillance for years, no one has been able to dig up enough dirt to shut them down."

"I read an article about this company," Theresa said. "Supposedly key people who work for their competitors have a tendency to 'disappear.'"

"Supposedly," Jo spat. "Yeah, right."

The other girls knew not to comment when Jo used that tone of voice. That tone meant she was thinking of her father, a Miami judge who was gunned down right before the fourteen-year-old eyes of Josefina Mercedes Carreras while trying to convict a drug lord. Four years had passed since, but time had done little to soften the blow. Sure, Jo could easily hide her pain behind her naturally fun and flirty facade. But mentions of murder usually sent her crashing and burning.

"Like most people who run an empire with this much money and power, they want only one thing: more," Uncle Sam continued. "And they'll do *anything* to get it."

"Real sweethearts," Theresa said glibly, rolling her eyes.

A picture of an older, distinguished-looking man filled the screen. "This is Mitchell von Strauss, president of InterCorp," Uncle Sam said. "One of the most intelligent— and ruthless—businessmen in the world. His accomplishments speak for themselves. Unfortunately his methods do, too. He *eliminates* his competition—some say literally. One magazine compared him to a dangerous dictator— someone who thinks he can use any means to achieve his goals. Even murder."

"Disgusting," Jo said. Her dark eyes shot daggers at

the image of von Strauss. Suddenly a new image appeared on-screen.

Jo's eyes instantly melted as she took in the vision of a tall, blond hottie with a deep tan and deeper dimples.

Ooh-la-la!

The one thing that could send Jo's caution, judgment, and common sense flying right out the window.

Ding!

"This is Ewan Gallagher, InterCorp's head of international relations," Uncle Sam explained.

"Relations?" Jo echoed. "Mmm. *I* can relate."

"He was a boy genius," Uncle Sam continued. "Graduated high school at fourteen, top of his class at Harvard at seventeen. Now, at just twenty-four, he's one of the most powerful men in international business."

Jo was practically drooling on the table.

"Wow," Caylin whispered. She looked as if she would hyperventilate at any second.

It wasn't like Caylin to be out of breath. But Jo sure couldn't blame her.

"Come on, you guys," Theresa muttered. "Can't you tell

he's a guy who'd sell his mother on the black market?"

"So?" Jo replied dreamily.

"So, do you remember Antonio? The guy you liked in London?" Theresa said. "Italian. Gorgeous. Charming. Liked to kill young female spies."

Jo scowled. "I remember."

"Theresa's right, girls," Uncle Sam said. "Don't judge this movie by its trailer. Gallagher is just as cold and ruthless as von Strauss."

Pouting, Jo tapped her high heels against the floor in frustration. She knew all too well how deceptive appearances could be—she'd had plenty of experience in that department. Still, for some bizarre reason she couldn't stop falling for dangerous guys. When she gazed up at Ewan's face on the screen, she didn't see cold and ruthless—just warm and guileless.

Note to self, she thought grimly. Get a clue!

She actually breathed a sigh of relief when a gray, sleek-looking building replaced Ewan's face on the screen.

"This is InterCorp's Prague headquarters," Uncle Sam continued. "Von Strauss and Gallagher relocated to the

Czech Republic's capital city just last week, presumably because an open-trade pact is about to be signed here."

"I love Prague!" Caylin said, ever the jet-setter. "It's so gorgeous."

"The New Russian Ballet likes Prague, too," Uncle Sam stated as footage of a gorgeous, dark-haired ballerina rolled. "This is Anka Perdova, age eighteen. She's the NRB's prima ballerina. The troupe is currently installed at Prague's St. Nikolai Theater."

"That's one big-buck investment," Caylin noted.

"Yes," Uncle Sam agreed. "And guess who is bankrolling their season in Prague?"

"InterCorp," Theresa replied.

"Exactly," Uncle Sam said.

"Why would InterCorp fund a ballet troupe?" Theresa asked.

"A tax write-off, probably," Uncle Sam replied. "And a smoke screen for their more devious doings."

Suddenly pictures of distinguished-looking men and women of all nationalities were flashing on the screen, rapid-fire. "In just eight days these dignitaries will be flooding

Prague to finalize the aforementioned open-trade pact," Uncle Sam said. "It's scheduled to be signed immediately following a performance at the ballet."

"Let me guess," Jo said. "Something's going to go down during the performance."

"I'm getting to that," Uncle Sam said as a close-up picture of an older, graying gentleman filled the screen.

"He looks familiar," Caylin said.

"This is Gogol Karkovic, the prime minister of Varokhastan—a small, newly democratic Eastern European country," Uncle Sam explained. "If he signs the pact, InterCorp stands to lose a fortune."

"Why?" Theresa asked.

"Varokhastan is rich with mines," Uncle Sam replied. "*Diamond* mines. InterCorp has a vested interest in the diamond industry—and they're very possessive. They would like nothing more than to lay claim to the diamonds of Varokhastan. And as I mentioned before, they do *not* like competition—something this open-trade pact would create."

A million glittering diamonds filled the screen.

"Heaven," Jo said in awe.

"Not really," Uncle Sam said gravely. "We believe an attempt is going to be made on Karkovic's life before the trade pact can be signed. And we believe InterCorp is behind this assassination plot."

Jo gasped. An assassination plot? She instantly regretted her last breezy comment as images of her father flickered before her eyes.

"How will they do it?" Theresa asked, concern etched on her face.

"That's for you to find out, Spy Girls," Uncle Sam replied.

"And for us to stop," Caylin added. She pounded a fist into her hand for emphasis.

"Exactly." Uncle Sam cleared his throat. "Don't forget who you're dealing with here. Men like von Strauss and Gallagher don't care who they destroy in their wake as long as they get what they're after."

"And that doesn't just mean Karkovic, right?" Theresa asked.

"You're right," Uncle Sam replied. Suddenly the image of Anka Perdova reappeared on-screen. This time she was smiling and signing autographs for a bunch of kids. "Who knows how far InterCorp's plans reach? They could endanger the whole ballet troupe. Everyone in the audience that night. The entire city of Prague. Young children, like the ones you see here. Karkovic may be their target but anyone anywhere near the theater will be in danger—unless you foil InterCorp's plans."

Jo's eyes teared up at the poignant image. To think that such an awful thing could take place during a ballet performance—it seemed impossible.

As Jo watched the talented ballerina smile for the young children her heart leaped into her throat. She and Anka, on the surface, seemed so alike. They both had long black hair; they both were eighteen; heck, they both were even lefties. And now they were both wrapped up in a horrible assassination plot.

"Karkovic's bodyguards won't have a chance," Theresa stated.

"So what's the plan?" Caylin asked, bouncing up and down in her seat. Ready to run, move, do something, *anything*.

Uncle Sam exhaled deeply. "Girls, your mission is to infiltrate the open-trade conference and stop the assassination of Karkovic."

Theresa raised her hand as if she were in grade school. "Uh, we *knew* that already, Sam," she said half sarcastically. "Don't you have any more for us to go on?"

"Negative," Uncle Sam replied. "You're entirely on your own."

Caylin's brow furrowed. "Why us?" she asked. "This is a big challenge. I mean, we're talking global impact and stuff. Why don't you just notify the pros and let them handle it?"

"You *are* the pros," Uncle Sam responded testily. "Besides, it's all speculation at this point. The exposure of a formal investigation can't be risked. And since most of the stagehands and interns are young females, we thought you would arouse the least amount of suspicion. Feel up to it?"

"Do we have a *choice*?" Theresa scoffed. But her gray eyes were dancing with excitement.

A slow, sly grin grew across Caylin's face. "Well, I *do*

love the ballet," she drawled. "And I've got *nothing* else on my schedule this week. I guess I can cope."

"Me too." Jo sighed dramatically. "So many evil schemes, so little time."

Uncle Sam chuckled. "Glad you're so confident, girls."

Theresa smiled. "Why's that, Sammy?"

"Because you ship out in two hours."

TWO

"So is Prague gonna be cold or what?" Theresa asked as she stood in front of her walk-in closet. The Tower dorm room she shared with Theresa and Caylin was a blur of flying shirts, pants, and dresses as the trio attempted to get appropriately attired for the long plane ride ahead.

"*Freezing,*" Caylin said with a frown. "Which wouldn't be so bad if there were any mountains to snowboard. But Prague's not exactly the ski capital of the world."

"Too bad," Jo kidded, bundling socks. "You'll just have to concentrate on the silly old mission, won't you?"

"Drag," Caylin replied with a smirk. "I hate when that happens."

Theresa unplugged her laptop and slid it into its padded case. Sunlight streamed through the massive windows— warmth she wouldn't be seeing for a while. She selected the stereo remote from the eight remotes on her night table and aimed it at the far wall. "I can't even hear myself think."

Miles Davis faded slightly. Theresa chose another remote and switched the channel from MTV to CNN, hoping to catch a glimpse of a global weather report.

"I'm going to miss this entertainment center." Theresa sighed. "We've got it all, but we only had two days to enjoy it."

"That's because you just had to rewire the whole wall before we left for London," Caylin said. "You're the only one who knows how to work everything. I mean, we have eight remotes!"

"They're labeled," Theresa explained.

"I still can't tell them apart." Caylin stared longingly at her snowboard, which she had mounted on the wall above her bed. "I just wish I could bring my board. What a bummer."

"I can't say I'm looking forward to icicles, either," Jo went on, folding a sweater. "After all, this bod's too dope to hide in a coat!"

Theresa giggled. "We're going on a *mission*, Jo. Not a vacation."

"A mission that we have *no time* to pack for," Caylin interjected. "What kind of wardrobe can a girl pack in no time?"

"Sometimes you guys amaze me." Theresa sighed. "A prominent world leader is about to be assassinated, and you two are worried about clothes."

Theresa gestured toward the giant TV screen. There Gogol Karkovic was being shown meeting young children who had been orphaned during the course of a recent civil war. Tears shone in the older man's eyes as he spoke in his native Varok.

The caption at the bottom of the screen read, *We cannot live in a world where guns make the law—where children are left to suffer alone.*

The room fell silent as Theresa clicked off the remote.

Jo squinted. Karkovic's message had clearly hit home with her. "Well, come on, we *do* have to wear *something*," she began, ignoring the heart-wrenching newscast. "Some help you are, Theresa. I still can't believe your mother is a fashion designer."

Theresa rolled her eyes. "I know, I know."

"I really *don't* get it, T." Caylin shook her head sadly. "How can you hate fashion when we have The Tower buying us clothes? You could get couture for the asking, sweetie darling, but all you want to do is wear jeans."

"I have better things to worry about," Theresa muttered, arranging her laptop and an array of peripherals on the bed.

"You and your toys," Jo kidded. "I'm gonna call Danielle and see if she has any last minute advice for us."

She went to grab the proper remote, but she could only stare, dumbfounded, at the lineup of controllers on Theresa's night table.

"Okay, T.," Jo growled. "I give up. Which one works the video chat?"

"Third from the left," Theresa replied without looking up from her hardware.

"I hate these things," Jo said. "Can't we just get one big remote?"

"It'd be the size of a mainframe," Theresa said with a laugh.

Jo sighed and punched in 11-12-80—the secret code to activate the video chat and Ryan Gosling's birthday. "Oh, Danielle, are you home?" Jo asked as the big TV came back to life with a flashing blue screen and the word *ringing* emblazoned across it.

Theresa couldn't help but smile at the mention of Danielle's name. When they were in London, the Spy Girls had seen a tall woman with short brown hair following them everywhere. They had been certain that "Short Hair" was working for the enemy and had tried desperately to learn her identity by snapping her picture with their secret cameras and chasing her through nightclubs.

"Boy, did I feel stupid when we found out Danielle was actually one of us," Theresa said.

"I know," Jo replied, dropping the remote on the bed. "I about had a cow when we got to the safe house and *bam*, there she was."

Theresa immediately retrieved the remote from the bed and replaced it on her nightstand. "I'm glad we've got her on our side. We're sure going to need her help on this mission."

A few seconds later Danielle's face appeared on the big screen. "Hello, Spy Girls," she chirped. "Ready to roll?"

"Hardly." Theresa moaned, pointing to the T-shirt and boxers she was still lounging around in. "I'm so clueless about clothes, I can't even figure out what to wear on the plane."

"You better get a move on," Danielle instructed. "You have less than an hour."

"I know," Caylin said, running a brush through her long blond hair. "Any Prague pointers?"

"Just keep a cool head," Danielle instructed. "This is a high-pressure mission, seeing as the pact signing is just over a week away. Stay focused and take it one step at a time."

"As long as those one-steps-at-a-time bring down InterCorp, it'll be *all* good," Jo said enthusiastically.

Danielle smiled. "Now, when you land, you need to tell your driver to take you to Josefská two-four-two, three-S. Is someone writing this down?"

"I am," Theresa said, grabbing the nearest pen and paper. "So it's what?"

"*J-o-s-e-f-s-k-a* two-four-two, three-S," Danielle repeated. "Got it?"

"Yep," Theresa said, writing down the letters in a sure, block script.

"I'll be there in thirty minutes to take you to the airport," Danielle said. "Good luck, girls!"

The screen faded to black.

"Hope we don't need it," Theresa muttered.

"Five minutes late." Caylin scowled as she hopped around impatiently in the designated Tower pickup area. "Danielle is five minutes late. Where is she?"

Jo whipped out her cell phone. She was just about to dial Danielle's digits when she heard the sound of screeching tires.

Delicious. Jo loved that sound. She could practically smell the burning rubber already.

A sleek, lobster-red blur roared around the corner, fishtailing and squealing to a halt in front of her.

Jo's tongue practically rolled out to the ground. There it sat, right in front of her. Jo Carreras's weakness number two—a gorgeous sports car. A brand-new Ferrari 458 Italia, to be exact, with Danielle grinning from the driver's seat.

"No way—a 458!" Jo gasped as she ran a hand over the sweet ride's shiny enamel. "Where'd you score this?"

"Didn't think I was this cool, did you?" Danielle opened the door and slid out. "This beauty was confiscated in a big drug bust a few weeks back. And when they plea-bargained the guy yesterday, the car stopped being evidence and started being mine. At least for a couple of days."

"You gotta let me drive, Danielle," Jo demanded, circling the vehicle like a lioness stalking her prey. *"Now."*

"No way." She shook her head. "The only one getting behind that wheel is me."

"Guess again, Sherlock." Jo swiped the keys from the ignition. "Direct fuel injection . . . German transmission—ohh, I *need* this."

"Say, Wonder Wheels," Theresa interrupted. "Where are *we* supposed to sit?"

"Yeah," Caylin agreed. "There're only two seats!"

Jo shrugged. "Cram in the back."

"With our *bags*?" Theresa asked incredulously.

"Come on," Jo grumbled, flipping the driver's seat forward and stuffing her bag in the tiny space behind it.

As Caylin slid uncomfortably into the Ferrari she glared at Danielle. "Couldn't get a limo, huh?"

"Who needs a limo when you've got a Ferrari?" Jo breathed. "We'll be at the airport in seven minutes."

"Seven?" Theresa exclaimed, eyes wide.

"Okay, six."

"Danielle," Theresa and Caylin complained in stereo.

"Don't worry," Danielle soothed. "I won't let Jo kill us."

Caylin and Theresa stuffed their bags—and each other—into the tiny space behind the two seats. Their heads were scrunched against the tan leather roof and their limbs tangled in their luggage.

"You do realize, Jo, that if we die now, no one will be left to save the world," Caylin stated dryly.

"Relax," Jo replied, smoothly slipping the car into gear. She revved the engine methodically. "With a V-eight, five hundred sixty-two horses, we'll go from zero to one-double-oh in three-point-four seconds."

"Is that with or without the air bag?" Theresa asked.

Jo gave her a grin, pressed her pedal to the metal, and peeled out. "Prague, here we come!" she screamed.

THREE

"This is it." Theresa surveyed the homes along the winding cobblestone street. She scanned the piece of paper on which she had scrawled the address. "I think."

"After an hour in customs I can't keep anything straight," Caylin said crankily.

Jo squinted at a map. "Malá Strana," she recited, ever the language expert. "The Little Quarter district of Prague. Our new home."

"Mozart used to walk these streets all the time," Theresa revealed. "But I doubt he lived *here*."

Theresa pointed at the door in front of her for emphasis. The number 242 was painted next to it haphazardly. Drop-jawed, she gazed up and up—the run-down building was five stories tall. Forbidding stone gargoyles stared down at her from the rooftop. "It looks so . . . old."

"Chances are, it is," Caylin quipped.

"Could this all be for us?" Jo whispered.

"Not," Caylin said, dropping her bags by her feet. "It looks like my aunt's apartment building in Paris. Didn't Danielle give a flat number?"

Theresa squinted at the crumpled piece of paper. "Three-S."

"There you go, Watson," Caylin said, picking up her bags and jaunting toward the door with a new spring in her step. "What did you think the three-S stood for?"

"Three spies, of course," Theresa said. "Hey, who's got the key?"

Caylin produced the envelope that a stern flight attendant had slipped to her during the flight. Inside were two keys. Caylin unlocked the heavy, hand-carved door and pushed it open. "Okay—I bet three means third floor," Caylin said, heading for the steep stairwell before them.

"No elevator?" Jo whined, looking disdainfully at the water-stained walls and worn gray carpet covering the stairs. "This is a far cry from the Ritz."

Indeed, the worn-down carpet and water-stained walls looked positively dilapidated compared to the decadent digs they'd dwelled in just days earlier.

When they reached the third floor and laid eyes on the scratched-up door marked 3-S, their expectations deflated even further.

"This is a nightmare," Jo said, her nose wrinkled.

"You can say that again," Caylin agreed, turning the key in the lock. But when the door swung wide, she gasped. "Check it out!" she cheered, spinning around to soak in the red velvet couch, the ornate woodwork, the abstract art on the walls, the giant aquarium.

"Can you say *delish*?" Theresa exclaimed. She slipped her sneakers off and ran her bare feet over the soft oriental rug. "The Tower has really outdone itself this time."

"Too cool!" Jo squealed, dumping her bags and dashing into a bedroom. "Whoa—a four-post canopy bed!" she hollered, prompting Theresa and Caylin to run in after her.

"Talk about perfect!" Theresa shrilled.

"Hurry up," Caylin prodded after scanning the room. "I want to see more!"

All the bedrooms had massive canopy beds and antique decor. The ceilings had to be fifteen feet high, with long windows framed by heavy red velvet drapes.

"Check out the new laptop in here," Caylin said, pointing into the middle bedroom. "Man, this room is totally equipped!"

Theresa gasped. *"Mine!"* She marched in and dropped her bag by the bed, gazing lovingly at the setup before her. "Mine, mine, mine, mine, mine! Ooh, I've been *dying* to get my hands on one of these!" Theresa plopped into the high-back wooden chair and punched away furiously at the keys. "Wow. A good computer can be so . . . *sexy.*"

Jo grabbed Theresa's arm and yanked her away from the laptop.

"Hey!"

"No net surfing till we see the rest of the place!" Jo ordered. "Let's check out the living room."

"And the fridge!" Caylin added.

En route to the kitchen Theresa spied a note resting on the corner of the massive antique dining room table.

"Uh-oh, gal pals," she exclaimed. "We have a love letter!"

As Theresa snatched up the paper, Caylin and Jo dashed over at lightning speed.

"Push the red button on the aquarium," Theresa read, glancing up at Caylin and Jo with a quizzical look in her eyes.

"Go for it," Caylin instructed.

Theresa pressed the red button on top of the aquarium. Nothing happened.

"Press it again," Caylin said, reaching for it.

"No, wait," Theresa replied. "Look."

The long side of the aquarium actually flickered. Gradually Uncle Sam's shadowed face appeared in the glass.

"That's so cool!" Theresa exclaimed, meeting Jo's and Caylin's gazes. "You can still see the fish. Is this an LCD or what?"

"That's top secret, Theresa," Uncle Sam replied.

"No fair."

The Spy Girls plopped down on the expensive-looking chairs and couches around the living room.

"Time to get down to business, ladies," he said.

"Cool," Caylin replied. She scooted to the edge of her seat in delicious anticipation. "Let's have it."

"There are three tablets in the drawer embedded in the base of the aquarium," Uncle Sam said. "Take notes."

Theresa ran over and retrieved the tablets and passed them out to her eager counterparts. "Ready, Sammy," she said, placing her fingers on the keys expectantly.

"You're all to report for duty tomorrow—that's Monday morning—at ten a.m.," Uncle Sam instructed. "Jo, you'll pose as Selma Ribiero, a Brazilian-American daughter of wealthy parentage. You're interning at InterCorp so that you can learn the ins and outs of big business."

Jo grinned wickedly.

"Already dreaming about rubbing elbows with Ewan Gallagher?" Caylin teased.

"No," Jo said lightly. "Just dreaming about saving the world, that's all."

Caylin laughed. "I do that, too, but it doesn't make me blush."

"Let's move on," Uncle Sam admonished. "Theresa,

you'll be posing as Tiffany Heileman, an American who's interning at the ballet in the props department."

"Tiffany?" Theresa scoffed. "Does a bleach job and frosted pink lip gloss come with that alias?"

Uncle Sam remained silent. While she couldn't see his face, Theresa could practically feel his glare.

"Sorry," she murmured. "Tiffany's . . . great. No complaints from me."

"Good." Uncle Sam cleared his throat. "Caylin, you're posing as Australian exchange student Muriel Hewitt, who's ushering at the theater for some extra cash."

"All righty, mate!" she replied in her best Aussie accent. "If I can't surf down under, at least I can talk about it."

"The information on where to go and who to report to is in the locked safety-deposit box under the sink," Uncle Sam continued, "and the key is taped to a sour spot in the refrigerator."

"Sour spot?" Theresa repeated. "Let's see—sour cream, sour milk, sweet-and-sour sauce. . . ."

Uncle Sam chuckled. "Your wardrobes will be delivered shortly."

"Whoo-hoo!" Jo and Caylin cheered.

"But answer the door *only* to those who use the secret buzz."

The intercom suddenly buzzed. Two short, two long.

Caylin rolled her eyes.

"I saw that!" Uncle Sam said.

"Saw what?" Caylin asked innocently.

"The eye roll, that's what," he said, thankfully not sounding *too* mad. "You're on video cam, too."

"Really? Where is it?" Theresa said, looking up, down, and all around to track the location of the hidden lens.

"You tell me," he dared.

Theresa went to the aquarium and began to inspect it inch by inch. "Check it out!" she called. "One of those fish swimming behind Uncle Sam is actually a camera."

"Okay, Sam, you got me," Caylin said as she looked directly into the faux goldfish's mouth, where a camera lens was hidden. "But isn't a secret buzz a little much?"

"Not if the people on the other side of the door have guns," Uncle Sam said.

"Good point," Jo admitted.

"Good point indeed. And good night." Uncle Sam's shadowy image dissolved into the aquarium's crystal blue water.

"This is totally wild," Jo said.

"I'll say," Caylin agreed. "I've always wanted to be an Aussie!" She broke into her best Sydney accent. "Let's go suss out that sour spot."

Jo and Caylin ambushed the fridge while Theresa checked out the equipment.

"This kitchen is loaded," Theresa noted. "Fresh fruit, juice machine, espresso . . . why go out?"

"Where's that key . . . ," Caylin grumbled. "Lemonade?" She examined the ceramic pitcher for the magic key. "Nope, no cigar. Maybe pickles?"

"What about lemon balls?" Jo proposed, looking bored with the search. "Do they have those in Prague?"

Caylin unscrewed the lid of the pickle jar. "Bingo!" she cheered, snatching the key from inside the lid.

"Now that all the secret bells and whistles are out in the open," Jo said, "I'm going to unpack and unwind."

The others agreed. An hour later essentials were

stowed, snacks were scarfed, and the Spy Girls were ready to rock.

"Okay," Jo began as she dabbed pink polish on her toenails. "Here's a little vocab lesson. There are about a dozen ways to say 'cute' in Czech, but I'll give you three."

"How challenging," Caylin called out from the kitchen, where she was whipping up a goulash dinner to celebrate their first night in Prague. "Just don't quiz me later, okay?"

"One, there's *roztomilý*, which is a charming kind of cute," Jo continued, unfazed. "Then there's *rozkošný*, which is *cute*-cute—you know, like 'that little big-eyed puppy is totally *rozkošný*.' And then there's *mazaný*, which is foxy . . . literally."

"Thanks, Jo," Theresa drawled. "I'm sure *that'll* come in handy the next time I'm in a bind."

Caylin jumped out of the kitchen. She clapped and rolled her eyes up melodramatically. "'Please, sir, don't kill me—I find you so . . . *mazaný*!'" she cried breathily.

"I'm just going to stick to my pocket translator, thank you very much." Theresa waved the thin, checkbook-size computer in the air for emphasis.

"You guys just don't know how to have fun." Jo sighed as she finished up her pedicure. "You know, it's amazing how the right polish and a kickin' toe ring can make the ugliest part of the body look fabulous."

Theresa looked up from her laptop. "You know, what's *really* amazing is how much time people spend painting their fingers and toes and faces. It just doesn't seem sensible."

"I think you've been surfing that web too long, my darling," Caylin called out. "Try some *real* surfing and you'll see the world in a whole different way."

"Sports and makeup." Theresa rolled her eyes. "Sorry, but I don't see the connection."

Buzz-buzz . . . buzzzzzzzz-buzzzzzzzz.

Jo jumped in surprise at the sound of the intercom. Thankfully her perfect polish remained intact.

"The secret buzz!" Theresa whispered.

"That's our wardrobe!" Jo exclaimed. She hobbled toward the door on her heels to avoid damaging her tantalizing tootsies. "Who *iiis* it?" she asked, peering through the peephole.

"Special delivery," the guy behind the door called.

Panting, she turned to Theresa and Caylin. "He's *foxy*!" Jo whispered.

"Don't you mean *mazany*?" Theresa and Caylin teased in stereo.

The "Mystery Date" song played in Jo's head as she opened the door, revealing a tall, muscular guy with long blond hair and a bright smile.

"I w-would like to, h-how you say, *greet* you," he mumbled in stilted English.

Jo held out her hand. "You mean, *hello*."

The delivery guy ignored her hand and squinted at her. "Yes . . . hello. I have boxes."

He turned and began unloading cardboard boxes from his dolly. Each box was marked with one of their names. The muscles in his forearms rippled like steel cables.

Mmm, *yummy*.

Jo grinned at the others, wiggling her eyebrows. "Those boxes look heavy," she said to him.

He stared at her feet. "Pink."

She showed off her pearly pink toenails. "You like?"

He gave her a strange look and walked out.

"What's *his* damage?" Jo whispered to her compatriots. Still, she couldn't help admiring his fair form as he brought in the last box.

"I go now," he said.

"Wait!" Jo cried.

The guy froze.

"Jo, the gentleman should *go* now," Caylin explained politely.

"I *know*, Cay, but I have to tip him, don't I?" Jo rummaged through her pockets frantically for the crowns she'd exchanged at the airport. She stuffed some of her cash into his big, strong hands.

"No, too much." He looked down incredulously at the wad she'd handed over.

"Take it," she insisted, hoping the tip would put a smile on his stony—but still gorgeous—face.

He simply shrugged again and left, wheeling his dolly down the hall with nary a peep.

"What, no *thank you*?" Jo shrieked as she slammed the door after him.

"I don't think he understood you," Theresa offered.

"But I was speaking the *international* language!" Jo complained. "How could he *not*—"

"Can't talk! Clothes!" Caylin screeched.

Jo instantly brightened, and she and Caylin ripped open their boxes like kids on Christmas morning. Theresa lagged noticeably behind.

"Prada winter wear!" Jo squealed as she surveyed her duds, grateful that posing as a socialite guaranteed her a delicious designer wardrobe.

"I've got more of the Banana Republic thing going," Caylin said, pulling out tan wool pants and beige fisherman's sweaters. "I guess it's that whole Australian safari vibe."

"I'm the Gap girl, thank goodness," Theresa called, smiling brightly as she held up basic after basic.

Jo held up a cream-colored blouse and sighed. "Well, sisters, one thing's for sure."

"What's that?" Theresa asked.

"Even if we *don't* save the world, at least we'll look good."

FOUR

"I feel like I'm in the middle of *Amadeus*," Caylin noted, Aussie accent in full effect as she led the way into the baroque city on a chilly Monday morning. "This city's a beaut, I tell ya!"

Peddlers made their way toward the town square, their pushcarts overflowing with everything from fruits and vegetables to handcrafted dolls and puppets. The spires and towers of the gorgeous Prague Castle dominated the skyline. Brightly painted houses—some dating back to the thirteenth century—lined the streets, contrasting with the stubborn gray sky.

Theresa smiled and nodded. "This place is about as far from Arizona as you can get, but it really *is* a beaut."

"It'd be a lot *more* of a beaut if it wasn't so freaking

cold," Jo grumbled through chattering teeth. "You're sure you know where we're going?"

"Yep," Caylin affirmed. The instructions they retrieved from the safe last night informed them that Josefská, the narrow, cobbled street they were living on, led straight to the main square. There the St. Nikolai Theater and InterCorp were only a few meters away from each other. Despite Jo's grumblings, Caylin had a definite spring in her step.

"I can't believe we're finally *doing* something," she cheered.

"Yeah, freezing our butts off," Jo commented. "This little faux fur number is *not* cold-weather compatible."

"The Tower issued you a *long* coat, Jo," Theresa said. "It wouldn't kill you to wear it."

"But I can't cover up this gorgeous quilted mini!" Jo cried. "You might as well call the fashion police!"

In the square an ancient clock chimed ten.

The Spy Girls froze.

"That's our cue, Sheilas!" Caylin announced.

"Sheilas?" Jo asked.

"It's Aussie for 'girls,'" Caylin explained.

"I know," Jo said with a smile. "I saw *Crocodile Dundee* enough times. You don't have to lay it on so thick when it's just us."

"Yes, I do," Caylin argued. "This is like method acting. If I don't do it right here, how can I do it right when it counts?"

"Point taken," Theresa said. "Let's split up, sisters."

"Good luck, you guys," Jo said.

Theresa smiled nervously. "You too."

"G'day, mates!"

Each Spy Girl moved off in a different direction.

Each with a different mission.

Each wondering if she could pull it off.

"And this is the grand tour," Josef Capek droned as he walked Jo through the halls of InterCorp Prague. "On the right, the employee break room."

"Exciting," Jo breathed. The first thing she had noticed about Josef Capek was his looks or, more specifically, his lack thereof. His short, stodgy frame, plain features, and receding hairline had thrilled Jo to pieces—not because she was into him but because she so *wasn't*. Since Capek's looks weren't the least bit lovable, Jo was able to concentrate solely on the InterCorp tour.

Of course, there was still that pesky matter of Ewan Gallagher to worry about. . . .

"You'll be required to perform general office duties— answering phones, running errands, that sort of thing," Capek continued as they walked down a long, narrow hall.

"That sounds fine to me," she said, effortlessly employing the accent she'd perfected while staying with relatives in Brazil.

As Capek directed her to her cubicle Jo was way tempted to ask where Mitchell von Strauss and Ewan Gallagher were. But Jo could tell that this was a busy office. Information would float through the air like confetti. She would quickly learn which bits were important and follow them through without arousing suspicion.

"This is your station," Capek announced as they approached a tiny cubicle already marked with a nameplate reading Selma Ribiero. "You will be assisting Alexander Gottwald, a vice president in charge of marketing. Why don't we meet him now?"

Jo nodded as she followed Capek down the hall. She kept her eyes glued to door after door, hoping to see a plate with one of the nasty names. Nothing. She stifled a sigh of disappointment.

Then she saw it.

Mitchell von Strauss, right there in plain letters. And his office was within sight of her cube!

Jo's mind spun. It told her to bug his phone, make friends with his assistant, send him flowers, offer to play golf with him, do *anything* to get on the inside.

She flashed the stern-looking woman at the desk outside von Strauss's office a smile. Jo received a frown in return.

So much for *that* plan.

Alexander Gottwald's office was two down from von Strauss's. Jo regarded the imposing man behind the large, cherry-wood desk carefully. Gray-haired, distinguished, and Armani clad, he was the picture of sophistication as he extended a hand toward her.

"Welcome aboard," Gottwald said in accented English.

"I'm thrilled to be here, Mr. Gottwald," she said, blessing him with her best thousand-watt grin.

"Well, we'll definitely keep you busy," Gottwald said. "With the open-trade pact coming up, things are really reaching a boiling point."

No kidding, she thought gazing blankly at him. "Open-trade pact?" she asked innocently.

"Yes—it's a very important event but I'll let Josef fill you in on all the gory details," he explained. He gave her a stern look. "You should read the newspapers more, my dear."

"Yes, I know," she said, her voice full of shame.

"For now," Gottwald continued, "I'm expecting two important calls. One from Ewan Gallagher and one from Vienna. When they come through, make sure you find me immediately."

Jo's heart sped up at the mention of Ewan's name. She would actually be talking to him that day! Her first big break!

"I'll show her how to put calls through right away," Capek promised with an efficient nod.

"I look forward to working with you, Mr. Gottwald," Jo called as Capek ushered her out.

"Likewise, I'm sure, Selma," Gottwald replied, turning his attention back to his paperwork.

Moments after Capek trained her on the phone system and left her to her own devices, Jo's cell phone went off, jolting her from her thoughts.

She looked around casually. Seeing no one, she slipped the phone out of her pocket and glanced at it.

Go to ballet box office . . . Pick up ticket for tonight's performance . . . Uncle Sam.

"Cool," she whispered.

"I'm Ottla Heydrich, director of ushers," a gray-haired woman told Caylin in fluent English. She extended a ring-adorned hand, and Caylin shook it briskly.

"Very nice to meet you," Caylin said. "Muriel Hewitt."

"Have a seat, Muriel." Ottla motioned to the chair in front of her desk.

While Ottla scanned "Muriel's" resume, Caylin looked around Ottla's office, which was tucked away in a far corner of the St. Nikolai Theater. It was a damp, dusky space filled with stacks of file folders, books, and ballet programs. Nothing too fascinating.

"Here from Australia, are you?" Ottla asked.

"You're not wrong about that!" Caylin laughed. "Aussie born and bred."

"Beautiful country," Ottla said offhandedly. She then took a deep breath. "As I'm sure you're aware, we're putting on *Swan Lake* right now. There are performances six nights a week. And our principal attraction, Anka Perdova, fills the seats night after night. Which means a St. Nikolai usher is a busy usher."

Caylin smiled, but she was bristling on the inside. She hated being talked down to. What was she, a third grader?

To Ottla she probably was.

"Let's go ahead and give you the tour," Ottla said. She rose from her chair and led Caylin out the door.

"It's a really beautiful theater," Caylin enthused. Hundreds of seats formed a sea of red velvet. Huge crystal chandeliers hung from above, and ornate moldings covered the high ceilings. The carpeting was bloodred, lined in gold. The stage was grandiose, and the air resonated with performances past. It simply oozed history.

"Yes, it is," Ottla agreed. "It was built in 1886, three years after the National Theater opened in 1883, and all renovations—up to the last one in 1988—have stayed true to the original design."

"Grouse!" Caylin exclaimed. Aussie for "very good."

Ottla gave her a confused look before handing her a piece of paper. "Here's a seating chart. You'll need to familiarize yourself with it immediately. You'll be seating people this evening."

"Righto," Caylin said, gazing down at the maze of numbers and boxes with confidence.

"We're getting ready to host all the dignitaries in town for the open-trade-pact signing in a week," Ottla said. "It will be the most important night of the year for us."

No kidding, Caylin thought grimly. "How exciting!" "Muriel" exclaimed.

"We'll definitely need your services that night," Ottla said, looking a bit worried. "The volume is going to be immense."

Caylin smiled. "Wouldn't miss it for the world!"

"The ballerinas are at a local school giving a concert this morning," Ottla explained, "so the theater is empty. Why don't you take advantage of it and acquaint yourself with the layout for a few hours?"

I'd like nothing better, Caylin thought.

Starting with backstage . . .

"So we have to touch up these three sets. The garden and great hall of Prince Siegfried's castle. And the lakeside. Do you have any questions, Tiffany?"

Hannah Shrum, a young American stagehand, was cheerfully training Theresa backstage. She'd already given Theresa a tour of the main theater. Now they were getting down to the real nitty-gritty.

Theresa examined the mammoth sets warily. "Does it take long to do this?" she asked. The artistry was extremely detailed—like paint by numbers times a million. Since Theresa was way more proficient in keystrokes than brush strokes, she was a bit intimidated.

"Depends," Hannah said, eyeballing the gigantic, varied

backdrops depicting huge oak trees and velvet couches and shimmering pools of water. "They have to be perfect every night, and sometimes the paint peels or cracks under the lights. The damage varies from show to show."

Theresa had already observed the out-of-date light system. But the lights weren't the only things that had captured her attention. She'd also noticed there weren't many people around. No ballerinas. Not even *Caylin* was anywhere to be seen. "How are the other people who work here?"

"Everyone is pretty cool as long as you stay out of their way," Hannah explained. "And not knowing how to speak Czech or Russian is a big handicap, although a lot gets communicated through pointing and hand signals. And even though our boss, Julius, can be a little temperamental at times, he's pretty laid-back once you get to know him. He's a British import—you know the type. Always wearing black leather pants and those clunky black boots. You'll meet him when he's back from that school thing."

Gotta snoop, Theresa thought. But how could she *not* be obvious? "Could you give me a backstage tour?" Theresa asked, cocking her head to the side. "I know you gave me that map earlier, but I'd like to see the real thing for myself. I don't want to get lost back there."

Hannah shrugged. "Why not?" she said, heading toward stage left and motioning for Theresa to follow.

"Here's the costume department . . . props . . . lighting . . ."

Hannah reeled off a laundry list of offices as they strolled down the dim hall and slowly passed each one. Their heavy footsteps broke the eerie silence. Theresa wrinkled her nose at the dank, musty smell that hung in the air—the walls were as dingy and water-stained as the ones in her new apartment building. The doors were constructed of heavy gray steel, giving the space an industrial feel. Theresa carefully tried to commit each door to memory.

"Here's Anka Perdova's dressing room," Hannah said.

A surge of adrenaline flowed through Theresa. She just knew she had to get in there . . . *somehow.*

I hope I can keep all these numbers straight, Caylin prayed as the audience started to file in for the evening's performance. Although she'd memorized most of the sections with no problem, she was still a bit freaked she'd mess something up. After all, an accent, alias, *and* new job were a lot for a girl to juggle all at once.

But after about twenty seatings Caylin's anxiety subsided. In fact, she found she was even enjoying herself. Seeing all the people dressed in tuxedos and long, flowing, elegant dresses was somewhat magical. Walking up and down the stairs again and again and again was way better than a workout on the StairMaster. Her assignment *did* have its fringe benefits, she had to admit.

"Seat forty-two-D," a familiar voice said, yanking Caylin from her thoughts.

"Jo!" Caylin gasped. "What are you doing here?"

"My *uncle* gave me a ticket," Jo said with a wink.

"Right this way," Caylin said, trying to keep her expression even in case anyone was watching.

"I never saw Ewan or von Strauss even once today," Jo hissed as she followed Caylin down the stairs.

"My day's been a snooze, too," Caylin whispered. "All aisle letters and seat numbers."

"Ewan was supposed to call my boss, but he never did," Jo said. "Talk about false hope."

Caylin pointed toward Jo's assigned seat. "Let's hope Theresa's having better luck than we are."

"We need one last touch-up on that tree over there, Tiffany," Julius demanded moments before curtain. "Go in the supply closet and get some more paint quick!"

"No problem," Theresa said, frantically sprinting to fetch the paint.

What a jerk! As far as Theresa could tell, Julius was nothing more than a short, ugly man with an even shorter and uglier personality. But maybe he'd grow on her . . . like a fungus! If he weren't head of the props and lighting departments, Julius would be one loathsome and useless human being.

She rounded the corner near the supply closet and slammed into something so forcefully, she landed on her butt.

"Whoa!" she muttered, shaking the Tweety birds away. "I'm really sorry."

Theresa stood up shakily and saw dark, almond-shaped eyes and beautiful black hair pulled back in a supertight bun. A tight white tutu on a body that was one of the most muscular and graceful she had ever seen.

Anka Perdova!

"Oh n-no, it's y-you," Theresa stammered. "I didn't even see—"

"Stupid American," Anka spat. She shoved Theresa aside and headed straight to her dressing room.

The door slammed.

Theresa stood there, gaping. For someone who danced so beautifully, Anka sure was nasty! The ballerina had looked so nice on video, signing autographs and smiling.

Maybe she should think about changing her name to *Sybil* Perdova, Theresa thought. Either that or double up on the Midol!

As the lights dimmed Jo settled back in her seat and took a deep breath.

Her father had always loved the ballet. It was a soft side few people saw of the no-nonsense, hard-line judge. He had always claimed that it relaxed him. Transported him.

So as the first note of music sounded Jo closed her eyes and let herself go. When she opened her lids, every concrete thought in her head was whisked away by the delicate beauty and grace of the dancers' movements. The ballerinas were talented, but Anka Perdova truly stole the show.

She glided across the stage effortlessly, leaping to the heavens and practically flying through the air. Uncle Sam wasn't kidding when he said she was the troupe's principal attraction. As far as Jo was concerned, Anka earned that title in spades the first five seconds of her performance.

It was hard to believe that in a week's time, this entire theater could be a bloodbath. How could InterCorp do such a thing?

The mere thought of InterCorp made Jo sick. Money. Power. All these things were bought with blood. Jo learned that at a very young age.

The ballet played on. Peaceful. Beautiful.

Seeing the talented ballerinas in action made Jo all the more determined to stop InterCorp and save Prime Minister Karkovic. She was willing to do whatever it took.

For the sake of world peace and for the memory of her father.

When the lights went up for intermission, Jo looked back and snuck a smile at Caylin, who was in the rear of the auditorium, directing people to the lobby. After Caylin met her gaze, Jo scanned the room for a glimpse of Theresa. She didn't see her.

But she did notice a gaggle of small children gathered near the stage, lined up for Anka's autograph.

How cute, Jo thought. But while watching Anka, tight-lipped and businesslike, scrawl her name on the kids' programs, Jo's eyes narrowed. Something didn't feel quite right.

She grabbed her satin clutch and hurriedly fished out her mascara cam—a minicamera concealed in a trademark pink-and-green tube of Great Lash, courtesy of The Tower.

Jo snapped a few shots just to be on the safe side.

She couldn't quite put her finger on it yet, but something was definitely wrong with this picture.

"I wish we could have stopped at the Malostranská kavårna," Theresa declared as she plopped down on the couch in their flat on Monday evening. "That's where Kafka used to hang out in the twenties."

"You know we can't be seen in public together," Jo reminded her, biting into a grilled cheese sandwich.

"I know," Theresa replied. "It just would've been nice."

The Spy Girls had made their way separately back to their flat after the ballet. Theresa had suggested that they use this time every night to share their information and theories. Though on this first night, they didn't have much.

"Leave it to you to know about who ate somewhere a zillion years ago," Caylin muttered through her ab crunches. Her blond hair was tied back in a ponytail, and sweat beaded her brow.

"So I like Kafka," Theresa replied. "So what?"

"The only person's eating habits I care about at the moment are *mine*," Jo said, chomping the grilled cheese. "I'm starvin', Marvin, and I can't deal with the cuisine. Can you believe they actually sell *deer* in the supermarkets here?"

"Well, at least you're not starving *and* in pain," Caylin said, glaring angrily at her Italian leather pumps, which lay on the floor a few feet away. "Those heels nearly killed me tonight."

"You'll live," Jo replied. "So what do you all think is up with this Anka chick?"

"What do you mean what's up with her?" Caylin asked in confusion, finishing her crunches and sitting up.

"Something's not right," Jo said. "I can't explain it, but when she was signing autographs, something weird was going on. Like she was all tight-lipped and sour faced. Nothing like she was in the video we saw."

"I accidentally bumped into her before the performance and she nearly took my head off," Theresa divulged. "She gave me a dirty look, then called me a stupid American."

"That doesn't fit what we know about her personality," Caylin said.

"That's what I'm saying," Jo insisted. "Something just doesn't fit here. I took a few snaps of her with the mascara cam. Maybe they'll tell us something."

"Psychic factor of ten!" Theresa exclaimed. "After my run-in with *Cranka*, I shot a video of her performance."

"No way," Jo replied, smiling.

"Way," Theresa said. "I just clipped my porta-cam to a broom propped against stage left and voilà, it was lights, camera, action."

She fished the black porta-cam from her coat pocket and showed it off—only a quarter of a pound and the size of a pack of gum. She placed it on the coffee table in front of them and sat down.

"Let's run it all through the video software," Jo suggested, slipping her mascara cam out of her red satin clutch.

Theresa agreed and set up her new laptop in front of them. She uncoiled the digital camera adapter and plugged the mascara cam into a video port in the side of the computer.

"This stuff is so cool," Theresa remarked, her eyes fixed and intent on the hardware. She punched at the keyboard furiously. Finally a crisp image of the theater appeared on the screen.

"Good shot," Caylin remarked.

"Good seat," Jo replied. "Wish I had that seat for the season."

Theresa clicked through the shots—four in all—of Anka Perdova signing autographs. There she was, grim and snarly.

"See what I mean?" Jo pointed out. "Not a happy camper."

"I see that she's grumpy," Caylin said "But that's about it."

"Let's zoom in on Anka," Theresa suggested, her brow furrowed in concentration. She moved the mouse and clicked away. Anka suddenly doubled in size.

"Nice pen," Caylin pointed out. "Mont Blanc."

"I'm so impressed," Theresa replied dryly.

"Wait!" Jo cried.

"What is it?"

"Can you call up that very first video we saw of Anka?" Jo asked. "The one where she's signing autographs with the kids?"

"Yeah," Theresa replied.

"Can you put the images side by side?"

"Yeah. What's the deal, Jo?"

"Just do it!" Jo ordered. "Hurry!"

Theresa clicked away. In minutes a still picture of the smiling Anka was next to the scowling one.

"Not much difference," Caylin stated. "Except she has a nice smile."

Jo chuckled. Then outright giggled.

"Jo?" Theresa asked.

"What is it?" Caylin demanded.

"Don't you *see* it?" Jo wondered.

"See what?"

"Right there in front of you!" Jo said, pointing and laughing. "That's the answer right there!"

"*What* is?" Caylin growled.

Theresa's jaw dropped. "I see it!"

"See *what*?" Caylin continued, her face reddening. "You two are killing me!"

"Cay," Jo explained, "you noticed the pen before. Compare the two pens."

Caylin took a moment. "They're the exact same pen, Jo. Exact. Except . . ."

"Yeah?" Jo asked hopefully, sharing a smile with Theresa.

"Oh, wow!" Caylin exclaimed, a lightbulb practically flashing on above her head. "That's it!"

"You see it too?" Theresa asked.

"Her *hands*!" Caylin said. "In the happy picture she's left-handed. In the nasty picture *she's right-handed*!"

"You win Final Jeopardy," Jo remarked.

"Well, maybe she's—" Caylin's brow wrinkled in thought.

"Ambidextrous?" Theresa finished.

"Yeah!"

"No. Anka Perdova's dossier says that she has been left-handed since childhood," Theresa said.

The Spy Girls shared a knowing look.

"That proves it, then," Theresa said.

"Right," Jo replied. "This can only mean one thing."

Caylin nodded. "The Anka we saw tonight is an impostor!"

"Good work, ladies," Uncle Sam complimented, his shadowy silhouette shimmering in the aquarium's screen. "I'll pass this info on."

"If InterCorp installed an Anka look-alike," Theresa said, "think how easy it would be to assassinate Prime Minister Karkovic. She'd have a clear shot from the stage. Bang, bang—he's a goner, and the real Anka—wherever she may be—is left holding the bag."

"Maybe InterCorp kidnapped her," Jo suggested.

"It's a theory," Uncle Sam replied.

"Maybe, maybe not," Caylin countered as she juggled a squirt bottle of water between her hands. "I have dancing experience, and if that woman's a killer, she's a darn good dancer, too."

"It *is* hard to believe InterCorp could find someone

that good," Theresa agreed. "And who looks so much like Anka."

"Hard to believe, yes, but not impossible," Jo reasoned. "Especially with the dough InterCorp's got. And hello— plastic surgery?"

"Plastic surgery is *that* advanced?" Caylin asked. "I mean, this is face transplant territory."

"Uncle Sam?" Theresa probed. "Is it possible? I mean, has The Tower done this sort of thing?"

Uncle Sam remained silent.

Jo shuddered. "Ew, creepy."

"Wait a sec. What if the real Anka has been murdered?" Theresa wondered. "That changes everything."

Jo shook her head. "She probably has to be alive if they're going to pin the assassination on her."

"Either that or the look-alike is the fall gal," Caylin offered.

"I agree with Jo on this one," Uncle Sam stated. "Odds are that Anka Perdova is alive and somewhere in Prague."

"Why do you think that?" Jo asked.

"If she's going to take the fall, she needs to be close to

the scene—that way she can be switched with the impostor without delay," Uncle Sam explained. "Finding the real Anka Perdova is now a priority."

Caylin grinned. Her whole body felt wired with anticipation. "Now we're cooking with fire!"

"Find out what you can, ladies," Uncle Sam said. "In the meantime, Theresa, I have something specific in mind for you."

"Shoot," she said, her calm voice not betraying her excitement. She rested her tablet in her lap, hands hovering.

"Anka Perdova has an online account with Artech, a European carrier," Uncle Sam explained. "Our records show that she has been online regularly from the theater. As recently as yesterday, as a matter of fact."

"Hmmm. The impostor knows her way around the web, huh?" Theresa noted.

"Does she have a computer in her dressing room?" Jo asked.

"Laptop, probably," Theresa replied, typing the info into her tablet. "She could be communicating with her boss."

"Exactly," Uncle Sam agreed. "Theresa, I want you to get into her dressing room and make a copy of whatever's on her hard drive. Files, incoming mail, the works. She might slip up and give us something good."

Theresa chuckled nervously. "Uh, not to be negative or anything . . . I mean, the hack is a snap. But how exactly am I supposed to break into her dressing room?"

"I was hoping you would ask that," Uncle Sam replied confidently. "Under the lamp in your bedroom you'll find a little item that just might help you out. Go get it, please."

Theresa hurried into her bedroom and returned with a key ring. It had one key and a square plastic attachment that resembled a car alarm remote. "Here it is."

"That key unlocks eighty percent of locks in the world," Uncle Sam explained. "It should work on Anka's door."

"Cool," Jo responded snagging it from Theresa's grasp. "Can we keep it?"

"Absolutely not," Uncle Sam replied. "And I'd be careful how you handle that key ring, Jo."

"Why?" Jo asked. "Will it blow up?"

"No. But if you snap your fingers, the metal edge of that

plastic remote becomes the business end of a very potent stun gun. The voltage is enough to stop a two-hundred-fifty-pound man."

Theresa yanked the key ring back. She stared at the dull metal plate on the stun gun and chuckled nervously. "Knowing my luck, I'll run into a guy who weighs two fifty-one."

Jo was sitting at the ballet during intermission, wearing a flowing green velvet dress. As she scanned the stage for the fake Anka she spotted Ewan Gallagher lurking by the front row.

This was her chance to meet him!

Practically floating on air, she made her way down toward the stage. As she got closer his immaculately combed blond hair came into focus. As did his square jaw and handsome, chiseled face.

He turned to speak to her, his ice blue eyes locking on hers.

Jo's heart pounded in her chest. She felt her cheeks flush. She awkwardly introduced herself as Selma Ribiero.

Ewan smiled and extended his hand. "Hello, Jo Carreras."

Her jaw dropped open in surprise.

How did he know her real name?

"Uh . . . my name is Selma. Selma Ribiero."

"Whatever you say, Jo," Ewan replied, his grin menacing. "Why don't we go meet the prime minister?"

Ewan grabbed her elbow and led her forcefully along the row of seats.

"Karkovic?" she asked, confused and panicked. "What's going on? Let me go!"

As they approached the prime minister the people around him—including his bodyguards—parted so they could get through. Jo recognized Karkovic immediately. She'd seen his picture a thousand times.

The prime minister rose to greet them, extending his hand and smiling. "Hello, Jo," he said, covering her hand with his. Karkovic's grip was firm and strong.

"Wha-what?" she stammered.

How did he know her real name, too?

He laughed and released her hand. But when he did, Jo heard a loud, earsplitting boom.

Something zipped by her ear. Too fast to see. A supersonic wasp. There was a simultaneous thunk. Like slapping meat with your bare hand.

Jo screamed, bewildered, as Karkovic was flung backward in agonizingly slow motion.

Blood erupted from his tuxedo shirt. Dazzling red on white.

He'd been shot in the heart.

When he landed in his theater seat, Jo saw a clear image of the wounded man.

It was not Karkovic.

It was *her father* lying there, blood pumping steadily out of his limp, lifeless form.

Jo sat up ramrod straight.

She blinked, her breath ragged. The room was dark. Shadowy.

She was in her bedroom in the flat. In Prague.

Safe.

It was just dream—a bad dream.

While she struggled to catch her breath, Jo had a sudden image of her father in his casket, so ashen and alien to her fourteen-year-old eyes.

She let out a deep breath and forced herself to lie back down. She gripped her pillow with her fists and made a silent vow.

She wasn't going to let Prime Minister Karkovic's family go through what she had gone through.

No way.

SIX

"Who could that be?" Caylin wondered as the phone in her room bleeped loudly on Tuesday morning. She wiped the sleep from her eyes and picked up the phone, careful to use her Aussie accent. "G'day."

"Hello, is Muriel there?"

"This is she," Caylin replied.

"It's Ottla calling," her boss said. "I'm afraid I didn't mention it yesterday with all the first-day confusion, but you don't need to be in until one o'clock from now on. I just wanted you to report early yesterday to get the seat numbers down, but it seems you got through your first night with flying colors."

"If there's anything that needs to be done around the office, I can always blow in early," Caylin offered, positively itching to nose around for some info on Anka.

"Well, I had planned to have you do some light office work in the afternoons and usher in the evenings from here on out, so there's really no need for you to come in early," Ottla said. "Unless, of course, you just want to."

"Righto," Caylin chirped. "Ten it is."

"Uh . . . okay," Ottla said.

But Caylin didn't particularly care if she confused Ottla or not. She was on a mission to find Anka's whereabouts, and digging up any information would definitely be a good start.

Time was already running out.

"He's working us like dogs!" Theresa whispered to Hannah. Julius had been watching them with barely concealed anger all morning as they touched up each and every set. Unfortunately none of their efforts had been good enough to win his approval thus far.

Theresa dropped her brush on the tree she was retouching and wiped her forehead with the back of her hand, utterly exhausted. "Man, what I wouldn't give to be in Jo's and Caylin's shoes right now," she muttered to herself. "This is slave labor."

As she finished perfecting the tree's paint job Theresa caught a glimpse of Fake Anka leaving her dressing room. Theresa checked her paint-splattered watch: 12:05.

"Finally," she whispered.

Lunchtime for the prima donna. That meant Fake Anka would be gone for at least an hour. Theresa shot Julius her hungriest look. Give us a lunch break, give us a lunch break, she silently commanded, hoping he'd catch her Psychic Friends Network vibes and let her get down to Spy Girl business.

"*Ach*, go and eat, you people," Julius finally growled. "Perhaps food will make you better painters!"

Theresa let out a huge sigh and dropped her brush into the thinner.

"Wanna join me, Tiffany?" Hannah asked, grabbing her coat from the corner. "There's a café down the street that has unbelievable soup."

"Thanks, but I need to run some errands," Theresa said

with an apologetic shrug. If breaking into someone's office counted as an errand, then she wasn't *totally* lying, she reasoned.

The second Julius made his exit, it was showtime. Looking around the halls to make sure the coast was clear, Theresa slipped into the costume closet, her heart pounding.

She locked the door and frantically searched the crowded racks for the right size bodysuit, tights, and slippers.

Deep breath, Theresa, deep breath! she commanded herself as she slid out of her Gap wear and into her make-shift ballerina suit.

As she pulled her hair haphazardly back into a severe bun Theresa reminded herself to grab the key ring and flash drive from her jeans.

It would totally suck if she forgot those.

She extracted them from her pocket, hoping she hadn't forgotten anything else.

Theresa took a deep breath. "Now or never."

She slowly turned the doorknob and poked her head out.

Looked right. Then left.

The hall was empty. She quickly slipped out of the costume closet and tiptoed down the hall.

I sure don't feel like a ballerina, she thought.

Anka's dressing room door was in sight. Just slip in and get the job done. Nice and neat. Better than Bond.

She pulled the magic key ring out and fingered the key. Her sweaty palms made the metal slick.

"Calm down," she told herself.

She began the final steps toward the door.

A maintenance man rounded the corner right in front of her. A surge of panic swept through her.

He gazed straight ahead and whistled softly. His belly jostled with each thick step.

Oh no!

Theresa ducked her head immediately. She held her chin in a southbound position and continued strolling down the hall.

Just another ballerina . . .

She prayed the maintenance guy wouldn't see her face and bust her undercover mission wide open. She knew he'd seen her around. She knew he knew who Tiffany was.

His hulking shape tromped by.

Theresa caught a whiff of tobacco. And intense BO.

Ugh! It was so bad, she had to cover her nose.

But thankfully the man's footsteps grew fainter and fainter.

Theresa sighed, grateful for the breath of fresh air. She was safe—for the moment. She chanced a glance over her shoulder. The maintenance man was gone. The hall was clear again.

"Man, did he reek!" she muttered as she backtracked to Anka's dressing room. Lifting the key up to her pursed lips and kissing it for good luck, she silently prayed Anka's lock wasn't one of the twenty percent in the world the key wouldn't open.

Slowly sliding the cold metal into the ancient knob, she held her breath and turned the key ever so slightly.

Nothing. It didn't budge.

New panic pumped through her. What if she couldn't get in?

She tried again. It still wouldn't budge.

Suddenly the sound of approaching footsteps filled the silence.

Theresa's mouth went dry as cotton. She froze.

What was she going to do now?

"Here's a list of people who will be at Sunday's open-trade-pact signing, Ms. Ribiero," Alexander Gottwald told Jo as he handed her a thick stack of paper right before lunch. "The caterer needs a final head count, so confirm these RSVPs ASAP."

"A-OK," she replied.

Gottwald didn't seem to get it.

As he disappeared into his office Jo quickly scanned the list. The name "Karkovic, Gogol" jumped out immediately.

He'll be dead meat if we don't stop this, Jo thought. Less than six days were left until the—

Someone cleared his throat behind her. Jo turned.

Ewan Gallagher!

He was even more gorgeous than in her nightmares!

Jo forced herself to stay cool, showing no signs of recognition—or lust—as she scoped him out.

Ewan's gelled blond hair was in tousled waves atop his head. His cold blue eyes were like icicles boring into her own. When he smiled, two adorable dimples dotted his cheeks.

And the devastating final touch—his Armani was a *perfect* fit.

"Can I help you?" Jo asked coolly.

"I'm Ewan Gallagher, director of international relations," he said. "And you are?"

She stuck out a Versace-covered arm and shook his hand. "Selma Ribiero, intern," she said, flashing him her pearly whites in what she hoped was a *friendly* and not *flirtatious* way. "Anything I can do for you?"

He smiled. "Actually, I was wondering if you could type up some memos for me. My secretary has gone home sick. Twenty-four-hour bug, we hope."

"No problem," Jo said, locked in his magnetic gaze.

"Can you type the top two in French?" he asked, eyebrow cocked.

Jo lowered her eyelids halfway. "I think I can handle that."

"I am impressed, Miss Ribiero," he replied, slipping a hand casually into his pocket. "Most Americans can speak only English."

"Well, I got around quite a bit in my youth," Jo explained, flashing her best smile again. "It's a small world."

"Indeed," Ewan replied. "And yet we receive small surprises every day."

"I surprise you?"

Ewan chuckled. "Perhaps you should get back to your memos, Miss Ribiero."

"Call me J—just Selma."

Oops. Steady, girl.

"Selma," Ewan repeated, eyes twinkling. "A very pretty name."

"Thank you," Jo replied, even though she *hated* the name.

He checked his watch. "Now I must go. Feel free to drop the memos in my in-box when you get the chance."

"Will you be in?"

Ewan smirked. "I doubt it, Selma. I get around quite a bit myself."

He turned and strode down the hallway. He turned the corner and was gone.

Jo let out a sigh. Then smiled slyly.

"I think I got him," she whispered.

SEVEN

Just open! Theresa silently pleaded as she tried Anka's dressing room lock.

Still nothing. Nothing but approaching footsteps and the pounding of her own heart.

The footsteps grew nearer and nearer. Faster, faster . . .

One more time, she told herself. Shutting her eyes, she tried to envision the door opening easily as she turned the key in the lock. Not that it would work, but . . .

It did. The tarnished knob turned and she was in.

Theresa quickly and quietly shut the door behind her. She pressed her ear against it, listening.

Her heartbeat intensified as the steps grew louder.

"I'm so busted," she whispered.

But the footsteps faded.

Whew! This spy business would kill her yet.

"Okay, Anka—or whoever you are, where do you keep your laptop?" Theresa wondered out loud.

She scanned the desktop, the floor, the bookshelves. No computer anywhere to be found.

"Don't tell me she took it with her," she muttered, flinging open every drawer in sight. She could have sworn Fake Anka didn't have any bags with her when she left.

"Okay, baby, be here." She yanked open the bottom desk drawer. There, underneath a tattered Euro edition of *Vogue*, was the elusive PC.

"Gotcha."

She hit the on/off button. As the familiar "ding" sounded Theresa smiled from the pure rush of adrenaline she felt. She felt like that chick from *The Matrix*—brainy, brazen, *and* babelicious.

"Internet, where are you . . . there you are," she said, double clicking on its accompanying icon. Her motions were fast-forward and precise now. She was in the zone.

"Okay, decoder, make me proud." She inserted her flash drive into the computer. A wordy prompt popped up on-screen. Theresa clicked "find password" and the decoder went to work. Hundreds of password combinations filled the screen in seconds.

"What's it going to be?" Theresa wondered. "Egomaniac? Prima donna? Impostorina?"

But no. The magic word was *pirouette*.

"Gotcha, part *deux*!" She replaced the decoder with a blank flash drive to copy the hard drive. The computer went to work, and Theresa leaned back to take a deep breath.

Just as the doorknob rattled.

She whirled around and gasped at the sound.

Indeed, the knob was rattling back and forth. Theresa's blood ran cold.

Someone was coming in.

And she, smart girl that she was, *forgot to lock the door behind her*.

"Oh, *pretzels*."

Theresa knew she had only one option. Her clammy hands frantically groped for the stun-gun key chain. And her eyes closed as she anticipated the absolute worst.

Depression set in as Jo went over the memos Ewan had asked her to type. She thought perhaps she might pick up some vital information from them. But no such luck. Reading the memos had been exciting for the first five seconds, but the thrill had long since vanished.

"Dear Sir, I must decline your dinner invitation," she read aloud as she typed away, rolling her eyes at the sheer inanity of it all. But after she printed the first letter, she decided to make a copy of it on her hard drive.

"You never know. . . ."

On the way to Ewan's office Jo spotted Mitchell von Strauss approaching. He looked exactly the same as he had in the video—tall, silver haired, and distinguished. She noted his serious expression as he slipped into his office and quickly shut the door.

"In the flesh at last," she whispered, slightly bummed about not scoring a personal intro. All in due time, she told herself. All in due time.

Jo was surprised to find Ewan at his desk. She smiled and entered without knocking.

"I thought you were out globe-trotting," she purred, dropping the completed memos on his desk.

He smiled at the sight of her. "Unfortunately work must intrude." His eyes scanned her up and down as he put the memos aside. "You're a lifesaver, Selma."

Jo blushed despite herself. "Don't mention it," she said, trying to keep her tone in that happy medium between professional and playful. "If you need anything else, you know where to find me."

"That I do," Ewan said, grinning wider.

She nodded and turned on her stilettos to exit without another word. But as Jo strolled out the door she felt Ewan's gaze upon her, watching her every step.

Theresa secured a vise grip on her stun gun.

The dressing room door slooowly inched open, creaking eerily the entire way.

Theresa fought off the urge to yell or scream or crawl under the desk and hide. She had to stand tall. Stay calm.

Yeah, right, she thought. Easier said than done.

A male head became visible through the partially

opened doorway. Not Anka, thank goodness. But who was it?

The smell hit her nose. Intense BO.

The maintenance man!

Theresa immediately turned her head so that he would only be able to see her from behind. The tutu. The tight bun of hair.

"Prosím," he mumbled—obviously in Czech.

She said nothing and shooed him away with her hand, hoping he'd just exit without an argument.

"Prosím!" he repeated. Only this time he punctuated the foreign statement with "Anka."

He thought she was Anka!

"Go away!" she ordered in her nastiest voice.

Ding!

Theresa jumped as the computer sounded. She could still feel the maintenance man hovering in the doorway. Tying not to shake, Theresa hit eject and slowly removed the drive.

The maintenance man uttered something in an angry tone and slammed the door.

"Man, do you *stink*!" she declared. Relief flooded her as she snapped Anka's laptop shut and placed it back precisely where she'd found it.

Seconds later she stuck her head out the door, looked right then left, and dashed to the costume closet, changing into her clothes as rapidly as the models she'd seen backstage at her mother's runway shows.

She exited the closet, bun halfway undone and attire slightly disheveled.

Someone clunked around the corner.

"Julius!" she called, trying to sound nonchalant.

"What were you doing in there?" he asked suspiciously.

"Uh, just looking for a safe place to stash my purse," Theresa replied innocently. "I, uh, went to the bank over lunch."

"Well," he snarled, "that room is off-limits."

Theresa triumphantly ran her fingers over the flash drive in her front pocket, giving Julius her most innocent "Who, me?" smile. "Sorry, Julius. It won't happen again. I *promise*."

• • •

"When Ottla told me the files were a wreck, she wasn't kidding," Caylin grumbled as she waded through a muddled sea of paperwork. Although she had gone through nearly every file in the office, Caylin hadn't yet run across one on Anka Perdova. And since she'd located a file for every single other ballerina, the absence of Anka's was a major red flag.

When Ottla returned from lunch, Caylin approached her.

"I've noticed some of these file folders are ragged and mismarked," Caylin stated, "and I'd like to dice them and create new ones for the troupe. Is there any way I could get a list of the performers, just so I don't leave anyone out?"

Ottla blessed her with a smile of approval. "Aren't we the industrious one?" She immediately sat down at her desk and printed out a list.

"And you know," Caylin continued innocently, "I can't seem to find a folder for Anka Perdova at all."

Ottla shrugged. "It must have been misplaced, I guess."

Try stolen, Caylin thought with a frustrated frown.

• • •

"You guys have been *busy*," Danielle said as she, Uncle Sam, and the Spy Girls shared a conference call on the aquarium phone later that evening.

"No kidding," Theresa replied. "Three heart attacks in one day is enough for me, thank you very much."

"Did you find anything that looked suspicious on the hard drive, Theresa?" Uncle Sam inquired.

"Sure did," Theresa said with a triumphant smile. "The only thing out of the ordinary was a piece of e-mail received yesterday morning. The subject was 'Danny Thugs I.'"

"What did it say?" Danielle asked, her image expanding as she moved closer to the video cam in anticipation.

"It said, 'Once hit, lights out,'" Theresa recited, looking down at her crumpled piece of paper. "'Escape route A. Subject in the dark. No implication.'"

"What's your take on that?" Uncle Sam asked.

"Obviously," Theresa replied, "'once hit, lights out' means once Karkovic is hit, the theater will go black."

"Good theory," Uncle Sam said. "Go on."

"'Escape route A' is a preplanned route for Fake Anka after she shoots Karkovic. 'Subject in the dark' I take to mean that the real Anka is clueless over who her kidnapper is. And 'No implication' means no consequences will be suffered because the kidnapper will replace Fake Anka with the real Anka immediately." Theresa took a breath, then stared directly into the fish lens. "So, what do you think?"

"I think it sounds like you're right on all counts," Uncle Sam said. "Very good job, Theresa."

"But what does 'Danny Thugs I' mean?" Jo asked.

Caylin shrugged. "Do you think someone named Danny could have Anka?"

"Or 'thugs' could mean there's more than one," Jo added.

"And I was thinking—since all this is going down at the theater, do you suppose the real Anka is being kept in there?" Theresa suggested. "It seems like the most convenient place, especially if the kidnapper—or kidnappers—plan to switch the two Ankas as soon as possible."

"It's possible," Uncle Sam said, "but we'll just need to keep our eyes and ears open and investigate to see if our theories are valid or not." He paused. "Anyone else make any progress?"

"Well," Caylin began, "I found out there's no file on Anka Perdova." She launched into the story of how every troupe member had one except Anka and that Ottla didn't seem too concerned about it. "I think someone stole it."

"Good to know," Uncle Sam said. "Keep up your probe. How about your day, Jo?"

"Well, I got the RSVP list for the treaty signing," she announced, holding up the copy she'd made for herself in front of the camera.

"Hey, I know," Caylin exclaimed, "why don't you check to see if there are any Dans or Dannys on the list? That could be our 'Danny Thugs I.'"

"Good idea," Uncle Sam replied.

Jo scanned the list. "There's one Dan—Dan Fields," she said, "and one Daniela—Daniela Fuentes. No one with the last name 'Daniel' or 'Daniels.' I'll find out who they are in the morning and see if they're legit."

"Sounds good," Uncle Sam affirmed. "Anything else?"

Jo read Ewan's memos aloud.

"They don't sound like much," Uncle Sam surmised when she was done, "but it's good you've established contact with one of the key players."

"I'll bet she has," Caylin teased.

Theresa rolled her eyes. "Don't tell me you've got a crush on this guy *already*!"

Jo scowled. "Mind your own espionage, girls. I've got things under control."

"You mean under your spell," Caylin corrected.

"What can I say?" Jo replied. "I don't spy and tell."

"That's quite enough, ladies," Uncle Sam scolded. "Jo, I don't have to remind you of your mission parameters, do I?"

"Absolutely not," Jo replied, shooting a scowl at Theresa and Caylin.

"Speaking of Gallagher," Danielle interjected, "how about bugging his and von Strauss's phones?"

"Jo, see what you can do about that," Uncle Sam ordered. "The bugs are in the kitchen in the canister marked 'flour.' And, Caylin, I'd like you to gain access to the theater's executive offices. They're not in use right now in preparation for some renovation project, but they still hold files there. Once you get in, ransack the area for anything pertaining to Anka Perdova."

"I'm on it," Caylin said.

"And I'll keep checking Anka's e-mail and try to locate a floor plan or any secret hideaways backstage," Theresa promised. "Who knows—maybe the true Anka is right under our noses."

"That would be nice," Caylin said solemnly.

"Remember your assignments, Spy Girls," Uncle Sam commanded. "Or Prime Minister Karkovic will end up like Abraham Lincoln."

"Yeah," Theresa replied. "Shot in an old theater for reasons that make no sense at all."

EIGHT

"Yes, this is Selma Ribiero from InterCorp Prague," Jo said into the phone as she sat in her cubicle on Wednesday morning. "Will Daniela Fuentes be attending the open-trade-pact signing?"

Jo posed the question in Portuguese, as she had noticed the international code preceding Ms. Fuentes's phone number was 55—Brazil. After Ms. Fuentes's assistant answered in the affirmative, Jo asked, "And could you please give me her full professional title?"

"Vice president of international affairs, Brazilian Council," the assistant replied, her tone implying it was a very stupid question.

Jo politely thanked her and hung up. Then, after making sure no one was within earshot, Jo immediately placed a call to the Brazilian Council to find out if Ms. Fuentes was indeed legit.

"Yes, this is Selma Ribiero from *Noticias Sudamericanas*," Jo lied to the Brazilian Council receptionist in Portuguese. "I'm fact checking an article about the open-trade-pact signing and was wondering if you could verify the spelling of Daniela Fuentes's name and the exact wording of her official title?"

It was exactly the same. Jo crossed Daniela Fuentes off her list.

Next Dan Fields of the good ol' USA. When a woman answered with "Dan Fields's office," Jo went into her usual spiel.

"Yes, he will be attending," the secretary confirmed.

"And can I get his official title?" she asked.

"Head foreign correspondent," she replied, *"New York Chronicle."*

"Thank you," Jo said, punching the *New York Chronicle* into her computer to see if Dan Fields's name was on their official website. After a few keystrokes "Dan Fields, head foreign correspondent" popped up on the virtual masthead.

"Oh, well," Jo muttered with a frustrated sigh. But one look at the clock was enough to perk her up.

Twelve thirty p.m. Ewan and Mitchell von Strauss would be at lunch.

"Get out your Raid, boys and girls," she whispered, dropping two pea-size surveillance devices in her pocket. "'Cause you got bugs."

Jo grabbed a thick stack of files and marched down the hall, looking busy.

Mitchell's office door was wide open and his secretary nowhere in sight. With a deep breath Jo pulled a bug out of her pocket.

"Here goes nothing," she whispered, heading for Mitchell's office. When a cleaning lady passed her way in the hall, Jo gave her a brisk nod and continued confidently on.

As she entered Mitchell's domain she smoothed her Dior suit and left the door just slightly ajar—a closed office door usually sent up a red flag of suspicion in the business world, she had learned.

Jo picked up Mitchell's receiver and expertly installed

the bugging device, her movements both fluid and precise. Bugging Mitchell's phone gave Jo the same rush she got behind the wheel of a race car—her blood pumped, her mind raced.

But when she heard Mitchell's secretary's voice seconds after she placed the receiver in its cradle, Jo felt more like she had hit a gigantic speed bump.

"May I help you?" the secretary inquired, her tone nasal and accusatory.

"Just dropping off these papers for Mr. von Strauss," Jo said, exactly as she'd rehearsed.

"With the door practically closed?" the secretary asked warily.

"Oh, did the door close behind me?" Jo recited from memory. "Must have been a draft."

"I'll make sure he gets the papers, then," the secretary promised, ceremoniously motioning her out.

"Thanks a mil," Jo purred, smiling in victory. But before she allowed herself to feel too cocky, she had one more stop: Ewan's office.

The coast appeared to be clear.

She plopped more papers down on his immaculate desk and placed a hand on his state-of-the-art telephone.

"Just what do you think you're doing?"

Jo spun around at the voice.

Ewan stood in the doorway, eyes narrow and deadly.

Jo's blood ran stone cold.

"I'll never be able to enjoy paint by numbers again," Theresa mumbled to herself as she applied a large stroke to the moat of Prince Siegfried's castle.

"What?" Hannah asked, a few feet to her left.

"Nothing," Theresa replied. The fumes and the mundane repetition of her painting duties were just getting to be too much. Theresa was *so* over it. But after a few more strokes Theresa experienced an instant attitude adjustment.

A door slammed. Feet stomped.

Anka had stormed out of her dressing room.

And she was headed *directly* Theresa's way.

"Have either of you seen my purse?" Fake Anka demanded. "It was in my dressing room, but now I can't find it."

Was it Theresa's imagination, or did Anka just put extra emphasis on the words *dressing room*?

Both she and Hannah shook their heads no.

She knows I was in there, Theresa figured. She has to.

"Well, *somebody* must have taken it," Fake Anka hissed, staring down Theresa and Hannah coldly before storming off.

"Somebody forgot to take her happy pill this morning," Hannah said, scowling.

She doesn't know the half of it, Theresa thought.

"Uh, Ewan, I'm just dropping off these papers for you," Jo blurted, snatching the papers from his desk and waving them in front of his gorgeous face. "Your assistant wasn't in. . . ."

"What were you doing with the phone?" he asked suspiciously.

"The phone?" she asked, oozing little-girl innocence.

But even under her best wide-eyed gaze Ewan's expression didn't soften. "Yes, the phone," he snapped impatiently.

"I was . . . I was going to leave you a personal voice

mail," she purred, turning on her flirtatious charm full force. "And I didn't want to do it from my cubicle—you know, where everybody could hear."

Ewan's expression froze for a moment, then softened. He cocked an eyebrow. "A personal voice mail?"

"Yeah," she replied sweetly. "To see if you wanted to get together sometime after work. I wasn't sure how proper it was because I'm an intern. But I figured it was a great way to learn. You know, I'd just *love* to pick your brain."

Ewan soaked up the attention like a sponge. "Well," he said, smiling, "that can certainly be arranged. In fact, tonight there's this gallery opening downtown. You should join me."

"That sounds great. What time?"

"Seven o'clock," he said, eyes sparkling. "Should be lots of fun."

"Yeah, lots of fun," she said cheerily, both excited and terrified. She'd never forget what had happened to her in London when she got too close to the enemy.

She'd almost lost her life.

Beauty is only skin deep, she reminded herself. That was one lesson she'd never forget.

Knock-knock-knock. Theresa rapped on Fake Anka's door, three times fast.

The door flew open.

"What?" Fake Anka growled.

"Just wondering if you found your purse," Theresa said, doing her best to come off like a Good Samaritan. After Hannah's comment about happy pills, Theresa had given some long, hard thought to the situation. Rather than treat Fake Anka like dirt, Theresa decided the best thing to do was treat her like royalty—be sweet, compliment her, suggest getting together for coffee.

In other words, kiss some serious butt.

After all, the closer she got to this carbon copy, the closer she'd be to finding the original.

"Yes, I did," Fake Anka replied, offering no explanation or apology whatsoever.

"I also wanted to introduce myself," Theresa said, trying her best not to let Fake Anka's cold demeanor affect her attitude. "I'm Tiffany Heileman, a huge fan of yours. I think you're just unbelievable."

"Thank you," Fake Anka said, her icy demeanor melting a half an inch.

"Um, I'd love to get together for coffee sometime and hear all about your experiences." She paused. "Maybe not."

Fake Anka sized her up for a moment before saying anything. Her expression was as sour as if Theresa had asked her to go on a blind date with the stinky maintenance man.

Theresa was about to turn and leave when Fake Anka finally answered.

"Perhaps . . . we will see."

"Seat fourteen-D—right this way, mate," Caylin told a ballet goer.

She was operating on automatic pilot. Even though her bod was in the theater, Caylin's mind was still on the office and the events from a few hours prior.

When Ottla had amicably agreed to take Caylin on a tour of the under-renovation executive offices, Caylin had thought it would be a piece of cake to ditch Ottla and case the joint out solo.

But that didn't wash. Although Ottla had been happy enough about granting the tour, Ottla had refused to leave Caylin's side. Each of Caylin's attempts at privacy—asking to realphabetize the files, reorganize the paperwork, even offering to clean the place—was immediately shot down.

"No one but authorized personnel is allowed in here without supervision," Ottla had replied, her tone implying Caylin was totally *un*authorized.

Caylin knew then that she would have to break in.

Her inner adrenaline junkie was so thrilled that even ushering couldn't bring her down. She bounced up the steps two at a time.

"Your tickets, sport?" she called as she rapidly approached an older gentleman with a much younger bleached blond on his arm. Whoa, wait a minute, she thought. The graying hair, the tall, lean frame—where did she know this guy from?

The guy handed her his tickets and smiled confidently, cockily. Of course—Mitchell von Strauss, head of InterCorp!

"Right this way, sir," she said, praying that her recognition didn't show on her face.

As she turned to show them to their seats her brain was buzzing with one big question: *Could they be here to finalize assassination plans?*

As they slid into their seats—first row, center—the bleached blond looked Caylin straight in the eye. "Could you tell me where the ladies' room is?"

Caylin glanced up at the growing group of people at the top of the stairs, all waiting to be shown to their seats. "I was actually headed there myself," she said, deciding to blow off her usherly duties so she could dig for potential dirt. "Let me show you the way."

"This artist is very big here in Prague, apparently," Ewan said as he and Jo strolled into Galerie MXM's small, dark interior.

"I can see why," Jo muttered, checking out the gigantic canvases dominated by wild colors and abstract images.

Good thing I wore black, Jo thought, looking down at her little velvet dress in gratitude. It seemed to be the color of choice for ninety-five percent of the crowd, so she fit right in.

"Maybe we should buy some of his work for the office," Ewan mused. "The Prague office is so bland compared to the American headquarters."

Jo nodded blankly in response. She desperately wanted to change the subject to Anka and the signing. She knew that she had to take it slow, however. Nice and easy.

As Ewan greeted a young, preppy-looking guy Jo soaked in the party atmosphere. Very glam, very Euro, very so-hip-it's-sick crowd. Lots of money in the room, obviously. Tuxedoed waiters offered glasses of champagne too tall to sip and tiny appetizers too beautiful to eat.

"*Rohlík?*" a waiter asked as he offered up a large tray of finger rolls.

"*Dekuji,*" Jo said in gratitude. She popped one into her mouth as Ewan turned to face her.

"An old polo chum," he explained, gesturing toward the departing male figure. "I would have introduced you, but he's quite boring."

"Then I guess I should thank you," she said with a laugh. "Where do you know him from?"

"Switzerland," he said. "Have you ever been?"

"I've been everywhere," she gushed, playing up the "socialite" end of her false identity.

"Oh yes, that's right." He laughed, curiosity obviously piqued. "Around the block a few times, correct?"

"Daddy had wads of money," she gushed. "Anywhere I wanted to go, I went."

"Then what was it that prompted your sky's-the-limit self to come to InterCorp?" he asked, his tone fun and flirtatious. "I'm dying to know."

"Well, although money's been no object throughout my life—well, perhaps *because* of it—I adore nothing more than earning buckets and buckets of it on my very own," she explained. "And I figured the best way to learn how to do this was at InterCorp." She smiled at Ewan coyly. "You are, after all, the experts."

"You definitely came to the right place," Ewan said. "In fact, you'll have the opportunity to rub elbows with every sort of financial mogul at the open-trade-pact signing next week. It's obscene how much cash these people have—almost *insane*."

"Almost," Jo replied with a wink. "Do you know much about the trade pact?"

"Only that it's a pain to even think about," Ewan said. "So enough about the financial world. What are your other passions?"

"There are sooo many," Jo cooed, momentarily bummed that he wasn't giving up any dirt on the signing. "The ballet, of course. I went a few nights ago, and Anka Perdova was amazing. Have you had a chance to see her?"

"She's genius, pure genius," he agreed, looking a tad uncomfortable. "And speaking of genius, the more I look at this art, the more I feel like it's seriously lacking."

"I agree, but I didn't want anyone to overhear and think I was a snob."

Ewan smiled. "Would you care to leave?"

Jo hesitated. "Where to?"

"Are you hungry?" he asked, a mischievous glint in his eye.

"Ravenous," she replied. What better place to pick Ewan's brain than at an intimate dinner for two?

"I don't feel like dealing with any crowds right now," he explained. "We could swing by my apartment and order in. That way we can really talk."

Uh-oh.

His apartment?

Jo didn't know what to say. Things were moving awfully fast. If Jo had been on a real first date—and not a secret mission—she would *never* go back to a guy's apartment. It was the baddest of all bad ideas.

Or was it?

She fingered the pea-size lump in the lining of her purse—the phone bug that she didn't get to install in Ewan's office that afternoon. Maybe she could get his home phone. . . .

With a sultry smile she slipped her hand into the crook of his elbow. "Ewan, I thought you'd never ask."

• • •

Caylin followed von Strauss's bleached blond friend into the lounge area of the ladies' room. "First time to see this production?" she asked, trying to sound like nothing more than a well-meaning usher.

"No," the woman answered curtly.

"Isn't Anka bloody amazing?" Caylin asked.

"Yes," the woman responded, lowering her gaze before disappearing into the bathroom area.

Did she lower her eyes because she doesn't want to talk to me anymore, Caylin wondered, or because she knows something about the true Anka's whereabouts?

She washed her hands and touched up her lipstick to kill time.

Then she had an idea.

She slipped her hand into her pocket and brought out her bottle of eyedrops. But it held a lot *more* than just eyedrops. In fact, it held exactly what Caylin needed right now.

When the blond emerged to fix her makeup, Caylin was ready.

"My blasted contacts make my eyes bone-dry!" she

complained, dropping one, two, then three drops in each eye.

Snap-snap-snap. The miniature camera inside the bottle clicked softly, taking frame after frame while drop after drop hit Caylin's pupils.

The woman again averted her gaze as she made her exit, totally clueless that her bathroom break had just turned into a Kodak moment.

"This place is unbelievable," Jo cooed as she looked around Ewan's obscenely large loft. The chocolate brown couches, cherry-wood furniture, and big-screen TV screamed "boy," but in a tasteful way. However, no framed pics or quirky touches personalized the space. The quarters were so generic, in fact, that the loft could have easily passed for a Pottery Barn showroom. "Not many personal touches, huh?"

He shrugged. "I've only been here a week. But I do have my high school rowing trophy up on the mantel. First place."

She eyed the silver award, unimpressed. Not that she

was expecting to find a ransom note for Anka on the refrigerator or anything, but she had hoped she'd find something more juicy than high school memorabilia.

Jo smiled. "I bet you miss your creature comforts from back home."

"Oh yeah."

"Which ones?"

"You know—the dog, the pool, the Lamborghini."

Jo gasped. "The *Lamborghini*?"

"I love it," he said. "But believe me, I'm not complaining. At twenty-four, I couldn't have it much better than this."

Jo fought off the urge to ask for a spec list of the Lam. She was slavering to know all about it . . . but there were more pressing issues at hand.

"Were you a boy genius or something?"

"I think I'll pick the 'or something,'" he said with a laugh. "Would you excuse me for a moment?"

Jo nodded and Ewan left the room. She heard the bathroom door down the hall close.

She breathed a sigh of relief. Now was her chance to bug

the phone. She slid her hand into her purse and retrieved the tiny device. Her fingers were shaking so badly that she almost dropped it.

Steady, girl.

Jo hurriedly grabbed his living room phone and inserted the bug in the receiver. But as she was putting the receiver back in position, she heard Ewan enter the room behind her.

"Who are you calling?" he asked.

"Checking my messages," she said, adopting her best panicked expression. "I'm sorry, Ewan, but I'm going to have to take a rain check on dinner. Something's suddenly come up."

"Oh," he replied.

Ewan's sad puppy-dog expression hit Jo right where it hurt—but she knew she had to leave before anything happened, for better or for worse. Still, poor Ewan seemed *sooo* disappointed. It was positively heartbreaking.

"Everything okay, I hope?" Ewan asked.

"Nothing life or death, but I do have to run," she explained.

"Let me drive you," he offered.

"No, I'll grab a cab," she insisted. No way would she let him drive her anywhere near headquarters!

Ewan shot her a quizzical look.

"I need to make several stops," she lied, "and I have no idea how long I'm going to be."

"Well, at least let me walk you out." He grabbed her little faux fur coat and held it out for her.

What a gent, Jo thought her heart temporarily melting. It quickly froze up again, and not because she was back out on the frigid streets. How could Ewan be a gent if he was mixed up in a psychotic assassination plot?

I have to do something about these hormones, Jo told herself.

Jo shivered while Ewan hailed her a taxi. "Remind me to never again wear a little black dress in subzero temperatures," she joked, teeth chattering.

"Little black dresses suit you," Ewan replied gently. "Better than power suits, at least from where I'm standing."

A cab pulled up and Jo felt a surge of relief. She was turning into a Popsicle.

As if reading her mind, Ewan attempted to melt Jo with a warm kiss as she slid into the cab.

She turned her cheek just in time.

"Thanks for a lovely evening," she said, shrugging out of his embrace. "I'll see you in the morning."

She slammed the door and the cab pulled away, leaving Ewan behind, sadness and confusion written all over his gorgeous face.

"Can you believe he tried to kiss me?" Jo asked Caylin and Theresa later that evening back in the living room of 3-S. Jo was sprawled out on the oriental rug while Caylin and Theresa lounged on the antique couches. Theresa's homemade mix of French pop blared from the speakers.

"Why is it you always end up with the guy adventures?" Theresa asked.

"Yeah, I'm wondering that myself," Caylin said, swinging her blond locks over her shoulder. "Absolutely no cute guys work in the theater offices. In fact, it's a *total* no-man's-land."

"Backstage is no boyfest, either," Theresa moaned. "Except . . . well, there is one guy. . . ."

"Really?" Jo asked, perking up.

"Who is he?" Caylin demanded. "We're all on a need-to-know basis, remember?"

Theresa burst out laughing. "Just kidding. He's a maintenance man. And he stinks! You never smelled BO like this! It's like bad cheese or something."

Jo groaned. "Gross!"

"Did you get his number?" Caylin asked.

"Har-dee-har," Theresa said. "He caught me in Anka's dressing room. I thought I was toast. At least Jo's target is cute."

"I know it sounds like I'm lucky," Jo insisted, "but I'm telling you—if this guy's involved with the Anka thing, he's pure pond scum. This was no date, trust me."

"Beats bad BO, that's all I'm saying," Theresa said.

"And taking pictures in bathrooms," Caylin added.

The ringing of the aquarium interrupted them.

"Uncle Sam awaits," Theresa said, reaching for the red button.

"Can't we let the machine get it?" Jo joked.

"I heard that, Jo," Uncle Sam replied, his dark silhouette coming into focus among the fish. "Anything to report?"

"I'll say," Jo began. One by one the Spy Girls delivered their daily reports. Once they were finished, Uncle Sam said he wanted them to listen to something. "And, Jo, I believe you'll find this particularly interesting. The first voice belongs to Mitchell von Strauss. The second, we're unsure about as of yet."

Jo scooted to the edge of her seat as a crackling static sounded, interrupted by a deep male voice:

> von Strauss: How is she?
>
> Voice 1: Fine. Sedated.
>
> von Strauss: No one's seen her?
>
> V1: Nobody but me.
>
> von Strauss: No one snooping around?
>
> V1: No.
>
> von Strauss: Keep it that way.
>
> Click.

The Spy Girls glared at one another grimly.

"So this confirms our suspicions," Caylin announced. "It's gotta be the real Anka they're talking about."

"It appears so," Uncle Sam said, voice grave. "Does anyone recognize the other voice? Someone who works at the ballet or InterCorp, perhaps?"

"Nope," the girls chorused glumly.

"Any more ideas about 'Danny Thugs I'?" he asked.

The girls again shared blank looks and shrugged, frustrated. "Nope."

"No more of this 'nope' nonsense," Uncle Sam growled. "There are only four days left. If we don't find the real Anka in time to save the prime minister . . ."

"Boom," Caylin replied softly. "They're dead."

"And so are we," Theresa added.

NINE

"I am just *too* dedicated," Theresa muttered to herself.

She had arrived at the theater around 5:30 a.m. Thursday morning, before Julius or even the stinky maintenance man made it in. But she wasn't there to get a jump start on retouching the great hall of Prince Siegfried's castle.

As if.

She just wanted some uninterrupted snoop time.

What do we have here? Theresa wondered as she surveyed the props closet. In the corner a tall roll of paper sat propped up against a stack of hatboxes.

It looked like a roll of wrapping paper, only it was beige and yellowed. Yet as Theresa unrolled the paper inch by inch, her smile grew wider and wider.

This was no wrapping paper. These were blueprints of the theater, dated 1988. The year of the last renovation, she remembered, flashing back to what Hannah had told her on Monday.

Theresa felt a surge of excitement. These blueprints could be the map that led her to the real Anka—if she was a prisoner somewhere in the theater, that is.

She studied the map for over an hour, taking in every millimeter of the centuries-old layout.

"Looks like an attic is right above the costume closet," she whispered, running a finger over the aged plans.

That would make a great hiding place.

Theresa rushed to the costume closet to check out the ceiling. Sure enough, there was a thin rope hanging from the rafters that, when pulled, would likely deliver a creaky staircase, like her attic door did back home.

Maybe she'd get lucky.

Theresa reached up on tiptoe for the flimsy rope. Her fingertips grazed the braided twine.

She heard heavy footsteps. And a low whistle.

Theresa gasped. She knew that whistle all too well—Julius!

What was *he* doing in so early?

Theresa frantically rolled up the blueprints and crouched in the corner.

The steps grew louder. The whistling was casual, as if Julius was simply making early morning rounds, finding dozens of imaginary faults in the set designs. For future torture of set painters, no doubt.

The steps paused right outside the door. Theresa held her breath.

What was he looking at?

The whistling stopped.

He'd seen something he didn't like, she knew. Did she leave some trace of her snooping?

Four heartbeats. Five. A dozen.

Finally Julius growled, "Stupid people . . . stupid, stupid, stupid people."

His whistling resumed and the heavy footsteps faded away.

Doesn't Julius ever sleep? Theresa wondered, letting out a sigh. So much for early morning snooping. She'd have to wait until lunch. And even then she knew she might not get much of a chance to see the attic.

Before she gently closed the closet door behind her, she gave the attic door one last searching look.

Please be up there, Anka, she prayed. Just be there.

"No way!" Jo whispered as she approached her cubicle Thursday morning.

In the middle of her desk sat a crystal vase containing a dozen red roses!

Trembling, Jo extracted the attached card from its envelope.

Selma,
Sorry our evening was cut short. Hope everything turned out okay and that I can honor that rain check you're holding. Free Saturday afternoon?
E.

"Take a chill pill, girl," Jo warned herself. This was actually bad news. She wasn't supposed to get too close.

But what an opportunity to get information!

"You can go . . . but strictly for research," she resolved,

skipping over to Ewan's office to accept his invite.

But when she spied his blond hair, those blue eyes, and that seductive smile through the doorway, she was overwhelmed by one supersize, super-scary realization—

I like him too much already.

Theresa froze. Panic coursed through her veins.

The attic stairs creaked like an old man snoring!

It was lunchtime, and she'd snuck back into the costume closet to take another shot at the attic. But as she tiptoed up the stairs the wood sounded as if it were ready to disintegrate beneath her.

She paused, listening. Nothing. No Julius, no Hannah.

She continued up, trying to step lightly. No dice. She'd have to risk it.

The attic was musty and damp, and the dim overhead bulb offered little light.

She took a step forward and kicked something. A thick cloud of dust erupted from the floor in front of her—just as she breathed in. A huge poof of soot shot straight into her nose.

She sneezed.

Ah-ah-ah-choooo!

This was no prissy little achoo. Theresa cranked out a whopper that rattled the rafters!

"Oh, man," she grunted, wiping her nose. "I'm dead."

She listened for a reaction from below.

Nothing.

Maybe she got lucky again.

She covered her mouth and nose and peered into the gloom. If Anka was up here, she knew she had company now, that was for sure.

"Anka?" Theresa called out.

She heard movement and froze. Could it be her?

"Anka?"

Theresa held her breath in anticipation. But instead of receiving a reply from the missing ballerina, she felt the pressure of little feet scampering over the top of her boot.

She shuddered. In the darkness she could just make out the shape of a giant rat scurrying toward a pile of boxes. Soon she heard a multitude of supersonic squeals.

"That's it," Theresa growled. "I'm outta here."

Theresa scrambled down the ladder and brushed herself off. Then carefully she poked her head out of the costume closet door and checked the hall.

No one.

She sighed and quietly closed the closet door. Slumping against it in frustration, she wondered where in the world the real Anka Perdova could possibly be.

"Rats," she groaned.

"'Danny Thugs I,'" Jo murmured as she wrote the letters down on the place mat. *Thugs* just seemed too obvious to her.

She had found a small, deserted café not far from InterCorp. It looked like a safe enough place to eat, think, and spy at the same time. The café was dark and silent with only three other customers.

Jo tore the paper place mat into eleven pieces and wrote a letter from "Danny Thugs I" on each piece. On a whim, she shuffled the letters around. But the more she reorganized the letters, the more she thought her exercise wasn't much more than a way to pass the time until her food arrived.

But still . . . it could've been a code.

She mixed up the letters faster.

The first combination she came up with was *thin gun days*.

"What's that supposed to be?" she muttered under her breath. A .44 trying to slim down to a .38?

An overweight waitress set a chicken sandwich before her, but Jo was too engrossed in her jumble to look up.

Shun Indy tag.

Unfortunately the Indy 500 was months away, and she doubted that Prime Minister Karkovic would be attending.

Duh Ginny sat.

"More like 'duh, Jo, this is pointless,'" she murmured.

Then Jo paused.

Could that be it . . . ?

She organized the letters one final time and smiled.

"Sunday night!" she exclaimed.

The night the assassination was supposed to take place!

Jo congratulated herself . . . on figuring out a piece of information that everyone knew already.

Her heart immediately sank. Suddenly she wasn't so hungry anymore.

"Am I glad to see you!" Caylin whispered as Theresa entered the theater bathroom after lunch.

Caylin grabbed Theresa's arm and pulled her into the nearest stall.

"Can I wash my hands before you abduct me?" Theresa pleaded. "You don't wanna know where they've been."

"Not a chance," Caylin replied. "You have no idea what I've gone through this morning. I've tried everything. Begging, conning, lying. But Ottla will *not* let me into those executive offices!" She kicked the side of the stall. "Got any ideas?"

"How about my key ring?" Theresa whispered, fishing it out of her pocket. "That's how I got into you-know-who's dressing room."

Caylin hefted the key. "That's great, but what about the guard by the door?" she queried. "If he sees me—*bam*, cover blown."

Theresa rubbed her chin, then smiled. "I got it," she

replied. "I'll ask the guard to come help me with something onstage. Then you slip right in."

Caylin returned a sly grin and wiggled her eyebrows. "Rock and roll, Spy Girl!"

Moments later Operation Distraction began.

"Sir, could you help me?" Theresa asked the unsmiling guard while Caylin crouched around the corner.

"No glop da English," he said, scowling.

Theresa smiled wanly. "Great. Where's Jo when I need her? Um, let's see. Could. You. Help. Me?"

"No glop da English," the guard repeated, more forcefully.

Theresa motioned him closer. When he leaned in, she took him by the arm and pulled.

"Please," she said in a timid, helpless voice. *"Por favor? Bitte?"*

"Bitte?" the guard asked, brow furrowed.

"Um, *ja!*" she piped. *"Bitte* give me a hand over here, okay?"

No response.

Theresa pulled on the man's arm. He took a step forward.

"*Ja! Ja!* Attaboy! *Bitte* help! With me. Over here. *Ja!*"

I feel like an idiot, Theresa thought. She *had* to get some language lessons from Jo, if only to avoid looking— and sounding—this stupid in the future.

But the guard actually followed her to the stage.

"I hope you don't freak when you realize I'm lying to you," she muttered to the man. She chanced a glance over her shoulder to make sure Caylin had made it through the locked door. *Bingo.* "Um . . . have you ever actually *used* that gun?"

"No glop da English."

"That's what I thought."

Caylin slid the magic key in the door. After a few jiggles it popped open.

Once inside she warily eyed the black filing cabinets lining the room. Six sprawling wooden desks were weighed down with books and documents, and several cheap prints of ballerinas hung crooked on the yellowed walls. The smell of old papers and dust hung in the air.

Caylin darted directly to the nearest filing cabinet and began flying through the manila folders, frantically searching for *Anka Perdova* or any name she didn't recognize.

There was nothing in *A*.

She immediately went for *P*.

She paged through the folders one by one. But nothing jumped out. She glanced at her watch. Three minutes had passed.

"Too much time," she whispered. "Come *on*."

She nipped through even faster, knowing she'd probably miss something. But she couldn't take the chance.

She neared the back of the *P* drawer and started thinking, which letter to tackle next.

Then she saw it.

A file marked *Alexandra Parsons*.

Caylin knew there was no such person in the ballet troupe. But she could've been anyone, an employee of InterCorp, a dancer long since gone.

She opened the file, anyway. It was the only name that was even close.

"Alexandra Parsons," she read. She looked over the

dancer's vitals and felt a surge of excitement. They matched Anka Perdova's. Exactly. Which meant that they would match the impostor's, too.

"This has gotta be her," Caylin reasoned. "It's just gotta be!"

The doorknob rattled.

Caylin's heart jumped into her throat. Was it Theresa? Or that security guard?

Caylin dove under the nearest desk.

The door creaked open.

"Muriel?" Ottla called. "Are you in here?"

Caylin held her breath, praying Ottla wouldn't actually come in.

"Muriel?" Her voice was closer now. "Muriel?"

Caylin's heart pounded. Her hands shook so badly that she had to ball them into fists.

Get out of here, Ottla, Caylin silently commanded. Give it up.

After a few seconds Ottla's footsteps retreated and the door slammed.

Caylin sighed in relief.

She waited a few moments and pulled herself up from beneath the desk. She slipped the file underneath her sweater. As she snuck out of the office Caylin crossed her fingers tightly, praying that she finally got her mitts on the money.

"The letters in 'Danny Thugs I' spell out 'Sunday night,'" Jo reported to Uncle Sam on her cell phone on her way back to the office. Her eyes darted all around her to ensure that no one from the office was on the sidewalk nearby.

"Well done, Jo," Uncle Sam proclaimed. "I'm glad you called because I want you to hear this call that came in late last night. The first voice is Ewan's. We don't know who the woman is yet."

The word *Ewan* was enough to spur Jo's interest. As a large truck rumbled past, Jo stuck her finger in her right ear in order to hear better.

Ewan: Hello?
Woman: Ewan, you are such a snake!

Ewan: What? What did I do?

Woman: You went to the gallery opening with some bimbo, that's what! I saw her! Who was she?

Ewan: Just a girl from the office—she's nobody.

Woman: Nobody—yeah, right. I'm coming over.

Ewan (sighing loudly): I'll be downstairs.

Click.

"A *bimbo*? Jo exclaimed. "A *nobody*? That creep show was lucky I even went to the gallery with him!"

"Hey!" Uncle Sam barked. "Keep your ego out of this, Jo. This mission is about stopping the assassination, not finding Mr. Right."

But Jo couldn't help it. She was so angry, she had to fight back bitter tears.

"Do you understand?"

"Yes," Jo replied stiffly.

"Fine, then. Do you have any idea who the woman is on the tape?"

Jo took a deep breath. "No," she said. "Obviously she's a jealous girlfriend, but I had no clue he was seeing anybody. I mean, he actually asked me out again for Saturday! The two-timing pig!"

"Any female pictures in his loft?" Sam asked.

"No," Jo replied. "And believe me, I was looking."

"She might know something about Anka's whereabouts," Uncle Sam said, his voice cutting out for a second. "Can you hold?"

While waiting for Uncle Sam to return to the line, Jo looked at InterCorp's building looming in the distance. Who wanted to go back to work when "Danny Thugs I" was meaningless and Ewan had a girlfriend that she—his prime investigator—didn't even know *existed*?

"Theresa and Caylin are conferencing on the other line," Uncle Sam stated. "So I'll talk to you tonight. Keep your eyes and ears peeled for any information on Ewan's girlfriend."

Jo hit end and scowled. Despite her nausea, she felt more determined than ever to go out and get the goods.

Nobody called her a nobody and got away with it.

Nobody.

"This is great work," Uncle Sam told Caylin and Theresa, who were conferencing him from two separate cell phones. Caylin was perched on a park bench near the theater while Theresa stood in front of an apartment building two blocks over.

"Alexandra Parsons, Anka Perdova—A.P.," Uncle Sam continued. "An unusual coincidence. Perhaps this `Ms. Parsons is the impostor in this scenario. But you had better FedEx the folder to me right now—there's a drop box three blocks north of the theater. Don't keep that information on you for longer than you have to."

"Got it." Caylin nodded, scanning the passersby to make sure no familiar faces spotted her. Most everyone was distracted by a marionette puppet show in the park; they didn't even give her a second glance.

"Should I snag those blueprints, too?" Theresa asked.

"Definitely," Uncle Sam replied. "You need to know that theater like it's your bedroom. And by the way, the ID on the pictures you shot of von Strauss's escort came back, Caylin. It's his daughter."

"His daughter?" Caylin echoed, aghast. "Oh, drag. That's so *non*-juicy."

"Afraid so," he said. "And knowing von Strauss's attitude toward his family, he would probably never put his own daughter in danger. It's unlikely she knows anything."

"Great," Caylin muttered, slumping against the park bench. "Another dead end."

"Want to go grab some joe?" Hannah asked Theresa after a grueling evening performance. The backstage area swarmed with dancers and technical people preparing to go home for the night.

Theresa had her eye on one superstar dancer in particular.

"Nah, I have to get going," Theresa said as she watched Fake Anka gather her bag and coat. "Rain check?"

"Sounds good. Catch you tomorrow."

"Every day," Theresa replied.

As she followed Fake Anka to the exit Theresa slipped a black cap on her head and tucked her tousled brown hair up under it. Her heavy black wool overcoat completed the ensemble.

"So long, Anka!" a dancer said as Fake Anka pushed open the door.

"Uh-huh," the impostor replied gruffly.

Theresa followed her out, lagging about twenty paces behind her.

"Time to find out who you really are," she whispered. She slipped on a pair of sunglasses just to be safe. Even though the sky was dark, she didn't want to chance being recognized. Besides, the lenses were dark enough to shield her eyes but light enough to see out of at night. The perfect stalking shades.

The night air was frigid. Anka headed down the back alley behind the theater toward the main street. Live jazz poured out from an open tavern door, but otherwise the streets were silent. A trio of cats scurried near a bank of trash cans, scavenging for food.

A trash can lid spun from beneath a cat's paws and clattered to the street.

Theresa gasped and ducked behind the cans.

Fake Anka whirled, staring.

Just the cats, just the cats, just the cats, Theresa silently prayed. Keep going!

Moments passed. Fake Anka stared out into the darkness.

One of the stray cats sniffed at Theresa's foot. She gave it a nudge toward the middle of the alley.

The cat meowed loudly and scurried away.

"Just a cat," Theresa whispered, hoping somehow that that would convince Anka.

It did. The impostor turned and continued on. Theresa slipped out from behind the cans and followed.

Anka turned the corner and marched down the street away from the theater. Theresa was careful not to get too close. In fact, Anka was walking almost too fast to keep up with.

"Man, she's in good shape," she huffed.

Then Theresa heard more footsteps.

Only this time they were *behind* her.

The hair on the back of her neck stood on end. Her stomach tightened, and she fought the urge to turn around.

The footsteps got closer while Anka moved farther away.

It didn't matter. Theresa had to look. Just had to. The tingling sensation at her back was almost too much to bear. She gulped and began a count.

One . . .

The steps quickened.

Two . . .

Two's good enough!

Theresa spun around. She saw a burly figure plunge into a shadowy alley, and her whole body went numb with fear.

"I'm outta here," she whispered, running to the left.

There—the tram station! She could lose him there! It was only two blocks away.

Could she make it? She knew she wasn't exactly Caylin in an all-out sprint.

She didn't have time to care.

She took off full tilt. Panic gripped her when she heard pounding footsteps behind her. Then she spotted the tram already at the station—preparing for departure!

No!

Theresa slipped a sweaty palm into her coat pocket and pulled out a tram token as she ran.

She had to time this perfectly. If that tram left . . .

She reached the turnstiles and fumbled with the token and the slot. She didn't look behind her—she didn't want to know.

"Come on, come on!"

The token slipped into the slot. The turnstile gave.

Theresa plunged through and jumped onto the tram just as the doors slid shut.

"All right!" she exclaimed, struggling for breath.

As the tram pulled out she searched around for the burly guy through the window.

She saw nothing.

Who could be following me? she wondered with a shiver as the train accelerated into the cold, dark night.

• • •

Back at 3-S, Caylin brought a bowl of popcorn to Jo's bedroom. "Look at the bright side, T.," she said. "At least you got away."

Theresa, sprawled next to Jo on her enormous canopy bed, smiled. "Very funny," she replied. "That dude was *huge*."

"You got a good look at him?" Jo asked excitedly.

"N-No," she stammered. "I could just tell. He was *huge*, that's all. No other distinguishing characteristics. Sorry."

"Intense," Caylin said. "Well, now that we found this weird Alexandra Parsons file, maybe we can get this sucker solved."

"Alexandra Parsons, huh?" Theresa said. "Think that's the impostor?"

Caylin shrugged. "Looks that way to me. But I guess we'll soon find out."

Jo took a handful of popcorn. "And at least we don't have to waste any more time on 'Danny Thugs I.'"

"Speaking of not wasting any more time," Caylin replied. "Aren't you glad you didn't waste any more time on Ewan?"

Jo rolled her eyes. "The freak. Calling me a nobody. *Me!*"

"Oh, the humanity!" Theresa cried dramatically.

"Oh, the *humility*," Caylin deadpanned.

Jo sported a smile as wide and evil as Godzilla's. "Yeah, well, freak-boy Ewan is about to find out how much damage a nobody can do!"

TEN

"Come out, come out, wherever you are!" Jo whispered as she scoped out InterCorp's halls for any suspicious-looking areas on Friday morning. Since Anka could be hidden *anywhere*—not just at the theater—Jo was making it her business to go over every square inch of the building with a fine-tooth comb.

As Jo approached a door marked Supplies she put her hand on its metal knob. A secretary in high heels clicked by, and Jo gave her a wave and a smile.

Once the woman passed, Jo tried the door again. Locked.

She used the magic key, and abracadabra, she was in.

"I have to get one of these," she whispered.

Jo scanned the room. Although there was no Anka to be found, there were no supplies to be found, either.

The closet was filled ceiling high with boxes marked Confidential and IRS.

"Wow," she mused. "Heavy-duty. Pay dirt, perhaps?"

She snapped some quick mascara pix of the boxes and bolted back to her cubicle before her boss could notice she was even gone. Once she got back and checked her e-mail, she was thrilled to find that Gottwald would be in a meeting for the next hour.

A whole hour.

Cool.

"Time to see what's in my boss's office," she sang under her breath.

Confidently striding into Gottwald's office with a packet of papers under her arm, Jo operated as if she had every right to be there. Who was going to say anything? She *was* his acting assistant.

Von Strauss's assistant poked her head into the office moments later. "Can I help you?"

Jo jumped in surprise. "Uh, just looking for a folder Mr. Gottwald needs. You know, for his meeting."

The woman nodded slowly. "I see."

"I'll let you know if I need anything, thanks," Jo said sweetly, shooting her a confident smile.

But after searching Gottwald's files for the next half hour, Jo was feeling anything *but* confident.

She found nothing.

Then she paused. She caught a flash of red poking out from under his computer keyboard. She lifted the keyboard.

A red folder marked Trade Pact. Right there. Hidden away.

Jackpot! Jo thought triumphantly.

Holding her breath, she opened the folder. It held only one piece of paper. But it was worth a thousand words. It was a confidential memo about the financial loss that InterCorp would suffer if the open-trade pact was signed!

Millions! Zillions! Enough to start another country in a really good neighborhood!

Immediately she ran the paper through Gottwald's personal fax machine and made a copy. Then she placed the original back in its folder under the keyboard. All before

Gottwald even returned, she thought smugly as she slid into her cubicle and stuck the photocopy in her Gucci briefcase for safekeeping.

"Whatcha got there, Selma?" came a voice.

Jo whirled and saw Ewan. She clicked her briefcase shut and forced herself to smile.

"Just a copy of an article I found interesting," she said automatically, shifting into flirt mode. "On money. My favorite subject."

"Really?" he asked, eyes narrowing. "What about money?"

Did he see me in Gottwald's office? she wondered.

No. She was just being paranoid.

"Best buys at Tiffany's," she quipped. "My first stop on my next jaunt to New York."

As Ewan looked into her eyes and smiled Jo felt just like Audrey Hepburn in Tiffany's—*Breakfast at*, that is. Like the smartest, most glamorous girl in the world!

As Theresa approached her locker she first saw a flash of white, then a bloodred psychotic scrawl.

What was it . . . a postcard. Taped to her cubby.

Her pulse raced. Who could it be from? she wondered, moving closer.

"*Pozor!*" it read in gigantic crimson letters. An army of foreign words had been scrawled in a madman's slanted script beneath it.

"Uh-oh," she muttered.

She slipped her minitranslator from her coat pocket and punched in the magic word.

Her blood ran cold.

Danger.

She quickly punched in the rest of the words from the postcard and wrote down their English translations one by one. When she'd deciphered the last syllable, her blood positively froze.

Stop snooping into things that are none of your business—or every one of you will die!

Everyone's dashing about like maniacs today," Ottla told Caylin as the office staff ran through the halls. "Two days until this pact signing, and you'd think the world was coming to an end."

Caylin laughed. "Everyone's gone troppo!"

Ottla gave her a blank look.

"Troppo," she repeated. "Aussie for 'crazy in the head.'"

"Right. Troppo," Ottla said. "Listen, Muriel, we need each department head to sign off on this." Ottla handed Caylin an interoffice memo outlining each department's responsibilities for Sunday. "This will take some legwork on your part," she continued, "but it needs to be done today."

"No problem," Caylin said, secretly thrilled to be able to snoopify some more. Even though Theresa had covered practically every inch of the place and found no Anka, Caylin was dying to take a crack at it herself.

After scoring Theresa's boss's signature and calling "Cheerio!" to her fellow Spy Girl, Caylin walked down the hall toward the head choreographer's office. En route she stopped short in front of what looked like a small utility closet.

Caylin regarded it with fascination. She had never even noticed it before. Seeing as how a simple utility closet had borne one of the most important pieces of evidence in the London mission, she was just itching to have a look inside.

"Wonder what's behind door number one?" Caylin whispered as she opened the unlocked door and entered the damp, musty interior. As Caylin reached out a hand to feel for a light switch the door slammed behind her.

"Uh-oh," Caylin moaned.

The closet was totally black. Caylin blindly groped for the doorknob. It wouldn't budge.

"Uh-oh squared."

A twinge of panic crept into Caylin's stomach. She was trapped. And she didn't even have her cell phone on her to call Theresa!

As reality hit, Caylin dropped her clipboard with a clatter and sank to her khaki-covered knees. She felt as if the walls were closing in on her already.

Claustrophobia—Caylin's worst enemy.

"Somebody help!" she yelled, kicking the door.

She blindly ran her hands along the door, searching for anything. But there was no keyhole, and the hinges were on the outside.

The only things she could find were a broom, a mop and bucket, and a fuse box on the wall.

Trapped.

Claustrophobia.

She forced herself not to think about it. She kicked the door again. But she couldn't help it. The walls were too close. She could smother, or be crushed, or the roof could collapse, the theater was so old. . . .

No!

Caylin took a deep breath and thought of snowy slopes, the wind in her hair, and her snowboard. It didn't help. The irrational fear gripped her tight. Her tumultuous tummy turned somersault after somersault.

Will anyone ever find me? she wondered with another aggravated kick.

And how would she explain herself if someone did?

Doubts and insecurities slam-danced around Caylin's brain as she tried to come up with a game plan.

Don't bother, you're nailed, they'll catch you and they'll kill you. . . .

"Shut up!" she commanded the taunting voices in her mind. She finally hit her forehead against the door in frustration.

"So we solved our last mission—so what," Caylin said bitterly. "The conference is in forty-eight hours, we still don't have one solid lead, and I'm stuck in a freaking closet!"

Ugh, I sound like a whiny brat! she thought, disgusted with herself. Caylin had always been a fighter. She was *not* one to give up. And she wasn't about to start now.

Self-pity abruptly transformed into unqualified rage.

She pounded on the door with unprecedented force. "Let me outta here!" she snarled, a caged animal.

After a few minutes of her furious pounding, the knob finally jiggled.

Relief flooded through Caylin's veins. Finally!

The door swung wide and she was met with a stench so thick, she could taste it.

"Ano?" a maintenance man asked in bewilderment.

Caylin squinted as the hall light blinded her.

"Ugh!" she replied, covering her nose in disgust.

"Ano?" he asked again.

"Nemluvím cesky!" Caylin immediately said. Translation: "I don't speak Czech!"

She scooped up her clipboard and slipped past him. "So much for a breath of fresh air," she added.

And so much for finding any more leads.

Let's see you thugs follow me now! Theresa silently dared as she strolled to Fake Anka's dorm on Friday afternoon.

Theresa had asked Julius if she could knock off at lunch, pleading that good ol' "time of the month" crampage. When Julius surprisingly obliged her request, she pulled her hair into a messy bun, donned some sunglasses, and hit the door double quick before he had a chance to change his mind.

She clutched the magic key ring in her pocket.

"Identification, please," the dorm security guard requested as soon as Theresa entered the lobby.

Without so much as glancing up, Theresa flashed the man her theater ID and rushed past him, beelining straight for the dormitory directory.

About eight lines down she hit pay dirt: *Anka Perdova— 5-E.*

Theresa scurried up the stairs, taking them two at a time.

"Here goes nothing," she muttered to herself as 5-E came within sight.

She slipped her magic key into the doorknob. "Open, sesame," she whispered, her heart filled with high expectations over the possible treasures hiding behind it. It swung open easily.

She stepped in.

An ear-piercing wail sounded, and Theresa panicked.

A burglar alarm!

Theresa spotted the beaten-up plastic keypad next to the door. It was loose on its screws.

Defuse it! she told herself.

The plastic cover came off in her hand. The wires underneath were old and frayed. One of them snapped in her hand, but the alarm continued to shriek.

Too much time . . .

The phone rang.

That was the last straw.

Theresa bolted. She slammed Anka's door shut and ran toward the fire door at the end of the hall. She heard the creak of a door opening behind her, but she didn't care.

She whipped open the fire door and dashed through it, finding herself on the fire escape. Anka's alarm wailed on and on inside.

Scrambling down the stairs, Theresa gasped as she nearly slipped on the icy metal.

Don't look down, she told herself, white knuckling the freezing rails for dear life. Five floors was a long way down.

She frantically descended the steps one by one. Her hands were freezing on the steel rails. Bizarre thoughts bombarded her brain: Would she be caught? Did Fake Anka know her identity? Was the mission blown?

Finally she made it to solid ground.

Theresa ducked into the nearest alley and peered back at the dorm.

Seconds later the security guard burst out of the dormitory doors, screaming incomprehensibly at the top of his lungs.

Theresa sighed. Now what? She needed to do something. Waiting around for the police to catch her was not an option.

Her gaze fell upon a hotel across the street from the dorm.

Theresa smiled.

"I need, um . . ." Theresa looked down at her pocket translator. "I need . . . *pokoj do ulice . . . na jih . . . poschodi . . . pet*," she told the hotel clerk in pidgin Czech. "A room facing the street on the fifth floor, south side," she followed up.

"Four thousand crowns," the overweight clerk said without looking up.

Theresa passed the woman her Visa, emblazoned with the name Camilla Stevens—a popular Tower alias.

The woman tossed her a key. The key was stamped with the number 555.

The magic key probably would have done the trick on the hotel room door, Theresa figured. But with the luck she was having that day, she'd probably walk in on two newlyweds.

As soon as she entered 555 Theresa marched to the window and jerked open the curtains.

"Yes!"

She had, as planned, a direct view of Anka's room.

"Let's zoom in," she said, digging around in her pockets for the opera glasses she sometimes used to check out the last act of the ballet from the balcony.

She caught sight of the security guard conferring with two Prague police officers. After a few moments they shut Anka's door and left.

The apartment sat empty.

"Guess there's nothing to do now but wait," Theresa muttered. She took a deep breath and flipped on the TV. The fact that there were only four stations to choose from didn't matter much.

Theresa couldn't understand a word anyone was saying, anyway.

Just as she was about to nod off from boredom, Theresa saw an overhead light go on over at Anka's.

"Gotcha!" Theresa cheered. Squinting, she saw two blurry figures enter the room. Pulse racing, she hopped up from the bed and scrambled for her opera glasses to get a better look at Fake Anka's companion.

"Who's your boyfriend?" she whispered into the

darkness, bringing the glasses to her eyes. As the fuzzy figures came into focus Theresa gasped at the man standing just inches away from Fake Anka.

Ewan!

They were arguing. They paced back and forth, their gestures angry and wild. Ewan raised his hand above his head and Theresa winced and closed her eyes, bracing herself for the blow.

But when she opened her lids, Ewan was giving Fake Anka a deep, passionate kiss.

Theresa's opera glasses hit the floor with a resounding clunk.

"I just can't believe they're a couple!" Jo cried back at 3-S. "So *she* was the one Uncle Sam got on tape!"

"Looks that way," Theresa replied.

The aquarium phone rang in the living room. Caylin immediately dove for it.

"Yo," she said.

"Hello, my superfly spies," came Danielle's voice. "Good news."

"We like good news," Caylin said, rubbing Jo's back consolingly.

"I've located Anka Perdova's family."

"Really? Where, in Moscow or something?" Jo asked.

"In Ohio."

"*Ohio?*" Theresa echoed, confused. "Whoa. I'm missing something."

"Yeah . . . we *all* were missing something," Caylin said, a smile creeping across her face. "Don't you get it? Alexandra Parsons *isn't* the impostor. She's the real deal."

Theresa gasped. "You mean—"

"Yes!" Caylin cried. "Alexandra Parsons is actually Anka Perdova! Right, Danielle?"

"Yes sirree," Danielle confirmed. "I guess it's some big secret of hers. Her mother is of Russian descent, but our Anka is baseball and apple pie all the way."

Jo gasped. "So she's been fooling everybody all this time? No way!"

"Affirmative," Danielle replied.

"She's a darned convincing Russian," Caylin exclaimed.

"We're talking Academy Award here," Danielle said.

"Apparently *everyone* was duped. I'm guessing that only the higher-ups at the New Russian Ballet are in on it—hence the lengths you had to go through to nab this folder. Who knows, maybe Alexandra thought she'd have a better shot at the NRB if she pretended to be Russian."

"Maybe it was her *only* shot," Caylin suggested.

"Exactly," Danielle agreed. "And maybe the execs finally found out her secret, so they're covering it up to save face."

Theresa took a deep breath. "It's just so hard to believe. . . ."

"And get this," Danielle said. "I paid her folks a visit, posing as a reporter. They said they haven't talked to her in a week and a half. And interestingly enough, they received a postcard from her just yesterday. I palmed it and e-mailed you a color scan."

"Danielle," Jo teased, "you sneak."

Theresa darted to fetch her laptop, then signed on. Within a matter of seconds she was staring at a downloaded file of the postcard.

"The handwriting's pretty shaky," Theresa noted.

"And she usually writes in a very neat script, according

to Mama," Danielle said. "Okay—postmark Prague, three days ago. Read along with me here and see what you think.

Hi, everyone, I'm fine but very busy. You know I'm not one to whine or anything, but things have been really hectic and I'm beat. Can't wait to see you on holiday.
Cheers,
Alex

"It sounds generic enough," Caylin said.

"What about the front of the postcard?" Jo suggested, staring at the screen intently. "Could you zap that over?"

"Sure thing," Danielle said. Her scanner buzzed in the background. A few seconds later the file appeared in Theresa's incoming mailbox.

The card featured a shot of a child ballerina with daisies in her hair.

"Magnify that." Jo brought her nose closer to the screen while Theresa blew up the image four hundred percent.

"What are those little splatters in the right-hand corner?" Jo asked, referring to five or six spots on the image.

"Is that just on the scan or on the original?"

Danielle paused. "Good eye, Jo—I didn't even notice those. It's definitely on the card. It's something red."

The Spy Girls shared fearful glances.

"Blood?" Caylin wondered grimly.

"I'll have forensics check it out," Danielle promised.

"Does the card have a smell?" Jo asked.

"A smell?" Danielle repeated. "Actually, it's kind of musty. Dank."

"Strange," Jo murmured.

"I just hope this means the real Anka is still alive," Theresa said, sighing deeply.

"Yeah." Caylin ran a hand anxiously through her blond hair. "But if we don't get on the stick, she may not be for much longer."

"And neither will Karkovic," Jo added.

Theresa shook her head. "Let's face it. We're all doomed."

ELEVEN

At least my heart doesn't skip a beat when I see him any-more, Jo thought as she looked into Ewan's eyes Saturday afternoon.

They were brunching at Luna, a hip eatery with fresh-cut flowers on the tables, colorful murals on the walls, and candles everywhere. Despite the Fake Anka revelation, Uncle Sam had told Jo to keep the brunch date and use the opportunity to pump Ewan for information. Although Ewan hadn't yet revealed anything over pancakes, Jo remained optimistic.

At some point the guy's got to slip, she resolved, lean-ing back in her seat and smiling wickedly. And when he did, she'd be right there to nail him.

"Are you excited about the ballet tomorrow night?" Jo asked, pulling up the sleeves on her black sweater.

Ewan's face paled so much, his skin looked lighter than his cream thermal. "The ballet?" he repeated with a gulp. "I guess so, but I'm more interested in the trade pact. For me the ballet is simply an appetizer to the main course."

"But Anka is just amazing," Jo exclaimed. "I can't wait to see her in action again."

"She is quite something," Ewan agreed. "It will be a lot of fun, I suppose."

"So what are you going to do now?" Jo asked, hoping she could score an invite to hang out with him for a bit longer.

"You wouldn't believe it if I told you," he said with a twinkle in his eye.

She grinned. Thirty-thousand watts. "Try me."

"You'll probably think it's stupid," he said, averting his gaze.

"I promise I won't laugh," she replied.

He paused. "Well, I'm actually taking a skydiving lesson. At two."

"Sk-skydiving?" Jo echoed. Although she loved flying down the freeway, free falling from ten thousand feet was an entirely different story.

"I'm trying to conquer my fear of flying," he confessed.

"By jumping out of a plane?"

He shrugged. "They say it works. Want to come with me?"

Jo hesitated.

Skydiving. Jumping out of a perfectly good airplane.

Should she put herself in danger to score some juicy details or stay on solid ground and possibly miss out?

"I'd love to," Jo finally replied, hoping she wasn't making a big, big mistake.

"Jeez, for an international impostor and potential murderess, your Saturday sure is a snoozer."

Theresa muttered as she watched Fake Anka exit a grocery store from a hundred feet back. Since the theater was closed to stage staff and dancers for pact-signing preparations, Theresa had spent the better part of her morning trailing the deadly diva.

So far it'd been one big laugh riot—the laundry, the gym, now the grocery store. What's next, the post office? Theresa wondered, taken aback by the fact that such a devious supercriminal could lead such a boring existence.

Theresa had been hoping to witness secret meetings, hidden hideaways, bang-'em-up car chases—*something* to revive the mission. But no such luck.

When she saw Fake Anka look around suspiciously and jump into a taxi, Theresa practically had a heart attack. Finally—a sign of life!

"Follow that cab," Theresa told a driver as she hopped into his taxi. "And step on it."

Ha! She'd always wanted to say that!

As they trailed Fake Anka's taxi over long, winding roads and across baroque bridges Theresa's interest grew with each mile. And her curiosity level went off the Richter scale when she observed Fake Anka's vehicle stopping in front of what appeared to be a neighborhood carnival, complete with rides, tents, and the whole nine.

"Guess it's time to get on the merry-go-round," Theresa mused.

"When the queen of England arrives, you curtsy," said Ms. Pontiva, the woman Ottla had hired to train the ushers and office staff on how to properly address government officials and royalty. All the tables had been pushed to the corner of the ballroom to give Pontiva enough space to work her magic.

Although Ms. Pontiva was very thorough, Caylin was having a hard time keeping the different customs straight. Such a hodgepodge of countries would be represented! The fact that the importance of this stuff faded in comparison to that of her mission didn't exactly boost her concentration level.

"What happens if we get confused?" she asked, looking up from her notebook.

"Just stay calm," Ms. Pontiva instructed, "and everything will be all right."

"Easy for you to say," Caylin mumbled to herself. "Miss Priss."

Then she froze. Ottla had just entered the theater.

She was accompanied by Prime Minister Karkovic!

Caylin's heart pounded as she laid eyes on the man she'd been sent to protect.

"Excuse me," Ottla said, "but I'd like you to meet Gogol Karkovic, the prime minister of Varokhastan."

With a nervous smile Caylin stuck out her arm to offer a firm handshake. A few other ushers followed suit while one bowed and another curtsied.

"We're still working out our greetings," Ms. Pontiva apologized with a laugh. "Welcome to Prague, Prime Minister."

"Yes, welcome," the group sang while Karkovic smiled ear to ear.

"G'day," Caylin called.

"Your theater is utterly breathtaking," he declared in a strong accent. "I am very pleased to sign pact that will have such enormous influence on our countries."

His aides quickly ushered Karkovic away, noting that his schedule was tight.

Caylin smiled as he said his good-byes. Even a few goose bumps dotted her flesh. He seemed to be such a good man.

Then her smile vanished. That good man had only twenty-four more hours to live.

Not if Caylin could help it. Now that she had met the man in the flesh, she was more determined than ever to keep him from harm's way.

• • •

"Okay, I understand," Ewan said into the special in-flight phone. He sat perched in the second row of the eight-seat InterCorp jet. The blue seats were made of plush velvet and the phone was state-of-the-art.

In the five minutes he'd been on the phone, Jo had been staring out the window, lost in thought.

Anka was somewhere in that world down there, she reflected. But where? How much did she know? Who else was with her?

When he hung up abruptly, Jo noticed Ewan had a strange look on his face.

"Everything okay?" she asked, secretly wondering if the call was about Anka, or Alexandra, or Fake Anka, or . . . whoever.

"Fine," he said, his expression indicating otherwise. As he looked deep into her eyes she felt a shiver up her spine.

His eyes were cold, vacant.

"What?" she asked in alarm.

He shook his head. "It's nothing, really," he insisted,

slapping a plastic smile on his face. "Let's get those parachutes on and get this show on the road."

As Ewan handed her a parachute pack and took one for himself Jo couldn't shake her uneasy feeling. For a terrifying moment she wondered if the parachute Ewan had given her was operable.

"Don't we have an instructor?" Jo asked.

Ewan shook his head. "I know all I need to know."

"Then could you ask the pilot if he can descend a few feet to relieve some of the pressure? My eardrums are about to burst!"

Ewan shot her a strange look before dropping his parachute on the seat and heading up to the cockpit.

While he did, Jo switched her parachute with his.

Just in case.

"He's descending to fourteen thousand feet for the jump now," Ewan announced. "Let's get into our gear, shall we?"

"Sure," Jo said, trying to sound brave. But she strapped herself in with shaking hands.

When Ewan studied his pack before putting it on, Jo panicked. Did he realize she made the switch?

"You know how you're always saying you love how Anka dances?" Ewan asked in an overly nonchalant tone as he adjusted the pack on his back.

"Yeah?"

"I was wondering why you mention her so much."

"What do you mean?" she asked. She secured her buckles, not meeting his gaze.

"Look, I *know*, okay?" he spat, his voice getting lower.

"You know what?" Jo asked, her mind spinning. That I'm a Spy Girl, she mused, or that I know he's dating Anka, or that I know Anka's an impostor, or that I know he plans to kill Karkovic?

"That you're living with someone who's been trailing Anka," he said accusingly.

"What?"

"And I know you copied the trade-pact memo," he grumbled. "Whatever it is you're after . . . you won't get it!"

The low, angry note in his voice triggered a memory— the taped phone conversation with von Strauss! It was *Ewan's* voice all along! He really was in on it!

Jo gasped. "You're the guy who—"

Before she could finish her sentence, Ewan lunged for her. Putting her self-defense training into play, she tried to use Ewan's momentum to roll backward and throw him over her. But the fat parachute on her back prevented the move.

They both hit the floor with a thud.

"Let me go!" she screamed, rolling to the side.

"Not on your life," he growled. He pulled her back and pinned her to the ground. "Prague is beautiful from this height. We'll jump together, Selma. You'll just love it . . . until I let you drop without a parachute."

"You mean *this* parachute?" Jo replied, yanking the cord that dangled from his pack.

Bellowing and cursing, Ewan disappeared under a sea of white nylon.

Jo struggled to her feet and lunged for the side door.

She fought to unlatch it. Growling, she yanked on the handle as hard as she could. It barely budged. Adrenaline coursed through her veins like hot lava, making every movement seem as if it were in slow motion.

Ewan's hands clamped around her ankles. He jerked his arms back, trying to bring her down.

"You're not going anywhere!" he cried.

"Is that what you told Anka Perdova?" she yelled back. She kicked his head as hard as she could, feeling a gratifying impact.

He groaned and loosened his grip.

With her last ounces of desperate strength Jo wrenched the door handle one final time and slammed all her weight against it.

It gave way.

The handle was torn from her grasp as a rock-solid wall of wind slammed her face. The air was sucked from her lungs. Her body was lifted in the air. Her stomach rolled.

Jo hurtled toward the earth at 125 miles per hour. Only one question screamed through her brain.

If the parachute in Ewan's pack opened . . .

. . . did that mean the one in hers *wouldn't*?

There was only one way to find out.

She pulled the cord.

And screamed.

• • •

Standing a safe distance from the carousel, Theresa fought a yawn as she watched Anka go around and around and around.

It was her third ride on the thing! How much longer can she take it? Theresa wondered in exasperation.

But a few minutes later Theresa's doldrums gave way to dismay. The hairs on her neck prickled—just like they had the other night when she was being followed.

She casually turned her head, scanning the crowd suspiciously, as the carousel continued on its circular path.

She froze.

There, behind a beat-up food stand, lurked the same burly guy who had trailed her the other night. She was sure of it. Even more sure when their eyes locked.

And he shot her a leering, vicious smile.

"Un-oh!"

Theresa hightailed it to the nearest tent. She threw some money at the attendant and plunged inside, hoping she would make it out alive.

Theresa dashed down a long hall, but she stumbled as her stomach heaved. Wha—?

The floor bubbled up and down like waves. Twisted reflections sprang up all around her, and she had to fight to keep on her feet.

Where was she?

Everywhere she looked, someone stared back at her. Tall ones, skinny ones, fat ones, deformed ones. But they all had wild brown hair and wore a long black coat. They were all *her*.

Of course! She was in the House of Mirrors!

Theresa glanced over her shoulder and gasped.

The burly guy! He was coming after her!

Theresa darted to the right and tripped over her clunky shoes. She quickly regained her balance.

After going through a few nauseating mirror rooms and hallways she was completely disoriented. She dodged other patrons, whirling at every movement she saw from the corner of her eye.

Was that him? she wondered, gasping. Her heart caught in her throat when she glimpsed a bald, portly reflection to her immediate left.

No—just a guy with his kid.

She had to keep moving.

She slipped into the next room. Rotating mirrors spun all around her. Her face appeared, disappeared, was fat, was thin, was monstrously distorted.

"I think I'm going to puke," she mumbled.

But her nausea left immediately when she spotted her burly stalker—over her shoulder in a mirror! He was only a few feet away!

His gaze locked with hers once again.

He stepped forward, smiling demoniacally. Theresa noticed with a turn of her stomach that one of his front teeth was gold.

Move it! She slipped between two spinning mirrors and through a black curtain.

Bad move. The room was pitch black!

Theresa cringed as someone grabbed her hand and forced it into what felt like a bowl of warm, wet grapes. A deep, menacing voice barked at her in Czech.

Of course, even without knowing a word of the language, Theresa knew *exactly* what the voice was saying:

"Feel the eyeballs!" She'd played that game in about a hundred haunted houses back in Arizona.

How refreshing to know some cultural trends were the same all over the world.

Theresa yanked her hand away and lunged forward, bumping the table and spilling the bowl of grapes.

The voice barked angrily. A complaint, she was sure.

"Sorry," Theresa cried out to the dark. She tossed a few bills in the air. "Here. Buy yourself some fresh eyeballs."

She kept on moving forward, not sure where she was going.

A flash of light came from behind her. She turned to see the burly guy's silhouette entering through the curtain. Then all was dark again.

Time to go!

Theresa fumbled into another curtain wall on the far side of the room. But there was no seam to slip through.

A scuffle erupted behind her. Her stalker and that feisty eyeball guy—she was sure of it. Theresa heard someone land hard on the ground with an "Oof!"

She had to find a way out fast.

Well, if she didn't have a seam, she'd have to make one!

She slipped her tiny penknife out of her pocket and slipped it into the black curtain material, sawing downward.

A beam of light sliced through.

She ripped the thick cloth apart and stuck her leg out.

Eyeball Man began shouting up a storm. At some point she was sure she heard a word that sounded like *police*.

"Yeah! Call 'em!" Theresa replied as she dove through the hole. "I could use some backup here!"

She landed with a thud outside the eyeball chamber, flat on the ground. She tried to get up, but her left foot was snagged in the black fabric. No—a hand! A massive hand had clamped down on her ankle with an iron grip!

She knew her stalker was hiding behind that black curtain. And she instantly knew he was as low to the ground as she since he had ahold of her ankle.

Instinctively she coiled up her body and drew her right knee toward her chest. With all her might she kicked out toward the moving bump in the black curtain—the stalker's head.

She felt a chunky impact through her boot.

She heard a grunt.

Her ankle was free! Theresa yanked her foot back, stood up, and sprinted around another corner, seeing more mirrors, more mirrors . . . and a sign for the exit!

She bolted for it full tilt. But as she rounded the corner just before the exit flap a huge, burly man blocked her way!

Her heart skipped a beat. How could he have gotten in front of her? Impossible!

The big man slowly turned around. Theresa took a step backward—then paused.

She saw a red nose. Huge painted lips. A white face. Frizzy hair.

A clown!

Theresa shuddered.

The clown leaned forward and offered the purple carnation pinned to the lapel of his green leisure suit.

She smiled. "Oh no. I'm not gonna fall for—"

Before she could finish, the carnation squirted her in the face with sugar water.

"Har-de-har-har-har!" the clown bellowed. He wasn't

laughing, though. He was actually *saying* "Har, de, har, har, har!"

Theresa licked her lips, lifted her boot, and slammed it down hard on the clown's oversize right shoe.

"Ow-ooo-ow-ow-ow!" the clown cried. He jumped up and down in a circle.

"Later, Bozo." Theresa dodged the clown, pushed the exit flap aside, and ran for her life toward the nearest tram.

Jo screamed at the top of her lungs. Something yanked her whole body, hard.

Her free fall was broken.

A loud flapping sound filled the air. She looked up in fear.

Her parachute had opened.

"Thankyouthankyouthankyouthankyou," she chanted frantically.

Jo felt herself soaring high in the sky. Her stomach lurched, and she felt as if she were choking on her heart.

What a rush!

Then she was dangling in the air, three thousand feet above the ground. She was frozen, with nothing to do but float. Another look up and around confirmed that InterCorp's jet was out of sight.

For a moment she felt completely free and at peace, as if she were a bird in flight.

Then Jo looked down.

All she saw were trees. A huge, endless sea of trees.

Her stomach instantly did somersaults. A hundred things could happen when a person parachuted into a tree. Deep cuts. Broken limbs—and not the ones with leaves. Brutal, unsanitary body piercings. Anything. Jo felt physically sick.

Stay calm. Just breathe, she told herself.

Once she had descended enough to see the trees for the forest, her panic subsided a bit. There were a few clearings down there. All she needed to do was steer her way over to one. As she tugged at her directional cords Jo gritted her teeth and crossed her fingers.

As she got closer and closer to the ground she realized with dread that hitting a tree was virtually unavoidable. She also realized that floating in the air was an illusion. As she neared the ground she knew she was *falling*, and parachute or not, it was still going to hurt. There was nothing to do but brace herself and hope for the best.

Suddenly leaves were whipping her face. Branches snapped all around her. Something tore into her left arm. Her body slammed into a tree trunk. Her body scraped against its ragged bark. The ground rocketed toward her.

But then she just stopped. She dangled.

Wha—?

Jo opened her eyes. The chute had snagged in the branches above her. She was stuck. The ground was about twelve feet below.

"Great," she muttered, wincing as she touched her torn left sleeve. She was bleeding, but not badly. She shook the straps of the chute, trying to dislodge herself. But no dice. There was only one way down: the hard way.

Jo slowly reached up to the chute clamps and prepared to unhook them. She took a deep breath. Maybe if she was careful—

Snap!

"Whoooaaa!"

Thud!

"Ow!"

Jo rolled to her side and coughed. The ground was frozen, and she felt as if her insides had been pureed. She lay there, her cheek pressed to the ground.

"Earth to Jo," she whispered.

She shakily attempted to move her appendages. Everything seemed to work.

"I'm going to feel this in the morning," she groaned. She stared at the gash on her left arm and grimaced. "So much for that little sleeveless number I was going to wear to the pact signing."

She scanned her surroundings. Nothing but woods.

"If I even *make* it to the signing," she added.

She looked at her watch. It was 2:30 p.m. The winter sun was beginning to descend toward the horizon. That was west. Jo remembered Ewan mentioning something about the pilot heading north of the airport.

That meant she wanted to go south. If she walked long enough, she had to hit *something* . . . right?

All she could do was brush herself off, take a deep breath, and walk.

The sun was getting ready to set when Jo began to

worry. She'd walked for over two hours and still saw nothing but trees. She had to have gone at least six miles. She was exhausted. And she knew if she got stuck out all night in this cold weather, she might not make it.

But just when she was about to give up hope, she heard something. A low rumble, getting louder. She took a few tentative steps forward, listening.

The rumble grew louder. Became a roar—as if something huge was coming.

Suddenly a tractor-trailer roared by, not twenty feet in front of her!

Jo gasped. A road! She plunged forward and broke through the trees. Indeed, two lanes of blacktop stretched to the left and the right as far as she could see.

And a pickup truck was approaching.

"I guess this means they're onto us," Caylin said as she swiftly and efficiently dressed the many scrapes and scratches covering Jo's arms and legs.

"You think?" Jo replied bitterly.

The Spy Girls were back safe in flat 3-S that evening.

They gorged on comfort food as a reward for their tough day while making a report to Uncle Sam at the same time.

"We're glad you're okay, Jo," Theresa said, her concern genuine.

"*Okay? You* try falling out of an airplane, landing in a tree, *and* hitching a three-hour ride in the back of a pickup truck in the freezing cold!"

"All right, ladies," Uncle Sam cut in. "You're alive, and we've still got a mission to accomplish. Jo, are you with us?"

Jo nodded.

"Good. The call Ewan received on the plane was from the impostor, who most likely told him she was being followed. Somehow they had figured out that you and Theresa live together."

"Right," Theresa chimed in, "and the guy chasing me was obviously one of Fake Anka's flunkies as well."

"You need to watch your backs," Uncle Sam warned. "In fact, I'm considering aborting the entire mission."

"Whoa, you can't do that!" Caylin pleaded. "We've come way too far already!"

"We can't let them get away with this," Jo said, fire burning in her eyes.

Uncle Sam sighed. "I hear you, girls. The truth is, aborting at this stage would trigger a chain reaction at InterCorp," he admitted. "The conspirators might close up shop. Right now they think they have you on the run. For this reason, I'm going to let you continue."

"All right!" Theresa cheered.

"We'll figure out something by tomorrow night," Jo promised. "We just *have* to."

TWELVE

Caylin headed out for the theater before seven on Sunday morning. It was going to be a long day, and she wanted to be around the assassination site as much as possible. Maybe she'd spot something important. Maybe she'd get a chance to search for the real Anka. Anything.

She was prepared for the place to be a zoo, but when she entered the theater office, she was surprised to find she was the first one there.

"Lazy bums," she muttered. She figured at the very least that Ottla would be there, making sure all the preparations were, well, *prepared*.

"Oh, well," she mused. "Maybe this Spy Girl can snoop around a bit more—"

A floorboard creaked behind her. Caylin's eyes went wide. Someone was—

A gloved hand covered her mouth and the sharp barrel of an automatic pistol was jammed against her temple.

"Move and die," a low voice growled in her ear.

Oh no.

Caylin's heart leaped. Her stomach shrank. She sighed, closed her eyes, and prepared herself for whatever would come next.

"I can't believe we have to work on a Sunday," Hannah moaned. Her hair was disheveled, and she looked half asleep.

"They want the joint to look tip-top, I guess," Theresa replied, eyes darting around. She had too many people to keep tabs on: Caylin, who had left the flat early that morning but didn't seem to be there; Fake Anka, who hadn't arrived yet; and the burly guy with the creepy gold tooth.

If either Fake Anka or Gold Tooth saw her, the jig was up.

And while most of the other dancers were milling

about, Theresa could only wonder about Fake Anka. Was she at ballet practice . . . or *target* practice?

"No way Ewan will be able to recognize me now!" Jo said to her disguised reflection in the mirror.

She had given herself a total makeover, complete with a corn silk blond wig, pale skin, blue contact lenses, and red lipstick. She completed the ensemble with a stunning black evening gown—with sleeves, to cover her cuts and bruises. The finished product looked nothing like the Jo— ahem, *Selma* that Ewan Gallagher knew.

"Simplicity is the key," she told her reflection. "I could grace five covers in one month with this look!" She blew a kiss at the mirror. "Too bad I can't have a hunky under- wear model on my arm. Going solo can be *such* a blow to the ego."

Once she was dressed, Jo again checked out her look in the mirror. It was so different from her usual image. The blue contacts looked so unnaturally natural to her, it was almost creepy.

But Ewan would never recognize her.

"Get ready, Mr. Gallagher," she purred to her reflection. "You're about to see the dead come back to life—and you won't even know it . . . until it's too late!"

"Where could Caylin be?" Theresa muttered under her breath. She smoothed out her deep blue velvet dress and checked her watch for the umpteenth time.

She and Caylin had arranged to meet in front of the costume closet at 5:00 p.m. But it was now almost 5:30, and there was still no sign of her. She hadn't even answered any of her texts.

With the ballet less than two hours away, the theater was an absolute zoo. There was a chance Caylin had gotten tied up, Theresa supposed, but it was unlike her not to call or text.

Something must have happened. Hot, unwanted tears burned behind Theresa's eyes as she imagined just how horrifying that "something" could be.

With Ewan and Fake Anka on the loose, no one was really safe. And after Ewan's attempt on Jo's life, nothing was impossible.

Theresa blinked back tears, sniffled, and made her way to the theater office. Ottla was there in her gown, applying some makeup.

"Excuse me, Ottla? Have you seen . . . er, Muriel?" Theresa asked.

"She still hasn't reported for duty today," Ottla growled. "Of all days! Are you a friend of hers?"

"No," she lied. "I just wanted to tell her I found a book of hers backstage."

"Whatever," Ottla said angrily. "If you see her first, please tell her to find me immediately."

Now I'm *really* freaked, Theresa thought as she left the office. She ducked into a hallway to call the flat.

No answer.

Maybe Caylin went straight to the preballet reception, Theresa hoped. But deep down she doubted it.

"She's probably chatting with Jo right now, wondering where I am," she whispered. "Please . . . please let her be there."

She dashed to the upper ballroom but saw no one after two exhausting laps. Panic gripped her.

Where *is* everybody? she cried to herself, desperate to find a familiar Spy Girl face in the crowd.

Someone bumped Theresa hard.

"Excuse me," a stunning blond said in a thick French accent.

"No problem," Theresa muttered. But a few paces later she paused. That dress . . . it was one of her mother's creations! The same dress she had loaned to Jo that morning.

Theresa stared hard at the blond woman. No. It couldn't be.

But when the blond glared straight at her with a big smirk on her face, Theresa couldn't help smiling with relief.

"Gotcha!" Jo crowed, cracking up.

Theresa pulled Jo close. "Look—no kidding around, Jo. Something's wrong. *Really* wrong."

Jo's giggles instantly ceased. "What?"

"It's Caylin," Theresa replied. "She's missing."

"What?" Her fake blue eyes widened in terror. "How?"

"I don't know," Theresa said. "Let's go over to the hors d'oeuvres table and try to blend. Who knows who's watching us now."

. . .

A few minutes later Jo lined up toast points on a silver tray while Theresa stirred a large vat of caviar with a mother-of-pearl spoon.

"How come when the best food is around, I don't feel like eating it?" Jo said morosely. "Caviar, the best champagne . . . talk about class."

"No one Caylin works with has seen her," Theresa went on, ignoring Jo's food fetish. "What could have happened?"

"Have you seen Ewan or Fake Anka?"

"No."

A toast point crumbled in Jo's hand as she shuddered. "I can't touch this stuff, I'm so nervous," she whispered.

Before Theresa had a chance to respond, Julius approached. His tuxedo was a far classier cry from the clunky boots and paint-stained clothes that she'd come to know.

"Tiffany! Thank goodness you're here," he said haughtily. "We need one bottle of merlot. Chop-chop."

Theresa's jaw muscles pulsed angrily. What a time to play fetch!

"Sure," she replied calmly. "Where?"

"Wine cellar," Julius said.

Theresa nearly dropped her spoon. She glimpsed Jo's fake blue eyes widening—she'd caught it, too!

"Wine cellar?"

"Left after props closet, down the hall, last door on the right. Go! Go!" he ordered, shooing her away.

As Theresa headed toward the exit Jo fell in step next to her.

"This place has a *wine* cellar?" Jo whispered. "Have you seen it?"

"No. I didn't even know about it. Are you thinking what I'm thinking?"

"Well, I'm thinking that the *real* Anka—"

"Reminded her folks that she's not one to *whine*," Theresa finished. "And those red splatters in the corner . . . "

The girls stared at each other.

"This is it, T.," Jo said. "I can feel it! Come on!"

THIRTEEN

"Left after props closet," Jo whispered, making a sharp louie.

"Down the hall," Theresa continued. They gleefully barreled down at top speed.

"Last door on right," Jo said.

Sure enough, they came face-to-face with an unmarked door.

"I always thought this was a dressing room," Theresa said. She grabbed the knob. It wouldn't budge. "Locked."

"Please tell me you have—"

"The magic key," Theresa finished, dangling the key ring from her fingers. Thank goodness she'd remembered to throw it in her evening bag. She fit the key in the lock, and with a turn of the knob they found themselves in what looked like a standard office, only the lighting was considerably dimmer. Its only distinguishable design element was a long, narrow hall that branched off from the far corner of the right wall.

"Down the hall. Chop-chop," Jo mimicked.

"Don't make fun of Julius," Theresa said. "If he hadn't commanded me to fetch that stupid bottle of merlot, we wouldn't *be* here right now."

Theresa motored down the hall. When she reached the end of the passage, she turned right—*right* into Ewan!

Theresa and Jo collectively gaped in amazement.

"Watch it, you idiot!" Ewan barked, stepping back and brushing off his designer tux. "What are you doing back here?"

"Allow *me* to explain," Jo said, stepping forward with her French femme fatale accent. "I was asked to help this stagehand select the best bottle of merlot in the house for Prime Minister Karkovic." She leaned in closer to Ewan and whispered, "This poor ignorant girl has no idea what good wine is, *n'est-ce pas*? Without my help she'd happily pour vinegar for the PM and call it a day."

Theresa blinked at Jo but remained deadpan.

Ewan raised his brows, but he didn't seem to recognize either of them in the dim light. A good sign.

"Don't worry," Jo said with a wink. "The peasant doesn't speak a word of English, either."

"*I'll* get the wine for you," Ewan grumbled, holding up a hand.

As he headed to the entryway of the cellar stairs Jo and Theresa followed.

"No," he blurted. "You wait here." He started down the stairs.

Once Ewan was safely out of earshot, Theresa swatted Jo on the head. "Peasant?"

"Hey, watch the wig!" Jo whispered indignantly. "So what's the plan here?"

"Think about it," Theresa said grimly. "There's only one thing we can do."

Jo nodded. She knew exactly what Theresa was thinking.

"Should you do the honors or I?" Theresa asked. Her hands trembled, and Jo could see the fear in her eyes.

Jo smiled. "It would be my pleasure, T."

She heard faint footsteps seconds later. This was it!

"Here's a merlot fit for a king, literally," Ewan said as he headed up the stairs. He reached the landing. "See? A very good year."

"Wonderful," Jo purred as he handed her the bottle. She gazed lovingly at the label. "Very nice." She hefted the bottle up and down in her hand, feeling its weight. "Mmm. And so *heavy*, too."

Ewan's icicle blue eyes widened in puzzlement. "Wha—?"

"Good night." Jo raised the bottle and slammed it down on Ewan's head as hard as she could.

Red wine and glass sprayed everywhere. Ewan's head snapped back and he hit the ground with a thud. His face was covered with wine and bits of glass. Small trickles of blood rolled down his cheek.

"Whoa," Theresa breathed.

"Hope it was as good for you as it was for me, Ewan," Jo muttered, brushing some glass off her pumps. "Hmmm. Lucky my dress is black."

The lights flashed three times fast. "The ballet's starting," Theresa piped. "We don't have much time!" They stepped over Ewan and headed down the stairs.

• • •

"This place is a maze," Jo whispered as they spun through the catacombs. "It's all dead ends. And who drinks this much wine?"

"Come on, this way," Theresa said. She pulled at Jo's arm.

"Anka!" Jo called out into the stale air.

"Caylin!" Theresa shouted.

Over and over again they kept calling. No answers came.

"Don't give up yet," Theresa told Jo as she continued to go up and down each and every aisle. A few minutes later Jo saw Theresa abruptly stop short.

"Wait," she said, perking up her ears. "Do you hear something?"

Jo stopped to listen. "Not a thing."

"Maybe it was just my imagination." Theresa shrugged and continued on.

After a few more minutes passed, Theresa halted again. "I definitely heard something that time," she proclaimed.

"What'd it sound like?" Jo asked.

"A cry of some sort," Theresa replied. "Over there, I think. By those magnum bottles."

Then Jo heard it. A muffled cry from deep behind a wall of bottles. They both moved closer and peered between the magnums.

"Look!" Jo cried, reaching between two bottles and feeling the wall behind them. "It's wood! A door!"

"Hello?" Theresa called.

The cries came again, louder this time.

"That's it!" Jo exclaimed. "We have to get through that door."

"Check out the floor," Theresa ordered. "There are wheel marks. The wine rack is on wheels! Grab an end."

They slowly rolled the massive rack of bottles to the side. The wheels creaked and moaned, but they moved. And sure enough, they had uncovered a stout wooden door.

"That thing must be a thousand years old," Jo surmised.

"Maybe," Theresa replied, fishing the magic key ring out once again. "But the lock is brand-new."

Theresa slid the key into the lock with a smile and turned. It didn't budge.

"Uh-oh," she said.

"What?" Jo asked.

Theresa jiggled the key. "Take a guess."

"Aw, no fair!" Jo cried. "It worked on all the other ones!"

"Not *this* one." Theresa slipped the key back in her purse and sighed. "Now what?"

"Well . . . ," Jo began.

"You have something?" Theresa asked.

Jo wiped her wine-stained hands on her designer dress and yanked a bobby pin from her hair. "What do you think?"

"I think we're doomed," Theresa replied glumly.

"It can't hurt to try," Jo replied sharply. She inserted the bobby pin in the lock and tried to jimmy it. "This always works in the movies."

"Jo, that's a state-of-the-art lock," Theresa lectured. "It has a complex series of tumblers that will only open to a specific computer-coded key. Not magic keys, and certainly not bobby—

The pin clicked and turned in the keyhole.

Jo giggled and beamed up at Theresa, whose jaw was practically on the floor.

"I'll accept your apology later, Brainiac," Jo said. She turned the knob and pulled the door open with a loud, grating squeal.

"Hello?" Theresa called. "Caylin? Anka?"

They peered into the dim chamber—then gasped. Both Anka and Caylin were sardined in the tiny crawl space, their arms and legs bound.

"You're okay!" Theresa wailed, tears of relief falling down her face.

"Ohmigosh!" Jo cried. She crouched down and hastily untied the ropes that bound them.

Theresa pulled Anka out, then Caylin. Both young women were sobbing. Caylin's burgundy formal was covered with a film of dust and grime.

"It's about time," Caylin complained through her tears.

"You're free now." Theresa wrapped Caylin in a hug. "I was so afraid you'd—"

"Not so fast!"

"Ewan!" Jo cried.

Theresa whipped around. Ewan stood behind them,

sneering as blood and wine dripped off his chiseled features. "Nobody's going anywhere!"

"And who's going to stop us?" Caylin growled, massaging blood back into her fists.

"Who do you think?' Ewan pulled an automatic pistol from his coat pocket.

"You shouldn't play with guns, Ewan," Jo warned in her Selma voice. "People could get hurt."

Ewan's eyes went wide. "Y-You!" he sputtered. He actually smiled through the blood. "Skydiving suits you, Selma. The impact did you some good. I prefer blonds."

"I think you've had too much wine." Jo pulled the wig off and tossed it aside. "I like myself just the way I am, thank you."

"I liked you, too, Selma," Ewan replied. He picked a shard of glass out of his cheek and regarded it momentarily before tossing it aside. "That's why I'll have to kill you first."

Ewan leveled the gun on Jo.

"Hey, lover boy," Theresa called out.

Ewan glanced at her and sneered. "Yeah?"

"If you're gonna take her out don't forget the keys to the car!"

Theresa tossed the magic key ring at Ewan. He reached out with his free hand and casually caught them.

He stared at the key ring and smiled. "What, no convertible?"

Theresa smiled. "I *knew* I forgot something!" She snapped her fingers for emphasis.

A blinding spark shot up from Ewan's fist. His face froze in shock and his whole body stiffened, quaking. The gun dropped from his other hand.

In a few seconds the stun gun shut down. Ewan hovered there for a moment, wobbling, fist frozen around the key ring. Then he collapsed in a heap.

FOURTEEN

"'Don't forget the keys to the car'?" Jo echoed, beaming. "Jeez, T., you couldn't come up with anything better than *that*?"

"Worked pretty well, I'd say," Theresa said matter-of-factly.

Caylin stepped forward and snatched up Ewan's pistol. "No more socializing," she commanded, tossing the rope Jo's way. "Help me tie this creep up. We don't have much time!"

"Okay," Jo said. "T., you take Anka upstairs. While we tie Ewan up, I'll search him for his key chain. Let's lock him up in that crawl space and give him a taste of his own medicine."

While Jo helped Caylin tie up Ewan, Theresa helped Anka run upstairs. They headed straight for the costume closet.

"Why are you taking me here?" Anka asked frantically as she swabbed at her dirty hands and face with baby wipes. "You're with Caylin, yes?"

"Yes, but I don't have time to explain—"

"Caylin already did," Anka said. "I know all about my look-alike."

"Then you have to change fast!" Theresa told her. "You have to go onstage and dance!"

"I don't know if I can," Anka replied. "The ropes cut into me because they were so tight. My feet are tingling too much."

They reached the costume closet. Theresa opened the door and shoved her inside. "Please, Anka . . . you have to try."

Anka stared at her a moment, then nodded. "I will. The audience out there deserves it . . . and so do I." She began shedding her dirty clothes. "I don't understand. How can someone look like me and dance like me?"

"This impostor—she had plastic surgery or something. Who knows, but everyone thinks she's you. When the lights go out for intermission, we're pretty sure she's going to shoot Gogol Karkovic from the stage."

"Caylin told me all that, too," Anka said as she cleaned her arms and legs. "It's *got* to be the craziest thing I've ever heard."

"I know it sounds like a bad episode of *The Twilight Zone*, but it's dead serious."

Anka struggled into her bodysuit. "Ewan kept saying I was going to kill Karkovic, but I couldn't understand how or why," she explained. "I thought it was because someone had found out my secret—that I faked being from Russia to get into the NRB. But what does that have to do with Karkovic? He's a good guy with a big heart. Why in the world would anyone want to kill him?"

"Because he's a good guy with a big heart, that's why." Theresa shook her head. "Oh, man, you must have been going crazy in there coming up with conspiracy theories. So why did you do it? Change your name and fake your heritage, I mean."

"Dancing is . . . well, it's the only thing I've ever been

able to do right, you know? If I couldn't dance for a living, then I didn't have another reason to live." Anka scrambled to find the right-size slippers. "Ever since I was little, I wanted to dance with the NRB. And I made my dream come true. I didn't do it to hurt anybody."

Theresa cocked her head to the side as she helped Anka fasten her skirt. "Well, it's pretty dishonest, but it doesn't mean you should be framed for murder."

"Seriously." Anka arranged her hair into a tight bun. "But then before Caylin got caught, I was all alone in that little room, thinking, *I'm getting what I deserve. I should be punished for what I've done. What Ewan's doing is right.*" She securely fastened bobby pins all over her head. "I thought I was going to go crazy. I was actually *agreeing* with that psycho."

"Oh, Anka, no," Theresa said gently. "No one deserves to be treated the way you were. No one deserves to be punished like this."

Anka shakily put on her stage makeup and turned to face Theresa. "This is beyond belief. But . . . well, the show must go on, right?"

"Right." Theresa smiled. "Everything's going to be okay, Anka. No matter what happens, you have witnesses to prove you weren't the murderer." She paused. "But now if only the murder *itself* can be prevented . . ."

"It's us," Caylin called as she pounded on the closet door.

Theresa let Caylin and Jo in and turned her attention to adjusting a net around Anka's tight bun. Theresa smoothed back the last few stray, matted strands of hair, and Anka was ready to roll.

"I say our only chance is to grab Fake Anka the next time she leaves the stage and replace her with the real Anka," Caylin said quickly. "Anka, will she leave the stage before intermission?"

Anka strained to hear what music was currently playing. "One more time, in about four minutes," she replied. "She'll exit for about ten seconds, stage left."

"We'll be there," Jo vowed.

"That is, if she doesn't shoot Karkovic within the next four minutes," Theresa said gravely. "Let's go."

The Spy Girls formed a human circle around the ballerina.

"Stay back, Anka. No one can see you yet!" Caylin insisted.

They inched their way toward stage left, praying they weren't too late.

The lights dimmed seconds later.

"Oh no!" Theresa gasped.

The girls collectively held their breath as they listened for a shot, but none came.

"It's just the end of the scene," Anka whispered as they reached a darkened, secluded corner at stage left—their final destination. "She should be coming offstage in a few seconds."

The resounding music started up again.

"Here she comes!" Caylin said.

The impostor danced toward them, oblivious . . .

Theresa placed her hands on Anka's shoulders. "Break a leg!" she whispered.

Both Ankas' eyes widened as they faced each other for a split second. But before Fake Anka could shriek, scream, or freak, Caylin tackled her to the ground while Jo gagged her with her black silk wrap.

The real Anka entered seamlessly into the scene without so much as missing a beat. A real trouper, she was.

"Do you want to be tied up or down?" Jo asked Fake Anka, who was kicking and struggling under Caylin's grip, her eyes glittering with fury. Jo crouched next to the impostor and offered her a satisfied smile.

As she bound Fake Anka's hands Theresa noticed that the dancer seemed to be frantically struggling to lunge to the left. Theresa scanned the area—the exit, the curtains, the table. . . .

The table!

A black box had been placed on top of the table. Theresa had used that table hundreds of times; she'd never seen that box before.

"What's that?" Theresa asked sharply. "It looks like a shoe box. What's in it?"

Fake Anka growled.

"Check out that box, Cay," Jo called as she secured Fake Anka's kicking feet. "Whatever's in it, Fake Anka here wants it pretty bad."

"It's probably her gun," Caylin said as she snatched

up the innocent-looking box and peeked inside. She did a double take. The box wasn't holding a gun at all.

It was holding a timer.

A *ticking* timer.

"Uh, guys?" Caylin called out.

"What?" Jo and Theresa asked in stereo.

"Does either of you know how to defuse a bomb?"

"What?"

Caylin held the box upright so Jo and Theresa could see the timer counting down from 3:34. "Looks like there's been a change of plans."

"Ohmigosh!" Theresa exclaimed, petrified. Jo just stared at it in horrified silence, saying everything by saying nothing at all.

"Talk to us!" Caylin cried, staring into Fake Anka's spiteful eyes. "I don't get it. It was *supposed* to be a *gun*."

"Maybe it wasn't," Theresa said. "We never knew for sure. Maybe it was meant to happen this way all along."

A few feet away the ballet continued. The music crescendoed as the stakes both on- and offstage grew higher and higher.

The timer hit 3:00.

"There's no time," Caylin said. "We need to disarm this thing *now*." Theresa searched in her purse. "I need something to work with!"

Jo produced a pair of tweezers. "Try these. They're great on eyebrows."

"Ungag her," Theresa demanded. "I need her to help."

2:47.

Jo yanked the scarf from Fake Anka's mouth.

"You better tell me how to disarm this," Theresa commanded, "or we're all dead meat."

"No, not us," Fake Anka taunted them the second she was ungagged. "Just Karkovic."

2:36.

"But I have the bomb in my hands," Theresa said, confused.

"You have the timer," Fake Anka explained. "The bomb is in the wine cellar. Where von Strauss is taking Karkovic right this minute."

"What about Karkovic's bodyguards?" Theresa asked. "Won't they—"

Fake Anka shook her head. "The bodyguards know all about this secret little meeting. And they don't suspect a thing."

Without a word Caylin hefted Ewan's gun and the magic key chain and took off running.

"Be careful!" Jo called.

"Why put a bomb in the cellar?" Theresa asked, indignant. "You would have killed Karkovic and Anka, too. You'd have no one to take the rap."

"Von Strauss was going to bring her up after he took Karkovic down," Fake Anka spat. "You did half our work for us. I should thank you."

"Don't bother," Theresa snapped. "Now tell me how to disarm this thing."

"Why bother?" Fake Anka asked flippantly. "We'll be okay. Who cares?"

"I think *you* will," Jo angrily chimed in. "Your boyfriend's down there, too."

"I don't believe you," Fake Anka said. She stared at Jo uncertainly.

Jo glanced at the timer as it passed the two-minute mark. She reached into her purse and held up Ewan's Lamborghini-logo key chain. "I believe this is the key I used to lock him in. Do you recognize it?"

"You're lying," Fake Anka snarled, eyes darting from Jo to Theresa and back.

"You know you love him," Theresa said. "Do you want him dead?"

"Why should I believe you?" Fake Anka screeched. "Why should I?"

Jo looked deep into her eyes. "Because if you don't, your boyfriend'll be dead and *you'll* be the only one to blame."

As Caylin dashed through the rows of wine she caught a glimpse of von Strauss racing toward the exit. Behind him she could hear Karkovic screaming and pounding on the cellar door.

She gripped Ewan's gun . . . but wasn't sure if she could use it.

She had a better idea.

She stuck out a foot and caught von Strauss as he sprinted by. The big man sprawled headlong onto the concrete floor with a cry of rage. Caylin smoothly stepped out of the shadows and tossed the Tower key ring at him. He caught it and stared in confusion.

"What are you doing?" von Strauss demanded.

"Saving the world from evil," she said, snapping her fingers.

"Wha-what?" he cried as the shock disabled him and he writhed on the floor in pain.

Caylin immediately scrambled to unlock the crawl space door and set Karkovic free. But she didn't have a key. . . .

Von Strauss did!

Quickly she patted his tuxedo pockets. Left. Right There!

She snatched his key chain from his prone form and frantically searched for the right one. "Go, go, go," she chanted. Her hands were shaking.

The fifth key worked. She hauled the door open and

saw Karkovic crouched next to the bound and gagged Ewan.

"Come on, sir," Caylin ordered, waving Karkovic out. "We have to get you out of here!"

:19

"Red or black, Anka?" Theresa pleaded, tweezers poised. "Red or black?"

The music escalated to a deafening level.

:16

Jo: "Tell me, Anka."

:13

Theresa: "Ewan's going to die."

:12

Jo: "You're a murderer."

:11

Theresa: "Red or black?"

:10

Jo: "You love him—you know you do."

:09

Theresa: "Just say it, *red or black*."

With eight seconds left on the clock tears of frustration welled in Fake Anka's eyes. A single tear rolled down her cheek.

"Red," she whispered.

Praying she wasn't bluffing, Theresa closed her eyes and gripped the red wire with the tweezers.

"Do it," Jo said.

Theresa clipped the red wire. The timer's LCD display faded to black.

While Fake Anka broke into sobs, Jo and Theresa hugged each other tightly.

"You did it," Jo whispered, squeezing her hard.

"No," Theresa said, pulling back to look into Jo's fake baby blues. "*We* did it!"

FIFTEEN

"As soon as I get von Strauss processed you're both going with me," Interpol Agent Johnson told Fake Anka and Ewan as he cuffed them to separate poles in a dark backstage corner. "In the meantime, Spy Girls, they're all yours. Off the record of course."

"Of course," Theresa repeated, smiling smugly. There were a lot of loose ends to tie up, and this was their big chance to get some answers.

"I cannot believe you two—two—women are the ones I was having followed," Fake Anka said, her English failing in her fury. She glared at Jo and Theresa.

Theresa glared right back. "How'd you even know to have us trailed in the first place?"

"The computer—you were fools," Fake Anka snarled. "After you break into my dressing room—you did not leave—log off—Internet," she said. "Dumb mistake. That is how I knew someone has been snooping around."

"Then she told me," Ewan said, "so I hired a private investigator."

"The big guy who followed me and left me that postcard, right?" Theresa asked.

"Yes," Fake Anka spat. "He saw you talking to the blond one, too." She motioned to Caylin. "She was first to come in today, so Ewan took her hostage. I was glad. I've always hated blonds."

Caylin narrowed her blue eyes. "You don't impress me all that much, either, thanks."

"And I guess this same investigator must have spilled the beans to you about my little gallery date with your pig boyfriend, hmmm?" Jo asked.

Fake Anka glared at Jo. Then at Ewan. Then at the floor.

"What I want to know is," Caylin asked, "why did you come up with this elaborate plan with the bomb in the cellar? Couldn't you have just shot Karkovic from the stage?"

Caylin received bizarre looks from all directions.

She cleared her throat. "Well, I didn't mean that would have been a good thing, but—"

"I wanted to shoot Karkovic," Fake Anka said. "I'm a good shot. My uncle, he teach me. I *told* Ewan, but he wouldn't listen." She jerked her head in Ewan's direction. "He said we can put Anka's fingerprints on the box and frame her in an easier way. Less people hurt, but she would still go to jail and die."

While Fake Anka described this setup, the real Anka approached. The ballet had ended to a standing ovation, and she still wore her stage costume. "But why would you get plastic surgery and pretend to be someone you're not to frame someone you don't even know?" she asked incredulously. "Did you do it for Ewan?"

"Of course not," Fake Anka said scornfully, glaring right back into the real Anka's eyes. She drew herself up and threw back her shoulders. "I'm Anna Poritzkova. You beat me out for my rightful place in the New Russian Ballet four years ago, and I swore I'd get revenge." She smiled bitterly. "I almost did. And I got to dance."

Anka's jaw dropped. The Spy Girls looked at one another in disbelief.

"Sorry to interrupt here," Interpol Agent Johnson said, "but I need to ask Ms. Perdova a few questions."

As he pulled her away Caylin noticed that Anka didn't once take her eyes off Fake—er, *Anna Poritzkova*.

"And it's curtain call for these two as well," Interpol Agent Zimmerman said, uncuffing Ewan and Fake Anka from the pole and commanding them to stand with von Strauss.

"Thanks for the memories!" Jo cheered. She winked at Ewan as he was led away.

"I'll get all of you for this," von Strauss threatened. "You just wait."

"Yeah, you would've gotten away with it, too," Caylin said in mock fear. "If it wasn't for us meddling gals."

Jo smiled sweetly and hollered for Agent Johnson to hold up. "Mr. von Strauss's going-away comment reminded me: You might want to check into InterCorp's secret tax files, too," she said. "They're hidden in the third-floor supply closet."

Von Strauss's face reddened with rage. "Why, you little—"

The Spy Girls were still laughing over von Strauss's expression when Ottla approached and introduced the president of the Czech Republic.

"I'd like to thank you for all your hard work," he said, shaking each of their hands. "You have done our country a great service."

The Spy Girls couldn't help but smile at one another.

"Cool," Theresa whispered.

"Thank you again," he proclaimed. "I just don't know what to say."

The Czech leader then turned to Karkovic. "Sir, would you like us to postpone the signing in light of everything that has happened?"

Karkovic smiled and shook his head. "Everything that happened is the biggest reason of all to go through with it," he replied. "We cannot let evil triumph over the goodness of humanity. I want to finish what I have started. After all," he concluded, "that's what freedom is all about."

• • •

"I can't believe I'm actually bummed to be leaving some-where so cold," Jo exclaimed over her suitcase back at 3-S. She'd grown to appreciate Prague and its quiet charm. She really was going to miss it.

"I know what you mean," Caylin said as she folded a sweater and placed it in her suitcase. "While I'm psyched to go home, a part of me wants to stay."

"Me three," Theresa agreed with a sad smile.

At that moment the door buzzer sounded—two short, two long.

"The secret buzz!" Jo said, rushing to the door to get it. "Hope it's the same delivery dude from last time!" She smoothed her hair before she opened the door.

"Special delivery for Caylin, Jo, and Theresa," a dark-haired woman announced. She handed Jo a folded paper bag before turning on her heels.

"What could this be?" Jo wondered. She set the bag down on the dining room table so they could open it together.

"Three cappuccinos to go!" Caylin announced. She

removed a trio of steaming cups from the bag.

"And that rare Nirvana CD!" Theresa squealed. She yanked the disc out so fast, she ripped the bag. "Now, who knew I was a total Kurt Cobain freak?"

"Looks like you're about to find out," Jo said, reaching for the folded note that had flopped out onto the table. "'Next stop: the birthplace of grunge,'" Jo recited, "'where you'll crack the code of the century—Uncle Sam.'"

"Huh?" Caylin muttered, utterly confused.

"Seattle!" Jo cheered, totally pumped.

"The coolest city in the universe!" Theresa chimed in.

Theresa passed coffees to Jo and Caylin and took one for herself.

"Lids off," Jo commanded, a twinkle in her eye.

They all removed their coffee cup lids.

"To our next taste of adventure," Theresa toasted.

Caylin smiled. "Ready, set, sip!"

And they did.

NOBODY DOES IT BETTER

To Dan and Jessica — congratulations

Josefina Mercedes Carreras—called "Jo" by anyone who wanted to continue life unhampered by a swift kick in the butt—strode down the tarmac of the Seattle-Tacoma airport Sunday night. The 747 express from the Czech Republic to New York had been a nightmare. The flight attendant had run out of snacks, Jo's book had been about as interesting as one of those complimentary airline cata-logs, and the two movies shown had been *Return of the Beach Nuts* and *My Invisible Stepmom*. Gag! Unfortunately the second leg of the journey—a direct flight from New York to Seattle—had been only marginally better. There had been snacks aplenty.

"Can anyone say, 'java'?" Jo asked as she gazed around the nearly empty airport in search of a coffee bar. "I think I feel a major case of jet lag coming on."

Caylin Pike set down her Louis Vuitton suitcase and tucked an errant strand of blond hair back under the black cowboy hat she was wearing. "Maybe we'll have an espresso machine at home base," she mused. "We *are* in the coffee capital of the world."

"Can we discuss decafs, cafs, and lattes later?" Theresa Hearth asked, peering over the large mirrored sunglasses she had put on before deplaning. "If I don't get into a shower and wash off this airplane grime pronto, I'm going to be labeled toxic by the U.S. government."

Jo nodded. Theresa was right, as usual. Now that she and her compatriots had landed in Seattle, downtime was *finito*. Uncle Sam would want them to get to headquarters, figure out their latest mission, and study any pertinent information—all before taking a moment for even a quick bathroom break.

And when Uncle Sam spoke, the girls listened. He was *el jefe más grande* at The Tower—plus he was their own private fearless leader, the man who had brought the trio together. Uncle Sam had guided the Spy Girls through their previous two missions, always offering words of encouragement. Ever mysterious—the guy's face seemed to be permanently obscured by smoke and mirrors—Uncle Sam held the girls' lives in his hands, usually via satellite. But Jo had mastered the difficult art of letting someone else call the shots. As a Tower agent she had learned that such sacrifices were often necessary. Ergo, she'd have to put her craving for a café mocha on pause.

"Duty calls," Theresa agreed. "Let's just hope this mish is calmer than the *last* one."

"I'll second that emotion," Jo said. "I've encountered enough Eastern European terrorists to satisfy my excitement quotient for a lifetime."

"Not I," Caylin declared. "Nothing is more appealing to me than kicking a bad guy from here to you-know-where."

"We know, Cay," Theresa drawled as Jo reached over and tugged on the brim of Caylin's cowboy hat.

Sometimes it was hard to believe that Jo, Caylin, and Theresa had known one another for only a few months. Sure, Jo had expected to make new friends when she'd been accepted to what she had *thought* was an elite East Coast college. Ha! College had turned out to be a top secret spy academy for which all three young women had been handpicked by the United States government. Jo, Caylin, and Theresa had been put through the most intense weeks of their teenage lives as they learned to work together to triumph over whatever evil of the week was threatening international security. Now they were like sisters . . . no, they were closer than sisters. The girls were practically conjoined triplets.

Smiling, Jo continued toward the baggage claim area. Uncle Sam had said they would find three limos waiting to whisk them individually to their local headquarters. At the relatively tender age of eighteen, Jo couldn't believe she had already become accustomed to limousines, disguises, and high-tech gadgetry. James Bond had nothing on Jo Carreras. Or Caylin Pike. Or Theresa Hearth. The Spy Girls.

"Does my scarf look okay?" Theresa asked. "I feel like I've got an *I Dream of Jeannie* thing goin' on."

Jo glanced at the hot pink scarf draped over half of Theresa's face and raised her eyebrows. "You do look a bit funky—but hey, this is Seattle. Anything goes."

Jo flipped her own scarf—long, black, gauzy, *très* cool—around the bottom half of her face. In her humble opinion the scarves were a bit over the top. But Uncle Sam had insisted the girls use at least minimal disguises and split up *pronto* when they hit the States. Apparently grunge locals couldn't be trusted.

The trio stopped in front of the double automatic doors under a ground transportation sign. Theresa skimmed the small note card that copilot George Watson had handed her as she stepped off the plane. "I get the white limo," she read. "Caylin is in the gray, and Jo has black to go with her scarf."

"Blah, blah, blah, rules and regulations," Caylin moaned.

"What?" Theresa asked. She was tearing the note card into mote-size pieces.

Jo grinned. "Are you suggesting we break ranks?" she asked Caylin.

Caylin smiled back. "We could all use a little fun after that dismal plane ride . . . and what harm could a limo switcheroo *really* do?"

"None at all," Jo declared. In lieu of a caffeine jolt she

would have to settle for some old-fashioned Spy Girl fun.

As one, Uncle Sam's angels stepped forward. The electronic doors whooshed open and Jo breathed in the cool, damp northwestern air. At the side of the curb stood three limo drivers. Man in Gray. Man in White. Man in Black. How cute.

Jo didn't hesitate. She walked straight toward Mr. Gray—light brown hair, great build, hundred-megawatt smile. What more could she ask for when the rubber hit the road?

"Why am I not surprised?" Caylin mused aloud as she headed toward Mr. White, who, Jo noticed, looked about as friendly as a python.

"Ta-ta!" Jo shouted. She brushed past the very hunky Mr. Gray and slipped into the plush backseat of the limo.

"Keep all hands and feet inside the vehicle!" Theresa called as she climbed into the black stretch ride parked at the head of the line.

Jo settled against the soft leather seat and closed her eyes. She half expected a laser light show to begin, the doors to lock, and Uncle Sam's shadowed face to appear on some kind of hidden TV screen. But there was only silence. Aha! The mission wasn't so pressing that The Tower felt the immediate dispatch of instructions was required. Good. With a bit of luck and a lot of Spy Girl style, this mission would proceed as smoothly as it had begun.

Of course, until the girls received detailed instructions from The Tower, they wouldn't know what they were facing. Jo knew that Theresa, girl-hacker extraordinaire, was hoping the mission would be computer based. Boring! Jo concluded. She prayed for some kicks before she started drowning in bytes and hard drives.

A few minutes later Jo leaned forward and glanced at the chauffeur's license attached to the driver's-side visor. "So where are we going . . . Travis O'Rourke?" she asked, inserting her patented don't-you-want-to-look-at-a-beautiful-girl-in-the-rearview-mirror-when-she's-talking-to-you lilt. Gazing out of the smoky glass window, she saw that they were speeding up a seaside highway, the Pacific Ocean so close that she could almost feel its cold, salty water.

"To 902 Stratford Road," Travis answered, pointing eastward. "We've still got a ways to go."

Good, cute-boy, Jo answered silently. Now she'd have even more time to entice him with her Spy Girl wiles. Yes, this was going to be a very pleasant journey—and one that would hopefully result in a date for dinner and a movie. Jo was in the mood for romance. . . .

"So where's a good place to—" Jo stopped speaking midsentence. One of her Spy Girl sensors had just been sounded.

Yep. There it was again. A distinct squealing of tires.

Jo pressed the button of the power window, waiting impatiently for the smoked glass to disappear into the door frame. Faster. Come on. Faster. At last the window was down. Jo poked her head out of the limo window. "What the . . . ?"

The white limo carrying Caylin was no longer heading east. The chauffeur had driven across the highway partition and was now racing west, toward the ocean.

This was bad. Jo had to follow. Fast.

"Turn the limo around and follow that car!" Jo screamed at Travis. "Step on it!"

Travis glanced at her in the rearview mirror. "I'm sorry, miss, but I can't do that. My boss would fire me if I didn't follow orders."

Aahhh. There was nothing more annoying than a man who was cowed by authority. Luckily Jo didn't have that problem at the moment. Which meant she needed a plan B. In two seconds Jo processed the situation and settled on a plan of action.

She unzipped the oversize bag she had carried on the airplane and groped through the contents until she found what she was looking for. Aha! There it was. The small, travel-size hair dryer she had laid down plastic for at the duty-free shop in the Czech Republic.

Sorry, Trav. Nothing personal.

She stuck the nozzle of the hair dryer against the back of the driver's head, grateful that he hadn't raised the privacy shield. "Pull over the limo and get out," she ordered. "I'm taking the wheel."

"What?" Travis's voice was high and thin.

"Pull over and get out. I'm driving." She nudged his head with the hair dryer. "Unless you want me to do something we'll both regret."

With a little more than a squeak, Travis slammed on the brakes. He had opened the door and tumbled out before the limo came to a complete stop.

Jo didn't waste any time. She climbed over the barrier between her and the front of the vehicle and slid into the driver's seat.

"I'm on my way, Cay!" Jo pressed the pedal to the metal and the limo surged forward. She would overtake Theresa's limo, grab herself some Spy Girl backup, and pursue.

The adventure had begun.

Scream? Cry? Laugh hysterically and assume she was on *Candid Camera*? Caylin couldn't decide on the appropriate response to the fact that her limo driver had just swung wildly off course.

Okay. Deep breath. Instinct told her to stay calm. Panicking would only make things—whatever *things* were—worse.

"Excuse me?" Caylin tapped semipolitely on the window that separated herself from the driver. "Where are we going?" Even if her driver couldn't hear her voice, Caylin was sure that he would notice that she was knocking on the glass.

The window lowered a couple of inches. "You probably want to know where we're going, huh?"

Caylin relaxed. The guy's voice was warm and friendly. "Yes . . . I mean, a second ago we were driving in the opposite direction."

The driver glanced at Caylin in the rearview mirror. Uh-oh. His eyes told a different story. They were dark, hard, and mean. "You'll see *exactly* where we're headed soon enough, compu-queen," he responded.

Yikes. This was trouble. Big trouble. Mr. Driver obviously thought that Caylin was Theresa. Anyone who knew anything about the Spy Girls knew that Theresa was Master of All Hackers. Or more accurately, Mistress of All Hackers. Which meant that the guy did, in fact, know something about the Spy Girls. And he knew that Theresa had been originally assigned to the white limo.

Oh, man. Something was seriously awry. Caylin had to get out of this particular moving vehicle ASAP.

She dove for the door handle.

Click. Click.

Caylin's heart sank even farther into her toes as she recognized the sound of power locks. A moment later the privacy screen closed again. She was trapped!

"Great. Perfect. Wonderful. Splendiferous way to begin my stay in the great Northwest . . . ," Caylin mumbled to herself. She scooted to the back of the limo and pressed her face against the rear windshield.

In the distance there were headlights. Could it be . . . ?

"Please. Please, let those beacons in the night belong to Jo or T.," Caylin whispered. Seconds later the headlights were closer. And then closer.

Caylin squinted. Yes! Jo was behind the wheel . . . and Theresa was by her side! And they were in hot pursuit of the white limousine. Things were definitely looking up. Jo and Theresa would save her.

Caylin shimmied back toward the driver's seat, pulled off her cowboy hat, and whipped off the huge Jackie O.-style sunglasses that had hidden most of her face. Disguise seemed pretty useless at this point.

"Hey, driver!" Caylin yelled, banging on the glass. "You are messin' with the wrong *chiquita!*"

He glanced at her again in the rearview mirror, his eyes amused.

"I'm serious!" Caylin yelled. "I've got friends in high places, buddy. And once they catch up with this overpriced hunk of metal, you're gonna be *history!*"

Adrenaline surged through Caylin's veins as she waited for Jo to come to the rescue. Stay focused, Pike, Caylin ordered herself. She had to think like a super-duper Spy Girl.

Description. She would need to give Uncle Sam a description of this guy.

Caylin leaned forward to get a better look at the driver. Black hair, dark eyes, major five o'clock shadow. He was attractive, but in a kind of ice-cold Ted Bundy serial killer way. Unfortunately the driver was cackling to himself, unconcerned by Caylin's warning of the fate that awaited him when her fellow SGs got ahold of him.

Caylin's eyes widened in horror as Captain Ice gripped the steering wheel and yanked it to the left. She noticed three things instantly.

One: The car was now hurtling down a very long wooden pier.

Two: There was a small tattoo of a rosebud on the back of Ice's neck.

Three: The limo was *still* hurtling down what was becoming a shorter and shorter pier.

Now, Jo. Now, T. I need you guys *now*, Caylin silently begged. She squeezed her eyes shut, repeating the mantra over and over. If they didn't hurry up *ahora*, they weren't going to be able to teach Rosebud a lesson in re: absconding with young maidens. Instead Caylin would be taking a long swim in some very cold water.

Seventy. Eighty. Ninety. Jo had watched the speedometer climb higher and higher as she struggled to overtake the white limo in front of her.

Picking up Theresa had been a cinch compared to this. Theresa's limo driver had been all too happy to relinquish his last passenger of the evening. If he had wondered about Jo's sudden appearance behind the wheel, he had kept it to himself.

Now Jo slammed on the brakes. The car fishtailed as she took a sharp left onto the pier.

"Careful!" Theresa cautioned, gripping the dashboard with both hands.

Jo forced herself to ignore the murky black water that lay on either side of the pier. One wrong move, one ill-advised tap on the steering wheel, and they'd both be shark bait.

Her eyes glued to the wooden slats of the pier, Jo pursued the white limousine. And then it stopped.

Jo screamed and stomped on the brake pedal. The gray limo screeched to a halt amid a terrifying squeal of tires.

"Omigosh!" Jo flung off her seat belt with a quick, practiced flick of the wrist. She threw the vehicle into park and opened the driver's-side door. A second later she was sprinting toward the white limousine—the back of which seemed to be bobbing up and down, resembling one end of a gigantic teeter-totter.

"Man. Oh, man. Oh, man." Jo tried not to go into full panic mode as she realized that the front half of the white limo was hanging off the pier. Jo reached the side of the white car and tugged on the left rear passenger door handle. Nothing. The automatic door locks were malfunctioning. Caylin was trapped inside.

Caylin yelled and kicked at the windows. Unfortunately the soft sole of Caylin's espadrille was no match for thick, bulletproof glass. Jo was also aware that the driver was also trying to force his way out of the car. She put his cries out of her mind and zeroed in on Caylin's frightened face. She had to help her friend. Immediately, if not sooner.

"What do we do?" Theresa yelled.

"I don't know," Jo responded. "Got any ideas?"

"We need a torch," Theresa stated. "We've got to get the glass to give way."

Jo didn't need to be told twice. She ran back to the gray limo and pulled a can of aerosol hair spray from her oversize canvas carry-on bag. She raced to Theresa's side and popped the top.

As Jo pressed the button on the top of the can, Theresa lit match after match from a pack the Spy Girls had picked up during their last dinner out in Prague. "Insta-torch!" Jo shouted, aiming the line of fire straight onto the back passenger-side window. Finally the heat of the makeshift torch caused the glass to crack.

Caylin kicked out the window and poked her head into the fresh air. "Heeelp!" she yelled.

Jo and Theresa dropped their tools and grabbed Caylin's arms. Seconds later she was free. The three girls stood on the pier, staring at one another for a long moment.

"What about . . . ?" Theresa pointed at the limousine.

"Yikes," Jo whispered.

Caylin's exit from the vehicle had caused the weight of the limousine to shift. The rear end of the long vehicle was inching upward to an impossible angle.

Theresa gasped. "It's going . . ."

"Straight into the ocean," Caylin finished.

As the girls stared in disbelief the elegant white car

slid off the pier and into the Pacific Ocean.

"He's gone," Caylin whispered as the rear of the limo disappeared into the black water.

Jo stared at the expanse of ocean. There was nothing but waves. The evil driver and all of Caylin's bags had just ceased to exist. And there was nothing the Spy Girls could do but shiver in the cold night air and try to be psyched that they were all still alive.

TWO

"What a night," Theresa said, sighing. "So much for the Seattle mish going smooth as butter."

"I almost died tonight," Caylin whispered for about the hundredth time in the last forty-five minutes.

In the backseat of the gray limo Theresa put her arm around Caylin's shoulders and squeezed. "We wouldn't have let that happen, Caylin."

"Yeah," Jo called from the front seat. "You're our only blonde. We need you."

Caylin giggled. "I'm surprised my hair didn't just turn white. I've never been so petrified in my life."

"Here we are," Jo said, pulling the car up to the curb of a very dark street. "This is 902 Stratford Road. Just as my pal Travis told me."

"Our home away from home," Theresa said. "Or in this

case, our headquarters away from headquarters."

Theresa peered out the limousine window to get a look at their latest digs. Huh. The shuttered storefront wasn't exactly as promising as the circle drive of the Ritz Hotel in London had been. Valet parking was out of the question.

The girls piled out of the limo. Theresa and Jo grabbed their bags and suitcases while Caylin shuddered, luggage-less, on the curb.

"You can borrow my clothes until you get new stuff," Theresa assured Caylin as Jo slid their Tower-issued key into the dead bolt lock at 902 Stratford Road.

Caylin stuck out her tongue. "Gee, how thrilling. I've always wanted to spend my days wearing a succession of outfits consisting of khakis and white button-down shirts."

Theresa snorted. "You're exaggerating." Caylin and Jo always teased Theresa mercilessly about the fact that she was fashion challenged—especially because Theresa's mom was a famous designer.

Jo opened the storefront door, and the girls walked in.

"Wow," Caylin said. "I guess this is what real estate agents refer to as a fixer-upper."

Theresa nodded. The room was dark, with high ceilings and a cold cement floor. Dusty tarps covered everything. There wasn't a thick fluffy carpet or velvet-upholstered settee in sight. "Well, at least we're safe," she allowed.

"I guess we all know what we have to do," Jo said, locking the door behind them.

"Call Uncle Sam," Theresa and Caylin chorused.

"And looky there . . . a speakerphone." Jo headed for the phone that was placed conspicuously on top of one of the larger pieces of tarp.

"They might not give us gold bathtubs or bidets," Theresa observed. "But you can always count on the good ol' Tower to provide a form of immediate communication."

"I guess we're going to have to tell Uncle Sam about the limousine switcheroo." Jo groaned. "But I don't think he's going to appreciate our fun and games."

"I'll make the dreaded call," Caylin offered. "Considering you guys saved my life tonight, it's the least I can do."

"Payment enough for me," Jo said, backing away from the telephone.

Caylin punched in Uncle Sam's top secret direct number.

They all looked at one another expectantly as the phone's ring blared out of the speakerphone.

"Girls?" Uncle Sam questioned the moment he picked up. "You're late."

"No shinola," Jo whispered, nudging Theresa.

"We, uh, had a little problem," Caylin answered. "It's really kind of funny . . . well, maybe *funny* isn't the right word. Um . . . one of the limo drivers might be dead."

Theresa nervously clenched and unclenched her fists. There was no point in beating around the proverbial bush. On the other end of the line Uncle Sam sighed deeply. As always, Theresa tried to discern something about the identity of their mysterious boss by listening to the sound of his voice. But all she could envision were shadows and fog.

"You better start from the beginning," Uncle Sam said. "And don't leave out any of the gory details."

Theresa and Jo gave Caylin encouraging pats on the back as she related the events of the past hour and a half to Uncle Sam. His silence throughout spoke volumes.

"And then we drove here," Caylin finished. "Minus my bags . . . and one driver."

For a long moment Uncle Sam didn't say anything. "Jo, get rid of the gray limo, and I mean *yesterday*," he said finally, speaking rapid-fire. "Wipe away all fingerprints and *any* trace that you were ever inside the vehicle."

"Check," Jo responded.

"Theresa and Caylin, prepare headquarters. I want you all ready to work first thing tomorrow morning." He paused. "If local law enforcement gets a sniff of tonight's events, we could have big, big trouble."

"Check," Theresa answered.

"And I need a description of the driver," Uncle Sam demanded. "I'll run a check on him and see if we can piece together an ID."

Caylin's face seemed to pale in the dim light as she recounted what details she could about the man who had tried to take her for a long drive off a short pier. "And he had a tattoo of a rosebud on the back of his neck," she concluded. "A small red rosebud." She shuddered. "Uh, sorry about the mishap," Caylin said. "We didn't mean to dump the limo driver into the ocean—honest."

"Let's just hope that the mission proves easy enough

to get you out of town before the you-know-what hits the fan," Uncle Sam answered darkly. "Cleaning up this mess is going to take all of my resources. I'll have to go to the highest levels of authority. I don't think you want to know just *how* high."

"Is that all, boss?" Jo asked. "I want to get to that limo before the sun rises."

"That's all—for now," he responded. "I'll give out the details of your mission when Jo returns."

"Over and out," Caylin said, pushing the off button on the speakerphone. She turned to Theresa and Jo.

Well. So much for getting to bed early. They were going to be up half the night just cleaning up their mistakes, not to mention preparing for the start of their mission.

"Ladies, assume your positions," Jo said. "I think we're in for a long haul."

"The word *oops* seems insufficient at this particular juncture," Caylin remarked. "We screwed up big time."

"We'll have to make it up to The Tower by performing our most heroic deeds yet," Theresa said. It was way too early in her career as a girl spy to get a big black X on her permanent record.

"I know this sounds weird, but does anyone else hope that Rosebud is alive?" Caylin asked quietly.

"Yeah," Jo answered. "I mean, sure, the guy tried to kill you and probably would have blown my head off given half a chance . . . but hey, I believe in karma."

"I don't want to kill anyone," Theresa stated simply. "Murder isn't in our job description."

Theresa sighed as she pulled off the tarp closest to her. At this rate the Seattle mission was going to be anything but a snap. As far as she could tell, the Spy Girls were looking at a snap, crackle, pop . . . and fizzle.

"Obliterating any sign that any Spy Girl was a passenger in the gray limousine is a fait accompli," Jo announced upon her return to 902 Stratford Road ninety minutes later. "They haven't invented the piece of high-tech equipment yet that could work its way through the amount of Formula 409 I used on that bad boy of a steering wheel."

Caylin rolled her eyes. "If you're done reveling in your cleaning prowess, Theresa and I have something to show you."

Jo tipped up the brim of her leather poor boy cap. "By all means, O Great Ones."

Caylin tugged at the electric cord she was holding and pushed the plug into the closest outlet. Instantly a bright green neon sign reading Seattle Sounds lit up the small store. "Ta-da!"

Jo whistled softly. Theresa and Caylin had totally transformed the fifteen-hundred-square-foot space during the past hour and a half. "A record store?"

"Correction," Theresa said. "A vintage music store. And an ultrahip one at that. I don't think you're allowed to buy stuff from here unless you have black-rimmed glasses and skinny jeans."

Jo glanced around the shop. There was more than a small chance that litters of hot guys would prowl these aisles in the a.m. The place had serious possibilities. "So where do we sleep?"

"Uh . . . I think we better call Uncle Sam for an answer

to that question," Caylin said. "There's no way I'm going to do the sleeping bag thing tonight."

"It's my turn to reach out and touch someone," Theresa said, stepping toward the speakerphone. "You two have had enough excitement for one grunge night."

Theresa quickly punched in the magic phone number and took a deep breath as she waited for Uncle Sam to answer. "Greetings," she said when she heard the line pick up. "We're ready for our instructions."

"Is it as if that gray limousine never existed at all, Jo?" the boss asked gruffly.

"You've got my word," Jo answered.

"Good." He cleared his throat. "Caylin, there are three electronic passkeys hidden in a Soundgarden CD case. Find them."

Caylin rifled through a row of CDs, picked one out, and pulled out three small, flat keys. She held them up.

"We've got the keys," Theresa informed the boss.

"Enter the door marked Warehouse," Uncle Sam said tersely. There was a click on the other end of the line and then nothing but a dial tone.

"Cloak-and-daggers continue," Jo commented as the girls dutifully filed toward the twelve-foot-tall steel door at the back of Seattle Sounds. She slid her electronic key into a small slit under the door's heavy metal knob. Instantly the door opened.

Caylin's eyebrows shot up. "Whoa. What looked like your basic music store . . ."

". . . is actually a front for a high-tech spy operation," Jo finished.

"What a surprise," Theresa added.

Jo stepped inside the center of operations and looked around. The place would have made even 007 weep. There were several computers, a dozen phones, and a bunch of weird screens and knobs on the walls. The room was a veritable electronic den. Jo stopped when she realized that a large part of the room's east wall was covered with a screen. And on that screen was a familiar shape—Uncle Sam's shadowy silhouette.

"Welcome, girls," Uncle Sam said. "Have a seat."

As always, his husky voice sent a shiver up Jo's spine. Would she ever see his face?

Jo turned off her hormones and plopped down on the long black leather couch in front of the screen. Theresa and Caylin sat down on either side of her.

"Spy Girls, this is your mission," Uncle Sam began. "You must retrieve and remove a volatile computer code from the mainframe at FutureWorks."

"FutureWorks?" Caylin asked. "It sounds like some kind of company that produces computer games or something."

"Hardly," Uncle Sam answered dryly. "FutureWorks is a Fortune 500 corporation that deals with Internet security."

"Web watchdogs," Theresa explained, looking from Jo to Caylin.

"They're *supposed* to be watchdogs," Uncle Sam concurred. "But in the last two weeks thousands of Internet users have had their credit card numbers stolen—all of whom had made purchases over the Internet using sites patrolled by none other than FutureWorks."

"The plot thickens," Caylin voiced. "But why is this a job for us? I mean, any local outfit could set up some kind of sting to catch whoever is responsible for the thefts."

"Yeah, credit card fraud doesn't seem like a big deal compared to our other missions," Jo observed. She wanted to use her skills and training to save lives, thwart world domination plots, and do her part to clean up the environment. A few stolen credit card numbers didn't exactly spell "global jeopardy."

"Trust me, retrieving this code is a matter of international concern," Uncle Sam said darkly. "Each time the thief—or thieves—steals and encodes another number, the code grows stronger. In a matter of just days every major bank in the world could be rendered powerless . . . and penniless."

Theresa whistled. "The global economy would be shot to you-know-where."

"Governments would collapse and chaos would reign," Uncle Sam corrected her.

"Consider our skepticism retracted," Caylin remarked. "This is the big time."

"So you're ready to hear how I want you to proceed?" Uncle Sam asked, his voice mildly patronizing.

Jo leaned forward. "Tell us everything," she said. The

rest of this mission was going to go off without another hitch if she had anything to do with it. One hijacked limousine and a possibly dead bad guy were all the impetus she needed to put her heart and soul into this mission from here on out. "We're ready to work."

Half an hour later Theresa's eyes were drooping shut as the girls signed off. But she couldn't think about bedtime yet. It was imperative that the girls go over Uncle Sam's instructions at least one more time before they went to sleep. No one wanted to risk making another mistake.

Theresa stifled a yawn as she headed up the narrow spiral staircase that led to their living quarters. "My alias is Tessa Somerset and I'm a new HTML operator for FutureWorks," she reminded herself aloud. "Tessa Somerset."

Jo followed up close behind, her feet clanging on the metal stairs. "And I'm Julia Martin, espresso maker extraordinaire."

"And I, dear friends, will be known as Courtney Hall, proprietress of Seattle Sounds, for the duration of our stay in the Northwest," Caylin called from the floor.

Theresa had to admit to herself that she felt just a teeny, tiny bit envious of Jo and Caylin. While she toiled away in some corporate cubicle, her friends would be chatting it up with local hipsters. Of course, the assignments made sense.

Mega Mocha, the café where Jo would be pouring coffee for foxy guys, was just a couple of blocks away from FutureWorks. There was no doubt that Jo—an expert in, uh, human relations—would be able to eke out pertinent information from FutureWorks employees who stopped by for a caffeine boost. And Caylin would do a great job of keeping the HQ vigil at Seattle Sounds.

"This mission would be a complete bust without you," Jo said, breaking into Theresa's thoughts.

Theresa nodded. Jo was right; Theresa—aka Tessa—was the only Spy Girl with the skills to retrieve the all-important code. Socializing could wait. Theresa had to save the world from financial catastrophe. She brushed away a mental image of the globe collapsing in on itself as she reached the top of the stairs. She opened a plain wooden door.

"Hey, nice crib," Jo said over her shoulder. If we didn't have to do our spy thang, we could throw a great bash in here."

"Do you think there's a Jacuzzi in the bathtub?" Theresa wondered, walking into the apartment. She was still dreaming of hot water and a fresh bar of soap.

Caylin followed Jo and Theresa into the large living room. "I just hope The Tower provided us with new wardrobes. I'm fresh out of designer duds, as you know."

"Let's investigate," Jo suggested. "Then we'll reconvene for the breakdown."

"Good plan," Theresa agreed.

By midnight the girls had deposited their belongings into the three bedrooms, brushed their teeth, and ground some decaf vanilla hazelnut beans for a pot of genuine Seattle coffee.

Caylin lounged on a short red velvet couch and sipped at an oversize mug of hot coffee. Jo perched on a white leather chair, and Theresa took a seat on the floor. Each girl wore her best let's-get-down-to-business expression.

"So we've all got to be on the lookout for Rosebud,"

Jo began. "Who knows—maybe the dude is still kickin'."
Uncle Sam had told them that Caylin's driver fit the description of Simon Gilbert, the twenty-year-old tech whiz who The Tower suspected might have created the code.

"And we've got to remember that Rosebud was after Theresa in a major way," Caylin said. "He called me 'compuqueen'—obviously he had our identities confused."

Theresa nodded. "Rosebud must have managed to hack into some of The Tower's computer files. He probably knew they were sending me to mess with his ultradevious plans."

"Totally," Caylin agreed. "Ugh—I can't believe that Rosebud guy could have created the code. I mean, how can a dude that scuzzy-looking be a genius?"

"*Evil* genius," Theresa stressed. "It takes all kinds."

"Yeah, and this Simon Gilbert dude could spell *b-a-d* bad news," Jo said. "He has a hard-core agenda."

Theresa tried to ignore the shiver that traveled down her spine. Simon Gilbert, Rosebud, *whoever* he was had wanted her dead. And if the guy was brilliant enough to create the code, then he was brilliant enough to have made plans to keep her from completing her mission—even if death intervened in the meantime. Sheesh.

Thank goodness The Tower had already installed an agent at FutureWorks. Agent Vince Trudeau—alias Victor Saunders—had been "working" at the corporation for several months. He had been assigned as an ultimate guard, his job to watch the watchdog. Apparently "Victor" had reported to Uncle Sam that he suspected a breach in security several days ago.

According to Uncle Sam, Victor was almost sure that high-level FutureWorks executives were in on the scam to build a code that would give them access to banks all across the world. He was working hard to uncover the corporate plot, but Victor needed a techie to help with the actual code retrieval. Enter Theresa. Victor would so-called hire her tomorrow morning. And then the fun would begin.

"Basically, Jo and I are in Seattle to cover your back," Caylin said to Theresa. "And to make sure you get out of this thing alive."

"Speaking of alive, let's turn on the news and see if a

body was fished out of the Pacific tonight," Jo said with a shudder.

Theresa grabbed the remote control off the top of the art deco coffee table and switched on the TV set. She flipped through three stations, each of which was showing the late-night news. As far as she could tell, the biggest news event of the day revolved around the new coffee shop that was having its grand opening at a fishermen's wharf in the morning.

"So far, so not so bad," Theresa said. "Nothing on Rosebud or a runaway limousine."

"Let's hope it stays that way," Caylin added.

Theresa turned off the television set. Caylin and Jo could hope all they wanted, but Theresa's gut told her that this mission was going to be their trickiest yet.

THREE

"Tessa Somerset, Tessa Somerset," Theresa murmured under her breath as she stood in front of 160 Fleet Street. FutureWorks dominated the entire block, as if the company were an ancient fortress from which soldiers could watch for enemies. Here, Theresa knew, *she* was the enemy.

Mentally sliding into calm, cool, professional Tessa mode, Theresa smoothed her tailored black skirt and tugged at the sleeves of the red Prada jacket she'd found, Tower-supplied and ready to wear, in her closet back at HQ.

Three, two, one.

She walked into the building and headed for the bank of elevators that went to floors twenty-one through thirty. Tessa Somerset, Tessa Somerset. She silently repeated the alias as if it were a mantra as the elevator ascended.

The door opened soundlessly at the thirtieth floor.

Theresa stepped out and found herself face to chest with a tall, elegantly dressed man in his late thirties. She knew immediately she was looking at Vince Trudeau, aka Victor Saunders. He had black hair with streaks of gray and a thin, dark mustache.

"Mr. Saunders, I presume," Theresa greeted him, holding out her hand.

"Wonderful to meet you, Tessa," he answered, giving her a firm handshake. "Welcome to FutureWorks."

And it was done. Theresa was an official employee of an official boss. No one else would know that both she and Victor were actually government spies—at least, not until after the mission was completed and all traces of Victor Saunders and Tessa Somerset were permanently erased by The Tower.

As Victor led Theresa to her cubicle he chatted about innocuous subjects: Seattle's relentless fog, the SuperSonics, the coffee fever that had gripped the city since Starbucks opened years ago. "We'll have lunch today to discuss other matters, yes?" Victor suggested eventually.

Theresa nodded. "Of course."

Satisfied, Victor stopped in front of a large cubicle. "Here is your work space, Ms. Somerset. Again, welcome aboard."

"Thank you, Mr. Saunders," Theresa said to her new boss's already retreating back.

"Vic isn't big on socializing," a deep voice informed Theresa. "He's pretty much a nose-to-the-grindstone type."

She turned away from her desk and gave the speaker a once-over. Cute, definitely cute. The guy—sandy brown hair, hazel eyes, and what looked like an athletic build— was sitting at an adjoining desk in her cubicle. His smile was warm and friendly. A welcome surprise.

"I'm Tessa Somerset," she said, shaking the guy's proffered hand.

He grinned. "Brad Fine, resident computer geek."

"Nice to meet you, Brad," she said. Very nice, she thought. Finally Theresa was getting some hot guy action on the job. It was about time.

She slid into her ergonomically correct office chair and booted up the state-of-the-art computer. There was already a pile of work in her in-box. Hmmm. It looked like her *real* work was going to have to wait a couple of hours.

Thank goodness Theresa could code HTML in her sleep. The job itself was going to be a bit tedious, but hardly a challenge. As long as she didn't go into a coma from boredom, she would have no problem finding time to crack the code. For several minutes Theresa worked in silence. She stopped typing when a message flashed on the screen of her monitor:

How about an early coffee break? I promise to keep
the geek factor at no more than a level five.
Brad

Theresa laughed and turned around. "Sounds great—but from one techie to another, you don't have to worry about being a geek around me."

"You mean I can talk about megabytes and RAM capacity?" he asked, his hazel eyes warm and intense.

"As long as you don't mind my obsession with nodes and VirusScan," she responded.

Brad stood up. "Let's blow this Popsicle stand."

Theresa followed without hesitation. After all, getting to know her colleagues was part of the mission. Who knew what kind of vital information was floating around in Brad's oh-so-fine-looking head? Besides, she actually wanted to have some fun. And a little romance wouldn't be a crime.

By eleven o'clock Monday morning Jo had reassessed the difficulty of her job as an international spy. As far as she could make out, working at a popular coffee shop under a boss who had armpit stains and a permanent caffeine high was much more stressful than chasing down assassins.

Mega Mocha was everything a hip café was supposed to be. Music blasted from speakers. Eighties memorabilia lined the walls. Young people filled the retro sofas and chairs. In a word, the place was *happening*.

"Am I supposed to twist this nozzle or flip that switch to get the foam to come out right?" Jo asked Doris Fain, a redheaded coworker who seemed to empathize with Jo's inability to make a decent latte.

Doris laughed. "Both." She watched Jo struggle with

the nozzle. "Are you sure you've done this before?"

"Sure, I'm sure," Jo said breezily. "But you know how it is . . . no two cappuccino makers are alike!"

Jo turned away from the stainless steel machine and eyed the three guys who had just walked in the door of Mega Mocha. Yum! Maybe hustling coffee had merits Jo hadn't yet considered. She struck her flirt pose—shoulders back, chin up, chest out—and sauntered toward table four.

"Now *this* I know how to do," Jo told Doris over her shoulder.

"Hey, gorgeous," the cutest of the three guys greeted her.

Jo flashed one of her best smiles. *Caray!* This mission would be a total blast—if only she weren't so freaked out about what had happened yesterday. It was hard to enjoy fun and games when she knew there was a distinct possibility that she had helped kill a man.

"I don't know if we have the Train Slashing Monkeys CD," Caylin said to the girl staring insolently at her from across the counter.

The girl snapped her gum. "You suck."

The customer is always right, Caylin reminded herself as she gave the girl a tight-lipped smile. "I'm sorry . . . I'm kind of new at this."

"What about the Mata Hari Misses?" a guy with a pierced nose inquired. "Do you have the sound track they did for *Evil Man*?"

Caylin shrugged. "Uh, check over there." Man, this job was a minefield.

Across the room a display of CDs crashed to the floor. "Uh, sorry." A skinny guy backed away from the pile and slunk toward the exit.

Caylin put her hands over her ears and squeezed her eyes shut. The names of a thousand bands she had never heard of before echoed through her brain. This was a nightmare. She'd only been able to slip back to the warehouse once to check for messages from The Tower, and taking a lunch break seemed pretty much out of the question. Worst of all, Caylin really, *really* had to go to the bathroom.

Aaarrrggghhh!

• • •

Theresa chewed on a piece of romaine lettuce from her Chinese chicken salad and listened to Victor intently. He had been speaking almost nonstop for the last fifteen minutes, filling in Theresa on details about FutureWorks that could prove extremely valuable over the next couple of days.

"So tell me more about the Monkey Room," Theresa said before biting into a piece of tender chicken. Mmm. The out-of-the-way, perfect-for-clandestine-meetings restaurant that the V-man had chosen served awesome food. So far today she'd had a good time with a cute guy and been treated to a delicious lunch. Maybe things were looking up.

Victor leaned back and tapped his fingers together. "Ah, yes, the brain center of FutureWorks—known by the peons as the Monkey Room—is the core of company operations."

Theresa nodded. Brad had told her as much during their forty-five-minute midmorning coffee break. She had guessed from Brad's reverent tone during their discussion that the Monkey Room was the key to the mission.

"So how do I get in there?" Theresa asked.

Victor smiled. "I thought you'd never ask." He leaned forward, glancing over his shoulder to make sure that no one was listening. "Unfortunately it's a delicate situation."

Naturally. Nothing was ever *not* delicate when a mission was hanging in the balance. "Tell me everything."

"Security is tight—very tight. Even I don't have clearance to get into the brain center." Victor pushed away his half-eaten Caesar salad and sighed. "And the place is wired like George Orwell's *1984*. There are cameras everywhere."

Great. Wonderful. Terrific. "I'll find a way inside," Theresa promised him. "I know I can."

Victor smiled. "I'm glad you've got such a good attitude, Ms. Somerset." He paused. "I'm handling the administrative side of this, er, problem—you don't have to concern yourself with any of the higher-ups. But you're the only person who can retrieve the code."

"And I will." Theresa wished she felt half as confident as she sounded.

"Just remember to get the code as quickly as possible," Victor said, lowering his voice almost to a whisper. "And then get *out*." He paused, his face growing grave. "I don't think I need to tell you that you're our only hope."

Theresa shook her head. The weight of the global economy was on her shoulders. From now until the time this mission was over, she had to focus on one thing and one thing only. The code.

Jo had learned more about coffee shops in the last several hours than she had in her entire lifetime. Among other tidbits of information, she had discovered what was commonly known as the midafternoon lull. Ah, yes. That amazing time of day when, apparently, almost no one in the greater Seattle area desired a caffeine jolt. The result of the onset of said lull was that Jo got to sit down for the first time in five hours. A hard, vinyl-covered bar stool had never felt so good.

"Alll III wanna dooo is haave some funnn . . . ," Jo sang along off-key as she mindlessly watched the soap opera on the television set over the bar. As far as she could tell, some very attractive guy was mad because some beautiful girl had been kissing another very attractive guy on a set that was supposed to look like a greenhouse but, in fact, looked more like an overgrown Chia garden.

Suddenly the screen went blank. The image of Very Attractive Guy One's angry face was replaced by a fancy logo reading Special Bulletin.

Jo automatically sat up straighter and concentrated on the plastic-looking anchorman who had just appeared on the air. Could be about anything, Jo reminded herself. Maybe there had been a bank robbery or some kind of natural disaster—a typhoon or an earthquake in southern California. Anything was possible. Without sound there was no point in jumping to alarming conclusions.

Again the picture on the television screen changed. The anchorman's face had been replaced with images— uh-oh—of a white limousine being dragged out of the ocean.

Yikes!

Jo's heart pounded as the footage cut to an interview with none other than Travis O'Rourke, her adorable limo driver. Ouch. As cute as Travis's face was, Jo wasn't thrilled to be seeing it on the small screen.

No, the situation was downright awful, Jo realized a

moment later. There, for everyone to see, was a police sketch of Jo wearing a headdress—a sketch artist's approximation of her black scarf—and a large pair of sunglasses. Her identity wasn't clear, but the disguise wasn't exactly stellar, either.

A Spy Girl conference was in order. Jo was a wanted woman. And she had no idea how long it would take the police to find her and blow The Tower's mission to smithereens.

FOUR

"Holy moly, Julia!" Doris exclaimed, breaking into Jo's frantic thoughts. "That chick looks just like you!"

"Uh . . ." Jo peered at the sketch even more closely. Oh, man. Doris was right. Any idiot could make a connection between the girl in the sketch and Jo. Words, horrible words, flashed on the screen at the bottom of the sketch.

Doris laughed. "According to the police, you're wanted for grand theft auto and first-degree murder." She patted Jo on the back. "Don't worry, hon. If you get life in prison, I'll bring you a fresh bag of hazelnut beans every week."

Prison. Metal bars. Big, mean women who liked to beat up eighteen-year-old girls. Ugly orange uniforms.

Jo dropped the mug she was holding. It fell to the floor and shattered, splattering coffee across the red-and-white-tile floor.

"Whoa!" Jo exclaimed with a nervous giggle. "Guess I've slammed too much caffeine today . . . my hands are shaking."

Doris nonchalantly glanced at her watch. "Your shift is over, anyway. Why don't you go home and have a cup of decaf?"

Jo laughed again. "Uh, great idea. Decaf. Ha, ha."

In under twenty seconds Jo pulled off her apron, grabbed her backpack from behind the counter, and fled Mega Mocha. She couldn't get back to the safety of HQ fast enough.

Caylin knew that her jaw was practically dragging on the in-need-of-a-sweep-and-mop floor of Seattle Sounds as she stared at one of the televisions that were mounted to the store's ceiling. The news bulletin had, in a phrase, rocked her world.

She was torn between scrambling around to find the remote control so that she could un-mute the sound and standing still so that she wouldn't miss any of the images on-screen. Temporary paralysis dictated the latter. Caylin was absolutely nailed to her spot behind the cash register.

"Who the—?" Yet another picture had flashed across the screen. Caylin had recognized Jo's limo driver, the vehicle, and even the police sketch of Jo. But she had *never* laid eyes on the guy whose picture was currently plastered on the television set. Who was he?

"Did you say something?" The only customer in the shop, a twentysomething guy wearing a University of Washington sweatshirt, glanced from Caylin to the TV to Caylin.

"Uh, no . . . I mean, yeah." She tore her eyes away from the television set. "I mean, man, there are a lot of wackos out there these days."

"You said it." The guy slapped a CD titled *Rain in July*, by a group called Fungus, onto the counter. "I'll put this on my Visa."

As Caylin rang up the sale—she had finally mastered the cash register sometime between three and four o'clock— thoughts raced through her mind.

There were too many questions. Way too many. Jeez, they didn't even know for certain that Rosebud was actually Simon Gilbert. He could have been anyone. And exactly how did he know to target Theresa? A simple "breach in security" didn't seem to be an adequate explanation.

Caylin tried to ignore the cold knot of dread that had formed in the pit of her stomach. But her gut instincts were usually accurate. And right now her gut was shouting, as if over a loudspeaker, that the disaster surrounding the Spy Girls was even bigger and freakier than anything they had imagined.

"See ya," College Guy said, taking the small plastic bag Caylin held out to him. "Watch out for the psychos."

"If you only knew . . . ," Caylin murmured. She followed the customer to the door, then double-locked it behind him. She didn't care that Seattle Sounds didn't officially close for another two hours. She had to retreat to the warehouse and contact The Tower. Like, yesterday.

"You can't beat a game of computer Risk," Brad said late Monday afternoon.

Theresa used her mouse to move the rest of her "men" into China. She and Brad had been playing Risk—the object of which was, fittingly enough, world domination—for almost two hours now. He was a formidable opponent and a great conversationalist. As much as Theresa loved Caylin and Jo, she missed being able to discuss the ins and outs of computers with the techie friends she'd had back in Arizona.

"I don't know . . . gaining access to a state-of-the-art mainframe might qualify as more fun," Theresa said. She was justifying her totally non-mission-oriented time with Brad by subtly pumping him for info about the inner workings of FutureWorks.

In the pocket of her jacket Theresa felt her cell phone vibrate. Probably Caylin and Jo asking her to pick up Chinese food on the way back to HQ, she surmised. Or texting to tell her something incredibly important that could have worldwide implications. Oh, well. She would assume the text was about dinner and continue her fishing expedition uninterrupted.

Brad moved his soldiers into Italy, then leaned back in his chair. "How about going out to dinner with me tonight?" he asked. "There's a great sushi place down at the fishermen's market."

"I'd love to . . . but I can't tonight," Theresa answered. A true enough statement.

"How about tomorrow night?" he pressed. "I can promise you the best yellowtail you've ever had."

"No . . . I don't think so." She wanted to say yes. Theresa really, really wanted to go on a nice, normal date with a nice, normal guy. But she couldn't—not in the middle of a mission.

"What if I told you that I could show you a mainframe that would blow your computer-lovin' mind?" Brad asked. "Please?"

Bingo. Brad knew something significant about the Monkey Room—she had guessed as much this morning when he had told her about it. Theresa could have her date and eat her mission, too. So to speak. "Well . . . okay," she allowed. She *was* human, after all.

"We'll leave right after work," Brad said. "It'll be a night to remember."

And then some. "It's a date," she declared. Smiling to herself, Theresa imagined the many ways the date could end. Maybe she could have some romance *and* save the world, she speculated. A girl could dream . . . later. Right now she had to conquer the rest of Asia.

"Did we text her, or did we text her?" Caylin asked Jo.

Jo shrugged. "We texted her. Twice." The girls had locked themselves into the warehouse, where they were keeping a TV news vigil. The Seattle police chief had announced earlier that he would hold a press conference at 4:45 p.m., and Jo and Caylin were waiting for it to begin. They had agreed to hold off on contacting Uncle Sam until they knew as much as possible about what was going on.

"Maybe Theresa doesn't realize how much trouble we're in," Jo suggested. "She's probably been locked in some tiny, over-air-conditioned cubicle all day."

"She should be here," Caylin insisted. There was strength in numbers, and the Spy Girls needed every iota of strength they could muster.

From earlier reports Caylin and Jo had pieced together the police department's theory of last night's events. Detectives believed that Jo, Caylin, and Theresa were part of a girl gang and that the crime had been a quote bizarre female gang heist unquote.

"I thought they quit using the word *heist* around the time that Bonnie and Clyde kicked the bucket," Jo commented.

"Call it whatever you want," Caylin responded. "They still think you're a cold-blooded killer."

Every word of the news report was imprinted upon Caylin's memory:

> "Last night members of a female gang
> wreaked havoc on the city of Seattle. One
> of the members stole a gray limousine
> at gunpoint, then, according to reports,
> proceeded on a mad car chase. This
> morning a white limousine was found in
> the Pacific. A man, identified as twenty-
> three-year-old Seth Armstrong, was
> found dead inside the vehicle. Police are
> looking for suspects as well as for the gray
> limousine. . . ."

Ugh.

"The man who died was definitely *not* Rosebud," Jo said for the fifth time.

"Nope," Caylin agreed. "I got a good look at Rosebud—*too* good. That guy in the picture they showed wasn't anyone I've ever seen before."

"Which means that the murder victim was probably Theresa's *real* limo driver." Jo chewed on her thumbnail and stared into space. Caylin could practically see her mind working overtime.

"Rosebud killed the driver," Caylin said. "That much seems obvious."

Jo shuddered. "And he would have killed you if he'd had the chance." She sat up straighter. "Hey, the press conference is starting." Jo leaned forward and turned up the volume on the television set. On the TV screen the stern-looking police chief, Officer Bascovitz, cleared his throat. "At the current time we are trying to locate three females," Officer Bascovitz announced. "Two are suspected of homicide."

"Two?" Caylin squeaked.

The police chief held up two sketches, and the camera zoomed in on them. They were clearly sketches of Jo and Caylin, although both wore their cheesy disguises.

"A third female may have been abducted from the scene of the crime," Officer Bascovitz continued. He held up yet another police sketch. This one was of Theresa, but most of her face was hidden by an enormous pair of mirrored aviator sunglasses. "An eyewitness claims to have seen one of the suspects order the third female into the missing gray limousine."

"Gulp," Jo said. "Could the news get *any* worse?"

"We have recovered a handgun from the scene," the officer informed reporters.

"Yes, things *could* get worse—and they just have." Caylin forced herself to look at the bright side. At least none of the Spy Girls' fingerprints could be on the handgun the cops found. Guns were *not* part of their Tower-approved paraphernalia.

On TV, Officer Bascovitz cleared his throat again. "We have found items belonging to one of the suspects in the white limousine," he said. "From an item of clothing discovered in those belongings, we will attempt to make a positive ID on the suspect. As soon as that ID has been made, we will put out an all-points bulletin."

Caylin froze. An item of clothing . . . oh no. Her lucky cap. Officer Bascovitz had been referring to her yellow Sunset Hill School baseball cap. Caylin was sure of it. She was dead meat. Stupid, stupid, stupid!

"A further search for bodies revealed nothing," the officer finished. "We can only hope that there will be no more deaths at the hands of these evil young women." He paused. "The public should be aware that these girls are considered armed and extremely dangerous. Treat them as such."

Mercifully the press conference ended, and Caylin switched off the TV set. Her lucky baseball cap . . . the one with the logo of her boarding school emblazoned across its front. Bringing the cap along on her Spy Girl missions had been a serious error.

"We might as well chop ourselves into tiny pieces and stuff each other into a garbage disposal," Jo said glumly.

"Rosebud is still out there," Caylin commented. "If he

had died in the limo, the police would have found him."

Jo sighed dramatically. "Uncle Sam isn't going to like this latest news flash—not at all."

"I take back wishing that Rosebud didn't kick it in the ocean," Caylin announced.

"I'm with you there," Jo agreed. "He could ruin the whole mission—not to mention our *lives*."

"We have to call The Tower," Caylin said. "Uncle Sam is the only person who might be able to get us out of this atomic situation."

"We'll get in touch with him soon," Jo agreed. "But first we need to talk to Theresa."

Caylin nodded. "The one thing we know for sure is that Rosebud wants Theresa six feet under. Until this blows over, her life is in grave danger."

She dialed the main number for FutureWorks, praying that Theresa would answer her desk phone. All the while Caylin kept avoiding the only reason why Theresa wouldn't respond to their texts. She wouldn't allow herself to think that Rosebud had already struck.

• • •

Theresa really didn't want to answer the ringing phone on her desk. She was flirting for the first time in months, and flexing the old womanly wile muscles felt darn good. Unfortunately she couldn't ignore the possibility that the call pertained to the mission.

She picked up the receiver. "Hello. This is Tessa Somerset."

"What are you *doing*?" Caylin squealed on the other end of the line. "Jo and I are *freaking* out. We thought you were *dead*!"

Theresa held the phone away from her ear for a moment's relief from Caylin's high-pitched screech. "Sorry . . . I've been, uh, busy." She glanced at the Risk board on her computer screen. Okay, maybe "busy" was an exaggeration. But still. There was no point in going postal.

"FYI, Rosebud is alive, Jo and I are wanted for murder, and the cops think we kidnapped you."

"What?" Theresa shrieked. She glanced at Brad, who looked alarmed. "I mean, what?" she whispered into the phone.

"You heard me," Caylin said. "Now get your butt back

to HQ so we can figure out how to proceed. Okeydoke?"

Theresa gulped. Oops. She'd never ignore her texts again. "I'll be there in twenty minutes," she promised.

Her hands shook as she hung up the phone. Brad was staring at her, questions in his warm hazel eyes. "My room-mate . . . says my cat is sick," Theresa explained lamely. "I, uh, need to take her to the vet."

Brad glanced at his watch. "We're not off for another half hour. They're pretty strict about the time clock around here."

Theresa locked eyes with Brad. "Well, since Victor and I are actually working together as international spies, I'm pretty sure he'll let me go home early." She winked.

Brad laughed. "Funny girl," he said admiringly.

She knocked lightly on the door of Victor's office, then poked her head inside. He was talking intently into the telephone, his voice low. When Victor saw her, he hung up the telephone immediately. "Yes?" he asked.

"Victor—I've got to go," Theresa said. "We're having something of a meltdown back at HQ."

Victor didn't ask any questions. He merely nodded. "I'm

handling things here. Go home and take care of business."

Theresa closed the door thoughtfully. Victor hadn't seemed surprised by her request to leave work early. He hadn't even inquired as to whether or not she had made progress with the code. Was it possible that he already knew about the allegations against Caylin and Jo? If so, why hadn't he told her?

Turning the question over in her mind, Theresa walked back to her cubicle and grabbed her small leather briefcase. "I got the green light," she informed Brad. "I'm outta here."

"Wow!" Brad exclaimed. "Victor must really like you. He's never let me go home early."

"What can I say? He's a cat lover." And with that cryptic exit line, she split.

FIVE

As the sun set over Seattle, Jo, Caylin, and Theresa locked themselves in the warehouse, away from anything that might distract them from their immediate goal: getting their butts out of some seriously hot water.

Jo stared at Uncle Sam's shadowy figure on the huge screen and wished that he would offer the girls a magic exit out of this giant pothole in their mission. No such luck. "At least you girls know that you're not responsible for anyone's death," Uncle Sam was saying. "Simon Gilbert is still alive."

"But the cops think we're *guilty*," Jo exclaimed. "We're being framed!"

"Calm down, Jo," Uncle Sam ordered. "The Tower will clear up this misunderstanding once the mission is completed."

"You want us to go ahead with the mission?" Caylin squeaked. "Don't you think that's a little unwise under the present circumstances?"

"So far, the police don't know who any of you are," Uncle Sam said. "As of now, I want you to proceed with the mission as planned."

Theresa looked up from the top secret computer decoding manual she had received from operatives at The Tower. "I met a guy at work who's going to show me around FutureWorks tomorrow," she informed Uncle Sam. "I think Brad knows how to get into the Monkey Room."

"The Monkey Room?" Uncle Sam asked skeptically. "Sounds like a come-on line to me."

"He's for real!" Theresa insisted. "Victor verified that FutureWorks plebs have nicknamed the main brain center the Monkey Room."

"How do you know this Brad can be trusted?" Uncle Sam asked.

Jo noticed a light pink blush spreading across Theresa's face. Hmmm. Interesting. Was it possible that in the midst of this turmoil Theresa was falling for a fellow computer nerd?

"I know how to judge character," Theresa insisted. "Brad's an upstanding guy—and he knows almost as much as I do about hard drives."

"Well, just make sure you don't get caught up in some kind of techie prank," Uncle Sam said.

Caylin snorted. "Yeah, the last thing we need is the Bradster trying to impress you by posting some fake letter from the president on some White House web page or something."

Theresa glared at Caylin. "We can quit discussing Brad now," she snapped. "I have one concern and one concern only. I'm going to get the code and get out."

"I don't think I need to emphasize that time is of the essence, Theresa." Uncle Sam's voice was stern—more stern than Jo had ever heard it.

"I *know*," Theresa said. "Sheesh, I'm doing everything I can."

"Stay safe, girls. Over and out." Typical. Uncle Sam wasn't big on warm and fuzzy good-byes. A moment after the succinct *sayonara* the screen went blank.

"At least the boss isn't totally wigging," Caylin commented. "I guess we should find comfort in his calm."

"Yeah, well, *he's* not the one being framed for first-degree, wham bam, see ya, wouldn't want to be ya, man." Since this afternoon Jo hadn't been able to get the image of herself in an ill-fitting jumpsuit and clunky leg irons out of her mind.

"He's also not the one with a psycho killer after his Tower tail," Theresa added.

Jo bit her lip, resisting the urge to chew her fingernails down to the quick. They couldn't despair. Not now. One false move could equal a major catastrophe . . . for them and for the world.

"Can we all take a moment and thank the pizza gods?" Caylin asked. "Aside from a chocolate bar and half a rank cup of blueberry yogurt, this is the first thing I've eaten all day." She took another bite of the now piping hot pizza they had found in the stocked freezer, savoring a thick piece of pepperoni.

Jo pushed away her plate. "I have no appetite. It feels like there's a Nerf ball in my stomach."

Theresa looked up from a Tower textbook titled *The Seven Habits of Highly Effective Hackers*. "I think it's time to call in the troops, if you know what I mean."

"Are you suggesting we put our pride where the sun don't shine and call Danielle?" Caylin asked.

Jo nodded. "You got it, babe." She looked from Theresa to Caylin. "All in favor, say, 'SOS.'"

"SOS," Caylin and Theresa responded in stereo. If Jo hadn't suggested calling Danielle, Caylin would have in a heartbeat.

Danielle, otherwise known as Glenda the Good Witch, was the Spy Girls' guardian angel. A veteran Tower agent, Danielle often swooped down to give the girls advice when they were stuck between a rock and a big black abyss. The woman was like a walking, talking international spy guide.

"I'll make the call," Caylin offered. She licked pizza sauce off her fingers and dialed Danielle's number on the nearest speakerphone.

A moment later the knightess in shining armor answered the phone. "Hey, it's the teen dream team!" she greeted them. "Caught any bad guys lately?"

The girls' collective groan was answer enough. "Uh-oh," Danielle said. "From the desolate tone of your youthful voices, I'm speculating that this problem is worse than a run in your panty hose."

"We're toast," Caylin answered. "We're burnt toast with butter and jam and the crusts cut off."

"Tell me everything," Danielle said.

Caylin started the story. Theresa supplied the middle. And Jo finished off with the bummer news that she and Caylin were wanted for murder and Theresa was quite possibly the target of a trigger-happy madman.

"I think it's fairy-dust time," Danielle said when they finished their tale of woe. "You girls need help in a big way."

"Exactly," Caylin said. "Got any suggestions?"

"The frame-up will get resolved in the long run," Danielle said. "As Sam told you, The Tower will make sure that you all are cleared."

"But in the short run we've got a bunch of local yokels with sheriff's badges wanting our butts in the electric chair," Jo pointed out.

"Okay, here's the plan," Danielle said in the crisp, firm voice that meant she was about to issue orders that she didn't want questioned. "Jo and Caylin, you two need makeovers." She paused. "I want totally new hair for Caylin and Jo. I want you girls to go heavy on the funky makeup and scanty in the clothes department."

"Uh . . . okay," Caylin responded. She wasn't thrilled at the idea of dyeing her hair, but it was a heck of a lot better prospect than sticking her thumbs in an ink pad at the police station.

"What about me?" Theresa asked. "Everyone at FutureWorks is going to think I'm nuts if I show up for my second day of work looking like an escapee from Hole."

"You're right, Theresa," Danielle agreed. "The police's ID of you is the least secure, and as far as they're concerned you've been hidden away somewhere. They won't be looking for you. So just continue at FutureWorks as if you don't have a care in the world."

"Check," Theresa said. "Not a care in the world . . . yeah, right."

"Good luck, Spy Queens," Danielle said. "I have every confidence that you all will come out of this with flying colors—and not just in your hair."

"I hope you're right," Caylin said. "But right now this feels like it could very well be our last mission."

"Don't let negative energy keep you girls down," Danielle said in her best pep-talk voice. "Go get 'em, and remember that a good attitude is half the battle."

Caylin clicked off the phone. "Looks like we need an all-night drugstore," she said. "Two boxes of hair dye coming up."

Theresa stood. "I'll go—the cops are combing the streets for you guys."

"The cops are combing the streets, and we'll be combing our hair." Jo laughed weakly. "It makes a certain amount of crazy sense."

"Let's hope a couple of new hairdos will be enough," Caylin suggested. "I'm not up for major plastic surgery." She felt the three pieces of pizza she had eaten congealing in her stomach. The Spy Girls were all safe for now. But as of tomorrow, they would be back out on the streets . . .

where anything could happen. A box of hair dye wasn't going to change that fact.

Theresa prowled through the aisles of an all-night drugstore, tossing items into her blue plastic basket. If the circumstances weren't so dire, this shopping spree would have been kind of fun. Purchasing large amounts of cheap makeup was liberating.

She surveyed the contents of the basket: all colors of eye shadow, mascara, and lipstick; temporary tattoos; black hair dye; blond hair dye; red hair dye; two streak kits. What else did she need?

Theresa kept her eyes glued to the stocked aisles as she walked. Who knew there were so many beauty products on the market? Bikini wax treatments, mustache bleach, blackhead strips, cucumber masks, fingernail strengtheners, eyelash curlers. There was no end to the number of items a girl could buy to make herself more attractive to the opposite sex. Theresa's own beauty regime consisted of soap and water and moisturizer, period.

"Ummph." Theresa bumped into a large, solid figure

next to her. Whoops. She had been so lost in her musings that she had mistakenly wandered into the men's hygiene section.

"Tessa?" Oh, man. Brad! Talk about dumb luck—or lack thereof.

"Brad! Hi!" Theresa smiled innocently, she hoped, and tried to mentally quell the quickening of her heartbeat. He looked even cuter in Levi's and an old T-shirt than he had in khakis and a button-down.

"How's the cat?" he asked.

The cat? Theresa racked her brain. "Oh, the *cat*." She giggled nervously. "Fluffy is fine. She just, uh, swallowed a hair ball . . . no problem."

He grinned. "So we're still on for tomorrow night? You're not going to have to keep a vigil by Fluffy's sickbed or anything?"

Theresa shook her head. "Absolutely not. She's back to her old self—she, uh, even killed a mouse tonight."

"So what are you doing here?" Brad asked.

"Who, me?" Theresa asked. "I was, um, out of tooth-paste. And shampoo. And a couple of other things." She took off in the direction of the pet food aisle. "Actually, I needed to get a new brand of cat food for Fluffy—one the vet suggested."

Brad glanced into her overflowing basket. "Are you also planning on opening a beauty salon?" he asked as they headed down aisle six. "I don't think I've ever seen so much makeup and stuff in one place."

She stared guiltily into her basket. "Um, I'm throwing a girlie party this weekend—you know, one of those chick-bonding nights when we get together and do each other's hair and makeup." She'd never done anything like that in her life, but the explanation seemed to satisfy Brad.

They reached the pet food aisle. Theresa tossed several cans of Feline Feast into her basket. Now *there* was something she'd never use.

"So, are you ready to pay?" Brad asked. "We can chat about gigabytes while we wait in line."

Think fast, Tessa, Theresa told herself. There was no way she could let Brad watch her pay for her loot. She had zero cash, which meant she had to use her Tower credit card. The leftover one from London that had the collective Tower alias Camilla Stevens stamped across the front.

"Uh, I've still got to pick up a few more things," she said.

"No prob. I'll keep you company." Brad put his hand on her back, as if to guide her toward her destination.

Theresa started to walk aimlessly. She *had* to get rid of him, much as she would have liked to stay and flirt. Brainstorm! She changed directions and headed toward the dreaded feminine hygiene aisle. Theresa stopped in front of a row of tampons and pads and started to do some price comparing. "Hey, Brad? Which of these do you think—"

Right on cue, Brad's face matched the red lipstick Theresa had stashed away in her basket. "I've, uh, got to get home," he said, averting his eyes from a box of Always with wings. "I'll see you at work tomorrow morning."

Theresa smiled. Thank goodness testosterone precluded the other half from being able to deal with a biological process that was as natural as breathing. Sometimes a girl needed to be left alone. Forget the pizza gods. Right now Theresa was praising the fertility goddesses. She was home free!

"I thought we were going to dye my hair *black*," Caylin moaned as she stared at her candy apple red hair in the bathroom mirror.

"You would have looked like Elvira if your hair were black," Jo pointed out. "Red suits you."

Caylin groaned. "I'd rather look like Elvira than Bozo the Clown."

Jo looked thoughtfully at her own makeover. A bottle-opening mishap had sent the superlightening blond color down the shower drain. Since the red hair dye had gone to Caylin, Jo had been forced to make do with both streak kits and the bottle of blue-black.

"I look like a skunk," Jo announced. "But I like it."

"Everyone in Seattle has weird hair," Theresa commented. "Don't worry about it."

"You wouldn't be saying that if *your* hair looked like something out of *The Simpsons*," Caylin said. "Brad might not like it if your luxurious brunette hair suddenly resembled a cheap, acrylic wig."

"Who knows?" Jo teased. "Maybe he's the kinky type."

Theresa sighed. "Can we shut up about Brad and do a final security check?" she asked. "Unlike you two, I have *real* work to do in the morning."

Caylin and Jo nodded in unison. The idea of going to bed was too tantalizing a prospect to pass up. "I'll do a twice-over on the windows," Caylin offered.

"And I'll check the doors," Jo said. "Again."

"Put me down for the alarm system," Theresa offered. "Thank goodness for motion detectors."

The trio filed out of the marble-tiled bathroom, and each Spy Girl headed for her designated security post. Caylin pulled on each of the apartment's windows, making sure that no intruder could get inside via the fire escape. At the last window she stopped and peered into the dark night. Rosebud was out there . . . somewhere. And until they knew who he was, where he was, and what he wanted, not one of them was safe.

SIX

"I said baaaybeee, are you gonna something-something saaave meee," Jo sang tunelessly as she carried a loaded tray to table twelve on Tuesday morning. Mega Mocha was packed, but Jo had more or less gotten the hang of her waitressing-slash-coffee-goddess gig. It was actually kind of a kick.

She stopped in front of the table full of preteens, who were most likely skipping school.

"Nice streaks," a tall blond guy commented from the next table. "You've got a total rock chick thang happening."

Jo batted her heavily mascara-coated eyelashes. "Thanks, blondie. Maybe I'll do *your* hair sometime." She shifted her attention to her customers. "I've got café au lait. I've got café mocha. I've got a double espresso." She set down the drinks in front of the kids.

"Hey, you're improving," remarked one of the girls. She had been in the café yesterday, at which point Jo had accidentally served her an iced coffee instead of coffee ice cream.

Jo grinned. "Thanks—and don't forget to tip," she suggested. "Gratuity is next to godliness." Man, it was nice to feel like a normal, teenage waitress. Sure, being a spy had tons of perks, but occasionally the concept of living a mundane life was enticing.

"Excuse me, ma'am. May I seat myself?" The overly polite question had been asked by none other than Theresa.

Jo turned around. "Why, yes, miss, sit wherever you like. There's a lovely table by the window." She waved her order pad in Theresa's face. "I'll be with you in a moment."

But Theresa didn't sit down. She was staring intently at something over Jo's shoulder.

"Cute guy at twelve o'clock?" Jo asked.

"Not exactly."

Jo pivoted and followed the direction of Theresa's gaze. Uh-oh. Chapter two. There was another news bulletin on the television set. From the images on the screen it was obvious that the station was offering an update on the so-called girl gang.

"Turn it up!" someone shouted from table nine. "This story rocks!"

"Yeah! We want to hear about the chick killers!" another customer yelled from a plush red velvet sofa.

"Okay, okay!" Doris yelled. "I give!" She switched off the music that had been blasting through the speakers and turned up the volume on the TV set.

"The blond female gang member has been identified as seventeen-year-old Caylin Pike," the newscaster announced. "Her name was traced through a high school yearbook from her alma mater, the prestigious Sunset Hill School." Instantly a photo of Caylin on her high school graduation day—looking *très* adorable in cap and gown—flashed across the screen.

"The suspect may look harmless," the anchorwoman continued. "But we stress that she and her cohort *are* considered armed and extremely dangerous."

Their cover was blown to bits. That much was clear.

"Is this really happening?" Jo whispered.

"Pike's parents were unavailable for comment," the anchorwoman continued. "But we will be sure to keep the public updated on the unfolding events of this most troubling story."

"This is happening, all right," Theresa said softly. "We'd better warn Caylin."

"I'll call her," Jo offered. "And you and I better steer clear of each other."

"I'll get my java to go," Theresa agreed. "Call me with developments."

As Theresa walked to the counter to order her coffee, Jo sped through the crowded café and parked herself next to the pay phone outside the women's bathroom. She pulled one of her tip quarters out of her apron pocket and dropped it into the coin slot. She quickly dialed the number for HQ, which she knew would also ring in Seattle Sounds.

The phone rang six times before Caylin finally picked up. "Hello!" she shouted. "Seattle Sounds, Courtney speaking."

"Hi, Courtney. It's Julia." Jo tapped her pen against the

side of the phone as she waited for Caylin to turn down the music.

"What's up?" Caylin asked a moment later. "And don't tell me you're in jail, using your one phone call."

From the other side of the café Jo could see Doris staring at her. Okay. She had to make this rap session quick and to the point. "Things aren't that bad—yet," Jo said quietly. "But do yourself a favor—don't watch the news today."

She hung up before Caylin could respond. Doris seemed to be genuinely friendly and on the level, but a Spy Girl could never be too careful. The last thirty-six hours had taught her *that* painful lesson.

Caylin dropped the phone into its Day-Glo orange cradle. Jo hadn't said much—she hadn't needed to. Caylin turned the music down even lower and cupped her hands around her mouth.

"I'm sorry, but, uh, Seattle Sounds is closed for the next hour," she announced to the customers, who were pawing aimlessly through the albums. "We've got an, uh, emergency plumbing problem."

Caylin couldn't see any reason not to close the store for a while. So far, her job had been more about ringing up sales and answering idiotic questions than it had been about gathering and disseminating information.

One girl drifted toward the door, hauling her boyfriend along with her. Two other guys kept flipping through albums as if Caylin hadn't spoken.

"I said get *out*," she seethed. Running a store took way too much patience. She'd had it with that stupid customer-is-always-right credo. "Now."

The guys looked at each other and shrugged. "Okay, Red, we get the message," one of them said. "Man, this town used to be *friendly*."

As soon as the guys were gone Caylin shoved the Closed sign in the window and locked the door. She walked to the back of the store and slipped into the warehouse, where she could watch the news in private. It didn't take long to surmise why Jo had called with the warning. Every station in the city was airing her high school graduation photo.

Tears sprang to Caylin's eyes when she flipped to a channel that was showing a different picture. In the photograph Caylin was standing between her parents, who were smiling proudly for the camera. She remembered having that photo taken—it had meant a lot to her to get a picture of the whole family together. Even though her parents' divorce had been as amicable as a divorce *could* be, moments of true togetherness were now few and far between.

Caylin grabbed the portable phone and dialed Uncle Sam's direct number. "I have to call my parents," she said as soon as she heard his husky voice. "The cops know who I am, and I'm sure reporters are hounding my mom and dad."

"Absolutely not," Uncle Sam said firmly. "Contacting your family at this juncture would be a critical error. There's every possibility that their phone lines are being tapped."

"So you know what's going on?" Caylin asked. "You know that they traced me to Sunset Hill?"

"We know everything," Uncle Sam said. "And we're

doing all we can. I know it's tough, but you've got to proceed as we discussed."

Caylin fought back tears as she hung up the phone. She felt utterly defeated. Reaching over to turn off the TV, she suddenly froze. There were her parents. Both of them. They were standing in front of the home she grew up in, and there were a dozen reporters sticking microphones in their faces.

"Mrs. Pike, where is your daughter?" one reporter shouted. "Has she tried to contact you in any way?"

"Were there signs that your daughter was involved in gang activity?" another reporter demanded.

"Caylin is innocent," Mr. Pike told the reporters. "That's all we have to say."

"Do you know where she is?" the first reporter asked again. "Are you aware that harboring a fugitive makes you an accessory to murder?"

"Our daughter has done nothing wrong," Mrs. Pike said, her voice strained but calm. "We have no further comment."

A tear slid down Caylin's face as she watched her

parents join hands and turn to walk back into the house. With every fiber of her being she longed to call and assure them that she was, in fact, innocent. She knew they were going through agony . . . they had to be. She reached for the phone, then dropped her hand.

"I can't call them," Caylin said aloud. "I can't disobey a direct order." She sighed deeply. The little girl inside her wanted nothing more than to crawl onto her mother's lap for comfort. But she wasn't a little girl anymore, and she couldn't pretend that Mommy could make everything all better. Caylin was a Spy Girl, and she had a mission to accomplish.

Taking a deep breath, Caylin prepared herself to go back into the store and reopen for business. There was work to do.

Theresa pushed enter on her keyboard and glanced at her in-box. Empty. She had completed her morning's work in record time. Which left Theresa free to go after the code.

Or flirt with Brad. She noticed out of her peripheral

vision that he had just pushed his chair away from his desk and swiveled in her direction.

"Hey, Tessa? Sorry I ran out on you so fast last night," Brad said haltingly. He ran a hand through his thick sandy brown hair. "I just, uh, realized I had to get home."

Yeah, right, she thought. The fact that he was standing in front of a panoramic display of tampons and maxi pads had nothing to do with it. "No problem," Theresa assured him.

"So, did you catch the news last night?" he asked. "There's some pretty disturbing stuff going on in this city."

"Um, yeah. I mean, no. I don't watch the news. . . . I, uh, prefer the Discovery Channel." She had no desire to get drawn into a discussion about local current events.

"There's like this wild girl gang on the prowl," Brad said excitedly. "They've killed at least one guy, and they may have kidnapped a girl."

Time to change the subject, Theresa told herself. Brad's inquiring mind needed to be stopped. "Um, what are you doing for lunch?" she asked, ignoring his comments completely. "I was thinking about going to that little bistro around the corner."

Brad's face fell. "I'd love to go with you, but I have an appointment."

"Oh, well," Theresa said breezily. "I'd probably be better off catching up on my employee's manual reading, anyway." Uh-huh, she added silently. She always spent her free time reading about the rules and regulations regarding worker dress code. Not!

In *veritas*, she was psyched to have some Brad-free hacking time. Cute or not, the guy seemed to have a million pairs of eyes watching her every move. Besides, they would have plenty of time to rap on their date.

"By the way, what have you got planned for tonight?" she asked.

Brad's hazel eyes sparkled. "That, my computer geek friend, is a secret."

Theresa raised her eyebrows. "Sounds fascinating."

"It'll be a night to remember, all right," Brad agreed. He reached into the pocket of his tweed sports coat and pulled out a tiny camera. "Say, 'cheese!'"

Before Theresa could respond, he had snapped her photograph. Terrific. This wasn't the best time for a photo op. "What was that for?" she asked quickly.

Brad slipped the camera back into his pocket. "I'm not at liberty to say . . . but you'll find out soon enough."

Theresa turned back to her monitor.

Hmmm.

Jo appraised her appearance in the small, smoky mirror over the sink in the women's bathroom. This would be her last chance to reapply lipstick before the lunch rush slammed every waitress in Mega Mocha.

Not bad. Not bad at all. The peroxide blond and blue-black streaks in her dark hair lent her a dangerous edge that appealed to her sense of adventure.

With this hairdo who knew what kind of thrills were in store for her? Anything was possible. Plus nobody would suspect a girl with much makeup of being an undercover operative. Farrah Fawcett, she most certainly was *not*.

Jo tucked the tube of Darkly Sensuous lipstick into her apron pocket, checked to make sure her high-tech mascara cam—an essential for any spy worth her weight in espresso beans—was still where she could get at it with one swift grab, and prepared to face the pit bulls. Seattleites desperately in need of a java fix were an angry breed.

She pushed open the door of the bathroom, sauntered back to the counter, and surveyed the crowd. Grunged-out teenagers lounged on sofas and fraying recliners. Young professionals sipped coffee as they thumbed through *The Wall Street Journal.* A few random mothers ordered bagels by the dozen as screaming babies tugged at their hair. Yep. As usual, the place looked alarmingly free of any kind of mission-related activity.

"Get a load of the guy at table five," Doris said, nudging Jo. "He is *h-o-t.* At least from this angle." She poked Jo again. "And he's sitting in *your* section."

Jo nodded absently. Yes, in an ideal world she would have nothing better to do than stand around and analyze the physical merits of every guy who happened to walk into Mega Mocha. But if something relating to the covert didn't happen soon, she was going to think this whole coffee-pouring gig was a bust. "Then again, I'm not sure

I dig that tattoo on the back of his neck," Doris said. "Creep-o-rama."

Jo felt her left eye twitch.

Tattoo.

Neck.

Was it possible in any way, shape, or form that . . . ?

No.

Jo glanced over at table five. Instantly her heart sped up to a rate of approximately a thousand beats a second. The guy sitting at table five had a tattoo on the back of his neck, all right. A tattoo of a rosebud.

Whoa. Hold the phone. Covert action had arrived with a bang.

While she stood with her mouth hanging open, a guy walked into Mega Mocha and plopped into the chair opposite Rosebud's. Jo didn't know who he was, but if the dude was here to meet up with Rosebud, he had to be bad news.

"Showtime," Jo whispered. Taking a deep breath, she went for it.

SEVEN

Access denied. Password not recognized. User not known.

"Dang," Theresa kicked the side of her desk with the heel of her black pump in frustration. FutureWorks didn't take many chances with its security system—well, security *was* their business, after all. A total genius must have programmed the mainframe. It was becoming all too obvious that she wasn't going to get inside the computer nerve center without some heavy-duty hacking gear.

There was a military-authorized pass code detector drive in her leather briefcase. Would it be safe to use?

She glanced around, looking for anyone who might be poised to see untoward behavior. There was no one.

She continued to sweep the area with watchful eyes. Huh. A smoke detector was mounted in a ceiling corner. The detector looked standard, but Theresa wasn't going to take any risks. Hadn't Victor told her that there were cameras all over FutureWorks? She stared at the smoke detector, rubbing one of her eyes as if there were something in it. There was no reason to arouse suspicions by ogling a hidden camera. Yep . . . there it was. A tiny red dot showed between the slats of the detector. Bingo.

Theresa turned back to her computer. She couldn't do any big-time hacking at her desk. She would have to take the show on the road . . . or in this case down the hall. She gathered up her belongings as if she were headed off to lunch. Just call me Sneaky Spice, she thought. FutureWorks was her stage. But she didn't want any spotlight shining on her . . . yet.

"That'll be twenty-six seventy-four," Caylin said to the brown-haired guy who stood on the other side of the cash register. She glanced at his album choice. *Chicago*. "Let me guess . . . it's a present for your girlfriend, right?"

He grinned. "How'd you guess?"

Caylin laughed, feeling something approaching lighthearted for the first time in two days. "Musical sound tracks aren't too popular among the male half of the species."

The guy took his purchase. "Have a great day."

Caylin waved good-bye, feeling slightly proud of herself. Sure, she had screwed up her parents' lives, put the entire mission in jeopardy, and was wanted for first-degree murder. But dang if she wasn't turning out to be one heck of a music store proprietress.

The bell over the front door jangled, and Caylin looked up from the receipts she was organizing. Two men walked inside. Correction. Two *policemen* walked inside, decked out in full men-in-blue garb, billy clubs at their sides. Talk about a sorry—no, *scary*—sight to see.

Police. Cops. Fuzz. The keepers of the thin blue line. She was in for it. Caylin was torn between standing up tall and proud as if she had nothing to hide and shrinking into her skin in order to be as inconspicuous as possible. She settled on a posture somewhere in between—head up, shoulders hunched. Not the best look for an international spy. And now the cops were heading straight in her direction.

I plead the fifth. I demand my lawyer, she told them silently. But Caylin didn't have a lawyer. Oh, well. Her heart pounded as the men approached. "Hello, Officers," she greeted them. "What can I do for you?" The best defense was a good offense, or so the saying claimed.

"Hiya, miss." One of the policemen held out his hand "I'm Officer Denver."

"Hi. Courtney Hall." Caylin shook his outstretched hand and thanked the beauty industry—and Danielle—for red hair in a box. She also gave a silent thanks to Jo for forcing her to put a huge butterfly temporary tattoo on her arm. The clip-on nose ring had been Caylin's own idea. The men didn't seem to recognize her. So far.

The other cop extended his hand. "Officer Barkman, ma'am."

Ma'am? That was a new one.

"What can I help you guys with?" Caylin asked, grateful that previous missions had given her experience in the my-voice-isn't-trembling-even-though-my-knees-are-knocking territory.

"We noticed that Seattle Sounds is a new shop in town," Officer Denver said. "We wanted to come by and welcome you to the neighborhood."

"Well, thanks, that was mighty nice of y'all." Caylin knew that stupidity could go a long way in the deception game.

"This is a great setup," Officer Denver continued. "Have you lived in Seattle long?"

Pound. Pound. Pound. "Uh, I'm actually relatively new to the area. I moved here from the East Coast." Not *exactly* a lie.

Officer Barkman glanced around the shop. "You must have been doing pretty well out there to be able to move and buy a store like this."

"You know, I, uh, got lucky in the stock market." Close. She had gotten lucky in the spy market. Right?

Officer Denver took a step closer. He was a hottie, no doubt. Blond hair, blue eyes, nice crisp uniform. "If you're new in town, maybe you'd like to get to know a strong young officer of the law who can show you all the best spots."

She wanted to say, "Yes, I would love a personalized tour of the greater Seattle metropolitan area." But hanging out with the fuzz would complicate matters beyond belief. And the mission came first. *That* fact had been driven home when she had resisted calling her parents this afternoon. Nonetheless, she needed to keep these guys on her good side.

"I would love to go out with you," she responded flirtatiously. "But I moved here to be closer to my boyfriend . . . and I don't think he would approve."

Officer Denver bowed. "Understood. But if you two call it quits, look me up."

Caylin nodded. "You can count on it." She twirled a piece of her newly red hair and smiled in a way that she knew highlighted her dimple.

"Make sure you lock the doors at night," Officer Barkman warned. "There are some pretty unsavory characters wandering around these days."

Again Caylin smiled her dumb redhead smile. "Will do. Thanks for the heads-up."

The policemen ambled out of the store, probably in

search of doughnuts and coffee. Caylin collapsed against the counter, limp with relief. Her disguise was a success. If two cops hadn't discerned her true identity, who would?

Jo stuck out a hip and tried to look uninterested in the conversation taking place between Rosebud and his cohort. "What can I get for you guys?" she asked, order pad at the ready.

Rosebud was staring at the chalkboard menu hanging over the counter. "I'll have an American coffee. Black." His eyes traveled from the menu to Jo's legs to Jo's face.

"Gotcha." Jo wrote down the order, keeping her face averted from Rosebud's dark eyes. Being recognized at this point could lead to some oh-so-ugly repercussions.

She turned to Rosebud's companion, who vaguely resembled a puppy in a shop window—soft, cuddly, and hopeful. "What can I get for you?"

"Café au lait, please," the guy responded politely. Jo noted a point in his favor. He wasn't staring at her chest *or* her legs. "Be right back with those, boys. Sit tight." Jo walked quickly back to the counter and handed her order to Doris, who was taking care of the coffee fixings.

So. Everything was fine. Rosebud hadn't recognized her. He'd been staring, sure, but lots of guys stared at Jo. The disguise was a go. She was, for the moment, safe.

"Were they nice?" Doris asked.

Jo shrugged. "I've met better." But I've never met worse, she thought.

Doris glanced back at the table. "Maybe you've met better, but it looks like they haven't."

Don't tell me, Jo thought. She looked back at the table. Oh, no. Rosebud and Mr. X had their heads bent close together, and they were most definitely gazing in her direction. And they were talking. Jo's stomach dropped into her carefully pedicured toes.

"Order up!" Doris announced. She placed the coffees on Jo's tray.

Back into the rats' nest. Jo carried the tray to the small table and set down the orders. "Here you go, guys. Happy java." She turned to go.

"Wait!" Rosebud put a restraining hand on Jo's wrist. "Have we met somewhere before?"

Jo looked him straight in the eyes. What choice did she have? Rosebud's dark gaze bored into hers with an intensity that she might have found mesmerizing under different circumstances.

Yeah, we met, she answered silently. You were wishing you could make it out of that giant pond in time to blow off the heads of me and my friends. Probably not the best approach.

Just the sound of Rosebud's voice made her skin crawl, but Jo clicked into Spy Girl mode and did what she had to do. She flashed him a dazzling I-want-to-go-on-a-date-with-you-more-than-I-want-to-do-anything-in-the-world smile.

"I wish," she replied. Jo gripped her tray with both hands and prayed the floor of Mega Mocha would open up and swallow her whole.

"I *know* we've met," Rosebud insisted. "Do you hang out at Murray's Bar at the pier?"

Proceed with caution, Carreras, Jo told herself. "I don't think so," she said in a breathy voice. "I, uh, don't go out much. I, um, spend most of my free time taking care of my sick aunt Rose." Rose? *Yikes!* She couldn't believe she'd used that word!

Rosebud continued to stare, unflinching. "It'll come to me, sweetie. I never forget a face."

Pound. Pound. "Well, I'm sure I could never forget *your* face, either . . . handsome." Oh, the things a girl had to say to get by in this big, bad world. "I'd love to stay and chat, but the crowds are demanding their caffeine."

Holding her tray in a strategic location, Jo grabbed her Great Lash cam from the pocket of her apron with her free hand. She was still within so-called shooting range, just feet from the table.

"You all enjoy that coffee . . . and the view," she said with a lilt. Ugh. Gross flirting made a chick feel dirty.

While Rosebud got visually reacquainted with her legs, she tilted the tiny camera toward his face. Snap. She tilted it toward Mr. X. Snap. Now they were captured on film. Finally. Jo had done something covert.

She raced back to the counter, gasping for breath. Inhale. Exhale. For the next fifteen minutes Jo paid very little attention to her other customers and watched

Rosebud and Mr. X in the least conspicuous manner possible. Nothing very remarkable happened—well, almost nothing. In a move so swift that Jo wondered if she had imagined it Rosebud handed Mr. X a piece of what looked like notebook paper. Interesting—perhaps. At last the guys got up to split.

Rosebud caught her watching him and waved.

"See you tomorrow?" he asked with a wink.

Jo gave him double-dimple action. "Maybe."

"Ooh, he has a *thing* for you," Doris whispered. "Their eyes met across the crowded café—it was love at first sight. . . ."

Just as long as he doesn't have it *in* for me, Jo thought as she felt the walls of the café closing in on her. The mission was getting more complicated and more dangerous by the hour.

Jo patted the mascara cam in her apron pocket for comfort. She was a Spy Girl. Danger was a major ingredient in her new life. She just didn't want tragedy spilling into the mix.

EIGHT

"Should I wear my khakis or the pale pink midi-skirt?" Theresa asked Caylin and Jo on Tuesday night. She held up both items of clothing for their inspection.

Jo slid off the bed and circled the garments in question. "Are we going for nice or naughty?"

Naughty. Hmmm. Theresa shrugged. "Somewhere in between." She threw the pink midi aside. Definitely too nice.

Caylin walked to Theresa's closet and pulled out an ice-blue silk shirt. "Wear Jo's black leather pants with this blouse," she suggested. "And you can top off the whole thing with some black platform tennis shoes."

"Black leather pants?" Theresa was horrified. She regarded the proposed outfit carefully. "Well . . . maybe . . ."

Jo flopped onto Theresa's bed. "Are we going to keep

discussing Theresa's wardrobe for her date—which supposedly isn't a *real* date but merely a fact-finding mission—or are we going to freak over my encounter with Rosebud?"

Theresa guiltily set aside the black pants. Jo was right. The mission was the most important thing in her life right now. "So he recognized you? Rosebud?"

Jo nodded. "He knew I looked familiar . . . he just didn't know *why*." She ran a hand through her hair. "Thank goodness for my skunk locks. I think these streaks saved my butt."

"Tell us about the guy Rosebud was with," Caylin said. "What did he look like?"

"He was young, cute, etc., etc. At one point Rosebud handed the guy a piece of notebook paper, but I couldn't get close enough to find out what was written on it." She sat up and snapped her fingers. "Duh! I *totally* forgot I took pictures of the dudes with my mascara cam. You girls can see Mr. X for yourselves."

"Let's waste no time, Spy Girls," Caylin said. "Hey,

Tessa, can you spare a few moments before your tête-à-tête to scan in the pics?"

"Of course." Theresa slipped into the chair in front of her laptop and booted up. "You know, Brad really *is* going to be a good info source—I think."

"Yeah, yeah. Computer geeks are notorious for helping out international spies with dangerous missions," Caylin said. "Happens all the time."

"Enough!" Theresa took the lash cam from Jo's outstretched hand and hooked it up to the computer. "In case you two wonder twins hadn't noticed, *this* computer geek has done plenty on the international spy circuit."

"Touché!" Jo called. "How did the pics turn out?"

"Hold on . . . I'll tell you in a second." Theresa watched as the digital photos appeared on-screen. "Oh my . . ."

Jo and Caylin peered over Theresa's shoulder. "That's Rosebud, all right," Caylin commented. "I'd recognize those coal-black eyes anywhere."

"But . . . but . . ." Theresa couldn't get the words out.

Jo waved a hand in front of Theresa's face. "What?"

"That's Brad!" she finally squeaked. "The other guy is *my* Brad."

"Your nerd?" Caylin asked. "He's the guy who was meeting with Rosebud?"

Theresa nodded. "Yeah . . . that's him." No wonder Brad hadn't been able to go to lunch with her this afternoon. When he'd said "appointment," she'd assumed it was with a doctor or a dentist. Not this. *Anything* but this.

"Does anyone know how 'The Funeral March' goes?" Jo asked. "I think we're going to need it."

Theresa shook her head. "Something isn't right. I *know* Brad is a good guy. I can feel it."

"You feel *lust*," Jo said. "If the geek—albeit *cute* geek—is meeting with Rosebud, then he's definitely involved in the No Good."

"Whether he's good or bad, this new development poses some interesting possibilities." Caylin twirled a strand of her red hair around a finger and stared thoughtfully at the digital photos.

"Please expound," Theresa said. "Right now I'm willing to try anything to get to the bottom of this nightmare."

"You can kill Brad with kindness . . . so to speak," Caylin explained. "If he really is one of the bad dudes, maybe you can coax him into giving you key data."

"And if he isn't, then I can grill him for information about Rosebud," Theresa concluded.

"Exactly."

Theresa pushed out the desk chair and walked back to the closet. "In that case, I'd better get ready for my date." She pulled her platform tennis shoes out of the closet. "I'm just glad Brad decided we should meet later in the evening. If we had left from work like we planned . . ."

"We never would have known that Brad might be a psycho," Jo finished the thought. "Meanwhile Caylin and I better put on our computer geek duds, too. We'll back you up all the way."

Theresa pulled on the silk blouse. "Phew! I didn't want to ask . . ."

"But it's always nice to have an extra Spy Girl or two

around when you're getting smoochie with a guy who might be planning to out you to Rosebud."

"You read my mind." Theresa laughed. Now. She was going to have to think about makeup. Evil or not, Brad deserved at least a little lip gloss. Cherry? Or strawberry? Hmmm . . .

"Is this place for real?" Caylin asked Jo on Tuesday night. "I feel like I've just walked into an episode of *Star Trek*."

"American culture has certainly taken a turn toward the weird," Jo agreed. The pair had followed Brad and Theresa to Arcadia, a twenty-four-hour, mall-sized, high-tech, video/virtual reality arcade. There were games everywhere, and the place was packed.

"How long are we going to have to sit in this virtual reality booth?" Caylin asked. "I'm getting a headache."

Jo negotiated her virtual car around a tight curve on a virtual freeway. "This is a perfect spot for the Rosebud Watch," she pointed out. "Besides, I'm having fun."

Caylin stuck her head out of the booth. "I don't think he's here. The scumbag would totally stick out in a place like this." She paused. "However, I think we're being checked out by two semihottie nerds who are playing the Ninja game."

"You don't say?" Jo's virtual Mercedes convertible spun out of control and she crashed. "Ouch." *Game Over* flashed mercilessly across the large screen in front of her. "Okay, okay, I can take a hint."

"Let's canvas the area for Rosebud," Caylin suggested. "Maybe he's hiding in one of the life-sized virtual boxing games." She slid out of her seat and stretched. Whew. No wonder people were drawn here. This was some intense stuff. Theresa was probably loving every second of it.

"Good plan. But we've got to keep a low profile," Jo replied as she stepped out of the machine. "Even if Rosebud is hiding in his lair tonight, I don't want the Bradster to get a gander of me."

The girls circled the area surrounding Brad and Theresa, who seemed engrossed in a game of electronic chess. They looked into every virtual reality booth, behind every video game, and even kept a short post next to the door of the men's bathroom. Nothing.

"I don't think Rosebud is here," Jo concluded. "We'd be able to sense his evil presence."

Caylin nodded. "I'm inclined to agree. I mean, what kind of malicious plan could be afoot for the night? I don't know too many crooks who warm up for illegal activity with a relaxing game of chess."

Jo giggled. "Theresa actually looks like she's having *fun*."

Caylin followed Jo's gaze. Theresa was laughing, her lip gloss shining effectively in Arcadia's techno lighting. "Different strokes."

"Well, remind *me* never to consent to a date with a computer geek," Jo said. "I prefer candlelight and slow jams."

Caylin sighed softly. At this rate it seemed unlikely that *any* of the Spy Girls *ever* was going to be romanced in a serious way. The idea of getting into a relationship was out of the question. Too bad. Caylin remembered what it was like to have a boyfriend—and she missed it.

"Sorry about that last checkmate," Theresa said as she climbed into a virtual reality game that promised to send her to the moon.

"Hey, I can take being beat four games in a row," he

responded, taking a seat close beside her. "I'm humbled . . . but very impressed."

"I, uh, play a lot of computer chess," Theresa explained as she put on the provided VR headgear. She knew most guys wouldn't find that statement to be terribly enticing, but Brad wasn't like most guys.

"Cool." Brad dropped several tokens into the slot and plunked on the headgear, and the ride to the moon began.

Theresa stared in awe as she flew through virtual outer space. She felt herself slipping into another state of being. She was no longer Tessa Somerset; she wasn't even Theresa Hearth anymore. She was Neil Armstrong, headed for that great big ball of cream cheese in the sky.

"This is awesome," Theresa said. "I can't wait to say, 'The *Eagle* has landed.'"

"Me neither," Brad agreed. He looked away from the screen and aimed his goggles in Theresa's direction. "You know, you're an amazing person, Tessa." Brad's voice was warm and sincere. "Most girls would think this kind of stuff is stupid."

Theresa navigated the spacecraft toward the cratered

surface of the moon. "Are you kidding? I'm in heaven."

No lie there. She *was* having a great time. Brad seemed like such a nice, normal guy. Was it really possible that he was involved with Rosebud?

Theresa racked her brain for an alternate explanation for his presence at Mega Mocha today. Maybe Rosebud was after him. Yeah, that had to be it. Rosebud had Brad pegged as a gullible guy who, with a little threatening and/or blackmail, would help him extract the code. That had to be it.

They were getting closer and closer to the moon. Now was the time to pry Brad for Rosebud info. He was totally entranced by the screen in front of them. Too entranced to be suspicious, hopefully.

"So there must be some pretty crazy characters hanging around FutureWorks." It was a statement, not a question.

"Yeah, I guess." Brad continued guiding them toward the moon's surface.

"Does anyone ever, like, try to take advantage of your vast knowledge of mainframes?" Theresa asked. "I mean, people try to do some pretty insane stuff with the Internet."

"The *Eagle* has landed!" Brad shouted.

Oops. She had missed her line. Oh, well.

"You know, people stealing credit card numbers and stuff right off the web." She negotiated her virtual self out of the space shuttle and took a step onto the moon. Unreal!

Brad took off his headgear. "Tell you what Tessa. Let's split," he suggested. "I want to show you something."

"But we're still on the moon." And I'm not done pumping you for information, she added silently.

"There's not much to see. Just a lot of rocks and dust." He stepped out of the booth and held out a hand.

She slipped off her headgear and took Brad's hand. "Where are we going?"

"Like I told you yesterday, it's a surprise." Brad gently placed his hand on the small of her back and guided her toward the huge red exit sign over one of the doors.

Theresa glanced surreptitiously over one shoulder. She couldn't see Jo and Caylin. But she was sure they would follow at a safe distance. And if they somehow got separated, then Theresa was confident she could handle Brad by herself. It wouldn't be *that* hard, would it?

"Say, 'supermodel,'" Jo cheered as the camera in the tiny photo booth clicked.

"Supermodel!" Caylin yelled. She stuck out her tongue and crossed her eyes. "Say, 'Uncle Sam'!"

"Uncle Sam!" Jo pursed her lips and tried to look semiseductive. The camera clicked again. "I love these booths."

Bored by watching the tedious progress of Brad and Theresa's fourth game of chess, Jo and Caylin had decided to explore the rest of Arcadia just in case Rosebud was hiding out in some heretofore undiscovered location. They hadn't found the tattooed one, but they *had* found a vintage, coin-operated photo booth. It proved the ideal tool for capturing their new makeovers on film for posterity.

"Too bad Theresa isn't with us," Caylin said. "It could have been a full-on Spy Girls photo session."

"Theresa! When was the last time we checked on her and the 'meister?" Even as she posed the question, Jo knew the answer.

Too long.

The girls stared at each other as the camera snapped one more time. "Let's go!" they chorused.

They more or less fell out of the booth and raced to the section of the arcade that housed the electronic chessboards.

Nothing. No one. Nada.

"They're not there," Jo said, stating the obvious. She looked wildly around the large arcade. By now the crowd had thinned out. The place was nearly empty, and there was no sign of Theresa or Brad.

"She's gone!" Caylin shrieked. Her face turned a peculiar shade that was somewhere between mustard yellow and pea green. "But we're not alone."

"Huh?" Jo was still scanning the room for a sign of Theresa's pale blue shirt.

"I just saw Rosebud—and he saw me." Caylin's voice was trembling as she spoke.

"Three, two, one, we're *outta* here!" Jo tugged on Caylin's arm and the girls fled.

• • •

"Now the real fun begins," Brad said as he led Theresa down a dark Seattle block.

"I'm intrigued." Theresa glanced around, taking in the sights. Huh. There was Mega Mocha. And now they were at the corner of Fleet Street.

"Is it my imagination, or are we walking to FutureWorks?" Theresa asked.

"You guessed it," Brad answered with a grin.

"Wow, you're a real romantic," Theresa joked. "We're going back to work for our first date?" But inside, she was shaking with a combo of excitement and nervousness. Was it possible that Brad was going to lead her straight to the code? It was. Unfortunately she couldn't ignore the fact that Brad could also be leading her straight to Rosebud and the barrel of a gun.

"I may not be great on the flowers and candy front, but I'm going to give you a night to remember," Brad said. "I'm going to show you what FutureWorks is *really* about."

Perfect, she thought. That was exactly what she wanted to hear. "I can't wait." And she meant that literally. The global economy was at stake.

"Take this," Brad said.

Theresa glanced at a rectangular piece of laminated plastic Brad had handed to her. Whoa. It was a fake security pass—complete with her photo! Okay, that explained the digital candid. But what was he up to? "Care to explain?" she asked.

He shook his head. "You'll just have to trust me."

At this point Theresa didn't trust *anyone*. Good thing Jo and Caylin were close behind. At least, she *assumed* they were.

"You're an expert," Theresa exclaimed, closely examining the pass. "This looks like the real deal."

Brad put his arm around her shoulders and squeezed. "I'm full of surprises, Tessa."

So am I, Theresa answered silently. So am I.

NINE

"Run!" Caylin yelled. "Run!" She could almost feel Rose-bud's breath on the back of her neck as she raced through Arcadia.

"I *am* running," Jo panted. "But he's still after us." Caylin pushed through a door marked No Entry and yanked Jo inside. They stopped in their tracks and looked around. Where were they? The room was dark and huge, with high ceilings. People wearing neon jerseys raced from side to side. Techno music blasted at an ear-shattering level.

"It's laser tag!" Jo said. "Let's find another way out!"

The girls joined hands and sprinted across the room. "Where's the exit?" Caylin shouted. She saw stairs and small *American Gladiator*–style barricades, but no other doors.

"I don't know—we just got more company!" Jo yelled over the music. Behind them Rosebud had slipped inside.

"I'm It!" Rosebud bellowed. "And you two are dead!"

Jo and Caylin ran behind an enormous speaker and squatted close to the floor. "There's got to be another exit!" Jo cried.

"I know!" Caylin shouted. "But it's so dark in here, I can't see anything!"

As Caylin's eyes adjusted to the dark room she peered out from behind the speaker. On the far side of the room she spotted a long, narrow staircase. She nudged Jo, pointing.

"Take the stairs!" Caylin screamed.

The girls darted out and raced across the room. They tripped up the steps two at a time. At the top Caylin realized they were on some kind of spectators' deck. She peered over the ledge. "Where is he?"

Gasping for breath, Jo staggered to Caylin's side. "There he is! Down there!" She pointed toward the laser tag floor. Yes! Rosebud was surrounded by a dozen angry nerds.

"Get off the floor, dude!" one of them yelled. "You're not in the game!"

"Beam him!" someone else shouted.

"I think that's our cue!" Caylin squinted and noticed a door at the end of the corridor marked Exit. "Jo! This way!"

Jo and Caylin ran down the spectators' platform and burst through the door. "We're safe!" Jo declared. They were in the parking lot of Arcadia, just steps away from their bus stop.

Caylin leaned against the side of the building, panting. "We may be safe, but we're stupid."

"Why? I mean, aside from the fact that we lost Theresa and Brad and almost got axed by Rosebud." She was holding her sides and blowing sweaty strands of hair off her forehead.

"The pictures," Caylin said flatly. "We forgot the pictures."

"Are we going where I think we're going?" Theresa asked, struggling to keep the excitement out of her voice.

Brad held Theresa's hand as they walked down a long, empty corridor on the second floor of FutureWorks. "Where do you think we're going?" he asked.

"The Monkey Room." She was almost breathless at the

thought. The Monkey Room. He might as well have told her he was taking her to Willie Wonka's chocolate factory. This was her golden ticket.

"Yep." Brad grinned proudly. "Impressed?"

"I'm in awe," Theresa responded. "How are we going to get in?"

"You'll see." Brad pulled Theresa to a stop in front of the security desk outside FutureWorks' center of operations. There were two guards on duty. One was deep into the latest issue of the *National Enquirer*. The other was dozing in front of a tiny black-and-white television set.

Well. Lax security or not Jo and Caylin wouldn't be able to scam their way past the tank-proof metal door blocking Theresa's path. If they were still tailing her at all, that is. Theresa was on her own . . . which was fine. Fine. Really.

"Hey, guys," Brad said casually to the rent-a-cops. "We're here for a virus check. The boss said there might be a glitch."

Security guard number one looked up from an article about aliens landing at the Mall of America. "Darn machines. We were better off without 'em."

Brad flashed his security pass, then indicated that Theresa should do the same. She held up her fake pass for inspection, but the guard barely gave it a glance. "Don't electrocute yourselves in there," he said. Then he pushed a small red button. And the door opened.

Brad clasped Theresa's hand and led her through. "This is it," she breathed. "This is the Monkey Room." Behind them the door closed with a soft whoosh. "I can't believe how easy it was to get inside."

"With the right tools, a souped-up PC, and a killer laser printer, *anything* is easy," Brad said proudly. "I got in here for the first time a month ago."

Theresa whistled softly. "This place is . . . incredible." And it was. They had entered what appeared to be a hermetically sealed chamber in which computers were the only decor. The floors were black marble, the walls hospital white. Everywhere Theresa looked, there was some kind of computer, monitor, or modem. On the wall were giant television screens, each of which showed a different site on the Internet. The place was like something out of a high-tech sci-fi movie. Watch out, James Cameron!

"We could do anything from here," Brad said, sitting down in front of one of the computers. "The hard drive of this baby feeds right into the Internet's mainframe. The information we could access is mind-boggling."

Theresa stood behind him, staring at the computer monitor. "Have you, like, tried to do . . . anything?"

Brad shrugged. "I've done a little hacking . . . nothing major so far." He paused. "If you want, I'll do a little sketch of the security blueprints I found. They're pretty radical."

"Great!" The more she knew about FutureWorks security, the better.

Brad pulled out a piece of notebook paper from the pocket of his khaki pants. Bells went off in Theresa's head as she stared at it. Brad was smoothing out the blank side of the paper, but Theresa was dying to see what was written on its reverse. "Hey, can I take a look at that?" she asked.

"Sure, Tessa. Whatever you want." Brad handed her the paper. "It's just some directions to some kind of game this guy gave me. He said I might find it interesting."

Theresa stared at the note, then pinched herself—

hard—on the arm. This was insanity. Written on the simple piece of notebook paper was everything Theresa would need in order to get the code. Sure, she'd have to do some pretty intense work, but the key parts were laid out right in front of her eyes.

"These are instructions," Theresa said. Should she say more? Biting her lip, Theresa decided to go for it. "They're instructions that could lead us to an extremely powerful code . . . or something."

"Wow." Brad stared at the writing on the page. "What do you want to do with it?"

Now *there* was a dumb question. "Let's follow the instructions," Theresa suggested excitedly. Was Brad really as clueless as he appeared? Or was he setting her up?

"I don't know. . . ." Brad's voice trailed off. "Those are some pretty intricate steps. I don't even know if I could make the transition from one instruction to the next."

This was the moment of truth. If Brad was playing dumb, it meant that there was a possibility that this whole situation had been engineered to Get Her. Maybe she would follow these instructions only to set off some kind of doomsday device that would blow her to tiny bits. But Brad was standing right next to her. Any harm she suffered would be suffered by him as well. Besides, time was running out. She had to go for it.

"I'll do it." Theresa slid into a chair in front of the computer. "Just get me a blank disc, and I'll take care of the rest."

Theresa's palms were sweating as she followed the first instruction. If all went according to plan, half an hour from now she would be able to say, "Mission accomplished."

"They probably went for a cup of coffee or something to eat," Caylin speculated. She was sipping a cup of lemon herbal tea and lounging on the leather sofa in a pair of sweats and soft cotton flannel. "Or maybe Brad wanted to show Theresa an all-night computer software shop."

"Yeah . . . I'm sure they're engaged in some perfectly harmless activity," Jo agreed. "Pretty soon Theresa will waltz in here all starry-eyed over the cyberkiss they shared." She stuffed half a sprinkled doughnut into her mouth.

"Right." So why did Caylin have that queasy feeling that usually meant trouble?

"Let's watch some tube," Jo suggested. "There's nothing like a bad sitcom to take your mind off body-art-ridden psychopaths."

Caylin glanced at her watch. "I'd love to spend a half hour watching the latest and lamest in prime time, but I think we'd better check out the news."

Jo sighed. "No rest for the weary." But she switched on the local news, anyway.

". . . And this just in from the AP," a perky blonde who had had one too many nose jobs trilled. "Brazen criminals change their appearances and smile for the camera!"

The anchorwoman's button nose was replaced with photographs of Jo and Caylin, resplendent in their new hair and makeup.

"No!" Caylin wailed. "Don't even tell me."

"Our quick pics," Jo stated. "The press got the prints from our impromptu photo session."

"How?" Caylin wondered, transfixed by the television screen. "I mean, we took those, like, an hour ago. How could the media possibly have gotten ahold of them?"

"Rosebud." Jo tossed the remote control at the television set and groaned. "He knew we were in the photo booth the whole time. And once we escaped, he went back and got the pictures."

"He's determined to get us arrested for that limo driver's murder," Caylin said. "And he's doing a pretty good job of it."

"That lout thinks he can frame us, get the code, and flee for who-knows-where with a Swiss bank account stuffed with zillions." Jo's voice was sad, resigned.

"That's what he *thinks*," Caylin growled, incensed. "But he doesn't know who he's dealing with."

Instantly Jo perked up. "Yeah . . . he doesn't know who he's dealing with!"

Caylin jabbed a finger toward the TV set. "We're the Spy Girls! There's no way we're letting him get away with that kind of bull."

"You said it, sister!" Jo jumped up, rallying. "Rosebud, prepare for jail! We're going to get you!"

Caylin hopped off the couch. There was a lot of thinking

to do. But before they could devise a plan, they needed one very important Spy Girl. Theresa. Caylin just hoped that Theresa was somewhere safe and happily hacking, not getting *hacked up*.

Forty minutes after sitting down in front of the computer, Theresa was sweating. Even with instructions she had to use one hundred percent of her brainpower to extract the code from the system. And now, as she pressed enter, she was prepared to see the end of the rainbow right on the monitor of the supercomputer.

"Enter," she whispered. The screen went black. "Dang!" She had railed. Theresa dropped her head in her hands and resisted the urge to cry.

Behind her Brad placed a gentle hand on her shoulder. "Wait—look!"

Theresa glanced back at the screen. Finally! There was the code—the be-all and end-all of this seemingly ill-fated mission—flashing right in front of her eyes. Yes!

Despair vanished and was quickly replaced with an intense rush of adrenaline. Theresa tapped the keyboard lightning quick, working deftly to store the code on disc. "Now it's time to say, 'bye-bye,'" she told the computer softly, her finger poised over the key that would extract the last little bit of information pertaining to the code from the mainframe forever. "But first, a word from our sponsors." How could she resist? By the time one of the bad guys got to her personal greeting, she would be *long* gone.

> So long, suckers!
> You won't be laughing all the way to the bank!
> Nyeah-nyeah!

Theresa saved the message on the computer, did one last check to assure herself that all useful information had been removed from the mainframe, then popped out the disc. *Finit.* She held out the disc for Brad's inspection. "Here it is. The key to the world's economy."

Brad took a couple of steps backward. "I don't think I want to be anywhere near that thing. It's, like, radiating power or something."

"I'll keep it," Theresa offered. Was this another trap? If so, Theresa was beyond caring. There was no way she wanted to let go of this disc no matter *what* travails she'd have to face. "Let's book."

"Wait—we've got one more stop," Brad told her.

Theresa followed Brad out of the Monkey Room, past the guards, and into the elevators, feeling increasingly nervous. What the heck was going on? Why was he taking her to the thirtieth floor?

"I'm stumped," Theresa said as she trailed Brad out of the elevator and down the hall to their shared cubicle. "Why are we back at our desks?" She had just experienced the most exciting hour of her life, and she was anxious to get back to HQ to fill in Jo and Caylin on the details. Plus she wanted to get the disc to safety ASAP.

"Getting into the Monkey Room is only step one," Brad explained calmly. "Now we have to make sure that the head cheeses never know we invaded their precious nerve center."

"This is yet another surprise, I take it," Theresa said, grinning at Brad. Why were his hazel eyes so sincere? Their warmth made it extremely difficult for her to maintain a healthy Spy Girl distance.

Brad nodded as he booted up his computer. "We've got to erase the digital security photos that were taken of us on our way in and out of the Monkey Room."

The guy thought of everything. Theresa had been *more* than satisfied with getting the code. But of course Brad was right . . . there was no doubt that whoever was in charge of Operation Money Grab paid close attention to who entered and exited the center of operations. She watched Brad's computer machinations, impressed.

"Like so. And so. And so." The digital photos that had filled Brad's monitor moments ago disappeared. "We're now nonpeople," Brad explained. "According to any record—official or unofficial—we never dropped by Ye Olde Monkey Room."

Theresa stared at Brad. Was this dude for real? He had given her a road map to the code. It was almost as if he had *wanted* her to find the answers she was looking for. Victor had tried to help, but he'd done little more than give her a few cryptic tips and let her off early from work when she needed to attend an emergency conference. But Brad . . . he had been an angel.

Hmmm. Could Brad actually be working for The Tower? Was it possible that he had been sent to meet up with Rosebud and garner information about the code *and* the frame-up? Truth be told, Theresa didn't know all that much about the guy. And it would be just like The Tower to install another agent without revealing it. They were masters of secrecy. Heck . . . the theory was worth a shot.

"Do you do a lot of, uh, covert computer work?" Theresa asked pointedly. "I mean, besides this FutureWorks stuff?"

"Um . . . one time I hacked into my older brother's e-mail," Brad answered. "But that was because I was really mad at him."

He wasn't biting. "Do you like, uh, James Bond movies?" Theresa asked. "I mean, I love all that *spy* stuff. The gadgets, the heroism, the secrecy—"

Brad snorted. "Are you *joking*? That stuff is *totally* unrealistic. Spies went out with the end of the cold war. Everyone knows that."

"Right. Right." Theresa felt her face turning crimson. Okay. Brad wasn't a Tower employee. That fact was all too clear. "It's just that I think you would make a great under-cover agent. You're so smart and, like, covert."

"Really? You think so?" Brad switched off his computer and took a step toward Theresa. "I've never had anyone tell me I'd be a great spy before. . . ."

His voice was soft, gravelly, mesmerizing. Brad was just inches from her now. And he was leaning closer and closer. Theresa closed her eyes. For one minute she was going to allow herself to be a girl, minus the "spy" she usually put in front of that particular label. She *was* human—code or no code.

A moment later Brad's lips touched hers. And Theresa forgot all about the code, the Monkey Room, and Rosebud. For now she was *really* enjoying being kissed.

"This is too much," Uncle Sam said over the speakerphone, his voice dark. "The Tower has never suffered such overt humiliation." For several long seconds the only sound in the room was that of Uncle Sam's heavy breathing. And then he spoke. "This mission is over. I want you out of Seattle at the crack of dawn."

Calling Uncle Sam had seemed like a good idea a few minutes ago. Emergency contact with The Tower usually resulted in at least one helpful hint. But Jo was beginning to question the wisdom of their decision.

"No way!" Jo exclaimed. "We can't abandon the mission."

Maybe they *shouldn't* have told Uncle Sam about the quick pics from Arcadia. After she and Caylin had taken turns describing the latest catastrophic sequence of events, Uncle Sam had exploded. And things were going from bad to worse. To worst.

"Besides, Theresa is out gathering info as we speak!" Caylin insisted. "We can't quit now."

"Give us a break, Jo," Uncle Sam snapped. "You and Caylin are having a high old time giving each other makeovers—and recording the whole thing for the world to see, no less."

"But Theresa—" Caylin interrupted.

"Theresa is out on a date," Uncle Sam said. "Victor told me all about it. You three are useless."

"No, we're not!" Jo shouted. "We can complete this mission. I know we can!" She took a deep breath and struggled to regain her tenuous, grip on calm. "We've just hit a few bumps in the road."

"This mission is over," Uncle Sam repeated flatly. "And so are the Spy Girls."

TEN

Theresa slipped her arms around Brad's waist as he pulled her closer. His lips were soft and warm and absolutely thrilling. Theresa melted into the kiss, savoring every moment.

Beep. Beep. Beep.

Dang. An annoying sound was invading the purity of her make-out session.

Beep. Beep. Beep.

Brad pulled away. "Is that your phone, Tessa?"

"Tessa?" Double oops. One little kiss shouldn't have made her forget her alias. "I mean, yeah. Yes!" She stepped out of Brad's arms and dug her phone out of the small handbag she had brought on the date. The text was clear: *911.* So much for smooching. She had to get back to HQ double-quick.

"Uh-oh, I gotta leave," Theresa told Brad.

"Why?" Brad was staring at her intently, arousing suspicion once again.

"It's my, uh, cat again. My roommate and I have a special cat-alert code." Theresa slipped on her jacket and smiled ruefully at Brad. "Sorry to kiss and run . . ." And she was even sorrier that she wouldn't be seeing him again. By this time tomorrow she would be halfway across the country.

"I'll walk you out," Brad offered, holding out his arm to Theresa.

"Thank you, kind sir."

Theresa followed Brad out of the office, thinking about their date from start to finish. The guy was too sweet to be evil. There was just no way that Brad was anything but a cute, semiclueless, but very endearing computer geek who was being used by Rosebud as some kind of weird pawn.

The trip to the ground floor of FutureWorks passed in a blur. Now that Theresa had recovered from Brad's spine-tingling kiss, her thoughts had turned to Jo and Caylin. What was the emergency? Cops? Rosebud? Well, whatever the problem was, they would handle it. Now that

Theresa had possession of the mission-completing information, they were home free.

Theresa trailed Brad out of the building, admiring the way his strong, broad back moved. It was too bad that ending the mission meant ending her romantic dalliance, but such was the life of a Spy Girl.

"Hello, kids." A dark figure stepped out of the shadows, blocking Brad and Theresa's path. "Nice evening, isn't it?"

A dangerous chill traveled down the length of Theresa's spine—significantly *less* pleasant than the chill she had felt in Brad's arms. Even in the dim light of the street she recognized Rosebud's face. There was no doubt that if he turned around, she would see the small, red tattoo on the back of his neck.

"What do you want?" Brad asked. "We were just leaving."

Rosebud sneered. "I want the disc, Brad." He paused, looking from Theresa to Brad to Theresa. "I believe you have it. And I want it now."

Brad stepped forward, blocking Theresa from Rosebud's view. "I don't have any disc, Simon," he said. "I don't know what you're talking about."

Rosebud laughed. "Yeah, right. There's no way you resisted going into the Monkey Room with that info I gave you today, geek. Why else would you be here late at night?"

"Tessa left her house keys in the office," Brad said. "Now I'd appreciate it if you got out of our way. We have a late date with a cat named Fluffy."

Theresa's heart was hammering in her chest. Brad certainly didn't appear to be in cahoots with Rosebud. And Rosebud didn't even seem to know who she was. She planned to keep it that way. Moving as if to take off her jacket, Theresa surreptitiously slid the disc into the waistband of her black pants. She would die before she gave it up to Rosebud.

"Trying to impress your girlfriend by showing her your big, bad computer skills, Bradley?" Rosebud chided. "I'm sure watching you hack got her all hot and bothered."

"Leave Tessa out of this," Brad said "Unless you want me to put my fist in your ugly face."

This encounter was *not* going smoothly. Theresa was going to keep her mouth shut, bide her time, and bolt. She hated to leave Brad on his own, but the entire world economy was at stake.

Ten, nine, eight, seven, *zero*. Theresa made a move to sprint.

Rosebud stepped in front of her. "You're not going anywhere, sweetheart. Neither of you is going anywhere until I get my hands on that disc." He pulled a small handgun out of the pocket of his trench coat. "Now get moving. We're all going back to work."

Going inside isn't an option, Theresa realized. This was her only opportunity to get away, and she was going to seize it—gun or no gun. Theresa faked right then ran. But before she got twenty feet away, Theresa felt the heavy blow of a cold, blunt object against the side of her head.

She crumpled to the sidewalk. Black dots floated before her eyes. A moment later the street seemed to be retreating farther and farther into the distance. And then her world faded to black.

"Why hasn't she responded to our text?" Jo shouted. "She knows a 911 means circumstances aren't just sticky, they're downright dire."

"Well, she didn't answer the text the other night,"

Caylin pointed out. "Maybe she just didn't think there was anything that could be important enough to take her away from her date." Caylin *wished* she believed a word of what she had just said. In truth, she was as panicked as Jo.

"Something is wrong," Jo said. "Something went seriously amiss, and Theresa needs our help."

Caylin had to agree. Drastic action was in order. But what? "We can't call Uncle Sam."

Jo snorted. "Ah, no. That would be, like, the worst idea in the universe."

Caylin stared into space, concentrating. Then she snapped her fingers. "Let's call Vince or Victor or whatever that Tower agent guy's name is. I'll dial."

Caylin pulled the speakerphone close while Jo went to the kitchen. She grabbed a tiny coded electronic address book—the one that held the direct numbers of all Tower contacts—from behind a flour jar.

Victor picked up on the first ring. "Yes?" Despite the semilate hour, Victor sounded alert and ready for action. Thank goodness.

Caylin briefed him quickly, explaining that she and Jo

were the agents working in concert with Theresa, his contact. The more she talked, the more she realized just how dangerous circumstances had become. She and Jo were wanted—makeovers and all—by every police officer in the state, and Theresa was effectively MIA.

"I can see why you girls are worried," Victor said when Caylin paused to breathe. "Clearly we must take steps to find Theresa."

"Yes!" Jo enthused. "Now you're speaking our language."

"I suggest you two meet me in front of FutureWorks as soon as possible," Victor said. "I don't want to go into details, but I have a hunch about what may be holding up your friend."

Hunches were good. Well, they weren't as good as actual concrete information, but Caylin wasn't about to argue. She and Jo were fresh out of ideas. "Well put together some quick disguises and meet you in twenty minutes," Caylin promised. She hung up the phone.

"Looks like we're going to have to go with the turban

and I-wear-my-sunglasses-at-night look," Jo said. "We've gone through everything else."

Caylin nodded. She would be willing to dress up as a Georgia peach if it meant they could complete this mission, redeem themselves, and live to spy another day. "Come on, Mata Hari," she said. "We've got lives to save."

Theresa blinked. She was dimly aware of a dull, throbbing pain in the back of her head. Slowly her surroundings came into focus. She was at her desk, in her chair. No, she wasn't just *in* her chair—she was tied to it! Theresa stared across the small office area and saw that Brad was bound in a similar fashion.

"Tessa?" he whispered. "Are you all right?"

She squeezed her eyes shut for a moment. "Um, aside from the obvious fact that I'm tied to a chair and my head feels like it's been booted up with an infected disc, I'm fine." Waking up a prisoner made her grouchy.

"Shut up!" Rosebud shouted at Theresa. "I'm thinking." He was standing in front of Brad's computer, pounding away at the keys. "It's gone. It's all gone. . . . I knew you extracted the code. I just knew it."

Theresa was beginning to regret the chirpy message she had left in place of the code. Apparently the computers at her and Brad's desks were more powerful than she had realized. Then again, Rosebud *was* the evil genius who had programmed the code in the first place. He didn't even need to go to the Monkey Room to assess the damage Theresa had done earlier.

A moment later the message flashed on the screen.

So long, suckers . . .

She didn't need to read the rest. Rosebud's face had turned a bright angry red, and his teeth were bared as if he were a bulldog going in for a kill. "Where is it Bradley?" he growled. "I know you have it. Give it to me. It's *mine.*"

"Wait a minute." Theresa looked away from Rosebud and confronted Brad. "You *knew* he was going to meet us here, didn't you?" she cried. "You're in on this! You had *me* extract the code so that you could give it to him and get off scot-free!"

Brad's eyebrows practically hit the ceiling. "Tessa, what are you—"

"That's it! You're *both* trying to frame me!" Theresa declared. "You wanted in on the deal, Brad, but you didn't want your hands to get dirty."

"*What* deal?" Brad shrieked.

Rosebud banged his fist on the keyboard. "I'd advise you to shut up *right* now, sister, before—"

"How much did he promise you, huh?" Theresa asked Brad. "Half? A quarter? Jeez, *one-sixteenth* of the entire world's economy isn't so bad when you think about it."

Rosebud picked up a monitor and threw it down with a crash. "Shut *up*!" he bellowed.

"How could you set me up, Brad?" Theresa asked tearfully, hoping waterworks would appeal to Brad's over-developed sensitive side. "How *could* you?"

Brad shook his head vigorously. "I swear, Tessa. I had no idea that Simon would do something like this. He just said it was a game, that's all. I—I mean, I don't really even know the guy. We met at a computer convention a few weeks ago and . . ."

"Quit your stupid yakking!" Rosebud screamed at Brad. He turned to Theresa with a smug smile. "Allow me to clear things up for you, *Theresa Hearth.* The computer geek never knew what hit him. *He* wasn't the one setting you up. I was. In fact, I was setting you *both* up."

Theresa grimaced. Rosebud had known who she was all along. And he had spent the last two days setting this trap . . . one she had walked right into and one that poor, gullible Brad never saw coming. "You're never going to get away with this," she spat out. "The Tower will stop you."

"Theresa?" Brad asked. "Who's Theresa?"

Rosebud backhanded Brad. "Shut up, dweeb." He turned back to Theresa. "I knew I had to get those instructions to you. You're the only person around with the skills to get the code . . . other than me, of course. But there was no way I could extract the code from the mainframe without getting caught—you and your idiot girlfriends were already on my trail. So I passed the info along to the doughboy over here and bingo! Here I am to pluck my code from your hands and be on my merry way. Now hand over the disc."

"I don't have any disc, jerk," Theresa insisted. "The code is gone. Vanished. I deleted it."

"And I happen to know that's impossible," Rosebud countered.

Theresa felt like puking. The code really *couldn't* be deleted, only transferred. Dang. Rosebud was right. He'd caught her. "Whatever," she managed to say. "There's still no disc. Why do you want it, anyway? Isn't the entire world economy supposed to turn over to you, like, by the weekend or something?"

"That's just the problem," Rosebud explained. "It *wasn't* going to turn over to me anymore. Someone else stepped in and decided to cut me out of the equation. So with your help, I'm taking the equation back."

The guy was so smug, so sure that he had won. And here she was, tied to a chair, powerless to stop him from winning this high-stakes game, and only falling deeper into his trap with each second.

Rosebud abandoned the computer. "Now that I've

proved that you did in fact get the code, I'm willing to bet the European economy that you've got it hidden on you somewhere." He walked toward Theresa. "I guess I'll just have to do a hands-on search."

Theresa closed her eyes. This was getting worse, worse, worse. She needed an SOS, and she needed it *now*.

"I'm glad you two were able to make it out tonight," Victor said as he hopped out of a taxi in front of FutureWorks. He seemed not to notice that both Jo and Caylin were wearing absurd outfits—pastel turbans, bell-bottoms, and giant sunglasses. They had decided that hiding in plain sight was the best way to avoid a cop confrontation.

"Do you know where she is?" Jo asked breathlessly. "Have you figured it out?"

Victor was calm, cool, and collected. "As I said on the phone, I have a hunch." He opened the door of FutureWorks with his passkey and motioned to the girls. "Let's go in, shall we?"

Energy was seeping out of Jo's pores as she followed Victor into the building. There was an electricity in the air that alerted her to some serious covert activity. Whatever they were about to find was going to make or break the mission.

They were all silent as the elevator rose swiftly and silently to the thirtieth floor. *Are you up there, T.?* Jo asked silently. *Are you in trouble?*

"This way, ladies," Victor said as they stepped out of the elevator.

"Let's hope for the best and expect the worst," Caylin suggested as they crept down the long hallway.

"Agreed." Theresa clenched and unclenched her fists, trying in vain to calm her fraying nerves.

"Aha!" Victor said as he turned the last corner. "I knew she was up here!" He stopped short. "But she's not alone."

Caylin and Jo stopped behind Victor. "Theresa!" Jo yelled. "I mean, Tessa!" Her heart pounded as she absorbed her friend's compromised position. Theresa was tied tightly to a chair, and Rosebud was looming over her like a vulture.

"Jo! Cay! Help!" Theresa's voice was desperate.

"What's going on here, Simon?" Victor asked Rosebud.

His voice had lost its cool, slightly British accent. He sounded more like Al Capone or John Gotti.

Rosebud stiffened. "I've, uh, captured these two. They were trying to get away with the code, but I stopped them. I was going to call you as soon as . . . well, anyway, the situation is under control, Chief."

Chief?

Jo glanced at Caylin, who was staring intently at Victor. "Are you thinking what I'm thinking?" Jo asked.

"You're lying!" Victor screamed at Rosebud. "You were trying to pull a fast one on me, Simon. And I don't appreciate that." He crossed the room and put his hands around Rosebud's neck. "That code and all that it stands for is *mine*!"

Caylin grabbed Jo's arm. "Yes," she finally answered. "I'm thinking *exactly* what you're thinking." She paused. "It's definitely time for plan C . . . or D . . . or F!"

ELEVEN

Victor pulled a gun from his pocket and pointed it at Rosebud's head. "You're not getting out of here with that code, Simon. And you're not going to see a dime of the cash I've got coming to me."

"Chief, I swear I was only trying to—"

"You're going to die tonight, Simon," Victor continued, his voice calm once again. "I had always planned to kill you—I just hadn't realized it was going to happen at this particular juncture. But so be it. We can't plan for all of life's little surprises."

Theresa gasped as the awful truth unfolded before her. Victor had been using her as a pawn all along. And he had used Rosebud, too. While Rosebud had thought he was going to outsmart Victor and get away with the code and the cash, Victor had planned from the start to do away with Rosebud when the time was right. Victor was the one who was trying to take control of the code—the executives at FutureWorks had nothing to do with it. Theresa wasn't going to shed any tears for Rosebud, but Victor's actions infuriated her.

"You're a traitor," she said quietly. "You're evil."

"And you're in deep, deep trouble, honey. Each and every one of you is going to die tonight," Victor said, waving the gun at Caylin and Jo. "One by one, you're all going to die!" Then slowly, methodically, he pointed the gun at Rosebud. "Then again, maybe I'll just put my tattooed friend in ICU. I think I can depend upon him to point the police in your direction."

Bang!

Rosebud moaned, grabbed his shoulder, and sank to the floor in a pool of blood.

Do something! Theresa silently urged her fellow Spy Girls—and herself. She struggled against her restraints, accidentally knocking over her chair in the process. As she fell, the all-important disc flew out of her waistband and landed at Victor's feet.

"Just as I suspected." Victor bent over to pick up the disc.

From her position on the floor Theresa watched as Caylin retreated several steps down the hall. Where was she going?

"Prepare to die, girls and guy." Victor slid the disc in his back pocket. "I have what *I* came for."

Behind Victor's back, Caylin assumed a sprinter's starting position. Then she *flew.* With a warrior-princess scream Caylin leaped onto Victor's back and knocked him to the ground.

Victor reached back and pushed his palm against Caylin's jaw. Her head reared, but she kept him pinned.

Jo raced over to Theresa's side. She cut away the binding ropes with a comb that doubled as a switchblade.

"Brad!" Theresa yelled. "Free Brad!"

Jo sped to Brad's side. Theresa shook out her numb wrists and hopped on her sleeping feet to help Caylin. Too late. Victor knocked Caylin off him. In a split second Victor was on his feet, waving the gun again.

"Cay! Look out!" Theresa screamed.

Too late again.

Bang!

Theresa heard glass shatter down the corridor.

Whew. Close call.

"Watch out!" Jo yelled from behind. She held a desk chair over her head, swung it back to gather momentum, and hit . . . Brad. Jo hadn't realized the guy was standing right behind her. He slid to the floor, unconscious.

"Brad!" Theresa yelled. "Oh, jeez!"

"Oops!" Jo turned to survey the damage.

"Too bad," Victor exclaimed. "You girls are mine now. Time to—"

Caylin jumped up on a desk and leapfrogged toward the office's low ceiling. She grabbed an exposed pipe. In a blur she swung and kicked her feet out. Bull's-eye. Her platforms smacked the creep in the head.

"—die." Victor's eyes rolled back and he fell forward in a heap.

"Get the disc!" Caylin yelled, dropping to the floor.

Theresa pushed aside Victor's coat and swiped the disc from his back pocket. "Got it!"

Jo grabbed the gun from Victor's fist and slipped it into her waistband. "Let's get the you-know-what out of here! Victor is starting to groan!"

Theresa paused. "What about Brad?" He was still lying on the floor, breathing easily but unconscious.

"We've got to leave him here," Caylin said, her hand on Theresa's shoulder. "He'll be fine. Without his gun Victor is powerless."

Theresa cast one last, longing glance at Brad and followed Jo and Caylin toward the elevator bank. Doors opened. Doors shut. Someone pressed "lobby." And they were going down, out, and away from the whole ugly scene.

Jo pointed at the gun hidden under her shirt. "You don't think it was a mistake to take Victor's gun, do you?"

Theresa shook her head. "We had no choice. Brad's life was at stake."

Jo nodded. "Yeah, you're right. Besides, what else could go wrong at this point? I think we've made all the mistakes we're going to."

"As long as we can get out of Seattle tonight, everything

will be fine," Caylin said. "We can't give the cops even twelve more hours to find us."

"Spy Girls unite!" Jo cheered. "Good-bye, Seattle!"

Back at headquarters Jo and Theresa paced as Caylin dialed and redialed Uncle Sam's number.

"It's no use," she said finally. "He disconnected our direct line to him." She threw down the phone and sighed deeply. "As far as Uncle Sam is concerned, we don't exist. The Tower receptionist pretended she didn't even know my *name*!"

"Danielle!" Jo shouted. "We've got to call Danielle before Uncle Sam gets to her and tells her not to have anything to do with us."

Caylin didn't need to look up Danielle's number. She had memorized it the *last* time the girls had called her frantic for help. Caylin couldn't even believe it had come to this: They had completed their mission and exposed a crooked agent, yet The Tower was freezing them out. What did it all mean? She hoped Danielle would explain it all. Unless she was freezing them out, too.

Jeez.

"While you all talk to Danielle, I'm going to transfer the code," Theresa told them. "We can save the information in my can of mousse—it's actually a hard drive."

"Good idea," Jo said. "I doubt any thief, double agent, or psychopath would go out of their way to steal our hair-care products."

Caylin punched in the last digit of Danielle's phone number in Washington, D.C. When she answered, her "Hello?" was groggy. Correction—it was near comatose.

"It's us!" Caylin said urgently. "Danielle, we need your help in the worst way."

"Victor is a traitor," Jo interrupted. "He shot Rosebud and tried to kill us. Well, he would have, except Caylin knocked him out first. Anyway, we're still wanted by the cops—you know, they've got out that APB on Caylin and me. And now Uncle Sam won't even talk to us! Can you believe that? And—"

"Slow down," Danielle interjected. "Take a deep breath and get ahold of yourself, Jo. You're scaring me."

"You've got to help us, Danielle," Caylin said, taking

over. "We need to get out of this state *pronto*."

"I sympathize with you girls," Danielle said with a yawn. "I really do . . . but unfortunately there isn't time for me to get to Seattle and lend you a hand." She paused. "You're on your own."

Theresa emerged from her bedroom, wielding her now precious can of mousse in one hand. "You've *got* to help us, Danielle!" she cried. "If you have to, abuse your authority or something. Please." She held the can of mousse close to her chest. "Just do what it takes to get us out of Seattle with the code."

"You have the code?" Danielle asked, her voice disbelieving.

"*Yes!*" all three chorused.

"Why didn't you say so before?" Danielle replied.

"Because we need to get out of here, like, yesterday!" Caylin said impatiently. "We need cash, and we need a car," she demanded. She was sure that Uncle Sam had canceled their Tower credit cards, and there was no way they would make it out of Seattle by plane. The airport was probably crawling with Feds. "If you don't provide those items, we're not going to be held responsible for our actions."

Danielle sighed. "All right, give me half an hour. I'll have a car and a couple of thousand in cash waiting for you outside HQ."

"Thank you!" Jo cried. "Thank you!"

"As soon as we're somewhere relatively safe we'll get on a plane to D.C.," Caylin declared. "You've got to meet us at the airport there so we can give you the code. It has to be you, Danielle. Sam won't even speak to us."

"Let me know when you're arriving, and I'll be there," Danielle promised. "But you girls better be careful. If there's any more trouble, even *I* may not be able to help you."

Caylin felt tears threatening to spill as she stared at the speakerphone. How could The Tower doubt their skills or their loyalty? Everyone made mistakes. Why were they being shut out?

"Danielle, you know . . . we really are good girls," Caylin began. "Don't believe anything that anyone tells you about us . . . because it's just *so* not true."

"Just get me the flight information when you have it," Danielle said. "We'll talk then."

Caylin hung up the phone, then turned to her fellow Spy Girls. "We've got a half hour to destroy any and all evidence that we were here."

Exchanging not another word, each girl set herself to the grim task. They had thirty minutes to erase themselves from Seattle, and they were going to need every second. This was the race of their lives. And a race *for* their lives.

Jo felt as if she hadn't taken a shower in a week, but she felt satisfied that no police raid on headquarters would ever reveal privileged information about the Spy Girls or The Tower. They'd dismantled, smashed, deprogrammed, and torn down everything. They'd thrown all volatile paperwork into the Dumpster in the alley and burned it to cinders.

All that was left downstairs was a normal-looking store with an empty cash register. There had been some moral quibbling over raiding it, but in the end all it yielded was about sixty-seven dollars. "No one pays cash anymore," Caylin had griped.

Part of Jo wondered why they were bothering to look

out for the interests of The Tower at all. Uncle Sam had turned his back on them, and yet here they were, busting their butts to protect the integrity of the agency.

We're working for a greater good, Jo reminded herself as she kept a vigil for the car that was supposedly arriving any minute. No matter how The Tower treated them, the facts remained the same. Jo was committed to saving the world from the kind of people who had gunned down her father when she was fourteen.

Through the window Jo saw a bright pair of headlights coming down the deserted block in front of HQ. "Let's go!" Jo yelled to Theresa and Caylin, who were throwing the last of their belongings into duffel bags. "The car is waiting!"

Theresa emerged from Jo's room. "I got most of your stuff . . . but we didn't have time to pack everything."

"Who cares?" Jo asked. "Right now I'm more worried about my life than my sundresses."

"Let's rock and roll!" Caylin shouted, entering the living room with two duffel bags slung over her shoulder. "The sooner we blow past Seattle city limits, the happier I'll be."

The girls fled the apartment without looking back. They clattered down the narrow metal staircase to the now decimated warehouse and raced through Seattle Sounds. When they hit fresh air, there was a collective sigh of relief.

A tall, dark, thin man—The Tower agent Danielle had promised them—stood next to a Cadillac sedan. In his hand was an envelope bursting with cash.

"I'll take that," Jo said, grabbing the envelope.

The agent balked. "As an agent of the United States government, I feel compelled to advise you to turn yourselves in. The Tower no longer recognizes you as an official entity. Once captured by police, you will have to go through the legal system on your own." He paused. "Make things easier for yourselves and give up now. The real truth will come out, one way or the other."

What? Give up? Get captured? Hope the truth will just eventually "come out" after Uncle Sam turned his back on them?

Never.

Jo pulled Victor's gun out of her waistband. "Forget it!"

she shouted, waving the weapon in the agent's face. "We're innocent!"

"Yeah!" Theresa yelled. "We were just doing our *job*. If The Tower is going to let us down, fine. But we're not going to let ourselves be sitting ducks for blood-hungry coppers!"

Caylin sprinted to the driver's side of the Cadillac and hopped in. "Get in, Spy Girls!" she called. "We're going, going, *gone!*"

Holding The Tower agent at bay with Victor's handgun, Jo opened the passenger-side back door for Theresa, who dove inside. Jo followed, and Caylin revved the engine. A moment later they roared down the street.

"Yeehaw!" Jo yelled. "Free at last!"

TWELVE

"California, here we come!" Jo sang Wednesday morning. "California dreamin'! Wish they all could be California girls! I mean, guys!"

Theresa rubbed her eyes and blinked at the bright sun rising in the clear blue sky. The side of her cheek was stuck to the Caddie's leather interior, and there was a sharp, shooting pain in her right thigh. Theresa shifted in the seat. The seat belt clasp had been digging into her leg all night.

"Where are we?" Theresa asked, stifling an enormous yawn.

"We just crossed the border into California," Jo informed her from the driver's seat. "We are now officially two states away from the source of our horrendous troubles."

On the other side of the backseat Caylin opened her

eyes and wiped some drool off her chin. "Did I hear some-one say, 'California'?"

"Yep." Jo honked the horn. "Whoopee!"

"I'm starved," Theresa announced. A moment later her stomach growled so loudly that Caylin and Jo burst into giggles. "I guess that frozen burrito circa four-thirty in the morning didn't fill me up."

"I, for one, could use about a dozen cups of coffee," Jo said. "Not only have I been driving most of the night, but I also think I got slightly addicted to caffeine during my gig at Mega Mocha."

Caylin pointed to a green sign on the side of the high-way. "Next stop: Peculiar, California," she announced. "It sounds like the perfect place for three tired, hungry Spy Girls to grab a little breakfast action."

Jo guided the luxury sedan toward the Peculiar high-way exit. She sped onto the ramp, then slowed the car as they reached a traffic light. "Which way?" she asked.

Theresa sat up straighter and glanced from left to right. "Let's go right," she said. "I see a sign for a place called Moody's Diner down the road."

Two minutes later Jo pulled into the parking lot of a small diner that appeared to be a converted gas station. The parking lot was full of dusty pickup trucks and ancient station wagons. "Looks like we'll be pretty safe here," Jo commented. "I don't think Bobby Jim and Billy Ray will be too interested in a couple of wanted Spy Girls."

"Yeah, we'll just do the hat, scarf, sunglasses thing," Caylin said. "It's all we've got on us, anyway. And if anyone thinks it's strange, we'll claim we're allergic to the sun."

The girls trooped into Moody's Diner and slid into a large booth next to the window. For a few minutes they stared at their menus with the kind of intense concentration that only three starving fugitives could muster.

"I think I'll have the Zip-a-dee-doo-da Breakfast Bagel," Caylin announced when a gum-snapping waitress arrived at the table. "And a side of fruit salad."

"Double chocolate pancakes, a side order of spicy hash browns, and a bottomless cup of coffee, please," Theresa told the waitress.

"Make that a bottomless *pitcher*, please," Jo requested. "And I would love to try the Northwest Mountain Sunshine

Plate. I've always wanted to have bacon, sausage, *and* ham during the same meal." She pushed her menu aside and stretched as the waitress retreated.

Caylin did the same. "Wow. I actually feel semi-normal for the first time since I set tail in that white limo."

"No kidding," Theresa agreed, pausing as the waitress set down a pitcher of coffee and three cups. "I think I could happily spend the rest of my life in a computer-free environment. I've had hard drives and mainframes coming out my nostrils." She had even dreamed about the mission during her not-very-satisfying night of sleep—encoders, decoders, and endless strings of numbers, letters, and passwords had raced through her brain as she tried to escape from a maze filled with treacherous Tower agents. It gave her the willies just thinking about it.

"I think we can say with some certainty that the worst is behind us," Jo declared, pouring milk into her cup of coffee.

"Yep. By tomorrow night we'll turn over the code, get back in The Tower's good graces, and be cleared of any miscreant deeds," Caylin said.

"Happy days are here again, let's smile, smile. . . ." Theresa's voice trailed off as she caught sight of the TV set that was positioned at the end of the diner's counter.

Wonderful. Right next to a lemon meringue pie under glass was the nine-by-thirteen-inch black-and-white image of Caylin's graduation photo. Man, she was starting to *hate* TV.

"Wh-what?" Jo stammered. "What is it, T.?"

"Um, scratch what I just said," she announced. "Don't look now, but it looks like our bizarro girl gang has just gone national."

Ouch. Double ouch. Triple ouch. What next?

Jo slipped quietly out of the booth and took a seat next to Theresa. She actually wanted to see what new horror the newscaster was sharing with the American public.

"Here you go, girls," the waitress said. She slapped each girl's order down in front of her. "I hope your mouths are as big as your eyes 'cause you three ordered enough food for five lumberjacks." She turned toward the TV. "Hey, there's a story about those crazy teenagers!"

Jo slid into her seat. I am invisible, she told herself. Caylin was invisible. They were all invisible. She stared at the TV through her eyelashes and held her breath.

"Turn it up, Charlie!" the waitress called to the cook. "I want to hear this."

Every head in the diner turned toward the small television set. "Police believe that the now infamous Terrorist Trio have fled Seattle," the newscaster announced. "Through a wiretap, detectives were able to recover a telephone conversation during which one of the female gang members demanded two thousand dollars in cash and a vehicle from an unidentified female."

As the incriminating phone call played, the station showed security cam footage of Caylin and Jo walking— then running—through Arcadia.

"Is it as bad as it sounds?" Caylin whispered.

Jo nodded. "Worse." Naturally, the police didn't happen to pick up the first part of Caylin's conversation with Danielle. There was no mention of Victor or the fact that they were being framed.

"We really are good girls," Caylin's voice blared over

the TV. "Don't believe anything that anyone tells you about us . . . because it's just *so* not true."

"Please tell me that's all they have," Theresa whispered.

Jo couldn't tear her eyes away from the small television. The newscaster was back on the air, reporting that an eyewitness had informed detectives that one Theresa Hearth had stolen important, highly sensitive information from the mainframe at FutureWorks.

"What eyewitness?" Caylin demanded. "Who?" It was obviously killing her that she couldn't see the TV from where she sat. Jo glanced at Caylin and saw that a vein in the side of her forehead was throbbing.

"It's Victor!" Theresa hissed. "That jerk."

Jo watched Victor being interviewed by a local Seattle reporter. He was in elegant mode, eminently trustworthy in a gray pin-striped suit and bowler hat. The louse.

"Yes, the entire situation was *quite* alarming," Victor said. "Theresa Hearth held myself and another young man hostage while she and her accomplices stole a disc holding a virus that could end the entire world banking system." He stared innocently into the camera. "They have already killed one man, shot another, and put countless people in danger. Those girls *must* be stopped—by any means necessary."

The newscaster reappeared on-screen. Thank goodness. Jo didn't think she could look at Victor's treacherous face for one more second without yakking.

"Evidence confirms the eyewitness account of events," the anchorman announced. Flash to FutureWorks security footage, obviously taken inside the thirtieth-floor elevator bank. A shadowy Theresa held what was clearly a computer disc. Another clip followed. Uh-oh. This one featured Jo waving a gun and shouting. Not good.

"One male cohort who failed to escape from the scene of the crime is being held in custody," the newscaster reported over the footage. "However, he claims to know nothing of the events that transpired, only claiming that he is innocent."

"Poor Brad!" Theresa whispered. "I can't believe I got him into this mess."

"If anyone sees these three young women, please contact the FBI immediately," the newscaster finished. "Once again, they are considered armed and dangerous." The plastic-looking anchor paused. "Alarmingly, that hasn't stopped teenage girls all over the country from taking up the cause of this mysterious Terrorist Trio. Parents are concerned."

Jo, Caylin, and Theresa stared at one another over the plates of rapidly cooling breakfast. None of them had taken so much as a bite of their meals.

"We're a *cause*?" Caylin asked softly. "What does that *mean*?"

"I think I'd laugh if our butts weren't on the line," Jo whispered. "I mean, they're, like, analyzing us. Caylin is the ringleader. I'm the brawn. And Theresa is the brains."

"We're like a cartoon," Theresa agreed. "Or a bad afternoon sitcom."

"Whoa . . . check this out." Jo turned back to the television. A group of teenage girls were on the screen, all decked out in Spy Girl disguise makeovers. Red hair. Skunk hair. Butterfly tattoos. Sunglasses. Scarves. The whole bit. The girls were also holding up signs for the news camera: It's Just *So* Not True.

"The Terrorist Trio, are, like, conspiracy victims," one of the girls, made up like Caylin, told a reporter. "The system is against us! Young women get *no* respect!"

Suddenly Caylin swiveled around to face the TV set. "You go, sister!" she burst out. "Right on!"

Jo cringed as every person in Moody's Diner turned to stare at their table.

She slid lower in the booth and prayed that the fact that each of them was wearing a hat, a scarf, and sunglasses wouldn't arouse suspicion.

Fat chance.

"The Terrorist Trio allegedly escaped Seattle in a midnight blue Cadillac Seville," the newscaster reported. "They are believed to be heading south."

In unison, the diner patrons craned their necks to look through the restaurant's huge glass windows. Jo knew what they were looking for. And she knew what they were going to see.

"Let's get breakfast to go!" Jo hissed. The girls picked up their food—plates, napkins, silverware, and all—and tore out of the diner.

"We'll send you the money for our bill!" Theresa yelled to the waitress as they ran.

"Yeah," Caylin agreed. "From jail!"

An hour later the Spy Girls were doing sixty-five down the highway. "Still no sign of troopers," Theresa reported from her lookout in the backseat.

"We're almost there," Caylin said. "The turnoff for Pirate's Cove is only two miles away."

"I know we all said we wanted to spend some time at your parents' summer beach house," Jo said as the Caddie raced toward the exit. "But I was hoping our stay would be under different circumstances." She cruised onto the exit ramp and followed Caylin's directions to the house.

"All we have to do is ditch the car and get in touch with Danielle," Theresa said. "Then we'll be outta there. Caylin's parents never need to know we stopped by without a formal invitation."

"Turn here!" Caylin instructed Jo. "The house is just a mile down the . . ." Her mouth dropped open. The usually deserted beach road wasn't deserted at all. First she saw the local channel nine news van. Then she saw the host of *American Investigator* sipping a cup of coffee. Then she noticed about a dozen cop cars.

"Curses! Foiled again!" Jo yelled. She slammed on the brakes. The Cadillac fishtailed as Jo did a one-eighty.

"Make a sharp left!" Caylin ordered. "I know a secret way back to the highway."

Jo drove the car onto a road that was little more than a trail, hoping for the best. In the distance she heard the unwelcome sound of sirens. "I hope you know what we're doing!" she told Caylin.

"I'll get us out of this," Caylin promised. "And then I'll take us to a place where I *know* we'll be safe."

"Where's that?" Theresa asked.

Caylin sighed. "It's a long story. I'll tell you on the way."

"Here we are," Caylin announced forty-five minutes later. "Mount Lassen."

Theresa was gazing out the car window and nibbling on a cold double-chocolate pancake. "All I see are trees," she said. "Are you sure there's an actual *house* here somewhere?"

"Take a right, Jo," Caylin instructed. She turned to look at Theresa. "Not just *any* house, *Tessa*. A mansion."

As Jo made the turn the woods opened up, revealing a huge log cabin built near the side of a mountain. A wide driveway led to what looked like a four-car garage. She whistled. "Your ex-sweetie lives well," Jo commented.

"Mike Takeshi isn't just an ex-boyfriend," Caylin said sharply. "He was my first love." Just seeing the oversize cabin caused a flood of memories. Caylin's first kiss. Mike carving their initials in the cellar wall. Picnicking in the moonlight. It all seemed as if it had happened a lifetime ago.

"Park here," Caylin instructed. "We can walk up to the house and make sure nobody is around."

"What makes you think no one is going to be there?" Theresa asked. She had polished off one pancake and moved on to another.

"The Takeshis are *never* here," she said. "Mike always flew out a couple of times a year to make sure the pipes weren't frozen or anything. But other than that, the place sat empty all through high school." She paused, staring at the house. "Except for one time . . . when a bunch of us came out for a vacation."

Jo threw the car into park, and the girls climbed out. "I hope there are a lot of canned goods in the cupboards," she said as they crept up the driveway. "I'm still hungry."

The girls neared the house and tiptoed to the windows at the front of the cabin. "Ssh!" Caylin ordered. "I'll make sure the coast is clear."

Jo and Theresa followed, giggling as they began to circle the property. Caylin heard a large branch snap behind her, then a loud "Ummph!"

She spun around. Jo had tripped over a fallen branch and landed face first. "Owwww!" she moaned, holding her ankle with both hands.

"Who's there?" A deep, masculine voice emanated from somewhere near the front door. "Tell me who's there."

So much for ultimate privacy. "It's me, Mike," Caylin called.

"Pike!" Mike Takeshi emerged from the house, every

bit as good-looking as she remembered. Tall, delectable, with a surfer's body, honey-tanned skin, and a poet's eyes, the sight of Mike had always made Caylin's heart race.

He walked toward Caylin, paused, and enfolded her silently in his arms. She inhaled the scent of him, savoring the sensation of his strong arms around her waist. At last he pulled way. "Are you okay?" he asked. "I've been watching the news. . . ."

Caylin nodded. "We're fine—so far." She glanced over his shoulder. "Are your parents here?"

"Nope. They're in Europe for the month." He paused. "Is it true?" Mike asked Caylin, his brown eyes questioning.

Caylin raised her eyebrows. "Got a couple of days?" she asked.

Mike took Caylin's hand and led them toward the house. "For you, Pike, I've got all the time in the world."

THIRTEEN

"I don't think I've ever fully appreciated the comfort of a leather recliner before." Theresa tipped back in the recliner and pulled out the footrest. "I could sleep for hours in this thing."

"Speak for yourself," Jo said. "I'm hoping Mike is going to offer me one of the many guest rooms this house has got goin' on." She gave him her most pleading, pretty-please look.

Mike grinned. "After the story you guys told me, I'll offer you a medal. You guys have been through hell."

"You believe us?" Theresa asked. At this point she was so used to being suspected of horrible crimes that she half wondered if Mike was going to pull out a gun and haul them off to prison.

Mike stared meaningfully at Caylin. "Pike has never

lied to me. I would never doubt anything she said."

Theresa and Jo raised their eyebrows. The affection in Mike's eyes was hard to miss. Hmmm. Caylin had apparently neglected to fill in her fellow Spy Girls on some of the juicier parts of her past.

"You can't tell *anyone* what I've told you." Caylin scooted closer to Mike on a comfy plaid flannel sofa. "Not now. Not ever. This is, like, as top secret as top secret gets."

"Don't worry." Mike reached over to push Caylin's bangs out of her eyes. "I won't tell a soul."

"If you do, we'll have to kill you," Jo warned. An awkward silence followed. Jo laughed nervously. "Okay, *not* the time to joke about murder and mayhem. Understood."

"Remember when we took the snowmobiles up the mountain during our junior year?" Mike asked Caylin. "You buried yours in a snowbank and it took me four hours to dig the thing out."

Caylin laughed. "Excuse *me.* I'm not the one who practically set the whole house on fire because I didn't know I had to open the flue in the fireplace."

Theresa looked from Mike to Caylin, appreciating the

warmth of their relationship. Maybe she and Brad would have the chance to form that kind of rapport . . . if she were still in Seattle and he weren't stuck in the clinker.

"You know what you need?" Mike began. "You need a good, old-fashioned four-wheeling adventure. It'll take your mind off this mess."

"I don't know. . . ." Caylin clearly wanted to go, but she looked hesitantly at Jo and Theresa. "Don't you guys think we should try to get in touch with Danielle?"

Jo shrugged, yawning. "I'm not doing *anything* until I've had a serious nap. Go have fun. We'll hold down the fort—or the cabin, as the case may be."

Caylin grinned. She looked happier than she had in days. "All right!" She pulled Mike off the sofa. "But *I'm* driving."

"You're pretty cute as a redhead," Mike said as he climbed into the Hummer parked in the garage. "I think I could get used to the new you."

Caylin's heart fluttered as she slammed the driver's side door shut. All of a sudden she realized just how alone she and Mike were. The souped-up army vehicle was its own private world, and Mount Lassen felt as if it were a thousand miles away from civilization.

"You look great, too, Mike. You always do." She stared into his warm brown eyes, seeing years' worth of good times reflected in their depths.

"When you broke up with me, you said it was because you needed space to find yourself," Mike said quietly. "But now that I know what you've been doing the past few months—or part of it, anyway—I have to wonder if you really wanted things to end. You know, between us."

Caylin swallowed painfully. "Don't make me answer that question, Mike. I can't."

He placed his hands on her shoulders. "You were trying to protect me, weren't you?" he asked. "Admit it, Caylin. You still love me."

"We were planning to go four-wheeling," Caylin said, her voice high and shrill. "Don't get all heavy on me now."

Mike sighed as he relaxed into the passenger seat and buckled his seat belt. "I'll let this go for now, Pike. But I deserve some answers."

Caylin threw the Hummer in reverse and backed out of the garage. She knew she was due for a serious talk with Mike at some point. But right now all she wanted to do was climb high in the mountains and drive her troubles away.

"Are you asleep, T.?" Jo asked. They had staked claim on two twin beds in one of the Takeshis' opulent guest rooms.

"No," Theresa answered, rolling over in bed. "I can't stop trying to figure out how everything on this mission went so haywire."

"Same here." Jo nestled more deeply into the down comforter and contemplated counting sheep. Or llamas. Or anything that might help her get a few hours of much needed REM.

"One good thing has come out of this whole thing," Theresa commented. "Mike and Caylin are reunited."

Jo yawned. "Yeah . . . Caylin is lucky. Mike's a hottie."

"No kidding. The guy makes Brad Pitt look like chump change."

"I'm the only one who hasn't got any lovin' on this

mission," Jo said, feeling cranky. "It's not fair." She had seen hot guy after hot guy waltz into Mega Mocha, but she had kept her hormones under control in order to complete the mission without unnecessary complications of the masculine sort. What a mistake!

Theresa groaned. "Please! You got action on the last two missions. And might I add that your judgment regarding the male half of the species isn't always the best?"

"Okay, time to change the subject." Sure, Jo had kissed a few bad guys. What agent worth her weight in designer duds hadn't?

"Fine. Let's talk about our next move," Theresa suggested. "We're both obsessing over it, anyway."

Theresa was right. There was no time like the present to map out a plan. Goodness knew they needed one. "We can't go to D.C.," Jo concluded. "The cops might have heard us telling Danielle we would meet her there."

"We'll have to tell Danielle to meet us somewhere else," Theresa concurred. "But where?"

Jo thought for a moment. They needed anonymity, and they needed freedom of movement. Yes, that was it. The

Spy Girls needed the ability to get lost in a crowd. They had learned from their Moody's Diner experience that taking the backwoods route wasn't a stellar tactic. "We'll go to Los Angeles," Jo said finally.

Theresa's eyes drifted shut. "Ah . . . L.A. Sand, beaches, sunshine. I like it."

Jo felt her own eyelids grow heavy. "Yeah . . . as soon as Caylin gets back we'll make the call. Tonight. Tonight we'll head south."

"And after this is all over we'll make sure Brad is okay, right?" Theresa asked, mumbling almost incoherently.

"Right," Jo murmured. She floated into sleep, knowing she would dream of herself in the arms of a buff, tan lifeguard. Maybe finding romance on this mission wasn't totally out of the question after all.

"I'm going to take that tree trunk!" Caylin shouted to Mike. "I want to see what this baby is made of!"

"Go for it," Mike told her. "The Hummer knows no limits."

Caylin pressed the pedal to the metal and flew over

a large, sawed-off trunk. She hadn't felt so relaxed in ages. With Mike she could almost forget that she was an international spy who had been disowned by her superiors. Unfortunately forgetting that a significant part of the American population wanted to see her hang wasn't so easy.

"Yes!" Mike yelled as they continued to speed up the mountain. "You haven't lost your touch."

The wind whipped Caylin's hair around her eyes and filled her lungs with fresh mountain air. I will prevail, she told herself. Correction. *They* would prevail.

"*Whooo . . . eee!*"

Suddenly Mike frowned. "What's that?" he asked.

Caylin glanced at him. "What's what?"

"That noise!" Mike twisted in his seat and gazed out the back of the Hummer. "Hey, someone is following us!"

Caylin gripped the steering wheel.

No. No way.

She peered into the rearview mirror, and her heart sank. Someone was gaining on them. She saw a tall, lanky figure astride a Harley-Davidson chopper, tearing up the mountain road. Victor! There was no way. How could he possibly have tracked them to Mike's house? Unless . . . unless someone had tipped him off?

"That's Victor," Caylin told Mike. "In case you don't already know that particular fact."

"How would *I* know?" Mike asked.

Caylin sped up the Hummer, shaking her head. "Never mind. Just stay down. Victor doesn't joke around." She would find out soon enough whether or not Mike had betrayed her. Maybe he had been lying all along when he had said that he believed their story. Maybe he thought she was a crazy murderer and that Victor was a good guy fighting for justice. Please, don't let that be the case, she pleaded silently. Caylin couldn't stand the thought of Mike doubting her.

"He's gaining!" Mike shouted. "We've got to do something!"

Caylin breathed a sigh of relief. Mike sounded sincere. "What? Tell me what to do!"

Mike ran his fingers through his thick, dark hair. "We've got to immobilize him. It's the only way we'll get away. That chopper can probably go a hundred and ten miles an hour."

Mike was right. At this point outrunning Victor wasn't possible. This road led straight to the top of the mountain, where Victor would have every opportunity to aim for her head. There was only one way back down the mountain, and it involved her turning around and retracing their progress. She would have to face Victor and win.

Caylin slammed on the brakes, reversed, and turned around. And then she headed straight toward the enemy. As they got closer to the motorcycle Caylin saw that Victor was steering the powerful bike with one hand. In the other he held yet another gun. This one looked bigger and more powerful than the last.

"Mike! Get out and run!" Caylin shouted. "If you bail now, you can make it back to the cabin safely."

"No way!" Mike shouted. "I'm not going to leave you alone with that psycho! I'll die first."

Despite the present circumstances Caylin smiled. Mike was with her. He was on her side, and he was going to help. Her faith in humankind restored, she started to formulate an insane, dangerous plan. "Do you have a rope?" she asked.

Mike unbuckled his seat belt and dove into the back of the Hummer. "I've got a bungee cord. Will that work?"

Caylin nodded. "Yep . . . now take the wheel." In a maneuver that she would have laughed out loud at if she had seen it in a Bruce Willis flick, Mike and Caylin switched places with the Hummer in motion. With Mike driving, Caylin was free to concentrate on bringing Victor down.

They met Victor head-on. He spun the motorcycle around, sped alongside the Hummer, and prepared to shoot. The terrain was bumpy, and he obviously was having trouble taking aim. But Caylin wasn't going to give him a chance to get off a shot. No way.

Caylin wrapped the bungee cord around her wrist and took a deep breath. She had one chance to bring down Victor. If she blew it, they would all die. She had no doubt that Victor would spare no one. The man was a cold-blooded killer.

Caylin threw back her arm and unleashed the bungee. The cord sprang out just as she had planned and wrapped itself around Victor's wrist. Caylin clenched every muscle in her body and held on tight. "Yes!" Caylin shouted.

Victor's face paled as he lost control of the motorcycle. The gun flew out of his hand, landing somewhere in the woods. A moment later Caylin was able to pull him off the chopper with the strength of the cord. He landed in a pile of brush . . . moving but groaning.

Mike hit the brakes and jumped out of the Hummer. "What are you doing?" Caylin yelled.

"I'm going to kill that guy!" he shouted.

Caylin leaped out of the Hummer and followed Mike into the woods. He was standing over Victor, wielding a large branch. "Got any questions for this dude, Pike?" Mike asked.

"Don't kill me," Victor whimpered. "Please, don't kill me."

"How did you find us?" Caylin yelled at Victor. She had to know. If he answered, maybe she would let him live. Maybe.

Victor groaned. "I traced your car," he grunted. "The agent who brought you the Caddie was in on this with me the whole time!"

Jerk. Idiot. "I should take you out right now," Caylin muttered.

Victor stared at her, "But you won't . . . will you?" he asked. "You girls are too pure to kill anyone on purpose."

He was right, darn it. Caylin didn't want blood on her hands—or on Mike's. "Don't test me," she said, anyway, hoping she sounded tougher than she felt.

"You can't escape me—not even if you murder me," Victor said. "You never had a chance. I've got contacts *everywhere*!"

"Can I do the deed?" Mike asked, waving the branch.

"No way." She paused for a moment. "But can you help me tie him up instead?"

Mike dropped the branch. A few short moments later Victor had been effectively hog-tied with the bungee cord.

"See if your 'contacts' can help you get out of *this* mess, dude," Mike taunted. He jogged toward the motorcycle, lifted the chopper upright, and rolled it toward the Hummer. "We're taking this with us. If you ever work your way out of those knots, we'll *all* be long gone."

Caylin felt her eyes brimming with tears. Mike had come through for her. She had needed him, and he had been there. The guy deserved to know the truth—it was the least she could offer. She ran to help him with the chopper.

"You know, Mike . . . you're right," Caylin said softly as she guided the bike toward the Hummer. "I didn't really want to break up with you. I never stopped caring."

Mike didn't respond. He began to lift the chopper. Caylin immediately got behind him and pressed her hands against his warm back to spot him. With one final grunt Mike managed to get the motorcycle into the back of the Hummer. He wiped sweat from his brow.

"Mike . . . did you hear what I said before?"

"Yeah," he replied, his eyes glued to the ground. "But you still need your space, right?"

Caylin didn't answer. She got in the driver's seat and revved up the engine. "Maybe someday."

Mike hopped into the front seat, put his hands on either side of Caylin's face, and planted a firm kiss on her lips. "Yeah . . . maybe someday."

With that promise in her heart, Caylin sped toward the giant log cabin. Victor was incapacitated, but he wasn't out of the game. Once again it was time for the Spy Girls to hit the road running.

FOURTEEN

The Spy Girls lingered with Mike in the small parking lot of the Motel 6, where they had spent the afternoon and evening hiding out and giving one another brand-new makeovers. Mike had proved himself to be an invaluable ally, having sacrificed his male ego in order to clean off the shelves at Rite-Aid of any and all beauty products that caught his eye. He was also providing the Spy Girls with another getaway car—this one a bright red Range Rover. It was the ultimate SUV.

"Do you have everything?" Mike asked. "Wet suits? Lotion? Surfboards? Self-tanner?"

"Check, check, check, and check," Jo answered. "Once we don our surfer babe gear and descend upon Venice Beach, no one will guess that the so-called Terrorist Trio is walking among them."

"Thanks again, Mike," Theresa said giving him a hug. "Without you Caylin might have been dead right now—not to mention Jo and me."

He laughed. "Hey, the last eighteen hours have been the most exciting of my life. I should be thanking you three."

Jo stepped forward and gave Mike a loud smack on the cheek. "You're an awesome guy, Takeshi—we'll get the Range Rover back to you when the madness dies down."

He shrugged. "No prob. Take your time."

Now that the easy good-byes were over, Caylin glanced significantly from Jo to Theresa.

"We'll just, uh, go ahead and get in the SUV," Theresa said.

As her fellow Spy Girls climbed into their latest getaway car, Caylin took Mike's hands in hers. "Thank you for . . . everything. Especially for believing in me. I'll never forget it."

Mike hugged her close. "Thank *you* for telling me the truth. Now that I know why we had to break up, I don't feel like the biggest loser on the planet." He leaned back and wrapped a strand of Caylin's now black hair around one of his fingers. "You were beautiful as a blond and adorable as a redhead . . . now you're sultry as a black-haired raven."

"Bye, Mike," Caylin whispered.

"Be safe, Pike." He let go of her hair, turned, and retreated toward the anonymous motel room. The plan was in motion now. Later, when the Spy Girls had been on the highway for a few hours, Mike would drive the Hummer to the house of a friend in Carmel, California. There he would lay low until the Spy Girls were able to prove Victor's treachery to The Tower.

Caylin hopped into the backseat of the SUV and buckled her seat belt. "Let's hit it!" she told Jo. Part of her wanted to wallow in sweet memories of the past, but she knew that getting wrapped up in some nostalgia trip would distract her from the task at hand—namely, the Big Handover.

"On the road again, I juuust caan't wait to get on the rooad again!" Jo sang from behind the wheel. "Next stop, Los Angeles, Califor-nye-yay!"

Dawn was breaking as the girls closed in on the City of Angels. Jo, Theresa, and Caylin were wide awake, trying in vain to map out the exact steps that would get them out of their mess of the week.

"So you guys talked to Danielle?" Caylin asked.

"Yes, for the third time," Jo answered. "We called her secret cell phone number. She agreed to get on a plane to Los Angeles. We're supposed to call again to establish a meeting place."

"When do we call?" Caylin asked. She was chewing on a piece of her now black hair, staring into the lightening sky.

"Whenever," Theresa answered. "Danielle's probably eating an early bird breakfast special as we speak."

Jo tossed Theresa the cell phone Mike had insisted they use during the last leg of their mission. "Reach out and touch someone," she told her fellow Spy Girl. "The sooner we know exactly where we're going, the faster we can make this whole *episode* a thing of the past."

"Do you think we'll have jobs once this mission is over?" Caylin wondered. "I mean, Uncle Sam is going to forgive us for those screwups, right?"

Theresa shrugged. She had been pondering the same

question as they sped through a long, dark night on the freeway. A week ago Theresa wouldn't have believed that The Tower could so easily lose faith in their loyal Spy Girls. But according to Jo and Caylin, Uncle Sam had been unrelenting on the telephone. Jeez. The guy had refused to take their calls for the last twenty-four hours! But maybe there was still hope. Maybe.

"If worse comes to worst, we can pool our limited resources and open up a private investigator agency," Jo commented dryly. "We can chase down stolen pets and deadbeat dads."

"Sounds thrilling," Theresa responded. "I can use my high-tech computer skills to flip through dusty files in some small town city hall basement."

"Just go ahead and make the call to Danielle," Caylin said. "I'm not willing to give up on The Tower yet. We've been through too much to call it quits."

Theresa dialed Danielle's secret cell phone number. The phone rang four times before Danielle finally picked up. When she spoke, her voice was almost drowned out in a sea of static. "Hello!" Danielle shouted.

"It's us. The Terrorist Trio." Theresa didn't think any further identification was necessary.

"I can't talk long," Danielle said. "There are . . . things happening here."

"Things? What things?" Things were bad. Things meant more trouble for the Spy Girls. Theresa could hear that much in Danielle's voice.

"Sam knows you all got in touch with me," Danielle informed Theresa darkly. "And he's not happy. This whole incident has put The Tower in a very awkward position."

"What are you saying, Danielle?" Theresa knew her voice was laced with a combination of panic, anger, and desperation, but she couldn't help it.

"The drop-off will be tricky," Danielle said. "We'll still meet in Venice Beach, but not in a café as we discussed—it's too risky."

"Where?" Theresa asked. "Just tell us where, and we'll be there."

The static on Danielle's end of the line was so heavy that Theresa could barely hear her. "Meet me in three hours at lifeguard stand number . . ." *Ssshhhh*. The static grew even louder.

"What? I didn't hear you!" Theresa yelled into the cell phone. "Which lifeguard stand?"

Click. The line was dead. "Dang," Theresa growled. She cut the connection, then immediately dialed Danielle's cell phone number again.

"The mobile unit you have called is not responding or is outside the coverage area. Please try your call again later." The computerized voice on the other end of the line repeated the message one more time. Then there was nothing but a dial tone.

"Well?" Caylin demanded. "What's the deal?"

Theresa bit her lip. Danielle hadn't sounded like herself—not at all. "I don't know. But I think we had better be prepared for the worst."

"What else is new?" Jo quipped, maneuvering the SUV onto the Pacific Coast Highway. "Los Angeles—ready or not, here we come."

• • •

The temperature had risen to a balmy eighty degrees when Jo turned the SUV into an all-day, five-dollar flat fee, public parking lot on Pacific Avenue and Venice Boulevard.

"Man. I dreamed about spending a day at the beach when we were freezing our butts off in Prague," Jo said, switching off the engine. "But I had pictured myself in a tiny bikini, lying on a blanket, with a trashy romance in my hand and a cooler of Diet Cokes at my side."

At least they were dressed for the locale. The girls had stopped at a gas station in Malibu and changed into their ultimate surfer girl wear. Now they looked like *Baywatch* extras.

"I know what you mean," Theresa agreed. "This wet suit is wedgy city."

Jo pulled out a tube of neon pink zinc oxide and slathered her nose. "If all goes well, maybe we can spend the afternoon relaxing in the shade of some hot lifeguard."

"I'm worried about Mike," Caylin stated for the umpteenth time.

"He called the cell phone when you were paying for

the last tank of gas," Jo reminded her reassuringly. "He's safely ensconced in Carmel, probably riding a tasty wave at this very moment." She, too, had been glad to receive Mike's phone call. Between him and Brad, the Spy Girls had managed to jeopardize the lives of two possible love interests. So much for danger being the great aphrodisiac.

The girls climbed out of the SUV, taking only what was absolutely essential—surfboards, sunglasses, a backpack holding the all-important mousse can and a few miscellaneous spy gadgets, and Mike's cell phone. They were silent as they traipsed across the parking lot and headed to Venice Beach, each girl lost in her own flood of tension and anxiety.

"Wow," Jo exclaimed when they reached the boardwalk. "This place is *packed*." There were people everywhere. Vendors had already set up shop along the boardwalk, selling everything from temporary tattoos to used clothes to five-minute massages. A psychic sat on a small crate, her tarot cards shuffled and ready for a customer. And there appeared to be about a thousand lifeguard stands. Danielle could be *anywhere*.

"What now?" Caylin asked, surveying the sea of people.

"We start looking," Theresa said. "And we don't stop until we find Danielle."

"We also keep an eye out for any and all suspicious persons," Jo said. "Victor could be here . . . or any number of his evil accomplices."

"Trust no one," Caylin said. "That's our motto."

The girls jogged down the beach, stopping at each life-guard stand to search for Danielle. There were a lot of hot lifeguards but no sign of the tall woman whom they had come to think of as their guardian angel.

Finally out of breath, the girls collapsed in the sand. "Yep, this is a real day at the beach," Theresa said. "This is my idea of re-lax-ation." She carefully inspected her arms and legs. "I think I'm getting a sunburn."

Jo pointed to a group of idle sunbathers who were lazing nearby on a huge beach blanket, listening to their transistor radios. "Listen up, girls. Those folks are tuned in to the news, and I don't think the news is good."

"Reports indicate that the Terrorist Trio have descended upon Venice Beach," the announcer read. "Undercover police have saturated the area. They have informed KFI radio that they are determined to catch the renegade girls by day's end. In other news . . ."

Caylin groaned. "Great. Just what we need. Undercover cops." She glanced over her shoulder. "Hey, is that guy looking at us?"

Jo and Theresa stared at a man standing nearby. He was dressed in surfer gear, but his skin was suspiciously pale. The guy looked like he hadn't been on a beach in years.

"Scatter!" Jo ordered. "Reconvene when it's safe at that lemonade stand over there."

"Check!" Caylin and Theresa chorused.

Jo sprinted up the beach, losing herself in a crowd of volleyball players. "We need a server!" someone shouted. Jo took this as a sign and grabbed the ball.

As she slammed it over the net she saw none other than Pale Man saunter past. He headed onto the boardwalk and disappeared into a burger joint. Her work here was done. She aced one more serve and tossed the ball to the girl next to her. "Your turn!"

Caylin bobbed in the ocean, waiting for the right wave to come along. Jo and Theresa might not like their wet suits, but hers felt like a second skin. She had known immediately how she was going to disappear. The waves were like home to her.

A perfect wave rolled toward her, and Caylin stood on her board. Seconds later she was riding toward shore with the sun on her back and the wind in her hair.

Heaven.

She hit the shore and saw Jo strolling toward the designated lemonade stand. Caylin jumped off her surfboard, tucked it under her arm, and jogged off to join her fellow Spy Girl. Missions came before tasty waves, unfortunately.

Theresa walked up to Jacie's Lemonade Stand and took a seat next to Jo and Caylin, who were sharing a jumbo frozen.

"What happened to *you*?" Caylin squealed.

Theresa glanced at her arms. "I had to *blend*," she exclaimed. She had spent the last twenty minutes getting a

NOBODY DOES IT BETTER **663**

henna tattoo from a woman with a pierced chin.

Jo giggled. "You look like something out of *The Guinness Book of World Records.*"

"Enough joking around," Caylin said. "Let's resume the search."

They got up, pitched the lemonade, and headed down the beach. At last Theresa saw a familiar head of shiny dark hair in the distance. "Danielle!" she said excitedly. "There's Danielle!"

"Of *course*," Jo said. "She's standing next to lifeguard stand number *three.*"

"We should have guessed," Caylin agreed, picking up the pace and running toward the stand.

As the girls neared the lifeguard stand Theresa felt as if the mousse can was burning a hole in her backpack. More than anything else in the world she wanted to deposit the code safely into Danielle's capable hands.

"Where is she *going*?" Jo shrieked.

Uh-oh. Danielle was walking toward a pier next to a tall, thin man wearing an oh-so-out-of-place long trench coat.

Theresa stopped in her tracks. "You don't think Danielle is in on this with Victor, do you?" she asked.

"She's been acting awfully strange . . . ," Jo offered. "Maybe . . . maybe she's betrayed us. No. No, she wouldn't do that. Would she?"

"The Tower agent who delivered the Cadillac and the money to us in Seattle was in cahoots with Victor," Caylin reminded them. "And Danielle was the one who sent the guy to us in the first place."

The girls stared at one another silently. The tension was so thick that it could have been cut with the proverbial knife.

"No," Theresa said finally. "Danielle would never turn on us."

"Never," Jo agreed immediately.

"No way. No how." Caylin's voice was firm, unwavering.

"Which means . . . that Victor is after her," Theresa concluded. "He's going to kill her and then come after us for the code!"

"Ohmigod! We've got to save her!" Caylin cried.

The girls jogged toward the pier, hot on Danielle's trail.

Two hundred yards away she hopped—or was pushed?—into a speedboat docked near the pier.

"If we go after her, the cops are going to notice," Theresa pointed out. "We'll be sitting ducks!"

"There's no other option," Jo yelled, sprinting toward the pier. "We've got to do this for Danielle . . . and for The Tower."

Nodding in mutual agreement, the Spy Girls raced toward the pier. Do or die. Do or die.

FIFTEEN

"Sorry, dude," Caylin said to a Teva-and-swim-trunks-clad guy who was about to hit the water on a Jet Ski. "Duty calls." She gave the guy a well-placed shove and jumped onto the Jet Ski. Beside her Jo and Theresa did the same to two other unsuspecting beach dudes.

"Rock on!" Jo yelled, revving up her engine. "Pacific Ocean, watch out!"

Each of the girls unleashed her Jet Ski from the pier and raced out to sea. The speedboat was gaining distance. Every moment counted.

Caylin was aware of nothing but pounding waves as she sped toward the boat. Come on, Danielle, she urged silently. Hang in there. Help was on its way.

Suddenly Jo zoomed up beside her, pointing toward

the shore. Several large men were each climbing onto a black-and-white Jet Ski. Cops!

"Hurry!" Jo mouthed, taking the lead.

The girls skipped over wave after wave, closing in on the renegade speedboat. Behind them the Venice Jet Ski cops were in hot pursuit. Suddenly the air was filled with even more noise. Caylin glanced up and saw a helicopter hovering over the speedboat.

Oh no! Danielle, in the arms of Victor, was being hauled up to the helicopter via a swinging rope ladder. Caylin saw the distinct glint of a gray metal gun shining in the sun.

No time to lose. The girls pulled up beside the now empty, idling speedboat. One by one each ditched her Jet Ski and climbed aboard.

"What do we do?" Jo yelled over the helicopter's roar. The copter still hovered above the boat.

Caylin caught the swinging rope ladder and held on with all of her strength. "We've got to go up there!"

"Victor had a gun!" Theresa screamed. "He could kill us all!"

"But if we *don't* go, he'll *definitely* shoot Danielle!" Jo shouted.

Theresa nodded. "We're goin' up."

Caylin climbed up the rope ladder, struggling to contain the overwhelming terror that gripped her. Each rung seemed a mile away as her muscles ached with the effort of climbing.

Up above, two large male hands shook the ladder back and forth. Caylin glanced down and saw that Jo and Theresa were still dangling beneath her, still holding on for dear life. But the ocean below was falling away. The copter was going up!

"Can you make it?" she screamed to her partners.

Jo's face was bright red, Theresa's sickly white. Agony was etched in their pained expressions.

"Yeeahh," Jo groaned.

Theresa managed a nod. Nothing else.

Caylin continued to pull herself up the ladder. She focused on the bottom of the helicopter, forcing herself to forget the huge, roiling ocean that lay thousands of feet below her.

Higher. The helicopter was moving steadily into the sky, making this mad journey more dangerous by the second. Rung by rung, Caylin approached her destination.

"Just *go!*" Jo screamed, her words almost lost in the wind. *"Go!"*

At last Caylin reached the door of the helicopter. She could see Danielle sitting inside on a built-in seat. The agent didn't appear to have been harmed. Which was the first good sign Caylin had seen in what felt like forever.

"Danielle." It was the only thing she could utter.

She hoisted herself up and searched wildly for Victor. Where was he? Flying the helicopter up front?

Jo appeared next. "Man . . ." She heaved herself up next to Caylin, panting. They crouched on the small floor of the craft, wedged behind the pilot's seat.

"You're not going to get away with this, Victor!" Jo yelled, regaining her breath. "I don't care if I have to rot in jail during a nine-month trial! You will *not* succeed!" She glanced around the tiny helicopter.

"Where is he?" she asked Danielle.

Before The Tower agent could respond, Theresa's head popped up. "The code," she moaned. "I've got the code."

Caylin and Jo grabbed her arms and pulled her over the edge. "You made it, T. You made it." But the helicopter was still ascending. The strong pair of hands that had been shaking the ladder moments ago could appear at any moment to push all of them out the open door.

"Where's Victor?" Theresa panted.

"Just give me the code!" Danielle shouted.

Caylin nodded to Theresa to go ahead. They were beyond the point of no return. To distrust Danielle at this point was unthinkable.

Theresa pulled off her backpack and stuck her hand inside. Finally she handed Danielle the can of mousse. Their fate was in her hands. Or Victor's. Or some other unknown person's who she was too tired to think about.

Danielle looked at the object in her hand. "I know I don't look my best," she said. "But am I really having *that* bad a hair day?"

The girls stared at Danielle in wonder. They were in a

life-and-death situation, and she was making jokes!

"We have to subdue Victor!" Jo shouted. "We're all going to die."

Danielle laughed. "Victor isn't here, Jo. He's in jail." She gestured toward a tall, thin guy who was lounging in the corner of the copter seat. "Meet Frank Grant. He's a good friend of mine . . . and a Tower agent."

"What?" Caylin shouted. "You mean he was the one who kidnapped you and was holding you hostage?"

Danielle laughed again. "Congratulations, Spy Girls! You've passed quite a test!" She was beaming, her eyes brimming with tears. "My Spy Girls, the heroines."

In the roiling water below the helicopter a dozen Jet Ski riding cops flashed the girls the thumbs-up sign. Their cheers were audible even over the roar of the copter blades.

"Those aren't real cops," Danielle explained. "At least not the kind you're thinking of. The Tower hired them to pursue you this morning." She paused. "And I knew Frank resembled Vince—aka Victor. He was a stand-in."

"Will someone *please* explain what's going on?" Theresa demanded.

"You were right about Vince," Danielle said as the pilot of the helicopter headed toward shore. "The Tower had suspected all along that he was working against us, but we had no way to know for sure without involving you three. Testing him was part of your mission."

She paused. "Initially Vince's plan wasn't to kill you, Theresa. After taking his position at FutureWorks he'd made a deal with Simon Gilbert—Rosebud, as you call him—for a percentage of the profits from the code. But Vince and Simon had a big falling-out and Vince knew that Simon was planning to take back possession of his code."

Theresa swallowed. "But where do I fit in here?"

"Victor thought that by enlisting you to extract the code, he'd turn you against The Tower," Danielle explained. "He figured you'd help him in the technical department in exchange for a few multibillions. But along the way Rosebud got clued in as to your arrival and had planned to kidnap *you* so that *you* could do the dirty work for *him*. And from that moment on, everything went haywire."

"So both Rosebud and Victor were trying to use me

in order to backstab the other." Theresa shook her head. "Weird."

"Where's the V-man now?" Caylin asked.

"The Tower caught up with him at the base of Mount Lassen. He's in custody." Danielle grinned again. "One more bad guy in the slammer."

"So Uncle Sam *knew* the V-man was bad the whole time?" Jo shrieked. "Why didn't he tell us?"

"It was imperative that Vince not suspect that you suspected *him* from the outset," Danielle explained. "We had to trust that you would figure out the truth."

"I don't understand," Theresa said. "Why didn't Uncle Sam tell us that once the mission went awry? I mean, he totally cut us off from The Tower like we were common criminals."

Danielle smiled. "Once the ball started rolling, Sam decided that the circumstances provided a perfect means to test all of your abilities. We wanted to know that you would come out of the mission on top without the backup support of The Tower—and you did!" Danielle leaned forward and patted each of the Spy Girls on the back. "You all put your heads together, achieved your mission, and remained loyal to The Tower under the most difficult circumstances. Bravo!"

"Talk about a close call," Jo murmured. "I didn't think we were going to make it."

"I was starting to consider enrolling in court reporter's school," Theresa agreed.

Caylin laughed. "I wasn't worried—not at all!"

The girls giggled with relief. They had really and truly proved themselves worthy of the Spy Girls name. Whew!

On Friday afternoon Jo, Caylin, and Theresa stood on the steps in front of the Santa Monica courthouse. Next to them, standing in front of a podium, was Officer Bascovitz. He had flown in from Seattle especially for the press conference that was currently under way.

"I am happy to announce that Jo, Caylin, and Theresa have been proven innocent," Officer Bascovitz boomed into the microphone. "The real killer has been caught and is now being held without bail."

"Thank goodness Brad was let out of prison," Theresa

whispered to Jo and Caylin. "When I called him this morning, he said a date with me should come with a warning label." She giggled. "But he *also* said that if I was ever in Seattle again, I should look him up." She paused. "Do you think we'll be back in Seattle anytime soon?"

"No!" Jo and Caylin whispered in unison.

"The law enforcement agencies of Washington and California would like to issue an official apology to these girls," Officer Bascovitz continued, gesturing toward the Spy Girls. "They were the unwitting victims of a criminal conspiracy."

In the large audience of reporters and supporters cheers erupted. "We knew you were innocent!" one girl yelled. She waved her sign—Hail the *Terrific* Trio—in the air.

Off to the side, TV reporters were already filing their stories for the evening news. "Although it is not known yet how the police came to realize that the supposed Terrorist Trio were innocent, the facts today speak for themselves." A blond, perky reporter smiled into the remote cam in front of her. "We'll have more at eleven."

Officer Bascovitz turned to the girls. "Would you like to make a statement?" he asked. "After all of this sensational media coverage, the American people want to hear your stories."

Jo stepped up to the podium. "I would like to thank our loyal supporters," she said, grinning at all of the teenagers who were holding signs and cheering. "We were in the wrong place at the wrong time, and we hold no grudge against the Seattle police department." She paused, smiling into the crowd. "And to all of you cute guys out there, *yes*, I *am* single!"

Caylin rolled her eyes at Jo's last comment and approached the podium. "I have two things to say," she announced. "The first is this: Mom and Dad, your love and support means everything to me. The second thing won't mean anything to a lot of you, but it will mean a lot to the person who matters." She leaned close to the microphone. "Thank you, Mike." Caylin stepped away from the podium and nudged Theresa forward.

"We're all looking forward to resuming our everyday lives now that this huge mix-up is behind us," Theresa said brightly. "We're just three *normal* American teenage girls . . . living three *normal* lives." She joined Caylin and Jo, who had retreated from the podium.

"Three cheers for three great girls!" a voice boomed out from the back of the crowd. The girls looked at one another. That voice . . . it was familiar.

"You don't think?" Jo said.

They stared in the direction of the booming voice. There stood a shadowy figure. He was wearing a long coat, the upturned lapels hiding most of his face. A white derby hat had been pushed low on his head. The man turned his face in the direction of the Spy Girls and flashed a quick thumbs-up.

"Uncle Sam!" Theresa cried. "It's him!" Even as she spoke, he disappeared into the crowd. And then he was gone.

"We never even got a chance to thank him," Caylin joked.

The girls retreated to the other end of the steps as Officer Bascovitz took questions from reporters. Talk about an action-packed week! It was going to take them a month of soap operas and bonbons to recover.

"Do you really think we're going to have to give autographs?" Jo wondered.

"We can't let down our adoring fans," Caylin pointed out.

"Dang! I wish I had practiced my signature." Theresa giggled.

Suddenly an eager face appeared before them. The young woman's short, dark hair was mussed, and she wore a fashionable sundress. In one hand she carried a LEAVE THE GIRLS ALONE! sign. Danielle in disguise!

"You guys are, like, my heroes," Danielle gushed in a singsong voice. "Can I, like, give you a present?"

"Why, yes, young fan, we would love a gift," Jo said, winking at Danielle.

Danielle placed a large snow globe in Jo's hand. Inside the crystal globe were miniature Swiss chalets and tiny porcelain skiers. As Danielle faded into the crowd of reporters the Spy Girls exchanged excited glances.

"Does this mean what I think it means?" Jo asked.

"Ladies, we're going to Switzerland!" Caylin squealed. "So much for our nice, relaxing beach vacation."

"Alps, here we come!" Theresa exclaimed.

The girls hugged one another close. This mission had been accomplished. But another awaited them. After all, they had a whole world to save.

Turn the page for a sneak peek at the next espionage adventure!

COVERT AFFAIRS 2

SPY GIRLS ARE FOREVER

by ELIZABETH CAGE

Beam me out of here," Jo Carreras muttered as she and Theresa Hearth entered the now familiar white plastic conference room of The Tower for another debriefing. "This place needs a major makeover. The latter-day mother ship motif is *way* out."

"Tell it to Uncle Sam," Theresa replied. She gently set her laptop on the pristine white conference table that stretched the length of the entire room. It had to be at least twenty feet long. "Maybe he'll turn you loose with The Tower platinum card."

"Yeah, right. Only if we save the world just one more time." Jo flipped her long black hair out of her face. Then she snatched a blueberry muffin from a small tray of juice, bagels, muffins, and other breakfast treats in the center of the conference table. The tray was the only thing in the room that hinted at warmth. Let alone humanity.

Actually, there was a time when the sight of this conference room/bad *Trek* set creeped Jo and Theresa out. Now it wasn't eerie so much as tacky. But back then, they were just raw recruits thrown together to save the Free World from Evil and other capitalized words. They'd been so green when the organization known only as The Tower had trained them as secret agents.

Naturally, their enemies underestimated three teenage girls. But the adventures had been intense. Dangerous. Thrilling. Terrifying. And exhausting. They had defused bombs, fallen out of airplanes, hacked into top secret computers, run from the law, and trotted the globe using false identities. They had used gadgets that would make James Bond drool. They wore fabulous couture that would make him drool even more. Soon they stopped being just girls.

They became the Spy Girls.

Jo glanced around and blinked her large ebony eyes. "Where's Caylin?"

Theresa shrugged.

Then they heard a high-pitched *"Kiii-yai!"*

The door at the opposite end of the room flew open, and Caylin Pike burst in, blond ponytail flipping, fists wrapped in athletic tape. She danced back and forth, boxing the air and twirling while she executed a series of wicked roundhouse kicks.

"It's about time," Jo murmured.

Caylin whooshed past Theresa and headed toward Jo's seat. She punched with each step—"Ya! Ya! Ya!"—all the way up to Jo. Then Caylin launched a final sidekick that came within an inch of Jo's nose.

"Now *that's* what I'm talking about." Caylin grinned, holding the foot in front of Jo's face. Jo didn't even flinch—except to wrinkle her nose.

"Ever hear of foot-odor spray?" she asked.

Caylin swung her foot back to the ground and stood in place. Her shoulders slumped. "I do *not* stink!"

"Your feet do," Jo replied with a wry smile.

Caylin ignored her, choosing instead to plop her foot on the conference table, bend forward, and stretch her hamstring. "This tae-bo stuff is unreal. It's total body kamikaze. You guys have to try it. You'll die."

"Just what I want out of a workout," Theresa said.

"No thanks, Van Damage," Jo added. "You work out enough for all of us."

"You don't even know what working out is," Caylin scolded, massaging her calf. She paused to snag a bottle of water from the tray.

"Working out?" Theresa asked, looking confused. She turned to Jo, shrugging. "Never heard of it."

"You know, weights, treadmills, ambulances," Jo quipped. "You've seen the infomercials."

Theresa widened her gray eyes in mock surprise. "*That's* working out? Ew!"

"God forbid you break a sweat," Caylin grumbled.

"You break the sweats, I'll break the codes," Theresa replied, patting her laptop.

"So what does Jo break?" Caylin asked.

Theresa grinned. "Wind."

"Hey!" Jo erupted, throwing a muffin. It exploded against Theresa's arm, sending chunky crumbs across the spotless white table. "You're supposed to be the quiet one!"

"*You* should try quiet sometime," Theresa said with a laugh, brushing crumbs away.

"Very funny," Jo said with an exaggerated toss of her dark hair. "The only thing I break is hearts, Spy Geek. Don't you forget it."

"Yeah, I heard that enemies of state all over the world are paying big bucks for the latest satellite pics of you sunbathing on The Tower roof," Caylin pointed out.

Jo blinked. "They are?"

Caylin and Theresa exploded in giggles and groans. "Yeah, *right*!"

Jo sighed melodramatically and shook her head. "It's so hard being beautiful, brilliant, and top secret."

"Ahem," came a deep voice from all around them, as if from within the walls.

The Spy Girls froze.

"Uh-oh," Caylin said, glancing about. "The Sam-man cometh. Cease all fun."

The lights dimmed. A large video screen emerged from the far wall, blinking and humming. Gradually the pixelated image of Uncle Sam, their boss, came to life before them. As usual, they couldn't make out any of his features.

"Greetings, Spy Girls," Uncle Sam said. "How are the debutantes of détente today?"

"My word, Uncle Sam," Jo gasped. "What have you done with your face?"

"I always look like this, Jo," Uncle Sam replied.

Jo rolled her eyes. "That was a joke. You know—what have you done with your face . . . like, 'where is it?'"

"I know what you meant, Jo," Uncle Sam replied dryly. "Do you think you're the first operative to come up with that one?"

"Yeah, yeah, yeah," Jo grumbled. "Dish it, Sammy. What's this week's crisis?"

"Well, it's a crisis, all right," Uncle Sam replied. "But it's a little different this time out."

"Different?" Theresa asked.

"Let me guess," Jo interjected. "Forty nuclear warheads have been stolen from Russia, and we have to infiltrate the Moscow mob. Dressed as nuns."

"No, that's not it," Caylin said. "We have to go to Nepal to rescue the Dalai Lama from a band of rebel Sherpas."

"Dressed as nuns," Jo repeated.

"If you two are finished?" Uncle Sam replied coldly.

"We have to go up in the space shuttle!" Caylin went on.

"Go undercover as Dallas Cowboy cheerleaders!" Jo countered.

"Now *that* would be cool," Caylin agreed.

"That's *quite* enough!" Uncle Sam exclaimed.

The girls paused, staring at the screen. Finally Jo muttered, "He is *so* decaf this morning."

"As I was saying when I was so *rudely* interrupted," Uncle Sam continued, "your next mission is a bit different. I assume you are all familiar with the Mediterranean principality Zagaria, along with its royal family."

"Princess Kristal," Theresa replied.

"Correct. The eighteen-year-old princess. Her mother, Queen Cascadia. And Prince Arthur, who just turned fifteen."

"Lucky kid," Caylin commented. "That's big bucks."

"Who'd want to be a royal?" Theresa scoffed. "Talk about lack of free will."

"Funny you should say that, Theresa," Uncle Sam said.

"Because it's exactly free will that has the palace in an uproar. It seems Kristal has been exercising her free will a little too freely these days."

"How so?" Caylin asked.

"Let me guess," Jo piped up. "It has something to do with her boyfriend, Rook."

"Exactly," Uncle Sam replied. "How did you know?"

Jo smiled. "I read the newspapers."

"Ha!" Theresa replied. "Like the *International Trasher*?"

Jo scowled. "That's *Tracker*, giga-girl! If you spoke any language other than Java, you'd *know* that it keeps its finger on the pulse of pop culture like no other newspaper."

"At a second-grade reading level," Theresa argued. "There's not enough soap in the cheesiest of operas to wash the dirt out of *that* rag."

"Ladies!" Uncle Sam said. "If I may?"

Jo and Theresa fell silent.

"Here's the situation: Kristal has run off to Schnell to do a little skiing in the Swiss Alps. The royal family is fairly certain that Rook is with her. Queen Cascadia fears that this could lead to more complicated—and permanent—romantic matters."

"Like marriage?" Caylin offered.

"Like marriage," Uncle Sam confirmed. "It's no secret the queen doesn't like Rook. If Kristal and Rook marry, the implications for the monarchy would be huge. Her Majesty has requested that The Tower locate the princess and return her to Zagaria."

"Schnell," Jo said in awe. "That's the most exclusive ski resort in Europe."

"With the best snowboarding in the world," Caylin added.

Theresa shook her head at her comrades' enthusiasm. "Doesn't the royal fam have bodyguards to handle this kind of stuff? I mean, why do *we* have to go?"

"Are you nuts, Theresa?" Jo demanded. "This is a cake-walk right into the jaws of luxury. It's *Schnell*!"

"The point, Theresa," Uncle Sam replied, "is that Kristal doesn't want to be found. Surely you know her reputation. She'd rather be the rock star that she is than a princess. She and Rook have been on the front cover of every tabloid in the world. This is her way of rebelling against her upbringing. Schnell isn't that big a town, but there are many intimate places for a girl like Kristal to hide. She goes there often, so she must have dependable people willing to keep her whereabouts discreet for a bribe. She would see royal bodyguards coming a mile away. On the other hand, three American girls who are fans just might be able to get close to her."

"Skiing and jet-setting," Caylin mused. "Sounds like a choice little mission."

"My advice would be to follow the paparazzi," Uncle Sam suggested. "They know the clubs where Kristal has been giving surprise concerts."

"Cool," Jo said.

"Lame," Theresa countered.

"What's your malfunction?" Jo asked. "Nothing's going to blow up, no one's going to die, and the world is still safe for democracy."

"That's the point," Theresa replied. "Shouldn't we be doing something a little more challenging? We've proven ourselves. Isn't there a *real* crisis out there somewhere?"

"Yeah, in your head," Jo muttered.

"I'm serious."

"T., we couldn't ask for a better mission." Caylin paused. "Actually, after our little fiasco in Seattle, we very well *should* ask for a better mission."

"Ask and ye shall receive," Uncle Sam said. "Theresa, relax and enjoy this one. If you pull it off, there's a whole week of rest and relaxation in Schnell for the three of you, courtesy of the royal family and The Tower."

"Are you kidding?" Jo squealed. "That is totally Gandhi of you, Uncle Sam! I take back all the things I said about your face!"

"Thank you, Jo," Uncle Sam replied. "But there is one thing. . . ."

"Uh-oh," Caylin moaned.

"Oh no," Theresa breathed.

"What, pray tell?" Jo asked.

The pixels in Uncle Sam's image multiplied into a mischievous smile. "You have to find the princess in seventy-two hours."

Theresa snorted. "Three days? Yeah. Okay. Sure. Nothing

like chasing a spoiled brat through a maze of clubs full of Euro-snobs smoking cigarettes that cost more than my haircut."

"We'll do it," Jo declared.

"No problem," Caylin agreed. "Sorry, T. You might actually have to go outdoors on this one."

"Ha ha," Theresa replied. She glumly raised her glass of orange juice. "Here's to world peace."

"Nah, here's to cool slopes and hot tubs," Jo shot back.

"Good luck, Spy Girls," Uncle Sam declared. "I'll contact you when you reach your home base in Schnell. I think you'll find your accommodations quite . . . accommodating."

Caylin stood and raised her drink as well. "Let's rock and roll, ladies!"

Two juice glasses and one water bottle clicked together. And then the Spy Girls were off.

ABOUT THE AUTHOR

Elizabeth Cage is a saucy pseudonym for a noted young adult writer. Her true identity and current whereabouts are classified.

NEW YORK TIMES **BESTSELLING SERIES**

SCOTT WESTERFELD

uglies pretties specials extras

A world where everyone's ugly.
And then they're not.

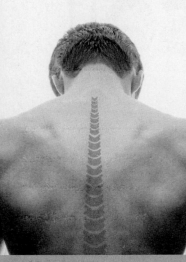

NEW YORK TIMES **BESTSELLING SERIES**

SCOTT WESTERFELD

 pretties specials extras

What happens when perfection isn't good enough?

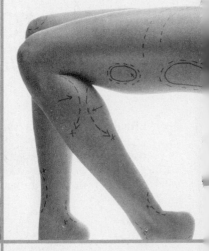

NEW YORK TIMES **BESTSELLING SERIES**

SCOTT WESTERFELD

uglies pretties specials extras

Frighteningly beautiful. Dangerously strong. Breathtakingly fast.

NEW YORK TIMES **BESTSELLING SERIES**

SCOTT WESTERFELD

uglies pretties specials extras

Where fame, popularity, and celebrity rule